Janet Louise McCartney was born and brought up in the beautiful Georgian town of Whitehaven, Cumbria which is located close to the Lake District. She is married to Gary and has a teenage daughter called Tamzin.

After thirteen years of having the initial idea she has finally written her first novel. Her life time ambition is to one day be able to give up her day job and write full time giving pleasure and entertainment to all her readers. With her debut novel now under her belt she hopes to go from strength to strength and produce the next international best seller.

J Lou McCartney

de Marco Empire

Vanguard Press

VANGUARD PAPERBACK

© Copyright 2008
J Lou McCartney

The right of J Lou McCartney to be identified as author of
this work has been asserted by her in accordance with the
Copyright, Designs and Patents Act 1988.

All Rights Reserved

A CIP catalogue record for this title is
available from the British Library.

ISBN 978 1 84386 439 4

Vanguard Press is an imprint of
Pegasus Elliot MacKenzie Publishers Ltd.
www.pegasuspublishers.com

First Published in 2008

Vanguard Press
Sheraton House Castle Park
Cambridge England

Printed & Bound in Great Britain

To

Diane

de Marco Empire

Hope you enjoy it!

love

J J McCartney

X

28/6/08

Dedication

With love to my husband Gary and daughter Tamzin
who have believed and supported me throughout the
entirety of creating my first novel.

Acknowledgements

Thanks to Pegasus Publishers, Vanguard Press, Mary Holmes and the Editorial team, Sandra Barber, Head of Promotions & Marketing Team, and everyone else involved in the production and promotion of my novel. A huge kiss to my daughter Tamzin for designing the book cover! Also special thanks to my personal development coach and friend Tommy Salmon for being instrumental in helping to unlock my true potential. And not forgetting my number one fans Leanne Fox and Karen Salmon who have encouraged me to continue writing more novels.

Prologue

It was the day of the preliminary hearing and the closed court room was for immediate family and close friends only. The press were banned from the building and the surrounding vicinity, which spanned three miles in every direction, but they had helicopter coverage, so hopefully if anything significant happened they wouldn't miss it. The whole process was being carefully monitored by the Metropolitan Police force. This was going to be a high profile case, one that the public would be very interested in the eventual outcome. The de Marcos were very well respected and had brought a lot of business and employment to the area over the years.

The plain clothes police officers had sneaked the defendant into the back of the building earlier that morning with the minimum of fuss. Since they had arrived they had been stuck in a private room for almost five hours, trying to amuse themselves as best they could. The young woman was a breath of fresh air and had instantly captivated them with her sophistication and natural charm. She talked to them at great length and showed a genuine interest in their family backgrounds asking what it was that had made them decide to become police officers in the first place. She was extremely easy to talk to and an excellent listener, wise for her years. They would have told her their deepest secrets if it hadn't been for the sudden loud knock on the door. It was the signal that they had been expecting; their colleague had finally arrived to take the accused to the dock to officially read out the charge.

"The Crown versus Saunders de Marco, everyone please rise," the usher announced in an authoritive manner.

The courtroom came to a sudden hush as the Judge entered the chamber and took his seat. He peered over his half rimmed spectacles at the young woman in the dock behind the bullet proof glass which had been specially erected. She was smartly dressed in a pristine black suit and crisp white blouse. Her long chestnut brown hair swept up into a neat chignon. She had the most startling blue eyes he had ever seen.

Clearing his throat the usher asked, "Are you Katherine Anne Saunders de Marco born on 22 September 1965, residing at the de Marco penthouse suites at Regent Park Square?"

"I am," she replied keeping her poise and dignity. The palms of her hands were sweaty and they trembled slightly as she smoothed down her skirt and tried her best to maintain her composure.

"Mr Jones." The judge signalled to the prosecution. "You may begin."

"Thank you, sir, the case is that Katherine Anne Saunders de Marco did conspire to murder her husband on the night of their wedding on 14 April 1990. As it is an indictable offence and taking into account the serious nature of the charge ..."

"Yes, yes the court understands, please get to the point, Mr Jones." The Judge was becoming impatient with all this waffling.

"As I was saying, considering the serious nature of the offence and the fear that the defendant may fail to surrender to custody, plus the risk that she may interfere with prosecution witnesses, along with the fact that she will be returning to her main place of residence which she shared with the victim, we request that bail should not be granted." Mr Jones was confident that Judge Wainwright would agree.

"Mr Carmichael." The usher invited him to begin.

"Sir, there is absolutely no risk that my client will not surrender to custody, she has deep roots in the community and several thriving businesses. My client is prepared to relinquish her passport and report to the local police station and also refrain from contacting any potential prosecution witnesses. I must also remind the court that my client's husband was shot dead on their wedding night and the defendant is of course innocent in the eyes of this court until proved otherwise. I therefore request for bail to be granted."

Katie held her breath. Matthew was a complete genius, and he certainly had a way with words. She looked defiantly around the courtroom, wondering who would crawl out of the woodwork first, as she was sure one of them would be here; they wouldn't be able to resist watching her public humiliation. Her father was sitting solemnly, arms folded in the gallery. She half smiled, grateful that he was there.

"Bail, are you stupid?" screeched the furious, wild-eyed woman in the gallery, arms flailing all over the place. "She is nothing short of a cold, heartless murdering bitch. Antonio was going to leave her and come back to me, his one and only true love, as I always knew he would, it was inevitable; but no, she couldn't stand to let that happen so murdered him instead, the man that I loved, to get her hands on his vast fortune no doubt!"

"How dare you, madam, this is merely a preliminary hearing not the trial itself," boomed the Judge. "I will not tolerate this kind of outburst in my courtroom, one more word and I'll have no option but to charge you with contempt of court!" He turned his attention back to the defence lawyer. "Mr Carmichael, do you have anything else to add?"

The defence lawyer continued, "As I was saying before this banshee interrupted." The onlookers couldn't help but stifle a laugh.

"Mr Carmichael, if you please." This was beginning to turn into some kind of farce. "This is not a circus, but a Court of Law."

"My client is previously of good character and has willingly given up her passport, we would ask if you would consider bail in this instance, pending the forthcoming trial."

"Your client is indeed innocent despite any speculation as that we have just witnessed in the gallery." He peered at the woman that had been extremely vocal.

"I must object, this woman could also be guilty." Mr Jones made one last attempt to sway the judge's decision to grant bail.

"And as Mrs Saunders de Marco has already been charged with conspiring to murder her husband this still has yet to be proven in a Court of Law. Furthermore this particular case could also be potentially classed as a 'crime of passion' therefore there is absolutely no reason to suspect that she would in fact be a danger to anyone else so, yes, I am in agreement for bail to be granted in this instance."

The woman began to sob uncontrollably and made a loud gasp as she dramatically put a well-manicured hand to her face and swooned back into her chair. One of the young male ushers who was standing by the exit door rushed over to help her. She was indeed very beautiful, a tall statuesque woman with huge breasts, big brown eyes and a mane of curly blonde hair. She was dripping with gold and wore a white designer trouser suit and black jumper, every inch of her was perfect, even, he noted, if she was obviously surgically enhanced.

That bloody woman should have been an actress. Katie mentally applauded her, bravo; the poisonous Sasha Breschnevsky hadn't changed a bit. The woman created drama wherever she went, always the centre of attention, even now, when Katie was the one about to stand trial charged with murder. Of all the people that could have turned up, she had least wanted to see that witch again. Why Sasha was still so obviously obsessed was beyond her, maybe she had just come to gloat, probably hoping and praying that eventually she would be found guilty.

It was love that had gotten Katie into this mess, but Sasha didn't know the meaning of the word "love" and forgiveness certainly was not in her vocabulary. Why was she still so bitter and engrossed with her, why could she not accept that she had been merely a trophy girlfriend, nothing more, nothing less? Antonio was dead, dead, so what was it that Sasha possibly hoped to gain by intruding into her life once more? They had history together, that was true, but it was ancient history as far as she was concerned and it no longer mattered, in fact nothing much mattered to her right now, only her freedom which was the only thing she had left.

The Judge interrupted her now throbbing brain. "This of course is a very serious allegation and having considered all the information before me I feel that in this case bail will be granted subject to the conditions outlined by the defence. I therefore confirm that you will be bailed to attend Crown Court on 25 August 1990. However it is my duty to warn you, Mrs de Marco, that if you fail to adhere to any of your bail conditions you will be liable for arrest and shall be remanded in custody for the remainder of the trial period."

Katie was shaking, she didn't know how to feel, but thanked God that she had been granted bail; she wouldn't last five minutes in prison.

"All rise please." The Judge stood up, straightened his wig and left the chamber.

The middle-aged officer gently guided Mrs de Marco back down the stairs and out of the side door, steering her down the corridor. "You best wait in here for the time being." He acknowledged the two young officers guarding the door. He'd seen a lot of people come through the Courts of Justice and this woman was definitely not typical of the cold blooded killers he'd seen sent down over the years. Still, he reminded himself, the gun was found in her possession, her finger prints were all over it and that was as good as guilty in his book. Sighing quietly, he wondered what had made her do it, what a waste. Perhaps he was getting too old for this; he just didn't understand the world anymore.

Matthew Carmichael strode purposefully down the corridor; he was determined there would be no case to answer. He was finally becoming well known in the legal world and his reputation would be unbreakable once he got Katie off, he grinned to himself. If anyone could find a way he could...

"Hey, Carmichael, the praying mantis isn't getting away with this, one way or another she's going down," the mean looking man snarled as he grabbed Matthew by the shoulders and shoved him hard against the wall.

"Everything ok, Mr Carmichael," shouted the young officer, noticing the commotion, not sure whether he should leave his position stationed at the door or not.

As he walked away the well dressed thug gave him a knowing look. "I'll be seein ya, Carmichael, real soon."

Carmichael was slightly rattled; noticing the scar which ran down the left hand side of his face reminded him of the very first time he met him. He worked for the de Marcos and was one of their more serious heavies. His reputation preceded him, but the police never managed to connect him to anything more serious than a parking ticket. Straightening his tie he took a deep breath. "I'm fine, just fine." He sighed realising that he probably hadn't seen the last of him, wondering what his next move may be.

The young officer opened the door for him. "We put her back into this room, sir, it has no windows and is totally secure. Jeff is with her just now."

Carmichael entered the room. "Thanks, Jeff, I'll take it from here, I'm expecting transportation in approximately forty minutes, just waiting for the paperwork coming through."

"Ok, sir, I'll let you know when it arrives." Jeff was conscious that he was somehow in the way and made a quick exit.

"Oh, Matt, what am I going to do, it's looking really bad?" Katie gushed as she jumped to her feet. "And look what they are calling me in the paper! I just can't believe this is happening to me." She handed him the newspaper, headlined "Premature demise of loving husband and popular business man Antonio de Marco brutally murdered by his wife, Katie 'praying mantis' Saunders de Marco."

He took the paper from her and tossed it into the bin. "Forget about the press, Katie, it's my job to prove your innocence and that's exactly what I'm going to do."

His voice was gentle and reassuring. "I'm still checking out the alibis of all Antonio's known associates, but I'm afraid I haven't discovered anymore than the police have, not yet anyway, but I intend to keep digging."

"But it was the day of our wedding, Matt, full of guests, it could have been anyone. I'm sure lots of people held grudges over the years." It was going to be like looking for a needle in a haystack; most people would have alibis and the Italian police were adamant that she did it and weren't interested in looking for anyone else.

"Listen, I've got a copy of the wedding guest list, I just need to work my way through it. We are going to have to sit down and discuss every single person on that list and if any of them had a reason for killing your husband."

"I don't deserve your help, Matt, really I don't, I was so dreadful to you back then, just when you needed me most and I let you down," she whimpered, burying her head into his warm chest, feeling the steady beat of his heart; it was strange that he still had that calming effect on her. He had always been there for her and she was grateful to have such a friend, especially now.

"Hush now, that's all in the past, let's discuss the conditions of your bail," he soothed as he slowly released her. Pulling up a chair, he opened his briefcase. "Do you have access to quarter of a million?"

"We had just set up joint bank accounts prior to our wedding, can you believe it, and now all of the accounts, including my personal ones, have been frozen, because of the suspicious nature of Antonio's death."

"Did you know that Antonio had life insurance amounting to thirty million pounds, which as his next of kin you would inherit?"

"Jesus, really?"

"But we both know that if you really did want him dead there would be a much easier way to do it. Why put yourself in the frame? You'd hire someone; make it look like an accident."

"Christ, Matt."

"I'm sorry Katie, just trying to face facts; in the long run it will all help in your defence to argue these points. And of course, where would you get hold of a gun?"

"I've seen it before, Matt; I think it was Antonio's."

"What, why have you never mentioned this to me before?" his voice was incredulous.

"I've barely had a chance to think straight, but I know that I didn't touch it that night. The evening before I stayed over alone, I mean Antonio wasn't with me, as is the usual tradition on the eve of anyone's wedding. I was looking for some clean towels and the gun was wrapped up in amongst them. I picked it up and then dropped it when there was a knock on the door."

"Who was it?"

"Sasha, just getting her last digs in, I suppose."

"Did you leave her alone at all?"

"Just briefly, my bath was running and I didn't want it to overflow."

"What was she doing when you came out?"

"Come to think of it she did look rather jittery, but to be honest I thought she was maybe going to try and sabotage my dress." Suddenly aware of what Matt was getting at she stopped. "Oh, my God, what are you suggesting?"

"I'm not suggesting anything, just trying to piece it all together."

"Oh, come on, Matt, Sasha adored him."

"Adored his fortune more like."

"Exactly, if she wanted anyone dead, it would have been me!"

"Do you think the shot could have been meant for you?"

"Me?" Katie gasped. "Seriously, you think that it could have been me they were after, why?"

"A million and one reasons spring to mind."

"No, really, you're wrong, nobody had anything against me."

"True, but there were plenty who had a grudge against de Marco, what better way to get at him than kill his bride on their wedding night." He watched her flawless face, waiting for her reaction.

"No, no, no!" Katie shook her head. "Impossible, he was on the phone, I went for a shower, when I came back he was dead."

"Mmm, ok we'll rule that out for the time being then." Matt looked thoughtful. "Getting back to the eve of the wedding, what happened after you had taken a bath?"

"I had a massage and a manicure, then I went downstairs and had dinner with Nina and the kids and Francesca and Alfredo."

"Did you tell anyone about the gun?"

"No, I just shut the box up and put it out of my mind."

"Then, what happened?"

"I decided to go for some fresh air and visit Pesaro, to try and relax and be on my own for a while." Katie noted his concern. "Pesaro is a horse, Matt."

"I see, did you check the gun on your return?"

"Yes, it had vanished."

"So, what do you think happened to it?"

"Well, the bed covers had been turned down and fresh towels were out, I just assumed that Francesca had removed it."

"Didn't you think that a bit strange?"

"Not really, I think she didn't want to worry me and that's why she didn't mention it."

"Jesus Christ, Katie, grow up, what the hell do you think a gun was doing hidden in his bedroom, he must have thought he may need it at some point?"

"Matt, I... I don't know, all I know is that I wanted to be his wife more than anything."

"What, at any expense, what the hell do you think a jury is going to say when they hear your story?"

"Probably the same as the Italian police, that I purchased it, hid it there and killed my own husband in cold blood on the night of our wedding." She began to sob.

"I'm sorry Katie, but this is just a taste of what the prosecution is going to put you through, I just don't know if you are strong enough to deal with it."

"Trust me, I will be, nobody wants Antonio's murderer brought to justice more than me."

"You have got to toughen up, Katie, it's the only way."

"Ok," she nodded, defeated and exhausted. "Can we please go now?"

"Soon, now, let's get back to the immediate obstacle in our path, how are we going to fund your bail, do you know anyone who has that amount of cash who's willing to help you?"

"The only thing I have left of any value is an emerald necklace and matching bracelet, Antonio gave them to me as a wedding present. But I just couldn't bear to part with them. It's the last thing Antonio ever bought me." Katie put her head in her hands and sighed.

"Ok, let's look at alternatives, what about Nina Valetti?"

"Nina? Oh, I don't know, I couldn't ask her for that much money, she has a family to think of."

"I think she's your best hope, after all she is your business partner."

Katie was finding it impossible to focus on what he was saying. "I'm going down for a long time aren't I?"

"No, not if I can help it, trust me I'll do everything in my power to keep you out of prison. I know you Katie and you're not capable of murder, of that I'm certain. But we have to establish who else could have a motive for killing him and what they would have to gain from his death. What I need from you is a list of everyone you can think of who was connected to Antonio in any way, and I'm thinking outside of the wedding guests."

Katie studied Matthew, he'd matured since she last saw him. She remembered how boyish he used to look, with his long hair and cheeky grin and that silly baseball cap that he virtually lived in. She wondered just for a brief second what their life together would have been like if she hadn't been swept off her feet by the dashing Antonio, damn him.

"I wish you had never got involved with that de Marco, I knew he would hurt you, you know that I would have cherished you...." His voice trailed off.

"I'll ring Nina, you're right; she will come up with the money." Katie interrupted him, swiftly changing the subject, hoping he wouldn't say another word about his feelings for her.

"Good, now what about going home? You could always stay with me; the house is certainly big enough."

"I don't think your wife will be keen on that, do you?"

"She's left me for a richer, but much older model." He looked very serious.

"Oh, I'm sorry." Katie didn't know what else to say to him, she wondered if he still saw anything of his little girl.

"Don't be, I'm not."

"That's a real shame, there's nothing worse than a broken home." Katie was thinking of her own predicament.

"So, will you be ok at the penthouse?"

"Yes, it's alarmed, I'll be perfectly safe."

"Good, then I'll drop you off; make sure that you really are ok."

"Please don't fuss, Matt."

"I also think it best if you had some kind of protection, I'll arrange some round the clock bodyguards from a reputable company I know of." It wasn't a question, he was telling her how things were going to be leading up to the trial.

"Whatever you think best."

"I'll do some work on the wedding list tonight and we'll talk tomorrow, you've had a pretty tough day."

Tough day, he must be joking, she didn't think anything could top how she felt right now.

Chapter One

It was mid July 1985. Katie and her best friend Lucy were getting ready for a night out to celebrate Lucy's twentieth birthday. They had been saving up for weeks and were going to the opening night of a prestigious new club in the city called "La Pregheira".

"God, you are such a skinny little bitch," Lucy teased her, as she watched her slip on her little black halter neck dress; it was totally backless and had diamantes edged around the neckline down to her cleavage. "You look fantastic."

Katie was 5ft 8, very slim with long shiny chestnut hair; she had spent ages curling it. The curls had now dropped and she swept the sides up with delicate, diamante combs; it was, she admitted to herself totally perfect. "I'll take the skinny as a compliment shall I?" she laughed as she stood back to admire her reflection.

"How do I look?" Lucy asked as she tossed her blonde hair off her face and walked seductively up and down the bathroom and stood in a supermodel type pose, hands on her hips, pouting her lips for ultimate effect.

"Totally voluptuous for sure!"

They both burst out laughing.

"I wish I was taller." Lucy said seriously.

"And I wish I had bigger boobs, I'm afraid I didn't get much in that department!" she half joked.

"Here then, have some of mine." Lucy pushed her ample breasts together and bounced them at her.

They both fell about giggling, mascara running down their faces; they were going to have a fun time tonight that was for sure.

The doorbell interrupted their high spirits. "That'll be Matt," they chirped in unison.

"I'll go, you'll need more time to get ready," teased Katie.

"Hey, you got the mascara all down your face, remember, you'll frighten the life out of him." Lucy thrust the box of tissues into her hands.

"Thanks, some best mate you are!" She dabbed the tissue under her eyes which Lucy had kindly shoved into her hands.

She opened the door. "Hey." She looked up into his face and smiled warmly.

"Hey, gorgeous, how are you?" Matt asked as he leaned down to kiss her. He was just over 6ft tall with an athletic physique. Katie loved his cheeky grin and shoulder length sandy brown hair, he was such good fun. She always felt comfortable and safe with him and he was always the perfect gentleman. They had been dating since they were teenagers and these days he was beginning to seem more like an elder brother to her. Their relationship had cooled down over the past six months yet neither of them wanted to admit it so they just plodded along, knowing that it was only a matter of time before one of them found a new love.

"I'm good thanks, how were your lectures today? Did you get your exam results back yet?"

"Yep, sure did, they said if I carry on like this then I will be an asset to the legal world!" he said proudly as he tipped the peak of his baseball cap. "Take a look, here's my diploma, fully fledged solicitor, cool huh?"

Katie took the envelope from him. "Passed with honours too, Lucy, that's brilliant news, congratulations, if anyone deserves it you do after all your hard work."

"And Jackson's Law Firm are interested in hiring me, they are one of the most respected law firms in London," he boasted.

"Wow, head hunted already, that's fantastic, but you do realise you'll need to lose the beloved baseball cap, get a haircut and buy some sharp suits if you want to look the part!"

Matt shrugged. "What, lose the locks and cap, not just yet! " Noticing the look of horror on Katie's face, "Ok, guess I will eventually, don't worry, I'll do whatever it takes, but one step at a time."

"Hey big, guy," Lucy yelled as she tottered across the room, grabbing the envelope from Katie. "You definitely got the brains in the family."

"Whoa take it easy in those heels; they look a little dangerous if you don't mind me saying so!"

As she was only 5ft 3 she had specially gone out shopping to buy new three-inch heels to boost her height; she, unfortunately had not been lucky enough to inherit her father's height, unlike her brother, who seemed to have inherited all the best things! "So, how do I look?"

Matt playfully ruffled Lucy's hair. "You'll do, but are you sure you're going to manage in those shoes, little sis, I have visions of you falling over and breaking something before the end of the evening?"

"Hey no problem. I've been practising for a few hours now, and please don't mess with the hair, I spent ages doing this," Lucy said crossly. "And you know how I hate it when you call me 'little sis'," she tutted, giving him a congratulatory hug as she passed back his certificate.

"If you beautiful young ladies are both ready I'll give you a lift, I'm afraid it's another night of study for me."

"Another, but you're qualified now."

"Yes, but I am not a qualified defence lawyer, which is ultimately what I want to do."

"What defend scumbags?"

"No, people who have been wrongly accused, silly."

"But how will you know if someone is innocent or guilty?"

"Hey, you're my sis, what can I say, I always know when you're telling porkies!"

"No, you don't, does he?" She looked to Katie for confirmation, holding her hands up, waiting for her response.

"Oh, no, keep me out of this, I'm not getting involved." She hated taking sides.

"Katie, help me out here," Lucy persisted.

"Ok, you asked for this, sorry but Matt does have a point."

"Why do you always take his side?" Lucy said grumpily.

"No, I don't do I, Matt?" This was going to turn into a major drama if Matt didn't come to the rescue and quickly.

"Thanks, Katie. Must say I do wish that I was coming with you, supposed to be an extraordinary night according to the papers." He changed the subject easily, which was just as well as Lucy looked as though she was just about to blow a gasket.

"Never mind, we'll give you a full rundown of the entire place tomorrow, let's go, taxi driver." Katie giggled as she pulled Lucy by the arm and pushed Matt unceremoniously out of the door.

Chapter Two

As Matt drove through the wrought iron gates and into the grounds his jaw instantly dropped in total awe; Club La Pregheira was something to behold indeed. He'd read about it in the local press and seen the pictures but it certainly didn't do it any real justice. The sight in front of him was absolutely amazing. The gravelled drive was lined with shrubs and various trees, there was a huge fountain just in front of the club, it was lit up with lights that danced and shimmered and as the sun began to set it looked almost magical. "Wow, what a place," Matt whistled. "These de Marcos must be multi millionaires to own something like this, if this is the outside, boy imagine what's waiting inside." He immediately noticed the security cameras dotted around the grounds and placed strategically around the building. Several burly doormen with walkie talkies were making their presence known as they checked the guests' handbags and coats.

One of the valets impatiently waved the car through and pointed for Matt to pull over.

"Yes?" Matt asked, winding down the window.

"Plenty of parking spaces to the left, or the drop off point is just over there," the valet informed him, pointing just in front of him.

Lucy squealed and clapped her hands in sheer delight. "Boy, this place is really something. It's so beautiful." Then it hit her like a thunderbolt.

"Oh, no, what are you thinking?" Katie dreaded what she was going to come up with, some insane idea no doubt.

"I'll have to try and bag myself one of these de Marcos," she half joked.

"Yeah, good idea, wouldn't mind a millionaire brother-in-law."

"Oh, Matt, don't encourage her, please."

"Only kidding!"

"Yeah, you're a right pair of jokers, you two." Katie shook her head.

"We are going to have the best time ever imaginable," Lucy enthused. "Oops, sorry, Matt."

"It's ok, really, I just hope they let you in," Matt laughed as he leaned over to kiss Katie on the cheek.

"And why would we not get in?"

"No reason, just have a lovely time and I'll see you both tomorrow; it's going to be another long night for me I'm afraid." He shrugged nonchalantly. Partying wasn't exactly his thing, his ultimate goal was becoming a top class lawyer and his name being sought after once he'd established himself. Everyone had a dream and that was his, that of course and then he would propose to Katie.

Katie gasped as she surveyed the majestic building, she had never seen anything like it. It was really impressive and although it had been recently renovated it still managed to retain its eighteenth-century charm. Apparently it had once belonged to a well-known business man back in Victorian Britain but had unfortunately fallen into disrepair over the years. It still oozed character from the outside, with its sandstone walls and statuesque pillars. The architecture was magnificent. The doorway had a huge white marble arch with columns on either side for support and above the door was a plaque saying 'Est. 1896'. She couldn't wait to see how the inside compared.

The entry line had begun to spread down one of the paths that led out into the vast garden area; they were going to have to try and get to the front somehow but it was looking practically impossible. They noticed the two big burly bouncers on the door, asking for the people with tickets to make their way forward.

Katie and Lucy looked at one another; shit, tickets, what tickets? No one had told them that they needed any tickets and by the look on the size of the queue they were extremely unlikely to get inside the club without them.

Lucy leaned over and whispered into Katie's ear. "It's going to be ok, I have an idea, follow me." She grabbed her arm and marched them both up to the front of the queue, ignoring the loud protests from the other guests still waiting in line.

"Look we're here about the croupier jobs," winked Lucy as she nudged Katie hoping that she would play along.

"Pull the other one, love, it's got bells on; you're slightly overdressed for an interview."

The other bouncer butted in. "Don't think so, girls, the jobs have already gone. It's opening night and if they were no croupiers, then the casino floor would not be open."

"No, no you don't understand, we are here as extra cover for when the other girls take time off," Lucy protested.

"Just a minute, let me check out this ridiculous story, girls." The bouncer talked into his walkie talkie. "Sorry to bother you, Veronica, its Fats here, are you expecting more girls for cover for the croupier jobs?"

Veronica was in charge of all three floors in the club, consisting of the restaurant, lounge and casino. She had been interviewing for weeks, and was fed up as all she seemed to get were either cheap tarts or girls who didn't have a clue about their type of business let alone gambling. She had even drafted in some temporary staff from a local agency and hoped if they were good enough to maybe offer them something worthwhile to stay on. She hesitated as she looked on the TV monitor. She was immediately struck by the petite blonde who would be very good for business; the brunette looked elegant enough but she looked far too reserved and unsure of herself. In this line of work you needed the right staff who had to ooze confidence from every pore of their being; it was vital to this sort of business. Maybe she should check them out, give them a trial, it wouldn't do any harm. And maybe in the process she would please her boss, Antonio. He seemed to have a thing for the blondes, they were like magnets to him and it was about time he swapped the Russian doll. After all she reasoned she needed to keep him on side, pleasing him would make her life here so much easier and anyway she had to admire their sheer audacity for blatantly trying it on.

"This is never going to work; they're going to rumble us!" Katie whispered.

"Shhhh, just hold your nerve, if we walk off now imagine how foolish we're going to look!"

Before Katie had a chance to answer, the huge bald headed bouncer signalled them over. "It appears to be your lucky day, ladies, Veronica will see you, and maybe you can let me know how you get on." He couldn't take his eyes off the cute blonde, she was just his type. "I'm Brian, what's your name, doll?"

"Erm, Lucy." She shuddered, smiling through gritted teeth. As if this big fat balding guy would really have a chance with her, the thought of it made her skin crawl.

"Go in, take a left down the corridor and someone will meet you," Brian said as he deliberately stepped in their way, leaving a little gap so that they had to squeeze past him. "See ya later, sweetheart."

"She was a bit of alright eh, Fats." Brian drooled rubbing his hands together. "I fancy a bit of that like."

"Put your tongue back in man," Fats shook his head, all he thought about was pulling a bit of skirt, he obviously wasn't getting any and looking at the state of him he probably wouldn't be getting any anytime soon. "Next?" He continued taking the tickets from the guests.

Brian turned to him. "We can't all have your physique mate, but what I lack in the looks department, I make up for down here." He grabbed his crotch. "Know what I mean?"

Fats was disgusted, he wasn't going to be able to put up with him for much longer, maybe it was time for pastures new, maybe another country, New Zealand sounded quite nice.

Lucy stuck her fingers down her throat to show her disgust. At least they were in the club now, fantastic. "Yuk, think I'm going to throw up!"

"You better not, now we're in what are we going to say to this Veronica person?"

"Ah, we'll just blag it as we go along!"

A tall scrawny looking guy walked towards them and beckoned them to follow him. He had narrow set eyes and a long thin nose, even the tuxedo he was wearing didn't do anything for him. He was the most revolting and yet oddest looking man they had ever seen. "Veronica is expecting you, come with me," ordered the strange weasel looking man.

"He looks like something out of a horror movie," Lucy whispered.

"Did you say something?" He turned around and stared at them with those eerie, unemotional eyes, which stopped them dead in their tracks.

The girls looked rather nervous as they continued to follow him down the corridor. "Don't worry, I won't bite!" he smirked sensing their discomfort, he seemed to have that effect on people and he enjoyed the feeling of power it gave him.

As their heels sank into the lush ruby red carpet that spanned the length of the corridor they paid particular attention to their lavish surroundings, anything to keep their minds off the weirdo in front of them.

The cream walls were lined with black and white photographs of fifties icons, such as James Dean, Marilyn Monroe, Elvis, Frank Sinatra, Sammy Davis Jr & Dean Martin, the latter three collectively known as the Rat Pack, all mounted in beautiful golden frames, their names etched on to plaques underneath the pictures.

"Here we are ladies," he pointed.

On the door hung a sign, 'Veronica Lamont, Club La Pregheira Manageress'. The strange man knocked loudly on the door and stuck his head in, announcing, "They are here, Ms Lamont, shall I show them in?"

"Please do, Eddie, and wait outside, I'll let you know when we finish."

Veronica surveyed them closely, mmm maybe not croupier material after all but waitressing, yes, why not? She was Antonio's number one when it came to hiring and firing and she knew exactly what kind of girl would be required to work here and in what capacity. She pushed her long jet black hair behind one of her ears, looking very pensive. Her make-up was dark and she always finished it off with her trade mark bright red lipstick which enhanced her full lips to the maximum.

"So, we have been advertising for quite some time, why have you come now on opening night?" she challenged them. "Well, I'm waiting."

"Err… we erm have only just recently moved here and only found out about the club," Katie stammered taken aback by this woman's startling oriental appearance.

"So?" Veronica pushed her for an answer.

"We want to be part of such a prestigious club as this and thought that perhaps once you met us and knew how hardworking we were, well you would give us a start."

Lucy couldn't believe that Katie was taking the lead, usually it was her. "That's right the place is sooo beautiful," she gushed. "We really are very impressed with what we've seen."

"Enough of the bullshit young lady, do you think that I am stupid or something? You just wanted to get in the club for free, admit it. I should just chuck you out on your arses right now!"

Neither of the girls spoke, the look on their faces said it all. Veronica felt a tiny bit sorry for them and seeing as how she was in a good mood, decided to give them a break.

"But on the more positive side I think you both have guts and I admire that, I really do. There may indeed be a place here for you both, but not croupiers, at least not to begin with, please sit." She barked the order at them.

They both obediently sat down in the red velvet chairs. The room was huge and they noticed the TV monitors, which appeared to access all areas inside and outside of the club. Veronica sat in the big leather reclining chair opposite them and folded her hands together. "Hmm, what am I going to do with you?" She sat there for a moment. "I think that we are alright for croupiers at the moment I'm afraid, but we always need more waitresses, if you are interested. Unfortunately for me girls come and go so we always have to employ extra just in case. We are expecting the owner tonight, Mr Antonio de Marco. He owns several prestigious clubs in the UK and is currently flying in from Paris as we speak. He has very high expectations of his staff, they have to fulfil a certain criteria; he likes style, intelligence and also honesty and politeness. It is not easy working here, you are on your feet most of the night and of course the customer is always right. But tell me, I am interested to know what you both do for a living right now?"

"Well, we have just recently finished college and have just started looking for work now that summer is nearly over," answered Lucy.

"What exactly did you study and I wonder, do either of you even have any bar experience at all?"

"A two year course in Customer Services covering hospitality and bar management and we did placements in actual bars and hotels as part of our course work."

"Good, good, so, what about we arrange for a meeting tomorrow afternoon, say 3 o'clock and tonight you can enjoy a few freebies and get a feel for the club and what it's all about. I'll happily organise a table for you both if you wish. We are expecting to be busy tonight and the boss will be arriving later this evening, so what do you say?"

"Really, that's brilliant." Lucy beamed at her, hardly believing their luck.

"That's settled then, but please remember I do not like to be messed around, so I expect that you are both genuine and will turn up to see me tomorrow. The wages are good and the tips are up to you. If you follow the rules you will make plenty of money here, do we have a deal?"

"Yes, of course."

"Good, Eddie, Eddie." Veronica shouted. "Get the girls names and addresses and then show them into the VIP area and arrange for a table in the restaurant, darling."

Eddie smiled showing a gold protruding tooth, which made him look even more sinister if that was even possible. He would do all the necessary checks too, just to make sure they were who they said they were. If they upset Ms Lamont in any way then it would be his job to sort them out, and boy would he enjoy sorting them out. She was putting her trust in them and he wanted to make sure they weren't going to let her down under any circumstances.

Chapter Three

Antonio wasn't in the mood for all the attention tonight, he just wanted to keep a low profile, but unfortunately in his line of work, publicity, albeit the right sort of publicity, was a must for his businesses.

"Antonio, darling," Drawled the large breasted statuesque blonde. "I cannot wait to see your new club, it is going to be soo exciting," she purred in a strong Russian accent as she stroked his arm. "I must look my best for the press."

Antonio wondered what he saw in this materialistic woman; to him she was just an accessory, a bit of fun, someone to have a good time with when he was in the mood. She was the latest in a long line of conquests. "I need to make a few calls, Sasha baby, why don't you pour us a drink while we wait for the limo?"

Sasha obediently walked over to the drinks cabinet, she knew when to keep out of his way, business, business, it was always business with him. In fact all he seemed to do these days was spend time working, he was no fun anymore. She would have to think of something to bring out the party animal in him because God knows where it had vanished to.

Antonio went into his office to make a quick phone call. "Stevo, is everything running as expected?"

"Yep, it's under control."

Antonio slammed the phone down, that was one less worry off his mind. He could do without all this crap, it was time to finish it before things really got messed up and Stevo was the man for the job.

All Antonio wanted was to make easy money, enjoy it and maybe even settle down and have a few kids, that's if he ever found the right woman. For now he would continue making those all important business deals and expanding whenever the opportunity arose.

Tonight he would be able to relax, enjoy his new club and have a few celebratory drinks among his select group of friends.

Chapter Four

Eddie was disappointed that the girls checked out, Ms Lamont would not be able to recruit them for her upper class clients. But there again some of the girls would do just about anything for extra money, they would just have to wait and see how they turned out.

"How did you know about the croupier vacancies?" asked Katie under her breath.

"You remember Sarah Ellis, the tall skinny girl who worked in Vaults Bar, well she's got a job here and apparently Ms Lamont was not impressed with the quality of the interviewees so she put some of the girls on trial and even had to employ some others from an agency," she explained.

They walked down the red carpeted hallway and made their way back into the foyer. It was getting pretty busy, and Eddie left them with a hostess called Tania Horrocks. Although a bit on the large side she was really beautiful, a shapely redhead with cat-like green eyes. "So, you are lucky to be having a tour and be given a free night, wonder what she wants in return," she said rather cynically.

"What do you mean?" Lucy didn't like her demeanour.

"Do you really think she will let you have this night for free, it will come out of your wages to cover the costs," she warned them. "Christ I've never known her to be so generous."

"Well maybe she knows talent when she sees it!"

"Exactly, it makes one wonder what talent she thinks you may have, because quite frankly I can't see it from where I'm standing."

"You cow, just who do you think you are?" Lucy was raging; all she wanted to do was yank this girl's red hair out by the roots.

"Hang on; we haven't even decided whether to take them yet, so there's no point in speculating." Katie protested.

"Look let's just enjoy the night and sort this out tomorrow, it is my birthday after all," Lucy reassured her, determined not to lose control of her temper.

Tania led them up the huge spiral staircase; you could still smell the fresh paint on the walls. In the entrance to the bar area was a delicate crystal chandelier which sparkled in the strobe lights, it was beautiful. The bar ran the entire length of the room and was all mirrored, the barmaids were all dressed in a white blouse and black skirt and the barmen in black shirts and white trousers, complete with a white tie, they looked really classy.

Tania told them to take a seat on the big red leather luxurious sofas in the waiting area. She beckoned to a young man. "Colin, this is Lucy and Katie, can you arrange a table for them?" She paused. "And, erm Veronica is footing the bill so there will be no charge."

Colin raised an eyebrow. "Really?"

"That's what I said, isn't it?"

"Sure, we have a table over near the bar or up in the right hand corner by the dance floor, which would you prefer?"

"Colin, I suggest you just stick them somewhere and make it quick, the place is starting to fill up and it's going to be hectic!"

The girls shrugged, it didn't really matter, both were in prime position and they would be moving into the restaurant later anyway.

"Ok, come on then."

Colin led them to the bar area, they would be able to see everyone coming into the club from here and anyone coming in would notice them straight away, that could only be good for business. After all they were both really pretty, he thought. Pulling out the chairs for the girls, Colin passed them the drinks menu. "I'll give you a few minutes to decide."

"I think that Tania is rather snotty, what about you?" Lucy asked once they were alone.

"Put it this way, I wouldn't want to get on the wrong side of her, if that's what she's like ordinarily."

The girls laughed. If they had known Tania's history they wouldn't have taken it so lightly.

Veronica was in the dancing girls' changing rooms, checking their costumes. "Smile, look gorgeous and most of all enjoy yourself, this is opening night!" She nodded her head in appreciation, there were twelve girls, dressed in purple leotards and matching feathered headdress; they looked divine. All they had to do was a cabaret style dance at different intervals during the evening, easy money for them. She also had Alice booked for later in the evening, she was a young coloured girl with a really husky voice, she sounded like just like Nina Simone, and if she was a hit with the customers then she would offer her a permanent position. Everything was running smoothly, thank God, it was a miracle.

Now, she must go and check on the restaurant and casino; hopefully there would be no problems there either.

Nicholas Carlotti ran the kitchen, Veronica had poached him from another very successful Italian restaurant, but here he could have complete control of the menu and he was such a natural. What a shame the owners hadn't realised his talents; they had stifled him, knocked the spirit completely out of him. Cooking had became a chore, but now all that had changed. That is how Nicholas thought she had managed to lure him away, by offering him a free run with no interference, only suggestions which he could take or leave if he wished. If only he knew what it had taken to get him here.

Veronica had spoken to the owners of the restaurant and they were very reluctant to let Nicholas go. In fact they were downright arrogant and pig headed. She had offered them a small fortune to secure his transfer to the de Marco's nightclub, but they would not accept any amount of money.

She had tried everything to secure his release; he was an up-and-coming chef with much talent. In fact the restaurant he worked for owed him everything, the only reason people came was for his enthusiasm and exciting menus. He ended up loathing his boss with a vengeance, after he stopped letting him plan and devise the menus.

Fortunately for Veronica the restaurant had mysteriously burnt down, an electrical fault or so the fire service thought. But she knew that if she spoke to Gianni and explained she was unable to employ the best chef in the city no matter how much money passed hands, he would sort it out.

Veronica had broken down in tears and told Gianni how disappointed she was in not being able to do a deal with the owner. Gianni loved a challenge and told her to leave it to him. That week the restaurant had burnt to a cinder, one of the cleaners had unfortunately been caught in the blast and ultimately lost her life after lingering on for many weeks; the family had of course been compensated. Veronica knew that Gianni had somehow been involved in all of it, but they never discussed it and probably never would. She did not want to know the details, but was thankful to Gianni in her own way.

Veronica didn't care about Gianni's involvement, instead she was delighted that Nick was finally working for them, and she had to admit that he was the first man she had been interested in for a very long time.

"How are we doing, darling?" Veronica smiled warmly at him.

"Fabulous, I am really enjoying the freedom, I feel like my old self again, young and vibrant, starting over and it's all thanks to you."

"No, it's thanks to your talent; I've merely given you the tools to do what you were born to do. Now, tell me, are there any problems I should know about?"

"I had to change a couple of tiny things on the menu because some of the ingredients were missing, so I improvised, but don't worry, it's nothing I can't handle." Nicholas kissed her hand and winked at her. He was very fond of Veronica and admired her immensely, she was a tough cookie on the outside, but he knew there was a softer side to her and he was looking forward to getting to know her more intimately.

"The menus look fantastic, darling, you have done a wonderful job, just as I knew you would. Perhaps we can get together later when you shut the kitchen down?" She hesitated. "For a glass of champagne and a bite to eat?"

"It would be my pleasure." Nicholas blew her a kiss and went to check on the preparations. "Until later then."

33

Veronica had very strong feelings for him and she hoped this could turn into something special. She had always had a thing about Antonio, loved him even, but he did not reciprocate her love. So she had accepted, a long time ago now, that she would never be his lover and had given up flirting with him. There was no doubt however, that Antonio appreciated her efforts in the club, and she knew deep down that he respected her as a business woman and an equal. Accepting that's the way it was she finally felt free to focus her attentions elsewhere. At last she was interested in another man and that was a turn up in her book. The future was looking exciting and Nick was the icing on the cake.

Chapter Five

Katie was enjoying herself, she felt like a celebrity, Club La Pregheira was something else. She had never been to a place like it before in her life and was intent on enjoying every single second.

"Wow, you look so relaxed, Katie, pity we will never be millionaires or marry one for that matter, I could certainly get use to this lifestyle," enthused Lucy wriggling out of her shoes.

"You never know, there must be a few in here tonight, cheers, big ears!" They chinked their glasses together.

"What's that horrible smell, have you taken your shoes off again?"

Lucy picked one of her shoes up and stuck her nose in it. "Smells fine to me, here smell." She tried to shove it under Katie's nose, but she was suddenly distracted.

Following Katie's gaze she noticed a commotion going on in the corner, staff were buzzing around everywhere and there was a waitress with a silver tray balanced on her hand with glasses of champagne.

"What's happening?"

"Must be someone famous."

"I wonder who it is, ooh this is so exciting!" Katie was straining to get a look.

Lucy was also intrigued, but being so short she couldn't see who the mystery person was. The staff were obviously expecting some big star by the look of it.

The waiters were rushing around the room urging everyone to be upstanding.

Veronica was in the middle of all the fuss trying to keep some calm.

There was a hush as the lights were turned up and all eyes were focused on the top of the stairs. A beautiful couple walked in and everyone started clapping. It was the man that caught Katie's eye. "Wow, he is gorgeous," Katie gushed. He was very tall, a good few inches taller than Matt. He looked lean, but muscular, he obviously worked out. He was immaculately dressed in a classic Italian suit and Prada designer leather shoes.

"Hey, you're spoken for, remember my brother, Matt, anyway that guy looks too smooth for my liking and what a dolly she looks in that pink dress with her tits bursting out everywhere!"

Katie's heart skipped a beat as the couple walked passed their table and this handsome man actually turned and smiled directly at her. She didn't notice the woman on his arm shooting a look of disgust in her direction.

"Who on earth is that?"

The waiter leaned over and whispered into Katie's ear. "That's the owner Antonio de Marco and his fiancée, Sasha Breschnevsky, they make a fine couple don't they?"

Lucy was right, that Sasha woman definitely looked like an underdressed Barbie doll. Antonio was drop dead gorgeous and definitely dressed to impress. Katie couldn't help wondering what on earth he was doing with a woman like that. "You have to admit that he's bloody gorgeous!"

"He was alright I suppose."

"Darling, did you really have to smile at that simpering little girl and encourage her?"

"Sasha, you have nothing to worry about I can assure you." Antonio heard himself saying the words, but really wondering why he felt an instant attraction towards this beautiful young woman; perhaps it was her crystal blue eyes, they were quite startling, he couldn't help wondering who she was.

"Antonio, darling, did you not hear what I was saying, shall we go straight into the restaurant?"

"Why don't I buy champagne for everyone to celebrate the opening night, Colin will arrange it." Antonio summoned the barman.

"Of course, sir, right away."

Sensing Sasha's annoyance Antonio kissed her on the cheek and remarked on how stunning she looked.

Sasha purred with delight, she loved compliments especially off Antonio because she knew that he had great if not exceptional taste.

"Excuse me, darling, I just need to go to the ladies room, I need to check my make-up."

"There's no need, you look perfect."

"I'm just going to do a quick touch up, shan't be long." She planted a kiss on his cheek and looked over to see if that girl was watching.

Colin sent champagne around all the tables with the compliments of the owner. He planted one on the girls table.

"What's this?!"

"Compliments of Mr de Marco."

Katie looked in his direction and blushed when he nodded at her and lifted his glass up.

"For me?"

"Don't be silly, he's bought it for the entire club."

Feeling rather foolish Katie had to make an excuse to leave the table. "Wow this wine is making me tiddly. Talking about tiddles, I need to go to the ladies, if I can find it." She murmured, pushing her chair back and almost knocking the champagne of the table in her haste.

"Toilets are just over there." Colin pointed them out. "I'm sure it was just for you, but he had to buy it for everyone in case Sasha went berserk with jealousy," he whispered in her ear. Antonio had certainly given her a meaningful look, one of admiration.

"Me too, let's go and find them together," Lucy piped up. "Then perhaps we better go and eat something, try and soak up this drink."

They both felt a little light headed as they eventually made their way to the ladies room.

Antonio couldn't take his eyes off Katie, admiring her slender frame as she walked delicately across the room.

Colin clocked his boss, he seemed to be quite taken with her, although he didn't know why as she was nothing like his current girlfriend. Ah, perhaps that was it!

Lucy rushed into the cubicle and proceeded to throw up, she wasn't much of a drinker and had obviously drunk the wine too fast.

Katie studied her reflection in the mirror, she was looking and feeling good.

"You look a little flushed darling, maybe you should just go home if you can't handle the house wine."

The high pitched voice grated through Katie's entire body. She turned around to see who it was who could make such an irritating noise.

"Let me introduce myself, I am Sasha Breschnevsky, Antonio de Marco's fiancée." She stressed the words as she flashed a huge diamond ring in her face.

"Congratulations, I'm sure you will both be very happy together."

"Yes, darling, we will. You see he adores me and would do anything for me, he treats me like a princess and he certainly wouldn't be remotely interested in someone like you. He is so lucky to have me, I am quite a catch you know."

"Yes, quite." Feeling lost for words Katie was relieved to hear Lucy flushing the toilet and opening the cubicle door.

"Enjoy your evening, darling, and don't set your sights too high, stick to the bar staff in future, they are more in your league." Sasha smiled at her as she renewed her pink lipstick and blew her a kiss on her way out. "Oh and by the way, don't let me catch you looking at him again."

"What a pompous bitch," Katie muttered.

"What was that all about?" Lucy enquired as she rinsed her face and tidied her hair up. "Damn good job I brought my foundation, I'll have to do my make-up from scratch."

"Sorry, Luce are you alright now?"

"Fine thanks, now tell me what the hell was going on with that foreign woman?"

"That was 'Antonio de Marco's fiancée'," she mimicked. "She even had the nerve to introduce herself to me."

"What, why would she do that?"

"She was making it clear that Antonio is clearly out of bounds! "

37

"Oh, well she must be worried if she's trying to warn you off already."

"Do you think?"

"So, I take it that you are interested in him, but what about Matt?" Lucy stopped what she was doing and looked her in the eye.

"You know how I feel about Matt, we've been going out since we were fifteen."

"Exactly, you two haven't exactly set the world on fire together have you?"

"Don't be like that, Matt's a lovely bloke."

"Yes I know, but just be careful, you don't want to mess with this woman, she sounds like a real handful, especially with tits like that," Lucy joked.

"There's nothing to worry about, Antonio isn't even an issue, I just don't know who that woman thinks she is, looking down her nose at me."

"Come on let's go and check out the restaurant, the night is still young and I want to have fun, girlfriend."

"You bet," Katie heard herself saying, but she couldn't stop thinking about Antonio. She couldn't help thinking that Sasha was quite right, what would Antonio see in her. In any case she was determined to enjoy the rest of the evening and put it to the back of her mind.

The restaurant was in a typical rustic Italian style with sculptures and pillars strategically placed. Private booths were situated on the edges of the restaurant and oval tables down the centre of the room. Gold candelabras were the centre pieces placed on cream laced table cloths. The red serviettes were in the shape of fans with detailed gold edging. To add to the ambience gentle music played in the background and it really did feel like a small piece of Italy.

"Names please."

"Lucy Carmichael and Katie Saunders."

"Oh, yes, we have a table for you in one of the booths to the right, Miguel our maitre d' will show you."

"This way, signoras." He led them to the booth and handed them gold embossed menus. "Can I get you an aperitif?"

"Yes, we'll have a bottle of your best house wine please," Lucy said in her most polite accent.

"Do you think that's wise?" whispered Katie, she was slightly merry now to say the least.

"Don't worry, I told you, the food will soak up the alcohol," Lucy whispered back.

"Everything ok, ladies?"

"Yes, smashing, thanks, just bring the wine," Lucy hiccupped.

"Very well, I'll see what we can do."

The menu was all in Italian and they were busy trying to work out what to have when a dashing young waiter brought a bottle of champagne over. "The menu is translated into English at the back, if it makes it easier for you."

"Oops, so it is."

"We didn't order that."

"Oh, compliments of Mr de Marco, you left it in the bar."

"That was very kind of him."

"No problem, I must attend to the other guests, so please ask your waitress if there is anything else you require, Gina will be over to take your orders in a short while. Enjoy the evening."

The food orders were coming thick and fast, Nicholas was thrilled to be so busy. He had a few problems with some of the starters, but everything was back under control. Now he was just waiting for the boss to order before he could finally relax. He knew he had to do something extra special to impress Mr de Marco and if he endorsed his food then his place here would be secure. The boss was a man of great taste and he had to make the dishes as authentic as possible, which given his background was not a problem.

The kitchen was a hive of activity, everyone pulling out all the stops; he had chosen his staff very carefully, picking the ones who were excellent cooks and able to cope under pressure.

"Nicholas, Nicholas, Mr de Marco is just coming into the restaurant," Gina announced excitedly.

Oh my God, this is it, he thought. "Just make sure everyone pays special attention once we get his order, we need to get this spot on, people."

Antonio and Sasha made their way to their table, where they were joined by their special guests, handpicked especially for the opening night. Tonight was purely for enjoyment and work was banned from the dinner table just for a change.

Stevo was getting really pissed off with Vince; he had intercepted him on the way to La Piacenza Club in Manchester. Vince ran the place for Antonio, but he had really taken the mickey. He was a dumb arse, how could he expect to get away with ripping his boss off. He had the nerve to do his dodgy dealings inside the club and he had to be stopped.

"You've been warned before, Vince and now your time is up pal. Where are the fucking drugs and where is the fucking money or have you snorted the dope and spent the money on that flash car and tarts?" Stevo was getting more angry.

Vince was petrified, he couldn't see a way out of his situation. It's true he had ripped off the de Marcos, but he couldn't help it, he was under pressure from everyone. "What do you want me to do, I'm sorry, I didn't mean for this to happen, I have great respect for Antonio, he's my friend."

"Not any more, Vince, he wants you out! Now let's go for a little drive mate." The poor little fucker was shitting himself, Stevo had to physically shove him into the car, he would take him somewhere real quiet, put a gun to his head and make it quick, as long as Vince provided names of the others involved in the scam.

Antonio noted who was in the restaurant. The usual socialites, who had nothing better to do than party. Antonio invited them purely for publicity as they would brag and boast to the world how fabulously trendy the club was and what a great host and friend Antonio de Marco was. Tonight he would compliment everyone, amuse them, ask their opinion about the latest fashion trends, fast cars and any tips for making his next million. They would end the evening totally thrilled by his hospitality and talk about it for weeks to come or at least until the next major event came along.

Gianni de Marco was enjoying Felicia's company, she was his fiancée and he loved showing her off to Antonio. There had always been strong rivalry between the two brothers and they had been known to steal each other's girls from time to time. Sasha was his ex but she had only been with him to get close to Antonio, and that annoyed Gianni. He wasn't bothered about Sasha, it was the thought that Antonio could have any woman he wanted without even trying. Gianni was impeccably dressed and looked every inch an Italian gentleman, but it was his vile temper that sprang to the surface every now and then that always let him down. And unfortunately he wasn't the type of guy to hold back if something or someone angered him.

Diana and Henry Brookstein loved dining with Antonio; he was one of the main investors in their art company and enthusiastically attended their gallery when a new piece had been successfully purchased. He was well-travelled and on his trips abroad he would encourage Henry to purchase the fine paintings or sculptures he had just discovered. Sure enough these pieces were snapped up at remarkable speed. Now Henry had a regular network of customers and it was all thanks to Antonio; he couldn't be more content with his life.

Roberto and Nina Valetti owned a most prestigious designer furniture store, their specialty was of course handmade Italian furniture. They certainly helped make the club look as authentic as possible, with advice and suggestions; they had agreed on simple, yet sophisticated décor and tableware. It looked very impressive.

Ralph and Lorraine Anderson had it all. Ralph was like Antonio a self-made millionaire, his lucky break came when he won a contract to design a hugely successful chain of hotels. He admired Antonio and was proud to be involved in the restoration of Club La Pregheira , it was definitely one of his masterpieces.

The champagne was already being opened, Antonio waited until everyone was ready. "A toast, to Club La Pregheira and it's ongoing success!"

"Club La Pregheira!"

"And a special thank you to my dearest friends without whom this would not have been possible, Roberto and Nina, Diana and Henry, Ralph and Lorraine and of course my brother and partner Gianni."

The toasts resounded around the table as champagne glasses clinked.

"And not forgetting the delightful Felicia and gorgeous Sasha for putting up with us during all the hard work and late nights to finally ensure the place was ready on time. I am sure you will all agree that it has certainly been worth it."

There was rapturous applause all around the table.

"Now, please enjoy the rest of the evening."

Chapter Six

The following morning, Katie was miles away as she made a pot of tea, she just couldn't get Antonio de Marco out of her mind. She wished that she had been sat at that table with him and all his friends, how thrilling would that have been. What did Lucy call him, yes smooth, but there was nothing wrong with that. She had to stop thinking about him and get back into the real world, as if she could ever be with someone like that as Sasha had pointed out. It was just a crush that's all, she'd forget about him in a few days. Katie would just have to pull herself together and stop dreaming, sort out her relationship with Matt once and for all. She did love Matt in her own way but it was a safe kind of love and she wanted a bit of excitement in her life, yearned for it. Her thoughts were interrupted by Lucy stumbling into the kitchen.

"God, you look awful, must have been all that boozing we did. Didn't you just love the food, the gnocchi in pesto was to die for, not to mention the creamy chicken cacciatore and stuffed garlic mushrooms, it's the best food I have ever tasted."

"I think I'm going to throw up." And with that Lucy rushed out of the room.

"Alcohol definitely doesn't agree with you," Katie shouted to her, hoping she was going to be fit for their appointment that afternoon.

Veronica was congratulating Nicholas, they had unfortunately missed out on the champagne celebrations the previous evening as it had been so incredibly busy.

While Nicholas was reading through his contract Veronica poured them a glass of champagne. "I think you'll find it a very attractive package, one you would be extremely foolish to turn down."

"I have no intention of turning it down, it's far better than I expected."

Veronica smiled sweetly as she handed him the glass. "I think we will do very well here, very well indeed."

Eddie knocked on the door. "So sorry to interrupt, Ms Lamont, but those two girls are back, are you able to see them?"

Veronica nodded. "Yes, just let me finish up in here and I'll be right out."

"No rest for the wicked, we'll catch up later, eh?" Nicholas kissed her fondly on the cheek.

Katie was hoping that Antonio would be there and was very disappointed when he was nowhere to be seen. Lucy was still feeling a bit rough and was in serious need of a mender.

"Hello girls, glad to see you came back. I have made the decision to take you both on, initially as cocktail waitresses, on a three month trial basis. If you are still interested in becoming croupiers you will need to be trained up, naturally."

"That sounds great, Ms Lamont, when do we start?" Katie asked eagerly.

"Just go and see Tania, she'll check the schedules and provide you with necessary uniforms. All I expect is punctuality and respect and we'll get along fine."

Veronica beckoned Tania and left them to it, she had more important things to attend to.

Tania knew they would be back, she just hoped they would be able to handle it and if not she would take great pleasure in getting rid of them. "Hi, come on over to the bar." She looked at Lucy. "I'll see if I can sort your friend out with a hangover remedy I know."

As Tania walked she continued to chatter to the girls. "The first couple of weeks will be hard work as we all have to wear these damn stilettos, but don't give up, if you can stick it out it will be worth it. Usually you will be assigned to certain tables for the evening, it is your responsibility to take the drinks order. You bring your order over to the bar where one of the barmen will get them ready for you. It's quite simple really, all the tips are put into this jar and shared out every evening. So you see, it is very easy. If you do encounter any problems then come to get me, I will be meeting and greeting at the front prior to the guests being seated at their tables. If they are dining, you will be notified when those tables are ready."

"You sound really knowledgeable, you must have done this before," Lucy noted.

"Yeah, I used to work in the Manchester Club, but got offered a better job here so decided to go for it." She still hadn't heard anything about Vince, but Stevo assured her that she had done the right thing.

Tania poured Lucy a glass of eggnog and told her to down it in one and waited for her reaction. Two seconds later Lucy turned a pasty colour and made a dash for the toilets. Laughing and shaking her head she poured two glasses of wine and passed one to Katie. "As long as you do what you're told then we'll have no problems. I'm in charge in the bar area, not Veronica, do you get my drift?"

It was a statement not a question. Katie just nodded.

"I've got your dress sizes off Veronica, they're on the way as we speak, just remember black stilettos, ok?"

Lucy returned looking even worse than she did before.

"Did you spew then?" Tania mocked.

"Yes, seemed to have done the trick that yellow stuff."

"Told you."

The girls had taken an instant dislike to Tania, there was just something about her that they couldn't quite put their finger on. Katie stuck with her instincts, they would have to watch their step around her.

Chapter Seven

Antonio was in his office with Stevo and Gianni discussing the Manchester club. "Did Vince tell you what we needed to know?"

"Eventually, he put up quite a struggle though, it took three of us to sort him. Turns out it's down to that little prick Driscoll and his gang."

"Driscoll, is he still hanging around like a bad smell? I thought we paid him off," Antonio sighed.

"Guess he just got greedy, he threatened to murder Vince's wife and daughter if he didn't help him, but I think Vince was enjoying the danger too much. That little bastard got him hooked on the coke and then he was like putty in his hands. He allowed Driscoll and his cronies back into the club and they were practically fucking running the joint."

Antonio was becoming more irritated by the situation and knew he had to do something about it, he couldn't have Driscoll anywhere near his club. He had a criminal record and he didn't need the police taking an interest in his businesses.

"I'll personally sort him out, it will be my pleasure," Gianni announced. "Me and Stevo will go up there and put the bloody frighteners on him."

"Don't be so fucking stupid, we need to keep a low profile especially now. We need to put the hard word on Driscoll, let him know who's in charge. I think we should make a personal trip to the club, unannounced of course, see if we can catch the little bastard at it."

Gianni admired Antonio's calmness. "I still reckon we should make an example out of him."

"We'll try and do it my way first, perhaps Vince's murder will make him think twice. Stevo, make the necessary arrangements, we need to get this sorted and sorted fast."

44

Chapter Eight

Matt wasn't sure about his sister and girlfriend working at Club La Pregheira, but they had tried to convince him that they only intended working there for the summer for some extra cash and a bit of fun. They wanted enough money to go on a tour of Australia before starting to look for a more suitable position. Matt was starting his new job and was intending to take time out and meet them at his uncle's house in Sydney. He knew that they would make a lot of money faster working there in tips alone, than in a steady nine to five job. It was only for about three months, so surely he could put up with it for that small space of time.

The waitress placed the steaming hot mug of coffee on the table. "Can I get you anything else?"

"No thanks," Matt answered as he looked at the cafe door and then his watch wondering where the girls were.

He was on his second cup of coffee when they finally arrived. "I was just about to give up on you!"

"Sorry, it took longer than we expected, we both start at the weekend," Katie told him as she sat down.

"I thought you would have been rough today, Lucy, but you actually look great."

"Yep, that glass of yellow stuff at the club certainly did the trick."

"Eggnog," Katie corrected her.

Lucy was really excited and couldn't wait to start working in the club. She would enjoy herself, make some good tips and maybe even pull herself a millionaire. Now that was a really nice thought, it would make a change from the usual arseholes she normally dated, which unfortunately were always bad boys. Typical love 'em and leave 'em types, messing around with other women while dating her. Even though she had been hurt many times, Lucy always believed that she would eventually find the right guy.

Chapter Nine

Friday night at last, it seemed to take an age for it finally to come around. The restaurant was fully booked so it was definitely going to be a busy night. Veronica came and gave the staff her usual pep talk and wished the new girls the best of luck.

Tania told the waitresses which tables they would be working for the evening and reminded them that they would no doubt have the odd millionaire in the house tonight and to treat them accordingly.

"Katie, Lucy, you have something missing, here." Tania handed them shiny, black badges with their names embossed in gold. "Sorry, house rule, everyone must display their first name, to show we have nothing to hide, that's Veronica's philosophy anyway. Just remember if you do piss anyone off they'll have your name and then its bye bye, nobody gets a second chance."

Reluctantly the girls pinned the badges to their blouses, the pressure was really on, if they messed up they could be out the door, just like that.

Tania pretended to reassure them, but her tone left a lot to be desired. "Don't worry you will be fine. Ok, the doors are opening in five minutes, everyone please take your places and good luck, and you two watch your step."

Katie was assigned to the first customers and took the drinks order; she didn't panic, despite Tania's words, and took it in her stride and managed perfectly. Tania noticed that she was an instant hit with the guests and even had them ordering the most expensive wine in the house. She was a natural, it amazed Tania how Veronica could have spotted this in her as Katie had seemed so reserved. Her performance and sales would reflect back on Tania's management skills and she would be happy with that for now as long as Katie didn't get any ideas above her station.

Lucy on the other hand started off very nervous and Tania had to give her a few pointers to help. Once the nerves had subsided she became more relaxed and started to enjoy herself. At least this one wouldn't be any competition, always being told what to do, how pathetic. Maybe she would befriend her and mould her for use in the future.

Yep they fit in really well, thought Tania and would definitely be an asset to the club. But she still had to watch Katie, that one was too much of a natural for her liking.

The bar telephone rang, it was Veronica. "Antonio and Sasha are on their way, can you make sure he gets the best waitress we have."

Tania reassured Veronica that it would not be a problem. Unfortunately for her it was Sarah's night off and she was the best of the best. Maybe she should call her and get her to come in. She certainly wasn't expecting him or that bloody snotty, Russian bombshell. Just because she was born into money and had had everything handed to her on a plate all her life she thought she could treat people like dirt. Who should she get to look after them, Katie, the demure politely spoken one or Lucy who she suspected would give Sasha as good as she got? But then poor Lucy would end up getting the sack on her first night. That's it then, decision made, it will have to be Katie, and if it looked like she was getting into trouble she would step in and diffuse the situation. On second thoughts maybe she would just let her get on with it, see if she was as good as she herself was. She very much doubted it.

She refrained from telling Katie which special guests she would be looking after this evening, the less she knew about it the better.

Colin and Kyle were the barmen for tonight, they were brothers and ran the bar exceptionally well. They loved working in these sorts of clubs and also loved casinos, although they still hadn't had the pleasure of viewing the one in here yet. It was a closely guarded secret and it was membership only open to the top business men which were either from out of town or very close friends of the de Marcos. Colin was certain that Veronica would organise a private showing for them if he played his cards right. He would turn on the old charm and she would be putty in his hands, or at least he hoped she would be.

Antonio and Sasha stepped out of the limousine. Sasha would not travel by anything else when she was in London, as far as she was concerned it was the only way to travel. She wore a dazzling white and silver strapless tiny dress with a white stole, silver stilettos, accessorised with a white and silver bag. Her blonde hair was scraped back from her face in a pony tail, she looked amazing, perfect as usual. Checking her complexion in her compact mirror Sasha applied a touch more blusher emphasising her high cheek bones in just the right places. She added her pink lip gloss and was ready to face the world, she loved making a grand entrance. Sasha was the type of women who attracted gasps from everyone she encountered and she adored it.

Antonio studied Sasha, she was the perfect woman on the outside but could be jealous and manipulative if it suited her. She certainly wasn't a woman to cross, as he had discovered when she found out about Gianni's little fling with an air hostess. Sasha had cut up his designer suits and went crazy with his credit cards; she even had her first boob job. She was totally obsessed with constantly improving her looks and kept a very close eye on her figure, making sure she never gained an ounce.

"Good evening Mr de Marco, Sasha." Tania showed them to their table. "I'll send your hostess over right away, have a pleasant evening."

"Katie, table eight please and ignore Sasha as she can be a right stroppy mare. Oops, sorry I forget you had a run in with her the other night, didn't you?"

47

"Sort of, but how do you know? "

"Nothing gets past me, remember that, Katie. Now the best advice I can give is to just ignore her, she treats everyone like that, even the boss!" Tania was loving winding Katie up, she couldn't wait for the fireworks to begin.

Katie turned her attention to table eight, oh my God, it was him, Antonio, her heart started thudding in her chest. She hadn't registered that obviously he would be with the dreadful Sasha. What was it about him that made her feel like this, she hadn't even heard him speak yet and she was a nervous wreck.

"You alright?" Tania questioned her, she was worrying that maybe she had made a big mistake in thinking that Katie would be capable; from what she heard of the toilet fiasco, Katie had stood up for herself. She certainly didn't need any aggro and wanted to stay on side with the de Marcos, they were very important to her, especially after they gave her this new job for helping them out.

Katie nodded and took a deep breath as she made her way over to the table. "What can I get for you this evening?"

Sasha didn't even look up, she was still busy checking out the wine list. Antonio looked at Katie and smiled that impeccable smile of his. She felt her face flushing and her heart was racing. He seemed to study her for ages before finally saying. "We'll have a bottle of my favourite wine." He winked at her. It felt like they were the only two people in the room. Then Sasha looked up.

"Hurry up then, girl, before we thirst to death. Aren't you supposed to be looking after us?" she tutted. "Get on with it then."

God that woman really got on her bloody nerves, she just wanted to slap her smug face. It was all she could do to contain herself. Gritting her teeth she made her way back to the bar; shit, what was his favourite wine she wondered.

"Bottle of his favourite, was it by any chance?" Kyle was already in the process of expertly opening the bottle. "Was the bitch giving you a hard time?"

"How did you guess?"

"By that pissed off look written all over your face."

"Is it that obvious?" Katie sighed.

"Just ignore the cow, everyone else does. She only gets away with her attitude cos of the boss, bloody rich bitch, got a fucking attitude problem. Just keep your head and you'll end up with a substantial tip tonight."

Katie laughed, she would love to stick the tip right up the snooty bitch's arse. Now that would be hilarious!!

Kyle laughed with her, wondering what Katie was thinking. Whatever it was he wished someone would bring that woman down a notch or two. No one would dare say a word though unfortunately, too afraid of upsetting the boss and getting the sack to boot.

Picking up the silver tray and its contents Katie walked slowly back to the table. She set the wine glasses down first. Sasha picked the glass up and studied it intently.

Katie was about to place the bottle on the table when Antonio reached over. He brushed her hand as he took the bottle from her, it was like an electric shock going through her entire body.

"What the hell is this, it's bloody filthy," shrieked Sasha. "Take it back immediately, you useless girl." She shoved the wine glass at her.

"I can assure you, madam, that there is nothing wrong with this glass."

"How dare you, you impertinent girl, have you no etiquette at all?"

"Have you?"

"What did you say to me?" Sasha stood up, towering over her. Antonio pulled her arm making her sit down.

Sasha was having none of it and glared at her. "Well, what are you waiting for, fuck off and clean it."

Katie looked at her, then at the glass. She had had just about enough of this goddamn woman. She picked up the nearest napkin spat on it and rubbed the rim of the glass. "That clean enough for you, madam, or do you want me to lick it too?" Katie slammed it down on the table.

Sasha nearly fell off her chair. "Did you see what she did, Antonio, are you going to let her speak to me like that? How dare you, you little bitch, you're sacked."

"Suits me, I'd rather serve a tramp than a stuck up cow like you. At least they would have better manners, of that I have absolutely no doubt." And with that Katie turned on her heel and stomped off.

Antonio roared with laughter, never, ever had anyone ever spoken to Sasha like that before; it was something to behold. Sasha deserved that for all the times she had treated the staff like something she had just trodden on.

"What the hell is so funny, you fucking idiot. She has embarrassed me in front of the entire club and I won't stand for it." Seething with rage Sasha signalled to Tania.

"Please make sure the limo is ready for me. I cannot bear to stay here for another second, not after that display, what were you thinking of employing that insolent little bitch?"

Tania dutifully escorted Sasha to the door. "I'm so sorry about your hostess, she will be severely reprimanded don't you worry, Veronica will sort it all out for you."

"There is nothing to sort out darling, I have already sacked her, I want her out. In fact I am going to have her personally escorted off the premises." She summoned Brian, the big burly bouncer.

Brian couldn't believe that she wanted to publicly humiliate this young girl, but what could he do about it, it was his job after all? When Sasha gave orders it was like taking them off his boss, he dare not argue or it would be him getting the sack.

Sasha smiled as the limo drove off, it was just a pity she would miss the show. No one would get one over on her, she would show that little cow, how dare she treat her like that.

Tania and Brian had no choice but to go and get Katie from the changing rooms. By this time half of the bar had noticed the scene, Sasha had been so loud and obnoxious. Finally, once Sasha was sure everybody was watching, she had stormed out of the club, pushing the staff out of her way and anybody else she came into contact with. There would be repercussions, there always were when Sasha was involved and it was also noted that Mr de Marco hadn't left with her.

Once Lucy finished serving her table she half thrust the tray into Kyle's hand. "Sorry, I need to see if Katie's alright, I'll be as quick as I can."

"Just hurry up, if Tania catches you, there'll be hell to pay."

Katie had just got changed and was putting her jacket on when Lucy came into the room. "What happened out there?"

"That psycho bitch…" Katie began.

"That psycho bitch happens to be engaged to the owner of this club, your boss. What were you thinking, are you crazy?" Tania was enjoying herself.

"Oh come on, Tania, Sasha did provoke her."

"Get back to work, Lucy, this is none of your business."

"But Katie is my friend."

"I don't give a shit, either get back to work or leave with her and don't come back." She glared at her, hands on her hips. "Well, what's it to be?"

"Go on, Lucy, it's ok, I'll talk to you later," sighed Katie.

Lucy had a fright when she almost walked smack bang into Brian who was waiting outside the door. "Anything I can do, love?" He gave her a sickening smile.

"Just fuck off." Lucy had to make him understand that she wasn't in the least bit interested in him.

"Now, that's not very nice is it?" Brian pushed her against the wall as she struggled wildly to get free.

"Get off me, you lousy bastard."

"Ah, don't be like that, just give me a kiss, you know you want to."

"In your fucking dreams."

"Brian, get in here, right now," Tania shouted. "Hurry up."

"What a shame!" His slimy tongue licked at her neck. "We'll finish this another time, sweetheart, really soon."

The horrible bastard, he made her skin crawl, she ran to the toilets and scrubbed at her neck, trying to get rid of the stench of him. Christ what was she going to do about him? He may do something much worse next time. She would have to talk to someone, get some advice.

"What do you want me to do, Tania?" Brian asked.

"Just get her out of here."

Brian started to take her towards the back entrance.

"No, Brian, out the front please," Tania smiled at Katie. "Well, you came in through the front door so you can leave through it, love."

Antonio was watching with great interest as Brian escorted Katie through the middle of the club like she was some sort of criminal. He would have to go over and rescue the poor girl, he couldn't watch her humiliation any longer.

"I'll deal with this, Brian."

"Ok, boss."

Tania started to apologise for the way Katie had behaved. "If Sarah was here this would never had happened, I've said it before we should never have trainees in on our busiest nights, its lunacy."

"From where I was sitting she was doing a great job."

"But, what she did to your fiancée was totally unacceptable."

Antonio was having none of it. Ignoring her he whisked Katie in the opposite direction. "Come with me, we'll have a little chat somewhere more private." There was something vulnerable about her that made his protective side come out. He had no doubt that she could look after herself, but he was intrigued to find out more about her.

"Look, Mr de Marco, I'm sorry that I upset you're fiancée, please just let me leave."

"I'll let you into a secret shall I? Sasha is a very demanding woman, she has been spoilt rotten all of her life and alas doesn't know any better. But that was the funniest thing I have seen in a long time, she needs to be brought down a peg or two every now and again and you certainly managed to do that." He chuckled as he unlocked his office door. "But it's not worth sacking you for, don't worry I'll smooth things over with her."

His office was of a similar design to Veronica's, Katie noted, just much bigger. He had a huge wooden cabinet filled with trophies. As if reading her thoughts he started to tell her what they were.

"Mainly golf trophies, I just play with the guys for fun. I always win the tournament, been playing since I was sixteen and was told that I had potential and could eventually have turned professional, but I wasn't really interested in it as a career path."

Katie was impressed. "Wow, just think you could have been up there playing alongside someone like Seve Ballesteros."

"So you are a golf fan?"

"Not really, my dad is, he plays a lot now that he is retired."

"I'll have to invite him to one of my friendly competitions sometime."

"Oh, that could be difficult, he lives in Australia now, since my mum died. He's got some family out there." Why was she telling him all this, she barely knew him.

"I'm sorry about your mum, what happened?" he asked gently.

"She had a sudden heart attack when I was seventeen."

"I'm sorry to hear that, you must miss her very much. " He paused. "Did you not want to go to Australia with your father?"

Katie shook her head. "No, not yet, my boyfriend Matt has just finished his law degree at University." Why on earth had she just mentioned her boyfriend.

"So, I guess you're only here on a temporary basis?"

"I suppose, but Matt's just got a job offer, so I don't really know what our plans are."

"So, this boyfriend of yours, what is he like?"

"Why do you ask?"

"Just curious to see what kind of man captured your heart." He smiled at her showing perfect white teeth. "Can I get you a drink?"

She could feel herself flushing now, he was just so charismatic, not like any man she had ever met before, he seemed so exciting. Maybe it was because of his Italian accent, the way he looked, or the fact that he owned all of this. "So, do you want me to go back to work?"

"Not tonight, we'll let all the gossip die down first." He handed her a glass of whisky.

She gratefully accepted the drink and sipped it slowly, not knowing where to look.

"Am I making you nervous, Katie?"

That was the first time he had said her name and for some strange reason it made her feel all warm and tingly inside. Perhaps it was the whisky, she wasn't sure which it was but it sure felt good. "No, of course not, Mr de Marco."

"Please, call me Antonio, I insist."

"I can't do that, you're my boss."

"Yes you can, I give you my permission." Antonio pointed to a black and white photo of a young woman in a gold frame. "You know, you remind me of my grandmother, you look just like her, when she was your age of course." He smiled again. "She was very beautiful, don't you think?"

Before Katie had time to answer Antonio's telephone started to ring; he looked at the phone.

"Aren't you going to answer that? It could be something important."

It was probably his brother, Gianni checking in. "They'll call back if it is."

But the phone continued to ring. Reluctantly he picked it up. "Yes?"

Katie saw a flicker of annoyance sweep across his face. It changed his handsome features and made him look quite menacing. It shocked her but it disappeared almost as quickly as it had came. She wondered if it was Sasha.

"I'm in the middle of something right now, I'll call you back."

"Everything ok?" Katie asked.

"Perfect, now, let me organise a lift home for you."

Katie tried to protest but Antonio put his hand up to stop her and pressed the intercom button. "Fred, can you bring the car round?"

Antonio opened the door and they walked towards the main entrance. "So, as I was saying, you have a foreign look about you, do you have..." The telephone was ringing once more. "Excuse me for one second." He answered it. "What?" Growling he cursed under his breath and slammed the phone down.

Katie looked at him, wondering what was going on.

"Just business, nothing to worry about, trust me." He smiled showing his gleaming white teeth as he nodded to the two bouncers as they left the building. He led Katie to the awaiting limousine.

Katie was thrilled and it must have shown in her eyes as Antonio opened the door for her, "Allow me, young lady," and gestured for her to get in. "Where do you live?"

"Er, I'm not sure if you should drive the limo up my street, you can drop me off nearby if you like."

"Why not?"

"Well, it is a little bit rough; I wouldn't want your lovely car to get damaged."

"You live in a rough area?"

"Yes, it was the only place we could afford the rent."

"You live with your boyfriend?"

"No, his sister, Lucy, she works for you too."

They can't be that much in love he thought, if they weren't even living together, it can't be serious then.

Katie gave him the directions and wondered what her neighbours would think when she turned up in a black stretch limo! The curtains would definitely be twitching, of that she was sure. She just hoped nobody thought she had came into a load of money and burgled her flat.

As they arrived at Katie's home Antonio leaned over, lightly brushing her cheek with the back of his hand. "I'll look forward to seeing you at work tomorrow evening and then perhaps, bella; we can arrange a proper date."

The limo sped off and Katie was left standing in the middle of the street, only moving when a car horn pipped at her and the driver yelled for her to watch where she was going. A date, what kind of a date, he was engaged and she was in love with Matt, wasn't she?

Antonio returned to his penthouse and dialled the number Gianni had given him. "What the hell do you want, I was having a pleasant evening until you interrupted."

"It's Vince, I mean his body, it's turned up in the river, a kid was throwing bread in for the swans and spotted his body, it will be all over the news. I thought I'd better warn you. It's only a matter of time before they identify him."

"Shit, thought we may have had more time, you got a water tight alibi?"

"Sure, what do you take me for? I'm no fool."

"Ok, keep me informed, I'll only contact Frank if they make a connection."

Frank was a close friend of the de Marcos and it wasn't the first time they had used him to help cover their tracks and he had a feeling it wouldn't be the last either. His position in the police force made him very valuable to them and they paid him well. But they never made contact unless it was an absolute necessity.

Chapter Ten

Katie was singing to herself as she brushed her hair in the mirror. She just couldn't get Antonio out of her head, he was the most handsome, most exciting man she had ever met in her life. There was a yearning in her that she had never felt before, her heart skipped a beat as she remembered the touch of his hand on her cheek.

"Hey, hey, Katie, snap out of it, I'm home!" Lucy clicked her fingers, clearly irritated by Katie's far away expression.

"Oh, er hi, Luce, I never heard you come in."

"Don't tell me, let me guess. You're thinking about him again, aren't you?"

"I don't know what you are talking about, I'm not thinking about anyone."

"Oh come on, it's written all over your face, you're mad for that Antonio aren't you? It will all end in tears you know."

"Look there's nothing going on, he, he just felt bad about how Sasha was treating me. That's all, really!"

"Ok, whatever, but just be careful I've been hearing a few nasty rumours about the de Marcos!"

"Whatever you've heard must be rubbish, the de Marcos seem perfectly normal to me."

"So, what did you have to do to get your job back then?"

"What, nothing, why."

"That's not what everyone's saying in the club, after we finished up Veronica announced that you didn't get sacked and were going to be back at work tomorrow night."

"Well, Antonio, I mean Mr de Marco said, it wasn't worth getting the sack for."

"Oh, did he now? And what did you give him in return for this noble favour?"

"Luce, calm down, this isn't like you."

Lucy burst into tears. "I'm sorry, that Brian pinned me up against the wall and was very suggestive, he frightens me."

"Oh, God, you poor thing." Katie put her arms around her. "Did he touch you?"

"My neck, he, he…" Lucy shuddered.

"Come on, it's alright, we'll have a word with Veronica, she won't stand for it."

"Do you think?"

"Yes, it will be ok, now can I get you a drink, hot chocolate or something?"

"No thanks, I'm just going to have a quick shower and get off to bed, I'm exhausted. I'll see you in the morning." Lucy left the room.

Katie got into bed and snuggled into her pillow. As she drifted off to sleep she dreamed of Antonio and his words, 'see you tomorrow, bella'.

Chapter Eleven

Antonio was reading the morning newspaper when his doorbell rang continuously. Jesus, who the hell was that? He strode to the door and before he had a chance to open it fully a man he recognised shoved his way into the apartment, closely followed by a policeman. Flashing his badge, Detective Constable Fearon aggressively began firing questions at him.

"Your employee, Vince Fraser, was found dead late last night, up in Manchester. It was obvious by his injuries that he had been tortured, broken ribs, face smashed in, very, very nasty death by all accounts. The estimated time of death has not been established yet due to the fact that he was found in the water. So it may take several days for the forensics to pinpoint the exact time of death and when they do, I'll need to know your whereabouts, Mr de Marco."

"Certainly, anything I can do to help, all you need to do is ask."

"I wonder who he pissed off to deserve such a horrific death, one of the worst things I have ever seen." He paused to catch his breath. "He was your trusted manager in your Manchester Club, who could have wanted him dead? What were they after? Someone mentioned that he was dabbling in drugs, what do you think about that then, Mr de Marco?" spat DC Fearon. He hated people like de Marco, Italian fucker comes to his city, thinks he is a big man, then to top it all the press sing his praises, think he's the best thing since sliced bread, it annoyed the hell out of him.

"Jesus, you trying to give yourself a heart attack or something," Antonio smiled politely.

Pulling a grubby handkerchief from his jacket pocket DC Fearon mopped his brow. "I'm glad that you find it so amusing."

"I'm just concerned for your health, that's all, can I get you a nice glass of water?"

He was really trying his patience now. "Are you trying to be obstructive, Mr de Marco?"

"Let me get you that glass of water." Antonio started towards the kitchen.

"I don't want a glass of fucking water."

The young PC looked embarrassed. "Sir?"

DC Fearon continued. "Aren't you bothered that one of your key employees has just been found brutally murdered?"

"You seem to have all the answers, you tell me. Now if you don't mind I was just about to take a shower." Antonio smiled coolly at DC Fearon.

"We'll be back."

"I'm sure you will," Antonio drawled sarcastically as he nodded towards the door. "You know your way out."

DC Fearon was really annoyed by this so called businessman of the year, Italian prick. There was something not quite right about him, he could feel it and he was intent on finding out exactly what that was. He might just do some delving into his past, see what he could turn up on this foreign fuck.

Antonio heaved a sigh of relief as they left. That DC Fearon was going to be a whole bundle of trouble, he could sense it.

"Hey, baby, what did they want? Why don't you come and have a long hot shower with me, darling?" Sasha put on her sexiest voice.

Antonio turned his attention to Sasha. She slowly dropped her silk dressing gown revealing her voluptuous body and huge, mountainous breasts. Antonio went to her kissing her passionately and running his hands all over her body. He felt himself hardening and wanted to take her right then and there. "Oh baby, you are so hot." Sasha moaned as she began to unzip his trousers.

The sound of her voice jolted Antonio back to earth with a bump. Just for a few seconds he imagined he was with the lovely, sweet Katie. He pushed Sasha away and hastily zipped his trousers back up. "Sorry Sasha, I er, I have to go into the club today, you know, business. I haven't got time for this."

"Suit yourself, darling. But what am I going to do for the whole day, I will be so bored?" she moaned.

Antonio grabbed his wallet and stuffed a wad of notes into her hand. "Get a facial or something, I'm sure you will spend it very wisely."

Sasha snorted as she looked at him and then at the money. "Whatever you say, darling." Still naked she picked up her dressing gown and walked off, tutting to herself.

She was a real pain in the arse lately he thought. It was time he got her out of his life, she was high maintenance and far too demanding. He was sick of it, she was slowly sucking the life out of him and he didn't want to end up cold and emotionless like her.

A real woman, with real feelings is what he needed, one who would respect him. He made a decision right there and then, he was going to make a move on Katie, he would romance her the Italian way and then he was going to marry her, it was about time he settled down. And once Antonio made a decision he stayed true to his word and nobody or nothing would talk him out of it.

Chapter Twelve

Veronica counted the takings. She was delighted with herself, everything was going smoothly, exactly to plan. Her little side line was paying well, some of the girls were more than just hostesses, but she had to be careful, very careful. If Antonio found out she would be in serious trouble and God knows what he would do. This was a legitimate business and he wouldn't stand for prostitution, not in his club. Club La Pregheira was too up market for something like that. She reassured herself that if the girls were willing and the clientele were happy, then why not. She wasn't doing any harm, after all she made the introductions for a small fee and then whatever the girls made, well after that it was up to them. That was the beauty of it, she never forced anyone into it. All Veronica did was make the suggestion to the girls she was almost certain would be up for it, and even though the majority of these women were single parents it didn't concern her. She planned to retire as soon as possible and gave herself an estimated five years. Veronica loved her job, loved the club and now she was getting serious with Nicholas, everything was fantastic. Pulling back the carpet she opened her hidden safe; she was in the middle of putting her stash back in when she noticed Antonio entering the building. It was certainly a great idea to install the security cameras, that was a stroke of genius, she would always be one step ahead; if she got caught then she would end up dead in the bottom of a lake somewhere, never to be found for years.

"How's my favourite lady?" Antonio said as he kissed Veronica on both cheeks.

"Brilliant, the club is a real success, we doubled our takings last night and I am confident we will go from strength to strength."

"What information do you have on the two new girls?"

"Lucy Carmichael and Katie Saunders?"

"Yes, have you done the background checks yet?"

"Of course, but it's quite boring really, they haven't done anything of any significance, why do you ask?"

"Nothing for you to worry about, Veronica, just send the files up to my office. You seen Gianni today?"

"No, not yet, should we be expecting him then?"

Antonio nodded and left the room making his way up the stairs to his own office which was situated adjacent to the casino. He had to work on a plan, a way to get rid of Sasha; whatever he did it was going to be painful.

Chapter Thirteen

Gianni was unperturbed that he too had had a visit from the local constabulary. What the fuck did it have to do with them? Vince was scum and got what he deserved. He was a coward and let the Driscoll drug gang into their Manchester club, he should have confided in him, sought his help. Then at least Gianni could have done something about it, maybe done a deal or something. Perhaps he would just have kicked the stupid bastard silly and destroyed the drug dealing mother fuckers once and for all, taken on the business himself. He didn't mind people dabbling in drugs, but there was a time and a place and blatantly dealing in the middle of their club was definitely not one of them. If you were clever enough then anything was possible. He grinned as he thought of his own little set up, it was perfect and thanks to his careful planning he was raking the money in. Discretion was the key though, if Antonio or Roberto ever found out then he would be in deep shit.

He drove to Club La Pregheira, hoping Antonio would be in a good mood, he heard about the drama with Sasha and the new cocktail waitress. But first he wanted to see Veronica, the bitch was doing things behind his back and she needed sorting out. Nobody made a fool out of the de Marcos, as Vince had just found out. God help her if she messed him around.

Veronica went white when she saw him coming towards her office. Just play it cool she thought, everything will be ok, he doesn't know a thing, she tried to convince herself as he burst through the door. "Gianni, what a surprise, it is so nice to see you, darling."

"Cut the crap, we can do this the easy way or the hard way, it's up to you."

Veronica stood her ground. "I'm sorry Gianni, you have lost me."

"Wrong answer, bitch." Gianni launched himself at her grabbing her roughly by the throat. "Fuck you, you fucking whore, I know what you have been up to."

Veronica was gasping for breath, her eyes bulged and she felt like she was going to pass out. He let go of her and as she slumped to the floor he kicked her in the ribs for good measure. Veronica writhed in agony, fighting for her breath. "Don't bullshit the king of all bullshitters, darling," he mocked. "Just give me the fucking money and we'll say no more about it."

"I, I don't know what…" Gianni kicked her again and grabbed her hair dragging her across the room.

"Please Gianni…"

"Was one kick in the ribs not enough for you?" He paused. "I'll ask you once more, where is the fucking money, you bitch!"

Veronica crawled to the hiding place and lifted the carpet. She couldn't speak, just pointed to the safe hidden in the floor.

"Combination?"

"Fifty five, twenty six, thirty six," she stuttered.

Gianni sniggered in her face. "Well thank you, darling, keep up the good work. Just remember if my brother finds out you'll be out on your ear. And if you think of telling him I will deny everything, after all the girls are all recruited by you, I have absolutely no involvement. I won't be greedy, let's say I take seventy five per cent, you can have twenty five, what do you say?"

"Yes, yes whatever you want," she muttered, holding her ribs.

"I'm so glad that we understand each other, nice doing business. Let's say we catch up once a week for the split. And don't even think of messing with me, I have someone watching you. So you see, fuck with me and that's the end of you and your pretty little sideline."

Gianni didn't need the money, he just loved showing that he was the boss, it gave him a real thrill; he wouldn't stand for any disrespect, not from this stupid bitch. No one did any deals without telling him about it, not a chance.

Feeling much calmer he was ready to go and face Antonio, take the shit off him. He could handle it, no problem, he would be apologetic and Antonio would forgive him, just like he had done all his life.

Veronica was puzzled, who the hell was watching her? Some bastard had dropped her right in it, God help them if she found out who it was. It would have to be someone close to her, was it Eddie, the assistant that frightened everyone with his mannerism and gold tooth? No, he would do anything for her, surely it couldn't be him! She remembered the old saying "keep your friends close and your enemies closer". Eddie was an odd sort of man, but he didn't have a nasty bone in his body and he certainly was not clever enough to spy on her! She had been good to him and it was she who had given him the job in the first place, nobody else would hire him because of the way he looked. It wasn't his fault that he looked the way he did, he was a man of few words but was totally trustworthy, and if he did know about her extra business opportunity then there was no way he would grass on her. She would have to tread more carefully in the future and keep a sharper lookout. That Tania Horrocks bitch had turned up out of the blue and was given a job without her consultation. It could be her, there again it could be anyone.

"Is it safe to come in?" Gianni asked sticking his head around the door of his brother's office.

Antonio shook his head in annoyance. "I take it you had a visit too?"

"Yeah, they don't know anything, it's nothing to worry about."

61

"You know we have to stay out of trouble, all the businesses are doing well and we don't need to get involved in this shit any more. All that is behind us now, we are totally legitimate and I want it to stay that way."

Just then Eddie Regan knocked on the door. "Veronica sent these files for you, Mr de Marco."

"What files?" enquired Gianni, looking at his brother.

"Just staff files."

"Is there anything else I can do?" asked Eddie.

"No, that's all for now, thanks, Eddie."

It was true that Eddie had been spying on Veronica but not under anyone's orders. He had been listening outside of the door and heard Gianni's attack on her. Eddie had wanted to go in and kick his ribs, see how he liked it, but he would not have been any match for Gianni. He had really hurt Veronica, maybe one day somebody would hurt him. Eddie hoped that he was around when that day finally came.

Gianni picked up the files and Katie's photograph fell out. "Mm just staff files eh? What's the deal with this chick then, she's not your usual type. Sasha ain't going to be very happy."

"Then maybe I've never had the right type of woman. There's just something about her, I can't quite put my finger on it, she just seems so familiar, like I've met her somewhere before."

"Boy, you sure have got it bad." He roared with laughter.

"I plan to marry her."

Gianni was totally dumbfounded. "You're totally serious about this aren't you?"

"You better make a good brother-in-law." Antonio joked.

"But you don't know anything about this girl, she could be another gold digger, or some kind of psychopath, what's it say in her file?"

"I very much doubt it, take a look, she's just a normal young woman."

"Well, it's your life, so I guess it's up to you."

"We could have a double wedding." Antonio was messing with him now.

Gianni looked mortified. "What, with me and Felicia? We're getting married in a couple of months time!"

"Well, I figured it was about time I settled down, don't you?"

"Hey enough of the wedding talk, you haven't even been on a date with her yet."

"I'll figure something out, but only after I tell Sasha it's over, after all that's the least I can do."

"Rather you than me bro, you know what she was like when I dumped her. Expect her to seek her revenge, cos you know that one way or another she will."

Antonio changed the subject. "You sorted out a replacement for Vince yet?"

"I thought I would take a trip up there, you know, show face, make sure everything is ok, do you want to come?"

"Yeah, sure."

"Ok, I'll make the necessary arrangements, we'll go tomorrow night, turn up unexpectedly, see if we can catch anybody out."

"Jesus, it comes to something if we can't even trust our own staff," Antonio contemplated.

"I'll say, but I never thought it of Vince, he just didn't seem the type."

"Well if it hadn't been for Tania we would still be in the dark and things could certainly have been much worse."

"True." But at least Vince was out of the picture for good, Gianni reminded himself.

Chapter Fourteen

Matthew was just getting out of his car when two men grabbed him and shoved him into the back seat. "I… I haven't got any money," he stammered.

"It's not your money we're interested in," Gianni de Marco said in a quiet but intimidating voice. "Just a friendly warning, dump Katie, she's way out of your league. You've got twenty four hours to break it to her."

"What do you mean, what's all this about?"

"Just do it, or maybe we'll take you out of the picture, permanent like," growled the man.

Matt couldn't help but notice the recently acquired pink scar which ran down the left hand side of his face.

"Do you understand?" The man pulled a knife and pressed it to his side.

"But I love her," was all Matt could say.

Lucy was on her way home when she spotted Matt's car and what appeared to be two men in it with him. All three of them were sitting in the back and Matt was in the middle of them, that looked a little strange to her. Curious to know what the hell was going on she hurried towards them.

"Oh look, here comes little sis, Lucy to the rescue. She's a pretty little thing, it would be a shame if something happened to her, you get my drift?" The thug looked at the knife and ran his finger over the glinting blade.

Matt nodded, unable to say a word. He was too shocked at what had just taken place.

Before she had time to reach her brother, Gianni and a man she had never seen before got out of the car, quickly crossed the road and jumped into a waiting vehicle which proceeded to drive off at a ridiculous speed.

"Was that Gianni de Marco, what's going on?" Lucy questioned. "Looked like they meant business to me, and what are you doing sitting in the back of the car?"

Matt just said the first thing that popped into his head and hoped that his sister would believe it. "Oh, they er, made me an offer, you know, family solicitor. But I turned him down, he's not the sort of person I would wish to represent."

"I'm not convinced, are you sure everything is ok?"

"Sure, I'm sure."

"Well, it's just kind of odd that he offers you a business deal in the back of your car."

"No, not really, that's how people like that do business."

"Are you getting out or staying in there for the rest of the day?"

"If you move out of the way, yes." Matt got out feeling slightly absurd.

"Come on, I'll make you a cuppa." Lucy linked him and they walked up to the apartment.

Nobody spoke until Gianni paid the hired man and dropped him off at his required destination.

"Are you sure you did the right thing, what will Antonio say?" Stevo asked.

"Hey, I'm his brother and I know him inside and out, remember? There's no need to tell him about this. I'm just speeding things up for him, when he's happy I'm happy and then everyone's happy."

"But surely he's capable of getting his own women."

"This one is different, she's the loyal type, not the sort to dump her besotted boyfriend and take up with another man. This way just makes it easier for them both, nothing to stand in their way now."

"Ok, I only want the best for Antonio."

"Me too, although I don't know what he sees in this Katie chick, she is just the girl next door as far as I am concerned."

"Maybe, that's the attraction, a normal woman just for a change."

"Who the hell knows? I don't really give a shit, but we better keep a close eye on Sasha, you know what she did to me!"

"No problem, what do you want me to do, rough her up a bit?" Stevo despised her and although he disagreed with violence towards women, he could quite happily make an exception in her case and give her a good slap.

"No, no need for that, I'll talk to her, trust me she won't do anything!"

"Do you think this Matthew guy will tell his sister about what just happened?"

"No way, if you had seen the look on his face when we mentioned his little sis. He won't dare risk it, especially when Jed pulled the knife, after that he knew we were serious!"

"She's something else, little Lucy I mean. I wouldn't want to see that animal hurt her!"

"So, you telling me that you've got a soft spot for her then?"

"I might have, but she doesn't even know who I am, yet!" Stevo laughed. "But all that's about to change."

"Shit, what the hell is it with the love bug, it's becoming contagious!"

"No, that's you and Antonio mate, I never mentioned the word love."

"You know me, I never had time for love, until I met Felicia of course, now she is a really classy lady. I got fed up with all those slobbering, doe-eyed girls, it did my head right in! I thought I would never settle down. It was a case of if a woman offers it on a plate, then why resist the inevitable?"

Stevo laughed haughtily. "You never cease to amaze me Gianni, your wild ways will have to stop once you're married."

Gianni laughed. "Of course, but it will be a damn shame for all those beautiful women out there to miss out on this!"

"Once you tie the knot, I'll remind you of what you just said, Gianni."

"You do that, I'll prove I'm perfectly capable of being faithful to one woman!"

"Ok, let's have a little wager on it, say a grand?"

"Make it two and you're on!"

"Whatever, it's your money man."

It was going to be a difficult task making sure Gianni stayed faithful and they both knew it.

Chapter Fifteen

"Isn't it great, Veronica just called me and gave me the night off, she said that Tania should have consulted her before giving me my marching orders."

"Why would she do that?" Matt was sure it was down to de Marco.

"To show Tania who's boss that's why!"

She was in fantastic form, all happy and smiling, completely oblivious to Matt's quiet mood. It pained him that she hadn't noticed, usually she would have known instantly if there was a slight sniff of anything being wrong.

"So, what should we do tonight then?" he asked her. "How about a movie and a restaurant." He waited for an answer. "Katie?"

"Oh, sorry, what did you say, I was miles away?"

"Fancy catching a movie and then a meal?"

Katie smiled at him. "Well, the thing is, Veronica has said that we can go to the club if we want, I just need to let her know so she can save us a table. Perfect opportunity for you to check it out for yourself."

"No, I would much prefer that lovely, atmospheric restaurant over on Rosamond Street, you know the one, it makes those fantastic steaks, how about it?" Matt was quite insistent, the club was the last place he wanted to take her.

"Oh, come on, you have never seen it from the inside, it will be so much fun and I'll get a staff discount too." Her voice was filled with excitement.

"You don't seriously want to go to the club, you work there, silly, you'll get sick of seeing the place."

"Don't be a spoilsport, if you're worried about the cost then don't be, I've got some cash, we'll both chip in." She looked at him with those big blue eyes of hers. "It'll be worth it, what do you say?"

Matt reluctantly agreed, hoping and praying that none of the de Marcos or their violent sidekick would be there. It was kind of ironic that he would be breaking the news to her in the club of all places, but just what was he going to say? It was breaking his heart thinking about it. His beautiful, sweet Katie, he could hardly believe that this would be their last night together as a couple.

"And another bonus is that Lucy's working tonight."

"Ok, ok, you win."

Katie threw her arms around him. "Brilliant, but I'll need a couple of hours to get ready."

"A few hours?"

"I've got to look my best in a place like that, trust me."

He wondered just who she was trying to impress and sadly doubted that it was him. "I'll pick you up at 7.30pm, Katie."

After Matt left, Lucy watched Katie intently. "I think he may be going to propose to you."

"What … don't be silly, what makes you say that?"

"Don't you think he was acting a bit weird, a bit fidgety and he had those puppy dog eyes, he couldn't take them off you?"

"I never noticed."

"Oh, come on, he tried to tempt you into going to that discreet little restaurant, you know the one over on Rosamond Street, and he was trying to be quite firm about it too, which is out of character for him."

"Do you think so?"

"Unless he's up to something else."

Katie started to panic. "But we decided on a long term engagement, marriage isn't even on the agenda… not yet!"

"I always thought you guys were made for each other and that one day we really would be blood relatives, I mean we are as close as sisters anyway."

"True and nothing will ever change that."

"Is there something that you are not telling me Katie?"

"Like what? I'm happy as I am, we both are, why change it?"

"This isn't like you, it's that de Marco, he has stirred something in you."

"Definitely not!"

"Methinks you protest too much, Katie."

"Just leave it, Luce, eh?"

"I think you should just break up with Matt, it would be the kindest thing to do. He worships the ground you walk on, but face it, suddenly you've changed."

"No I haven't, I'm still the same Katie that I ever was."

"Ok, well how do you explain these?" Lucy shoved her into the small kitchenette.

There was a huge bouquet of red roses. Katie's face beamed as she ran over to smell them. She tore open the card. 'Bella, dinner tomorrow night 8pm and I won't take no for an answer, A."

"Oh they are so beautiful," Katie gushed as she read the card.

"See, you are smitten with him, just admit it."

"Oh, it's true, I am attracted to him but I don't want to hurt Matt."

"You know that I don't approve Katie. If you intend to go on this date then please just finish it with Matt tonight, promise me."

"Oh Matt." Katie looked genuinely upset. "But what will I tell him?"

"Just the truth Katie, that's all I ask and the sooner the better as far as I'm concerned."

68

Chapter Sixteen

Katie looked amazing; she wore a knee length red strappy dress, her long dark hair glistened under the low lights in the restaurant.

"You look stunning." Matt was proud to be seen with her. He was determined to make the most of the evening. He could never usually afford such an exclusive place as this, he wanted it to be a night to remember and with the use of his overdraft and Katie's staff discount he could make it happen.

Matt listened as Katie talked about the décor, she was totally at ease. He realised that she really had changed virtually overnight; this is where she belongs he thought. But how was he going to break the news to her, would she crumble and be devastated or would she not really care? Once he knew her so well, but this new-found confidence Katie had really threw him. Something had happened to her, he knew she was no longer his Katie. Perhaps he was doing the right thing, letting her go. He looked around, if anyone deserved all of this Katie did. What could he offer her right now? Nothing that's what. She was ready to move on and he wouldn't stand in her way. The love of his life was moving on without him, the thought of losing her totally saddened him. In fact he admitted it was positively breaking his heart. He nervously knocked back his double Southern Comfort.

"Whoa, slow down, is everything ok?"

"Sure, I just need to use the gents, be right back." Matt needed to go and compose himself, he wanted to get through the farewell meal and then break it to her as gently as he could.

As soon as he left the table Lucy rushed over. "You told him yet, is that why he took off?"

"No, I don't know how to tell him, he's been so good to me, I don't want to hurt him."

"And how do you think he'll feel if you go on this date tomorrow and he finds out?"

"I know, I just don't know if I can."

"You better had or I will."

Just then Veronica walked over with a bottle of champagne. "This is on the house. Lucy, will you be a dear and do the honours once your brother comes back?"

"I didn't tell you that he was my brother!" Lucy exclaimed.

"There isn't anything that I don't know, trust me darling," Veronica winked at Katie and walked back over to the bar.

"What the hell is going on here?" Lucy was flabbergasted; terrified that Matt had ordered it to go with his proposal of marriage.

"That's what I would like to know," Matt said as he sat down. "What's with the champagne?"

Christ, he doesn't know anything about it thought Lucy; the look on his face was one of total surprise.

"Er… apparently it is complimentary or something," Katie smiled.

"Do all staff get this treatment on their days off?" Matt softly asked.

"Just enjoy it," Lucy said impatiently. "I need to get back to work." She popped the cork and slowly poured the champagne into the tall flute glasses. She leaned over and whispered into Katie's ear. "Just remember what I said."

"So, where were we?" Matt asked.

"I don't know, you seem a bit edgy, why don't you tell me what's wrong?"

"Katie," Matt said seriously as he held her hand and looked into her eyes. "You know that I want the best for you, don't you." He didn't wait for an answer. "There's no room for you in my life right now, I just can't offer you anything. I think we should go our separate ways, for a while anyway. I am going to be really busy what with the new job and everything. Jackson's have already lined up several cases for me and I'm going to be working longer and harder for the foreseeable future. I also need to move closer to the company, so that I am on hand when needed. There'll be no time for socialising, it's for the best." His words were final.

"You… you what?" Katie could scarcely believe her ears. She felt so guilty, why hadn't she the courage to tell him her real feelings. Tears welled up in her eyes.

"Katie, please don't cry. Remember I will always be there for you, no matter what. I just want you to be happy."

"But… but I am happy," she protested.

"No, not really, you'll make something of yourself here and you don't need me tying you down. I have to go, I'm sorry I have a meeting and it won't wait." He had to get out of here, right now, before his real feelings came flooding out.

Katie couldn't speak, she just watched him walk away, out of her life.

Veronica caught Matt just as he was about to go out the door. "You did the right thing, for everyone, you'll see."

"My God, what am I doing letting Katie get mixed up with you people. If anything happens to her I swear to God ..."

"Brian, see this nice gentleman off the premises. And make sure he is never allowed in here again under any circumstances." She turned to Matt. "Nice knowing you Mr Carmichael."

"You win some, you lose some, just the way it is mate." Brian opened the door for him, Matt hesitated for a second. "Don't even think about it."

Matt wimped out and got into his car and sat there with his head in his hands as one single tear trickled down his cheek. What had he just done? It was too late now,

Katie was left to the mercy of that psychotic family. He had a horrible feeling that he had just made the biggest mistake of his life and worse still left Katie smack, bang in the middle of some kind of mafia gang.

He decided right then and there that he would look out for Katie at all costs, watch her from a safe distance. One thing he was absolutely certain of was that it was all going to end in tears. And when it did he vowed he would be there to pick up the pieces.

Chapter Seventeen

Club La Piacenza was back to normal, thank God, Antonio thought. Vince's death obviously scared off the drug dealers big time, especially when the police had been sniffing around, poking and prying into everyone's business. Already they had a few prime suspects, but nothing concrete. The heat was off and they would be alright, at least for the immediate future anyway.

"Do you think Harry is the trustworthy type?" Gianni wondered.

"Sure, I think he will do a great job, we should have made him the manager from the start. Then at least we would never have had this aggravation. I hate to say it, Gianni, but you made a bad choice in Vince."

"Yeah ok, bro, no need to rub my face in it. Still I sorted it out in the end didn't I?"

"I wish it had never come to that."

"We had no choice, remember, he was bleeding us dry. It was only a matter of time before the Driscolls moved in and then where would we be?"

"Yeah, well, we will just have to live with the fact that we left his wife a widow and his daughter growing up without a father."

"It had to be done, Antonio, there was no other way. They had him in their pocket, good job I found out when I did."

"Yeah, your little spy did good, I'll give you that. Is she going to keep her mouth shut?"

"I have installed her as head waitress, she'll keep a watchful eye on things, don't you worry." It was thanks to her that he knew all about Veronica's little scam.

Harry came over and interrupted their conversation. "Boss, why didn't you tell me you were coming? I would have laid out the red carpet." he joked.

"No need for that, Harry, everything seems to be running smoothly, how would you like to become permanent manager? I think you've earned it."

"Sure, Mr de Marco, I am totally enjoying it."

"Any problems need sorting out?" enquired Gianni.

"Erm… yeah we have this little scumbag that comes in, not dealing himself but overseeing his errand boys, just kids really, you know what I mean?"

"So, why not just bar the little shit?" Gianni said impatiently.

"He personally hasn't actually done anything wrong. He comes in about 10.30pm, same table every Friday and Saturday, I'll give you the nod when he arrives."

"Keep up the good work Harry, you need any more muscle, let me know and I'll send reinforcements," Antonio laughed.

"You sure he is the right guy for the job then?" Gianni was doubtful.

"He's a good guy, we have no problems there." He gulped down his whisky chaser.

"I guess we can just relax then and have a bit of fun, brother to brother talk maybe."

"What do you want to talk about?" Antonio knew what was coming, Gianni knew him so well, even though they were like chalk and cheese in many ways. But blood was thicker than water and he needed Gianni's approval. After all he was the only sibling he had left in the world. They were last of the de Marcos and the family line had to carry on.

"You sorted anything out with this Katie chick yet?"

"No, but I may have a date with her tomorrow, if I'm lucky she'll accept my invitation."

"You told Sasha then?"

"In a fashion, I left her a note to be out tonight!"

"Jesus, you'll go back and she'll have fucking torched the place."

"No, I got Stevo on the job, he'll make sure she'll go without any fuss."

"Well, I admire your confidence. She poured paint stripper on my car and trashed my apartment, remember?"

"How could I ever forget?"

"You have to admit Sasha is one very unpredictable lady!"

"Hey, she doesn't worry me!"

Harry was trying to get the de Marcos' attention. They were so engrossed that they didn't notice the young wide boy come in and strut his stuff like he owned the place. Harry was getting frustrated, he didn't want the little shit clocking the owners were in, as he was sure he knew who they were by sight. He wrote a short note and discreetly shoved it into the waitresses hand and pushed her into the brothers' direction.

"Jesus, what's this, you coming on to me H?"

"For fucks sake, here's fifty quid, just get over there as quickly as possible," he said smacking her arse for good measure.

The cocktail waitress put on her best smile and seductively walked in the de Marcos' direction. She had the hots for Gianni, but he had never noticed her before, so she was going to make the best of this opportunity. There was just something exciting about him, something dangerous. She shoved the note into Gianni's hand and looked meaningfully into his gorgeous brown eyes. Boy he was awesome she thought, she would just love to fuck him tonight. And she bet by the way he returned her look he was up for it too.

Gianni read the note and passed it to Antonio. "What's your name, sweetheart?"

"Honey."

"I hope you taste as sweet as you look, darling." He rubbed her arm. "What's a cute chick like you waitressing for? You should be in the movies or something, you sure got the looks for it."

Honey giggled, if only he knew she had starred in a couple of x-rated ones.

"So, Honey, what's your real name?"

"Honey of course," she teased him. Her real name was Heather, but she always intrigued the guys when she said her name was Honey, it worked every time. She was feeling really horny and knew by the way Gianni looked at her that he would be hers tonight. The thought excited her, she couldn't wait to see what kind of lover he was. She was very experienced and expected Gianni to match her in the bedroom.

"So, what time do you get off?"

"Whatever time you like, baby."

She could feel someone looking at her and clocked the arrogant little prick on table twelve. "I got to go and serve, but I'll be back later, you can count on it," she told Gianni.

It wasn't the first time the little prick had tried to get her attention; he was so desperate to get into her knickers, but unfortunately for him, he made her skin crawl. Any other time she would be more than happy to oblige, there was just something about this greasy little shit that she didn't like. But to him Honey was a challenge, he was used to getting what he wanted, and he so wanted her! When he tried it on as he always did, she hoped Gianni was watching, he would sort it out, of that she was certain.

Gianni was watching intently, this chick was hot and there was no way he was going to let a little squirt like him take advantage. He saw him pull Honey close to him and slip his hand up her top. Honey squealed and tipped his drink over him. The little prick grabbed her by the throat. Gianni was just about to intervene when Harry went over to his table and had a word. Things settled down and Gianni couldn't help but feel slightly disappointed, he really wanted to smack the little fucker.

Antonio leaned over. "You'll get your chance, but just not publicly, you get me?"

"Sure, no probs, bro."

Gianni was delighted when he saw the little shit follow Honey, now was his chance to have a little chat with him, warn him off and kill two birds with one stone at the same time.

Antonio sat back to watch his brother in action, he could take care of himself. "Be careful."

"No problem, bro." Gianni was confident of handling this by himself, what could be simpler?

Honey was on her way to the toilet when Pete grabbed her from behind. "Come on, darling, you know that you are gagging for it, what say we fuck right here, right now?"

Honey tried to get out of his grasp but with little success, so she bit his arm. Pete grabbed her by the hair and forced her head down. "Suck on this, slut!"

Just then Gianni turned up. "Suck on this pal!" And with that he shoved his fist into his face, bursting his nose. Blood spattered all over his glistening white shirt and on to the wall behind him.

Antonio looked on from the corner, not wanting to be spotted.

Pete was on the floor. "You broke my fucking nose, man, Jesus!"

Gianni leaned over him. "This is my club, you little shit, and I own everything in it, including the girls, now if you know what's good for you, you'll take your business along with your scrawny little arse and get out of here and never come back!"

Pete defiantly spat in his face, "What, you wanna beat me up over some fucking slapper? You dickhead!"

Gianni pulled him off the floor. "Get out of here, Honey," he snarled at her. "You want me to spell it out for you just so you understand, drugs you little fuck, d r u g s, get me or do you need a fucking translator?"

Honey rushed past Antonio, she was hysterical. Antonio stopped her before she made it back into the club. "Sort yourself out, love, do me a favour and keep this to yourself, I'll make it worth your while."

She nodded in agreement and made for the ladies toilets. Gianni had defended her, he must really fancy her she thought, what a guy, nobody had stuck their neck out for her, ever. This was the beginning of something, and she couldn't wait until she finished her shift.

Before Antonio knew what was happening, his brother was on the floor, blood spurting from his foot! The little bastard had a knife and wasn't afraid to use it! Antonio seethed, nobody messed with his family. He ran over picked up the knife and slammed it into the little shit's heart! The startled look on the boy's face was like a deer caught in car headlights. Antonio, realising what he had done, dropped the knife like a hot brick.

"Is he dead?" Gianni asked trying to feel for a pulse.

"I think so," Antonio stammered, he had never killed anyone before, but it was either him or his brother and he just couldn't let that happen.

"Get Harry, he'll sort it."

"You need to go the hospital."

"No, don't worry about me, I'll be fine."

Gianni left by the back door and was whisked off to see a private doctor, one that wouldn't ask any questions as long as the money was to his liking.

Antonio went to Harry's office and changed his shirt. "Get that blood cleaned up and quickly, before anyone notices."

"What about the body, Antonio?"

"Use your fucking imagination, Harry; just make him disappear, permanently."

Harry brought two of the security men to get rid of the body. Antonio would have to pay them a hefty wedge to keep them quiet, he was glad that the men who worked for him were handpicked, loyal to the club and the de Marcos.

Antonio calmly went back to his table and acted normally, or at least as normally as he could. He had just taken a young boy's life; he had never given it a second thought. Was he just like Gianni after all, he wondered? He had tried his best to lead a normal life, but somehow violence followed them around and he had to deal with it as best he could.

Pete was taken to a new housing development a few miles down the road, dropped into the foundations and covered in cement. It would be several years before his body would be discovered.

Gianni was feeling sorry for himself. Harry had organised a doctor to sort out his foot; he needed seven stitches all because of that little shit who thought he could take a de Marco on.

Honey arrived at his hotel, delighted that he had sent for her. "My poor babe, I feel so bad for you. What happened to Pete?"

"Never mind that, get your fucking clothes off and I'll give you the ride of your life, baby." He opened his trousers and pulled out his throbbing member. "Come and sit on this, help take my mind off my bloody foot!"

Honey obediently obliged, he had the biggest cock she had ever seen. They fucked all night, despite the obvious pain Gianni was in. She had to admit he had brilliant staying power. At that moment all Honey wanted was to make him delirious with desire for her.

Antonio was distraught, he had killed a boy, how was he going to live with himself. He picked up the hotel phone.

Katie was wakened up by the constant ringing of her phone. Stumbling out of bed she put on the light and went into the sitting room.

"Hello," she murmured, bleary eyed.

"Hi Katie, it's Antonio."

"Antonio? How did you get my number?"

"You're on the staff files, remember?"

"Do you have any idea what time it is?"

"I'm sorry for the hour, just wanted to speak to you that's all."

"Oh, is something wrong?"

"No, I was just thinking about you. I can't wait to see you tomorrow, you are coming aren't you?"

"Of course."

76

"Good, I'll send Fred for you, my darling. See you soon."

And with that Antonio hung up, wondering why he had felt the need to hear her voice.

What was he doing phoning her at that time of night, was she dreaming? She went back to bed and fell into a deep sleep, her dreams were full of Antonio calling for her, but she didn't know why.

Chapter Eighteen

Lucy certainly had a bounce in her step, she was on cloud nine. Something had put a smile on her face, or someone, Katie thought. "Hey, what's with the smiley face?"

"Oh, I shouldn't be allowed to be so happy when Matt is so miserable."

"Lucy, there's something you should know, Matt finished with me."

"No way, he would never do that."

"I'm sorry, Lucy, but he did, I can't understand why though, I thought he would be devastated. It just doesn't make any sense to me."

"What, Matt actually finished with you?" Lucy was aghast.

"Yes, it's true."

"I don't believe it, wait until I see him!"

"Just leave it, Lucy."

"It's that champagne that did it, he must have lost his nerve."

"What is that supposed to mean?"

"Well, I was convinced that he was going to propose to you, he seemed so jittery."

"It just shows you how wrong you can be."

"And he was totally cool about it, what did he say?" She still couldn't believe it.

"He just wants to concentrate on his career, that's the most important thing to him right now."

"Anything else?"

"It doesn't really matter now, Lucy, I just wish him all the best. Anyway, stop changing the subject, I'm dying to know what's going on with you."

"It's funny how you can just meet someone and in the blink of an eye be totally smitten."

"And just who are you smitten with?"

"Stevo, he's just really cool."

"Stevo, he's a very close friend of the de Marcos isn't he?"

"Yes, he came in late last night to see Veronica about something and we just got talking."

"Oh, yes?"

"And he's really interested in getting to know me better."

Katie was still thinking about Matt, and Lucy knew she was distracted.

"So, I went back to his place and we made mad passionate love all over his flat, you know, on the kitchen table, in the shower, you name it we did it."

"That's nice."

"Katie, what did I just say?"

"Oh sorry, what?"

"You're still upset about Matt aren't you?"

"Of course."

"Out of the two of us he was always the sensible one, a career and family was what he said he most wanted out of life and in that order."

"I just can't help feeling that there's more to it than that." Katie was perplexed.

"It just doesn't make sense to me either."

"Do you think he found out about the roses?"

"No, how could he? I didn't say anything if that's what you think."

"I know you didn't. I just hope that this won't spoil our friendship."

"Matt is my brother and I have to stay loyal to him, although I do feel torn between you both."

"I understand how difficult it must be for you," Was all Katie could say.

"I'm sure things will turn out how they are supposed to, but I still don't understand what was going on in Matt's head."

"One thing is for sure we will always care about each other, no matter what." Katie still felt terrible about the events of the previous evening.

"Let's change the subject."

"What time did you come home?" Katie asked.

"Oh, about an hour ago!"

"You wanna talk about it?"

"Not really, just that I think I am madly in love." Seeing the look of shock on Katie's face Lucy was quick to defend herself. "Nothing happened, we just had a few drinks in the club after most of the staff had left, we talked all night and then went to this little café for a coffee."

"What's he like?"

"Lovely, very down to earth and good fun."

"It's nice to see you've met someone, good luck."

"Thanks, Katie, and good luck to you too, I hope you have made the right decision about Antonio."

"It's early days, yet he makes me feel like I am the only woman on the planet."

"I don't want to rain on your parade but what about Sasha?"

"Oh, I've no doubt that she is history right about now."

"I hope you are right, she seems like trouble to me."

"Don't worry about me, Lucy, Antonio will look after me."

"I hope you don't ever regret giving Matt up for him, seriously I hope it all works out."

"Lucy you can't help who you fall for. Matt was always good to me, I think we must have just outgrown each other. We both want different things now. Promise me you won't hold this against me."

"You are my best mate, Katie and always will be."

Lucy put her arms around her. "Just be happy, that's all I ask."

Katie was overwhelmed at how well her friend had taken the news. She had been so scared of losing her friendship for good and she would have hated that. "You know Lucy, we will always be mates, no matter what."

"Best mates forever then."

Chapter Nineteen

Sasha couldn't believe that Antonio had ditched her. He couldn't even tell her to her face, instead he left a note telling her that it was all over and that he wanted her out of his apartment before he returned from Manchester. The bastard would pay, she decided.

She summoned Fred. She'd teach him a lesson he would never forget, how dare he treat her this way.

"Where do you want to go, Ms Breschnevsky?"

"I intend going for a long expensive massage, a sauna, a facial, a manicure, a pedicure and an all over body tan. Then, darling, I will have my hair done. After that, the jewellers on Bond Street and perhaps Harrods, I am going to shop, shop, shop until I drop."

Fred opened the limo door for her, he knew Antonio had finished their relationship and had expected her to react like this. As soon as they drove off, the locksmith turned up and got to work immediately. Now all Fred had to do was just drop her at her desired destination and hopefully that would be the last he would ever see of her. She was the worst woman out of a bad bunch that Antonio had ever dated. Quite frankly he was delighted to finally see the back of her.

"Stop here, you stupid, stupid man, did you not listen to a word I have said? Marie Bouvard Beauty Salon."

Fred apologised and politely opened the door for her. "Would you like me to wait for you?"

"No need, darling, I will call you when I am finished, just make sure you are on time if you don't want to be fired."

"No problem, Ms Breschnevsky." He tipped the peak of his cap. Thank God, that whining voice was sending him stir crazy. When he got back to the office he rang Antonio. "Everything is going according to your requests."

"Good, good, just go back to the apartment and pay the locksmith, oh and Fred, don't even think of going back to pick Sasha up. One last thing, make sure her cases are packed and send them on to the Regent Hotel, I'll make the necessary arrangements."

"Ok, boss." Fred couldn't help feeling extremely smug. He had a funny feeling Sasha wouldn't take this lying down, there would be hell to pay, only this time he secretly hoped that he would be witness to it.

Sasha was greeted by Sandy, her usual beauty therapist.

"Oh, it is so nice to see you, Ms Breschnevsky, are we having everything today?"

"Of course, darling, and please pop open a bottle of champagne."

"Sure, are we celebrating anything exciting?"

"If you could call being dumped in a note by a complete louse, then yes, we are celebrating. I want nothing less than your absolute best today, the most expensive bottle you have, do you understand me, darling?"

"Certainly, Ms Breschnevsky." Sandy knew that it was going to be a goddamn awful day, Sasha was in a really foul mood and after a couple of glasses who knew what havoc she was about to wreak. "Lydia will show you into the room, I will be with you directly."

"Yes, yes, just get a bloody move on and make sure the champagne is chilled to my specific requirements."

Sandy scuttled away cursing under her breath. It was going to be hell looking after this bloody woman today, minding her p's and q's. Sandy reminded herself the only reason she endured being treated like a dog was because of the huge tips Sasha always gave her. Tolerating her rudeness was a small price to pay.

Antonio and Gianni were on their way back from Manchester.

Gianni noted how Antonio was grinning from ear to ear.

"Ok, spill the beans what have you been up to then?"

"Well, Sasha has now left the building and she's in for a couple of nasty shocks."

"Like what?"

"Oh, just got the locksmith to change all of the locks for starters."

"And?" Gianni wondered what else his brother had been up to.

"I asked Fred to drop her off in the city and told him not to go back for her under any circumstances."

"Jesus, she will go ape shit!" exclaimed Gianni.

"Ah, but that's not all, I have cancelled all her credit cards and sent her belongings over to the Regent hotel, which, of course, being the perfect gentleman I have decided I will happily cover the costs, just as long as it doesn't break the bank."

"You're something else, bro!" Gianni roared with laughter. "Just watch your back, you know what she's capable of."

"Do I look like I am worried?"

"Not at all."

They travelled the rest of the journey in silence. Antonio was thinking about the young boy he had killed.

Gianni was safe in the knowledge that there were no witnesses and the security tapes had all been deleted. The body would never be found and therefore no crime to answer. He couldn't get Honey out of his mind; she was perfect as a bit on the side and that's all she would ever be, his entertainment on tap whenever he wanted it!

Chapter Twenty

Veronica was running around the club like an idiot. Shit, both brothers were coming tonight and some of the girls hadn't turned up, again. She had been on to the agency, but had had to pay extra as it was so short notice. She could throttle Janine and Marsha, they were a waste of space. They would have to go, she decided, in fact they would never set foot in the club ever again.

"Tania, make sure Antonio gets a private booth, for two people. Arrange for Alice to sing something nice to him at approximately ten o'clock, I'll give you the nod. Just make sure she is aware of it darling."

"Who is it for, him and Sasha?" probed Tania.

"No, no it's not, it's for the new lady in his life and one he is quite taken with or so it seems." Her voice sounded sad. "Now run along, I need to see Nicholas."

Tania nodded and obediently did as Veronica asked, her mind wandering back to Katie and Sasha's little tiff from the other night.

Colin was polishing the glasses when Tania interrupted him. "We got both Gianni and Antonio tonight and apparently he has a new woman."

"Who, Gianni?" Colin tutted.

"No, Antonio. It should be an interesting night, I wonder if Sasha knows about this."

"Probably not, can you imagine if she turned up. It certainly would be good entertainment."

Tania had a wicked thought; Colin could see the mischievous look in her eyes.

"Oh God, you're not going to tell her are you?"

"As if I would!"

Colin never said anything else, he just prepared for fireworks. He couldn't wait to tell Kyle, he would love all the drama.

Tania couldn't wait to tell Sasha about Antonio bringing a new date to the club. She rang around until she finally reached her at the beauty salon. Sasha had totally freaked out, she was determined to find out who this bitch was. She had a feeling it had something to do with that little twit Antonio drooled over. Things had never been the same between them since that night. If it was her, she would make her life a total misery, what did she have that was more exciting than her? She just couldn't understand it, Antonio had worshipped her, showered her with many gifts over their two years together. She would wreck this relationship, she decided, after all if she couldn't have him then absolutely nobody else would.

Sandy returned to the room and handed Sasha her credit card. "I am so sorry but this card has been declined."

"You what, are you fucking kidding me?" Sasha searched through her handbag and pulled out her gold card. "Try this, darling," she ordered.

Three credit cards later and Sandy had to call the police. Sasha was going ballistic, screaming and smashing up the place, she was furious.

The police escorted her off the premises, they had to lock her up until she calmed down. They were aware of who she was and let her off with a caution. Sandy would be reimbursed once Antonio sorted out this unfortunate incident.

Sasha was even more furious when Fred did not answer her call. After numerous attempts she finally got through to him, ordering him to collect her at the police station. Fred announced in no uncertain terms that her belongings had been sent to the Regent Hotel. What the hell was going on, what was Antonio doing to her? She would sort this goddamn awful mess out. Yes, go and check into the hotel, put her glad rags on and turn up to the club; she was impatient to wait until eight o'clock. Perhaps she would wait until about ten when things were getting really intimate. She would teach him not to treat her like that. Sasha knew how to make an entrance and boy what an entrance it would be, she could barely wait. A woman scorned was a dangerous one and Antonio didn't seem to know what he was dealing with. Wait until her father found out, he would cut his balls off! No one messed his daughter around especially a business associate who, if it wasn't for him, would never have been so successful in the first place.

"Nana, oh, Nana." Sasha sounded desperate.

"What's wrong, Sasha, has someone hurt you?" her father anxiously asked.

"It's Antonio he has thrown me out, what should I do?" she cried.

"You can't just move from one brother to the next, you know that sweetheart, is that what it is all about?"

"No I have a horrible feeling that he has met someone else."

"What do you need, money?" He knew that was usually the only reason that she called him.

"I got a message saying that my bags had been sent to the Regent Hotel, can you believe that?"

"I think you should come home for a while, calm down and get over this break up."

"No, not yet there's something I need to do first."

"I'll transfer some money into your account, in the meantime don't do anything rash."

"As if I would."

That was just it, he knew she was going to seek revenge. He had been amazed that Antonio had stayed with her for so long. He had hoped that she would marry one of the de Marcos and prayed that it would be Antonio. Antonio was smart but Gianni had a dark side to him. "When you get to the hotel call me and let me know how you are doing."

"Thanks, Nana, you are the best."

Chapter Twenty One

Lucy turned up for work only to find Stevo waiting for her, he was charming and she hoped that something special would come of this. It was very early days and she wanted to play it cool.

"Hey, what time do you want to meet up later?"

"I'm going to be really tired tonight, especially as some of the girls haven't turned up. I may just want to go home," she teased him.

"Is that a no then?"

"We'll see."

Stevo grinned, she was playing hard to get, but he liked that. It was usual for him to pull any girl he wanted because of his connection to the de Marcos. It would be fun chasing this one though, who knows; maybe this was the start of something big.

Just then Veronica appeared. "Don't harass the staff, Stevo."

"Hey, I wasn't!"

"Hum, we are fully booked tonight and Lucy doesn't need any distractions."

Stevo leaned over and whispered into Lucy's ear. "You can distract me anytime you want."

Lucy blushed and made a quick exit.

"Stevo, come on get out of here," Veronica said impatiently.

Stevo saluted her and did as he was told. He didn't want to mess with Veronica, she had nerves of steel and was a formidable woman to deal with if you upset her.

As Lucy was getting changed she overheard Tania talking to one of the girls. What was she saying, Sasha was going to turn up and cause a scene? Oh no, she would have to warn Katie.

"Hey Lucy, you ready? You're needed at the bar they are running behind, make it quick," Tania ordered.

Bloody hell, how was she going to get a message to Katie now? Damn it, she would try to use the phone behind the bar if possible, the least she could do was warn her friend!

"Ok, Colin, what do you want me to do?"

"Well, all the table cloths need to be put out, the ashtrays, candles and of course the tables all need wiped down first."

"Oh, is that all?" Lucy said sarcastically.

"Come on, Lucy what's wrong with you today?"

"Nothing," she sighed and made her way over to the nearest table. Poor Katie was going to be dressed to the nines and Sasha was going to ruin everything. Lucy was on pins thinking about what would happen, she hoped to see Stevo to tell him to try and warn Antonio. She would tell whoever turned up first, but suspected that they would both arrive together. Maybe she should inform Veronica. Eventually it slipped Lucy's mind as she had several obnoxious customers who kept her on her toes most of the evening. In fact she didn't even notice when Antonio and Katie came in and immediately went into the restaurant.

Tania was delighted with herself and nudged Colin.

"What?" Colin was rushed off his feet, the drink orders were coming thick and fast. It was only early and he was feeling the stress of trying to keep the customers happy. Kyle had arrived late and that's why Lucy had come to the rescue, making drinks and serving them as well, she was working her little butt off.

"Just noticed Antonio and his new girl arrive," Tania whispered.

"Why don't you just leave it alone, Katie is a lovely girl, don't tell me that you're jealous." Colin was becoming impatient and it showed.

"God, sorry I spoke, I have nothing against Katie but Jesus she has muscled in pretty quickly and with Sasha barely out of the picture," she tutted.

"Well I have decided that I like her immensely she will be the making of Antonio de Marco, trust me."

"Whoa, take it easy, I was only kidding."

Tania was annoyed and it showed, she was always jealous of anyone who looked like they had a better future than her. She was so shallow at times. There were two sides to her, the nice polite woman who would do anything for you and the back-stabbing bitch who was really just out for herself and didn't care who she trampled on to get it. Colin had sussed her out pretty quickly, unlike his brother Kyle who just liked women full stop as he could totally relate to them. He could be quite bitchy at times but also very sensitive. Colin hadn't had a chance to tell him about the events which were going to unfold some time that evening.

Veronica welcomed Antonio and the "English rose" Katie, as she decided Katie could pass for royalty, she just had that regal grace about her. It had surprised her how elegant and ladylike she looked. Heads had turned but Antonio had wasted no time in getting into the restaurant as quickly as possible. "I'll send Sarah to serve you, any problems, you know where to find me."

"Thanks, Veronica, we'll be perfectly fine." Antonio pulled out Katie's chair.

Katie looked a little alarmed, she certainly wasn't used to being fussed around, not like this.

"Please." Antonio's voice was firm almost commanding.

He had arranged for Fred to pick Katie up in the limo as he was running late. Meeting her at the door, he remarked on how she looked even more beautiful than he remembered, if that was possible. His mind started wandering back to the previous evening, all he wanted to do was forget it had ever happened, lock it in the back of his mind and throw away the key.

"Are you ok, Antonio?" Katie asked gently.

He looked into her deep blue eyes, the hairs on the back of his neck stood on end. There was something about that calmness in her voice, that gentleness that sent him wild with desire. "I'm fine, just a little weary from yesterday."

"You didn't really say why you called me so late."

"I told you, bella, I just wanted to hear your voice, it soothes me."

"Why, why did you need soothing?"

"Enough questions, my darling, let's have some champagne."

Antonio could be so sweet to her yet there was something dangerous about him, something he didn't want her to see.

As Antonio poured the champagne all thoughts of what had happened the night before quickly disappeared.

Katie was enjoying his attentions and felt like she was in another world, a wonderful happy world. They talked endlessly about music, food and art. Antonio had been pleasantly surprised to discover she knew a lot about Italian furniture. Little did he know that she had been studying all day long just so that she could impress him with her knowledge, Veronica had helped her out.

Katie ordered Insalata Toscana, a tossed Italian salad with diced mozzarella, tomatoes, red onion and olives in a parmesan dressing.

"Excellent choice," Antonio said not even looking at the menu, why would he, he knew it like the back of his hand. "I'll have Proscuitto di Palma Con Dolcelatte."

"And for your main course?"

"Allow me." Antonio smiled at Katie. "Two Pollo Rusticano."

"May I say that you have chosen well, Mr de Marco, as usual."

Sarah gathered the menus and hurried off into the kitchen.

"Ok, what is this Proscuitto dish, I know it's some kind of chicken, naturally."

"Wait and see," Antonio teased her. "It will be worth waiting for."

"Noooh, no way, I want to know right now." Katie put on her best little girl voice. "Please tell me."

"Oh, how can I resist when you ask me in that way?"

"I'm still waiting," Katie giggled.

"Ok, you win, its pan fried pieces of succulent tender chicken breast with roasted mediterranean vegetables, served on a garlic crouton in a mushroom and sweet marsala wine sauce."

"My god, I am starving," Katie laughed so hard her eyes watered and her cheap mascara started to run.

Antonio handed her his handkerchief. "Don't worry it is perfectly clean."

Katie was horrified; she must look an almighty mess. "Oh, I better go to the little girls' room and er fix my face."

"Katie, you look absolutely stunning, just use your compact honey, it's only a little mascara, except that you look kind of like a panda," he joked with her.

"You pig, you've got me totally paranoid now." Katie delved into her handbag to find her mirror and checked out her eye make-up.

Antonio watched her as she dabbed gently beneath her eyes, he was totally mesmerised by her. She was so dainty, so elegant and intelligent too. He was completely oblivious to the starter being served.

"Errm, ah erm," coughed Sarah as she surveyed Antonio, he was completely bewitched by Katie, it was so obvious. She thought that he and Sasha made a handsome couple, but these two it seemed were perfect for each other. She quite envied them, the beginning of a new and exciting love affair.

It was Katie who noticed Sarah's arrival or perhaps it was the aromatic smell of flavours making her look up. "Oh, sorry, Sarah."

"That's no problem, Katie."

"I think that is a little too familiar, Sarah."

Katie interrupted. "But I do work here, Antonio and we all call each other by our first names."

"Not anymore, my darling." He waved his hand for Sarah to leave.

"What on earth do you mean, and did you have to dismiss her like that?"

"Eat, eat while it's hot, darling, we'll talk later."

Sarah practically ran back to the restaurant, she was all red faced and out of breath.

"My God, Sarah, is it the food, what on earth is wrong?" Nicholas yelled. "Have I made someone violently ill or something."

Veronica was just making her usual check of the night when she overheard the commotion. She immediately grabbed Sarah and shook her hard. "Well, speak girl, what is it?"

"It… its Katie," she panted.

"What about her, has she upset Antonio, I'd better go and see what's happening." Veronica was just about to rush out into the restaurant all guns blazing.

"No, no, it's not what you think."

"Out with it, girl." Veronica was really starting to get annoyed.

"Mr de Marco, he, he told me that it wasn't appropriate for me to call Katie by her first name and, and when she said that we all call each other by our first names, well he said, not any more anyway."

"Good gracious, girl, is that what all this is about?"

"I think, I think that she won't be working here anymore, Ms Lamont."

"So, tell me something that I don't know," spat Veronica. Shit nothing ever happened in here without her knowing about it, apart from Tania of course, who seemed to be the exception for some bizarre reason, a law unto herself.

Nicholas didn't know what the hell they were talking about, he just thanked god that there was nothing wrong with his food. "Will someone please explain what on earth is going on?" he demanded.

"It's quite simple really, Antonio is in love and I have heard that he plans to marry Katie, sorry Miss Saunders, as soon as possible."

"But that's totally insane!" Sarah exclaimed.

"I wouldn't let my brother hear you say that!" Gianni had been watching the whole spectacle, unbeknown to the staff. "I would mind your own business if I were you and get back to work."

"Gianni, darling, where did you spring from?" Veronica asked sweetly.

"Thought I'd pop in early to see you, Veronica darling." He put his arm through hers and walked her out of the kitchen through the back and down the corridor towards her office. He waited until she unlocked the door.

Veronica opened the safe and obediently handed over the takings from the escort girls, hoping that he would be satisfied; her ribs were still recovering.

Gianni counted the wad of money, took his cut and thrust the remaining notes into her hand. "Nice doing business, see you later, darling."

Veronica hated Gianni with a vengeance, he had ruined her retirement plan and one day he would pay for what he had done to her.

Gianni met Felicia coming out of the ladies room. "Come on, sweetheart, let me introduce you to Antonio's new flame."

"I hope you don't mind me saying, but that was awfully quick, considering he only turfed Sasha out this morning."

"Yep, well the lady got what was coming to her. She can't treat my brother like shit and expect to get away with it forever, her time was up."

"Oh, I see, what is this Katie like?"

"You're just about to find out."

By this time it seemed most of the staff were gossiping about Antonio's new future wife. It was absolutely incredible to think that he was in love with this girl, he barely knew her, she wasn't even his type. Colin decided that the world had finally gone mad.

Lucy was flabbergasted when one of the girls whispered the news to her. "Don't be absurd, as if, they've only just met. Just ignore it, it's only a rumour." She doubted herself, she had never seen Katie like this before, she positively glowed.

Gianni and Felicia walked up the stairs and were greeted by Tania. "Is no one working tonight or what, get everyone back to work at once."

Tania was about to protest when Gianni gave her a frightening dark look.

"I'll see to it right away, Mr de Marco." Tania rushed over to Sarah and Sarah in turn told Colin and Kyle, who then told everyone else that Gianni was in the building.

Normality resumed in the restaurant, it had been mad panic for about ten minutes. Luckily Antonio and Katie hadn't noticed the gossip mongers, they only had eyes for each other.

"Hey, bro, aren't you going to introduce me to your beautiful young lady?"

"Of course, Katie, meet my brother Gianni and his fiancée Felicia Carmine."

"Pleased to meet you I'm sure," Katie said in a polite quiet voice.

"Hi, I love your hair, who's your hairdresser?" Felicia enquired.

"I, I erm did it myself."

"Wow, so much talent, I certainly don't have the patience. My hairdresser is Roberto Castalini, he's quite near here, why don't I give you one of his cards? I expect you will be too busy from now on to have enough time to style it yourself." She handed her a gold coloured business card.

Gianni took Katie's hand and kissed it. Katie blushed.

Noticing her discomfort Antonio laughed, "Hey Gianni, hands off my date!"

"Don't worry, Katie, you have nothing to fear, I am totally smitten with my gorgeous fiancée." He kissed Felicia adoringly on the cheek.

Katie somehow doubted his sincerity, his reputation as a ladies' man preceded him and she could see why they all fell for his charms.

"Come on, Gianni, our table is waiting, why don't we meet up after dinner in the bar for a nightcap?"

"That's an excellent idea," Antonio agreed.

They made a swift exit. "That was a nice stroke of 'hey you need a hairdresser' darling, very subtle."

"But, Gianni, I was being totally genuine," she insisted.

"Of course you were." Gianni was starving and in need of a double whisky.

Chapter Twenty Two

Sasha arrived at The Regent Hotel, she was still in an extremely foul mood. Her mind was in turmoil as she wondered how she was going to get into Club La Pregheira . She forced her way past the other guests waiting to check in. Sasha had never stood in a queue in her entire life and she wasn't about to start now.

A young mousey-haired girl greeted her at the desk. "I'm sorry, madam, you'll have to wait your turn."

Sasha leaned over the counter and snarled, "Do you know who I am, darling?"

"No, madam, I'm sorry, I don't."

"Well, if you want to feel my wrath, I would be happy to oblige. You see my fiancé has just taken up with a younger woman, he has thrown me out of our beautiful home and frozen my bank account. You see where I'm going with this, I have lost everything in one goddamn day." Her voice was verging on the edge of hysteria.

"I am so sorry, madam, what name is it please?" The young girl didn't know how to deal with this woman, but decided the best bet was to get her out of the foyer as quickly as possible. She certainly didn't want a scene with this crazy woman, especially in full view of the other guests.

"Sasha Breschnevsky, and I would appreciate it if you could check to see if my luggage has arrived yet."

"Ah yes, you are booked into the Ambassador Suite which has marvellous views over the city, the room is just beautiful."

"Darling, I really don't give a damn I have just spent two hours in a police cell, so I advise you to process me right now. Just give me the damn key and send my luggage up, I'll find the room myself."

The young woman passed her the key; snatching it out of her hand she stormed off towards the lifts. Once she entered the apartment she burst into tears, why oh why had Antonio done this to her? She adored him, well she adored his wealth and the freedom to spend whatever she wanted whenever she wanted. Nobody had ever treated her like this before, she was adored by so many men, always receiving admiring looks, or so she thought. It was really because she looked like a real life barbie doll, all plastic and bleached hair. And of course, most people who knew her just wanted to rip her arms and legs off, just for the fun of it.

She ran herself a hot bath to try and calm down. As she immersed herself in the soothing bubble bath she rang reception. "I would like a bottle of chilled champagne and some caviar darling." She purred.

She decided to contact her friend in the film industry, Rhianna would be able to help her get into the club she thought. She hadn't seen Rhianna for years, since they used to star in soft porn movies. In those days when she was about seventeen years old she had jet black hair, no tits and a big hooky nose. She was unrecognisable now, ever since her plastic surgery. She revelled in the fact that no one even knew about it and probably never would. Antonio would have had a fit, had he known, but she had worked under a false name, just for the fun of it, she enjoyed sex. Her father thought that she was touring Europe but secretly she was filming in Amsterdam, wearing false wigs and exotic costumes, she had thoroughly loved it. The money hadn't mattered as she was loaded anyway. It all happened after her mother had died and she needed to get away. Rhianna had been a wonderful friend showed her the ways of the world, opened her eyes and taught how to take care of herself. She knew that she would be able to depend on her, as she owed her. Sasha had saved her from being deported by paying off the local police. She was looking forward to seeing her again, part of her still longed for that lifestyle, the sex, the drink, the excitement of it all. Remembering the times on the luxury yachts, the sex parties and no hassle in her life. She pulled herself together, that was a whole lifetime ago, one she should never, ever think of again. Anyway she was way too old for it now. Hopefully Rhianna would arrive from Amsterdam within the next hour or so with her bag of goodies.

As she sank back into the bath and sipped on her champagne she thought how much fun it would be to see if she could get away with one of her long lost alter egos. When she did eventually arrive at the club she wondered about what she was going to do, how she could win Antonio back! What the hell, she would just go with the flow, take it as it comes, she could handle it, after all she was Sasha Breshnevsky.

Chapter Twenty Three

Antonio was intent on finding out just how many boyfriends Katie actually had. She was quite shy with him, but he was determined for her to answer his questions. He knew about Matthew Carmichael, but he would never be able to look after her like Antonio was going to. He wondered why he had never met anyone like her before; he wished that she had been a part of his life sooner.

"Oh, stop, Antonio, does it really matter, I'm with you now."

"I just wanted to know how many times you have had your heart broken."

Katie sighed. "That's just it, never, but I have broken someone's heart."

She sounded so sad, Antonio felt his jealousy about to rise to the surface, he bit his tongue. "I can't believe that you would hurt anyone intentionally."

"But I have."

Antonio was annoyed at the dreamy faraway look she had, he was going to lose it if she was still in love with this guy. "Don't you want to be with me, bella?"

"Oh, it's not you, it's just I feel bad for the way things ended with Matt, his sister Lucy is my best friend and it's kind of awkward."

"Darling, don't worry he'll move on and meet someone else."

"I know, I just didn't expect to meet someone like you."

Antonio was flattered. "Listen, darling, I have something to cheer you up." He reached into his jacket pocket and produced a black velvet box. "Give me your hand."

Katie trembled, oh my god, what if it is an engagement ring, she wasn't ready for that, what would she say?

Antonio pressed it into her hand. "Go on, darling, open it."

Katie slowly opened the box, she sighed with relief, it was the most beautiful necklace that she had ever seen, it was a heart shaped pendent encrusted with diamonds. "Oh, my god, it's, it's so incredibly beautiful."

Antonio was delighted with her response. "Here, darling, allow me." He swiftly stood up and took the pendent out of the box. Scooping back her hair he gently fastened the necklace, kissing her ear as he did so.

Katie gasped, he sent a shudder down her spine, making her feel like she had never felt before, she ached for him. She touched the necklace and gave him the most amazing smile. "Oh, thank you."

"My darling, this is just the beginning, trust me."

Everything was going like clockwork he thought, this was going to be a perfect evening and hopefully she would be in his bed tonight. He nodded to Tania.

Tania hurriedly rushed over to Alice. "That's your cue."

Alice obediently grabbed her mike; she was getting a special payment for this personal performance. The lights went down and her husky voice came over the microphone, softly, sexily, she serenaded them. The spotlight was over her now, she stood at their table and sang to them, as if they were the only two people in the whole room.

Katie was absolutely thrilled; Antonio leaned over and held her hand, the attraction between them was intense. He stroked her hand as they listened to the gentle tones of this wonderful singer. They were besotted with each other, the spark between them was just waiting to be ignited. Sexual tension enveloped them, waiting to explode, it was going to be an exceptional night.

Chapter Twenty Four

Rhianna had just arrived at the Regent Hotel; she couldn't believe that she had to lie to her husband about a sick relative. He knew nothing of her past and that's the way she wanted to keep it. She owed Sasha, but after this, that would be the debt well and truly paid. As she made her way up to the suite she wished she had never agreed to meet her, she hated deceiving her husband. She patted her tiny bump and smiled at the new life she would be bringing into the world in about six months time. Her life had completely changed and if Charlie ever found out it would finish them, she was taking an immense risk. She knocked hard on the door of Sasha's apartment.

"Oh, darling, thank god, I was at my wits end, did you bring the stuff?"

"Yes."

"Good, come in, we haven't got much time, I need to be ready in less than an hour. Can you do this?"

"You know me, of course, Tatiana!" exclaimed Rhianna.

"Please, never call me that again darling, not even as a joke, that part of my life is well and truly over."

Rhianna was only messing around, but she could feel the venom oozing from every pore in Sasha's body. The sooner she did her job and was on her way the better; she could do without this shit.

"Ok, I brought a suitcase, see what you like and I'll get you ready."

"Thank you, darling," Sasha grabbed the case from her and started throwing wigs and outfits all over the place. "Help yourself to a glass of champagne, darling."

"No thanks, I don't drink any more."

"What, ten years later and you are teetotal. I don't believe it."

"It's true Tatiana, I mean Sasha, I'm expecting a baby."

"Oh, poor you, how inconvenient for your body, what about work?"

"I've been out of the game for many years now, probably as many as you."

"My God, who would have believed it; you've turned into a right little housewife haven't you?"

"And what's wrong with being a little housewife, I'm happy if that's what you mean." Rhianna was getting annoyed. "Do you want my help or not?"

"Calm down, darling, your secret is safe with me."

"As is yours with me, darling." If she fucked with her, Rhianna wouldn't think twice about throwing her out of the fucking window.

They set to work and discussed just what Sasha was going to look like and what she should wear, the taxi was coming in less than forty-five minutes, there was no time to lose.

Chapter Twenty Five

Alice had just finished her personal rendition; she was pleased that they looked totally happy. She was in for a huge tip tonight and was grateful that she could finally pay off her loan shark.

"Well done, Alice." Tania was pleased that everything had run smoothly, at least for now, she smirked to herself.

The entire restaurant was delighted with her performance and gave her a massive round of applause. Later that evening in the bar area there was going to be further entertainment in the form of dancing girls followed by music for the rest of the night for those still full of energy. Tania had done her job and just wanted to go home, it seemed that Sasha was not going to turn up and that disappointed her despite the efforts she had made to get her there. It was well after ten thirty and she was knackered.

Katie and Antonio could feel the smouldering heat between them. It was inevitable that they would end up in bed together but it remained unsaid. No words were needed, they both knew what they felt was all-consuming want and desire for each other like they had never felt before. Katie was excited at the prospect but also scared, she wanted to please him and be everything he wanted in a woman. She was going to give herself to him, totally, willingly with all her heart and soul.

Lucy waltzed over and interrupted the two lovebirds. "I'm so sorry Mr de Marco, but I need to speak to Katie rather urgently, is that ok?"

Antonio looked at her, he was rather perplexed. He didn't want Lucy whispering in her ear and spoiling their perfect evening. "As you can see, Lucy, we are having a rather intimate dinner, just the two of us and we really don't want to be disturbed."

Lucy looked at Katie.

"Can it wait?" Katie asked her.

"No, not really."

"Antonio, do you mind?"

"Go ahead, darling, but don't be long, it's time we were leaving." He gave her that look and she knew what he was thinking, because she was thinking exactly the same thing.

Katie reluctantly left the dinner table and followed Lucy to the ladies. "Ok, what's all this about? I was really enjoying myself."

"It's Sasha, she knows, I heard that she is raging about you and Antonio and is hell bent on revenge. Apparently she is going to turn up tonight and ruin your evening. I just wanted you to know so that you can be prepared if she does turn up."

"Lucy, don't worry about me, I can take care of myself, after all what could she possibly do to me, anyway it's getting late if she was going to do something she would have done it by now."

"Maybe, but I just have a feeling about this."

"That's really sweet of you, but honestly I am with Antonio, she wouldn't dare do anything in front of him and anyway she won't even get into the club."

"Well, don't say that I didn't warn you, anyway I must get back to work or that Tania bitch will have my guts for garters."

"Thanks, Lucy, don't wait up for me, I may not be back until the morning!"

"You are kidding, right?"

Katie looked deadly serious. "I think I am head over heels for him Lucy. Incredible to believe I know, but there's just something about him, it's so exciting."

"Jesus, you've only know him five minutes."

"Talk about pot, kettle black? What about you and Stevo?"

"Hang on, I haven't rushed into anything, certainly not slept with him yet, it's way too soon!"

"Sorry, I wasn't saying that you had, I just meant if it felt right then why not?"

"Ok, point taken, just don't get in over your head."

"I won't, trust me."

"And maybe I won't be home tonight either!" Lucy exclaimed.

They both laughed heartily and hugged, both understanding each other.

"Well, just don't do anything that I wouldn't do!" Katie grinned.

"There's no chance of that!"

Just then Tania popped her head around the door. "I am so sorry to butt in but we are getting rather busy and you're needed, Lucy." Her voice full of sarcasm.

"I'm on my way." As Tania left the room Lucy clicked her heels together and did a salute. "Yes, ma'am, right away."

Katie roared with laughter. "You better hope she didn't see that or you'll be getting the sack."

"No I won't, you are now officially the Princess of Club La Pregheira and nobody will upset you or they will have Antonio to deal with." She curtsied.

"Yes, very funny, anyway I think he may have a proposition for me, he mentioned something about me not working here anymore and look at the necklace he gave me." She hardly stopped for breath.

"Oh, my god, it's beautiful, it must have set him back a bit."

"I know it's cheesy but I just feel all warm and content when I'm with him and I know he feels exactly the same way, it's like we were meant to be together." Katie looked all dreamy.

"Well, the rumour going around the club is that he is going to propose to you tonight." And with that Lucy left the ladies room.

Propose, Katie laughed, someone must have spotted the little black box he had given her and made incorrect assumptions. Touching up her make-up she stifled a laugh, for a split second she had thought the same thing too, what an idiot.

Antonio was sitting anxiously waiting for her. "Everything ok?"

"Yes, just girl stuff, nothing really. She was telling me all about Stevo."

"Oh, yes, what has he done?"

"Nothing, just asked her out on a date."

"He kept that quiet."

"Well, he doesn't have to tell you everything just because you're his boss."

"We're friends first and foremost."

"Oh?"

"Yes, we grew up together; he's like another brother really."

"That's nice, why don't you tell me a bit about where you come from?"

"I have a vineyard in Italy, inherited from my parents; it's been in the family for hundreds of years." He paused and then had a sudden brainwave. "I would love to take you there, what do you say?"

"I would really like that, whereabouts in Italy?"

"It's a little place called La Pregheira, literally translated it means 'the prayer'."

"So, that's why you named the club La Pregheira, I wondered what it meant, it's a lovely name."

"You will love the green heart of Italy."

"What is that?"

"La Pregheira is in Umbria, Italy."

"Wow, so we'll be going to 'the prayer' in the green heart of Italy."

"You got it!"

Katie could hardly wait, how fascinating and romantic!

Chapter Twenty Six

Sasha was unrecognisable in her short dark bobbed wig, she wore little make-up and a school madam outfit, long black skirt, white blouse and black jacket. She removed all of her jewellery. "Well, will I do?"

Rhianna started laughing.

"Ok, what's the problem?" Sasha demanded to know.

"I'm sorry; it's just usually you would have worn a tie and had a leather whip. I guess it just brought back memories."

Sasha laughed too, she put on a pair of black rimmed spectacles and looked at her reflection in the mirror. Rhianna had done an excellent job; she had even applied a strategically placed mole just below her lower lip. She was sure she would get in undetected, she would have to be quiet as a mouse and try to sneak in the back door, hopefully no one would realise it was her until it was too late. She knocked back her champagne for dutch courage.

The hotel phone rang, it was reception, the taxi had arrived.

"Well, this is it, thanks for your help, Rhianna."

"Here's the stuff you asked for, just use it in moderation. Remember that Norwegian guy?"

Sasha laughed. "That fat old bastard got what he deserved, it wasn't my fault that he had a full blown heart attack."

"He died remember, I just don't want you to end up in prison or something, you are in the UK now."

"Ok, I'll be very careful."

"That's our debt repaid, no offence but please don't ever contact me again, I hope that you will be happy one day."

"I'll be happy once I show that bitch she can't take Antonio away from me so easily."

Sasha had never changed, still the poisonous, venomous bitch. "Good luck." And with that Rhianna left the hotel suite, glad to be finally out of her grasp once and for all.

As Sasha got into the taxi she was excited at the thought of what she was going to do. She checked her handbag for the stuff. She would throw it right into the bitch's face and then give her an almighty punch and hopefully knock her out. Maybe she would get Antonio at the same time. But the bouncers would probably be hauling her out by then. She could hardly wait for the journey to end, it seemed to take forever. Luckily she knew the code number to get in the cleaners' entrance at the back of the building, Antonio wouldn't have changed that already, or so she hoped, if he had then she was screwed. He thought he had been so clever, but he will wish that he never dumped her in the first place. She couldn't wait for him to crawl back to her on his hands and knees, he would have to beg and plead with her and flash the cash big time. He always said he admired strong women and now she would show him what a strong woman she really was.

Chapter Twenty Seven

Antonio got a message to say that there was an urgent phone call for him, which he had to take in his office. Excusing himself from the table he informed Katie that he would be back in a flash.

It wasn't unusual for him to receive urgent calls, but he was very annoyed when there was nobody on the other end of the phone. He immediately knew that there was something very wrong, but he wasn't sure what it was. He just knew that he had to get back to Katie as soon as possible; it would take him a good five minutes to walk down the long corridor and back into the restaurant. He got on the walkie talkie to Brian and Stevo. "Look, there's something going down, just keep an eye out for trouble."

"Like what?" Stevo was scanning the area, looking for anything remotely suspicious.

"Just look damn it, I'll be there in a minute."

Katie had been sitting daydreaming when she felt a presence; she looked up and briefly saw a figure of a woman she thought she recognised. Some kind of powder was thrown into her face, her eyes burned and she starting coughing really hard. The pain was unbearable and she was frightened that she had permanently lost her eyesight. Whilst trying to catch her breath she felt the ice water poured all over her.

"Nobody steals my man."

Unable to see a thing she panicked, recognising the grating voice immediately. It was Sasha, how could she do this to her?

Veronica had been at the bar area when she noticed a tall dark haired woman walking over to Katie's table. There was something familiar about her, but by the time she realised who it was, the event was all over. She couldn't believe the scene in front of her and raced over to try and do something to help. "Get off her, you fucking maniac are you insane?"

Gianni saw some kind of disturbance going on but didn't know who it was. Felicia got out of her seat to see what was happening. "No, stay here, I'll deal with this."

"But, that girl looks in trouble, I should go and help."

"No, I told you to stay here." And with that he rushed towards the scene, he hated trouble in the club, it was bad for business, and where the hell was Antonio, while all this was going on?

Gianni grabbed the woman by the hair and the wig immediately came off in his hand. "Christ, Sasha, you lunatic, you've blinded the girl." He grabbed her by the

104

arms and viciously started to shake her. "What the fuck have you done, answer me woman or I swear to God..."

Lucy had dropped the tray of drinks when she saw the commotion. "Oh, my God, someone get an ambulance quick." She screamed fearing the worst.

Kyle grabbed the phone and called an ambulance just to be on the safe side.

Brian and Stevo ran over and released Gianni's grip on Sasha telling him that they would deal with her, after all that's what they were paid to do.

Lucy was pushing her way through. "Stevo, let me past, I need to see if she's ok."

Stevo moved out of her way, glad that he wasn't high profile like the de Marcos or this could have so easily have happened to her.

"It's ok, Katie, I'm here, you'll be fine."

Katie was trying to talk, but she couldn't get the words out, her eyes felt like they were on fire and her clothes were soaking wet making her shiver.

"It's going to be alright, an ambulance is on its way, try not to worry." Lucy tried her best to comfort her.

Veronica arrived with a damp towel to put over Katie's eyes. "Try to relax, dear, take slow, deep breaths, put your head back, I'm just going to put a damp towel over your eyes to see if it will help."

Stevo snatched Sasha's handbag and emptied out the contents to see what she had used, but he found nothing. "You better tell me what was in it you, bitch!"

"Fuck you!" Sasha wasn't going to tell them anything.

"Right that's it."

"What are you going to fucking do to me?"

Stevo and Brian literally dragged her through the club by her arms as she kicked and flailed, screaming to be let go.

Throwing her on to the street, Stevo shouted. "You better pray that girl doesn't go blind."

Sasha laughed hysterically, ranting in Russian, nobody understood her and nobody cared.

Just as Stevo was about to contact Antonio he saw him rushing past. "I told you to tell me if anything happened."

Eddie had watched the whole thing on the TV monitor in Veronica's office, he too had been fooled, until Gianni had pulled the wig off. It would be too late for Antonio to do anything though, that was a great shame, the poor girl, she didn't deserve that. However he had been able to tell Antonio that whatever it was Sasha used she had kicked under the table.

"Let me through." Antonio was very worried. "Katie, are you ok?"

"What..." Katie spluttered, "...has she done to me, Antonio... she's completely... insane."

"Don't worry, darling, I'm here now, you're going to be ok," he soothed holding her tight.

"The paramedics are here, Mr de Marco."

The paramedics raced towards the table. "Does anyone know what was thrown into her face."

Antonio suddenly remembered Eddie telling him to look under the table. "Wait, there's something under the table." He quickly found a small bottle with no lid on it and wondered what the hell had been in there. He passed it to the paramedic.

"It looks like pepper." He sniffed the remains and immediately sneezed. "Yes, it's pepper all right, mixed with something else."

His partner stuck his finger in and tasted it. "Cayenne pepper to be exact, mixed with salt."

"Does that mean she will be ok?" Antonio wanted to make sure there would be no permanent damage.

"We'll take her in anyway, sir just to be doubly sure. She'll need to get it all rinsed out, with a special solution, but there should be no lasting effect, perhaps just red and swollen eyes for a few days."

"Thank God, come on, I'll go with you, darling."

"No … I want Lucy to go… like you said… I will be… fine."

"Ok, whatever you want as long as Lucy rings me to let me know you will be ok."

Lucy nodded at him. "Of course I will."

By this time, Katie was shivering either with shock or the effects of the ice bucket being thrown all over her. Antonio put his dinner jacket around her. "Here's my jacket, don't worry, you're going to be fine, darling."

Katie was overcome with emotion, that bloody Sasha woman was trying to maim her for life. She let out a huge sigh of relief and felt tears welling in her eyes, which inevitably made them sting even more.

"I am expecting you to look after her for the next few days," he said turning to Lucy. "And don't worry about your shifts, you'll still get paid, it's the least I can do."

Lucy was extremely grateful. "Thanks, Mr de Marco."

"Now, go on, get out of here, both of you."

Lucy helped Katie up and one of the paramedics took her other arm. Ten minutes later the ambulance arrived in casualty.

On thoroughly checking her, the doctor, told her that she was lucky, it was a potent mix alright. He mixed up a special solution and poured the drops into her eyes. It stung like hell.

"Please rinse your eyes out in lukewarm water as often as possible. Over the next few days you will have red, puffy, watery eyes. It will be slightly uncomfortable but don't worry it's only temporary."

Thanking him, they left accident and emergency. Katie could barely see. She heard a familiar voice; it was Fred, the limo driver.

"Evening, Miss Saunders, Mr de Marco asked me to wait for you and personally take you home."

"Oh, Fred, thank you, that was so thoughtful of him."

"He really does care about you, miss."

"I know."

Fred opened the passenger door for the girls. "Allow me, ladies."

Antonio was sitting in the limousine which surprised Lucy. Boy he really does care about her she thought, maybe she had got him all wrong.

The first thing Katie noticed was the strong, yet distinctive aftershave; Antonio was there. "I'm sorry I still can't focus properly, but there's no permanent damage."

"You don't know how relieved I am to hear that."

"Thanks but you didn't have to give us a lift home."

"It's my pleasure and I won't take no for an answer."

Antonio put a protective arm around her and pulled her close to him. "Thank God, you're ok. That woman needs locking up."

Lucy agreed with Antonio, but Katie just wanted to forget about the nasty incident.

As they reached their destination Lucy noticed Matt's car, he must be in the apartment already she thought. She had managed to make a quick call to him, when the paramedics were getting Katie into the ambulance and fussing over her. Hopefully Antonio would have no intention of going into the flat.

"I'll call you first thing tomorrow, darling, but ring me if you need anything."

"I will." Katie was still shaking. "Here's your jacket." She started to take it off.

"No, just hang on to it for now." He rubbed her arms and felt her whole body shivering. "God, you're freezing."

"Yes, she needs to get out of those icy clothes and have a hot bath right away."

"I couldn't agree with you more, Lucy!"

"Ok, enough, both of you, I hate being fussed over," Katie butted in.

They all said their goodnights and the two girls made their way up to their apartment.

Katie was surprised to find that Matt was there going frantic with worry. "Good grief what on earth happened?" He was going crazy. "Who is this psychotic idiot?"

"Please Matt, I appreciate your concern but all I want to do is go and have a long soak."

"Sure, I understand," he said rather impatiently.

As Lucy was helping Katie run her bath, Matt was pacing the floor. Who could want to hurt her, what had she done to anyone, she had such a lovely nature, there was no way this was her fault. He couldn't wait to speak to his sister, damn it, he couldn't help but feel that he was to blame. If he hadn't given up on her so easily then none of this would have happened.

Chapter Twenty Eight

Antonio was on the phone to Gianni. "Get that fucking bitch on the next flight back to Russia, or I swear to God I'll kill her with my own hands."

"Already sorted, when I explained to her father he was very sympathetic and agreed she would be better off with him until things calmed down."

"Very fucking generous of him, I'm sure." Antonio fumed.

"Just remember how we started off, bro, gun trafficking ring any bells? We would have ended up in the clink if it wasn't for him. You gotta realise we owe him and that's why we can't touch his little girl, you got that?" Gianni snapped.

"Ok, ok, calm down, when does she leave?"

"She's got a mid-afternoon flight tomorrow."

"Is that the best we could do?" Antonio was becoming more irate by the second.

"I'm afraid so."

"Do me a favour, Gianni, put her room on guard, she doesn't go out and nobody goes in!"

"Great minds think alike, bro, got two of our guys on it as we speak."

Antonio was grateful to him; he never wanted to see that damn woman ever again.

Lucy was explaining everything to Matt as best she could. The only reason they could come up with was that Sasha was a woman scorned and wanted to exact her revenge and what better way of doing it than in a public place for all to see. Matt was still angry and wanted to know exactly what it was that had made this woman completely flip out.

"She's just some kind of psycho bitch; I heard that she had done something like this before."

"If de Marco knew she was a nut job then why didn't he break it to her more gently, I mean what the hell was the rush?"

"Matt, I think they have fallen in love."

"You've got to be kidding me, right? They've only just met, I mean how many dates have they had, one for goodness sake!" He wished she hadn't told him that, he suspected as much but didn't want to accept it.

"Matt, it wasn't too long ago when you and Katie felt the same, remember. I know it hurts like hell, but she is so happy with him."

"I thought you hated the de Marcos, you've soon changed your tune."

"No, I'm still not sure about them, but I'm prepared to give Antonio the benefit of the doubt and so should you."

Wearing her bathrobe, with a towel wrapped around her hair, Katie appeared at the door. "Yes, Matt, just let me get on with my life, anything there is to find out about Antonio I will find out for myself. I'm all grown up now, believe it or not, so just let me be happy."

Matt was taken aback by her tone, this was so unlike her, standing there looking all determined with that don't mess with me glint in her eyes. "I'm sorry, how are you feeling?"

"A little better, my eyes don't sting as much. I need a hot mug of cocoa though to warm up; I can't seem to stop shaking."

"I'll make it, Katie, you go and sit down, relax."

"Thanks, Lucy."

The doorbell suddenly rang, startling them all. Who the hell was that at this time of night? Matt went to answer it. He was surprised to see a young man delivering one red rose and a card. He took it off him, it was for Katie, no doubt it was from Antonio.

He walked over to her. "From a well wisher I believe."

She looked a little awkward as she took the card from the envelope. She couldn't make out what it said but knew that it was from Antonio, it had a faint smell of his aftershave.

"Well, who is it from then?" Matt asked.

"Erm… it's from Antonio."

"What does he say?" Lucy immediately regretted asking it, forgetting that Matt was still there.

"I can't really make it out, my eyes are still sore." She rubbed them, making them itch even more.

Matt was feeling more and more uncomfortable with the situation. "I think it's time I went and left you two to talk. Just try and take it easy, Katie."

"Thanks, Matt, I will."

After Matt left the flat Lucy apologised profusely. "I'm so sorry Katie, I wasn't thinking. You know what I'm like, open my big gob and put both feet right in it."

"Here, what does it say?" Katie passed her the card.

"My beautiful Katie, get well soon. Looking forward to our trip to the green heart of Italy, Antonio."

Katie was shaking with cold, she could barely stand up.

"Come on, Katie, I'll make you that hot cocoa now, that will do the trick. A couple of pain killers and an early night, you'll be fit as a fiddle in the morning."

Katie went to bed with a fever that night, she would be ill for almost a week thanks to that dreadful woman. She snuggled into her pillow and dreamed of Antonio rescuing her, it was a dream she would continue to have for years to come.

110

Chapter Twenty Nine

Sasha had been calling Antonio nonstop, but it always went straight on to his answer machine. She was becoming increasingly irate. She decided that there was nothing else she could do, other than turn up at his apartment. Grabbing her things she rang reception demanding a taxi. The young man on the desk told her that it wasn't possible. "What do you mean, not possible?" Sasha screamed down the phone. "Do you fucking know who I am?"

"I'm sorry, madam, I am under strict instructions." He was told that the woman was dangerous and about to be sectioned, but not until the following afternoon for some strange reason.

"Whose instructions are they then?"

"I am not at liberty to say."

"Just give me a goddamn taxi number and I'll book it myself."

"I'm sorry madam, I can't do that." He replaced the receiver.

Sasha was beside herself now, what could she do? She got out her little gold compact and cut herself a line of coke and snorted it in a split second. She fell back on to the sofa enjoying the feeling of euphoria that she always felt when she took it. She wasn't an addict but admitted to herself she was taking it more and more these days, thanks to her early days with Gianni who had introduced her to it. He very occasionally still dabbled from time to time. She picked up the hotel phone, she'd show that son of a bitch if it's the last thing she did. This time a woman picked up the phone. "Get me an outside line please."

Ringing the operator she got a couple of taxi numbers. One was on its way and would be with her anytime. Pulling her jacket on she straightened her hair and checked her make-up. She reckoned she would do. Opening the door of her suite she was stunned to see two guys standing there. "Out of my way," she screeched.

The two men smiled at her. "Not a chance, please go back into your room."

"I will not!"

They were being observed by the maid just coming out of the suite opposite.

"Are you ok, madam?" she enquired, concerned for the woman's welfare.

"No, call the police; they are trying to kill me!"

"Everything's ok, she's just been released from a psycho ward and we need to keep her here overnight. She is a danger to herself and others."

The maid was rather alarmed and quickly scuttled off, there was no way she was getting involved in this, especially on the paltry wages she earned.

The two men got hold of her arms and dragged her kicking and screaming back into her suite. She was a quivering wreck. "How dare you, get you're fucking hands off me, do you hear?"

"Message from Mr de Marco, your flight is 2.45pm tomorrow, back to daddy. You are not to leave the hotel until it's time catch your flight. You try anything else, bitch, and I'll gladly crush your windpipe, just like that." Jed clicked his fingers for effect.

Sasha was trembling with fright and could hardly speak; the man with the scar was a mean bastard. "What is he paying you, I'll double it," she gasped.

"I don't give a fuck, lady." He shoved her onto the sofa and whispered into her ear. "Watch yourself tonight, love, I may come in and give you a right good seeing to."

Sasha's face was ashen with fright, her eyes big and wide. She was used to being in charge in any situation, but she knew if she dared to utter a word this man would rape her in an instant. He was the only man to ever frighten the life out of her like this. Reluctantly she nodded to the men, letting them know she understood what they were saying to her.

After they left she had another line of coke to ease her aching brain. That goddamn bitch Katie, she would have her revenge, one way or another she would pay for the misery she had caused her. Maybe she would hire an assassin, she started laughing hysterically. The thought totally amused her, an assassin, she didn't know any. She laughed until her sides ached. But she knew somebody who did, her father; he would do anything for her. She couldn't wait to see him, now she had something to look forward to, something to keep her going through all this. Once Katie was out of the way, she would be back in Antonio's arms. Exhausted she climbed on to the king size bed and fell into a deep sleep.

Jed had phoned Antonio to tell him about Sasha's mission to escape. Antonio had been very grateful; he was a fool to have got involved with her in the first place, especially after he knew what she did to Gianni. "Just escort her to the plane tomorrow and make sure she gets on it."

"No problem, boss."

Antonio was in his office at the club, he had a desire to do some gambling tonight, just to vent his anger. It was either that or he would do time for that bitch. He decided he would play roulette and bet big. It was going to be a long night. He called Gianni. "Fancy doing some serious gambling in the casino tonight?"

"Sure, give me half an hour, bro."

Antonio didn't gamble very often, but he was upset and wanted some kind of release. If things had gone according to plan then he would have had Katie in his bed making love to her round about now.

Chapter Thirty

Matt was really frustrated, there was nothing he could do. He was starting his new job on Monday and hoped that it would be a good opportunity to do some digging. The de Marco brothers were dodgy, he had a gut feeling that there was more to them than met the eye and he was determined to find out everything he could about them. He was worried for Katie and wanted her to know what she was getting into. He still loved her and wanted to protect her at all costs. Matt was beginning to regret the day Lucy and Katie first went to that goddamn club, he wish he had put his foot down. But unfortunately that wasn't in his nature. He just had a horrible feeling that something terrible was going to happen. If it was in his power he would stop it if he could, his sister and ex-girlfriend were very important to him and he would protect them, even put his life on the line if he had to.

Lucy phoned Matt as soon as Katie went to bed. "She is quite ill at the moment."

"What, are her eyes no better?"

"She still has puffy, sore eyes, but she has a chill. I think she is coming down with something, it could be flu."

"Lucy, I'm not convinced about this Antonio character."

"Look, Matt, it's really none of our business."

"I know, you're right, I just worry about you both. And you still haven't told me about this Steve guy."

"Oh, Stevo you mean. He is wonderful to me, but it's early days, I don't really know him that well, we are going for lunch tomorrow."

"So, you called it off tonight then?"

"No, we didn't really arrange a proper date, which is just as well after what happened in the club."

"Ok, sis, just take care and I'll speak to you soon."

"You worry too much, Matt, you'll get frown lines if you're not careful." Lucy joked.

"Night, night." Matt put the phone down. He looked at himself in the mirror, Lucy was right, he had to stop fretting or else it would age him. He was only a young bloke with the rest of his life ahead of him. From now on he would keep his head down, give his all to the law firm and work his way up through the ranks. There would always be a place for Katie in his heart no matter what. He doubted that he would ever love anyone like that again, it was sad but he knew he had to move on.

Lucy called the doctor out in the middle of the night, Katie had a fever and her temperature was high. The doctor arrived forty-five minutes later. He advised Lucy that Katie had picked up a flu virus that was unfortunately going around.

"Just make sure that she has plenty of fluids and I'll prescribe her a course of antibiotics, she should rest for the next few days. It should clear up in about a week or so."

"Ok, thanks, Dr Clark."

Katie didn't remember the doctor's visit; she was hot one minute and freezing cold the next. She felt like shit and looked like hell, zapped of energy she was barely able to get out of bed.

For the next few days she spent most of her time in bed; she refused to see Antonio as she didn't want him to see her at her worst. Every day she received a single red rose and a card with a different message on it. She knew that he really cared about her and couldn't wait until he fulfilled his promise to take her to Umbria. That kept her occupied, in between bouts of her body aching and her throbbing headaches. Her eyes had cleared up in a couple of days but her body had borne the brunt of the ice bucket that Sasha had so enjoyed tipping over her. All she could do was keep warm, take the tablets and try to recuperate as soon as possible. The roses kept coming, the phone kept ringing, but Katie wouldn't speak to Antonio, she was embarrassed by the whole situation. She told Lucy to tell him she was resting and would ring him as soon as she was back to her normal self. Lucy willingly obliged and hoped that this was the end of Katie and Antonio's romance once and for all. Matt was right, there was more to the de Marcos than met the eye and he was right to be concerned about her.

Chapter Thirty One

Antonio had an extremely lucky night, he had cleared the table. Gianni had only seen his brother like this once before. He knew that he liked to gamble but that was in the distant past. That's how they got involved in the gun trafficking with Sasha's father. They had been in an illegal casino in Moscow, Antonio had been a bit wild then since their parents and sister had died and he needed an escape of some sort. He went off the rails, became crazy. He owed Sergio a big wedge of money. Sergio had taken him to one side and made the proposition of gun trafficking or else he would pay with his life, nobody would dare mess with the Breschnevsky family. Antonio had agreed. Initially they transported the guns via his Italian furniture and art dealing connections, unbeknown to his business partners, the Brookstein and Valetti families. That was almost ten years ago; there was no way that they would ever find out now as it was all in the past. He had repaid Sergio tenfold, set him up with various contacts. And anyway the de Marcos were totally legit, no illegal dealings anymore; they were one hundred per cent clean. But Antonio knew that Sergio still had that hold over them.

The brothers went back to Antonio's office to discuss the events of the night. Gianni comforted his brother. "Come on, bro, you're stronger than this, since when did you ever get upset by a woman?"

Antonio was swigging back the whisky. Gianni was starting to get worried the last time Antonio was like this was when their parents and only sister died in a car crash. He had to get him home as quickly as possible before he did something he regretted. He was in a black mood. Gianni told Eddie to get Fred. Five minutes later they were in the limo on their way back to Antonio's penthouse.

Gianni put his brother to bed. He was in no fit state to be left alone tonight. He called Felicia and told her that he was staying over to look after him. She was very understanding, like she usually was, that's why he loved her so much. He could do whatever he wanted with no questions asked, safe in the knowledge that Felicia would always be there for him. He could swing for Sasha; she had turned Antonio into a quivering wreck. He didn't know what he had ever seen in her, she was poison through and through.

Sasha was oblivious to the turmoil she had caused. She would go back to Moscow, retreat and recover and put her next plan into action, no one got one over on her, especially the de Marco brothers.

Chapter Thirty Two

Stevo was beside himself; he decided to pay Lucy a call, just turn up. She would either turf him out or be grateful for his company; he was willing to take the chance.

It was about two in the morning by the time he arrived. Lucy fell into his arms and they made mad passionate love for the first time. She was everything he had expected and much more, this was the woman for him. After all his conquests he knew that she was different and belonged to him, giving herself willingly. Thankfully, Katie was sound asleep and never heard a thing.

"Stevo, do you think we have a future together?" Lucy was nestled in his arms all warm and totally loved up.

"You bet, you are the best thing that has ever happened to me, trust me babe,"

"Oh, I do. No offence, but please make sure you are gone before Katie gets up, she'll be mad if she knows that you stayed over."

"Why would she be mad, babe?"

"She just feels let down by everyone in the club; you know it shouldn't have happened."

"I know, but if it's any consolation that Sasha bitch will be on a flight home tomorrow afternoon, it's all sorted, babe."

"What do you mean?"

"Nothing, babe, just go to sleep, honey."

Stevo wrapped his arms around her and held her close. It was the happiest he had ever been with a woman and hoped that it would last.

Chapter Thirty Three

Veronica was feeling extremely horny; the events of that evening had sent her into a frenzy. All she wanted was Nicholas, to feel him inside her, she craved him badly.

He was finishing off in the kitchen when she walked in. All the staff had gone home, she sent the bouncers and Eddie home too, she told them that there was no need for them to stay any longer.

But Eddie was still in the building; he fancied Veronica something rotten and wanted to be with her, comfort her. He knew that she only had eyes for Nicholas and that he would never, ever have a chance to be with her.

He was watching on the TV monitor as Veronica walked into the kitchen. She hitched her skirt up, showing Nicholas she wasn't wearing any underwear. He wished that he could zoom in, see everything close up. His dick was throbbing; he wanted to fuck her so badly it ached. Veronica grabbed Nicholas and started kissing him passionately, she wrapped her legs around him. "Take me baby," she ordered him.

Eddie couldn't make out what they were saying but understood as Nicholas willingly obliged her.

Veronica groaned in total ecstasy. "I want to feel you right now!"

Nicholas lifted her on to the preparation table, he took her fast and hard. She was screaming and sticking her claw like nails into his back and writhing with ecstasy.

"Oh my god, Nick, where have you been all my life?"

"I'm here for you, my sweetheart, don't ever forget it." He buried his face in her ample breasts.

They made love all around the kitchen, enjoying every inch of each other. Finally when they were both spent they opened a bottle of wine.

"To many more times like this," Nicholas toasted her.

"Wow, that was fantastic, you have certainly excelled yourself in the kitchen tonight," she giggled as she gulped back the chilled wine.

Eddie was sitting in Veronica's chair watching them, wishing it was him taking her. He was overcome with jealousy, this was as close as he would ever get to having Veronica, he knew that. Next time he would video them, take it home for his bedtime pleasure. He smirked to himself, yes, that's what he would do. He left the office before he was discovered, pity there was no sound on the TV, he could tell that Veronica was a real goer though, a very sexual, powerful woman.

Veronica was totally elated; no man had ever made her feel like that before. They just had this connection and it was one hell of a connection.

117

"Baby you were fantastic, I wish you had done this sooner."

"If I knew how big your manhood was, darling, I would have had you months ago."

They both laughed, Nicholas pulled her up off the kitchen floor and bent her over the table. "Ready for some more,"

Before she could answer he was inside her once more. She screamed with delight. "You are a bad boy, Nick."

Chapter Thirty Four

Antonio was flat out, Gianni couldn't believe that he was in this state. It was so unlike him, he was the sane, sensible one. A woman had finally tipped him over the edge. But what he saw in this Katie girl was beyond him, elegant maybe, but not the marrying kind. He would do whatever it took to make his brother happy and that's why he had put the hard word on Matthew Carmichael. Antonio would never have done it and if he found out he would be blazing with him. He knew that he could trust Jed implicitly, if the price was right. There was no doubt in his mind that he had done the right thing. Whatever his brother wanted he would make sure by hook or by crook he would get it. It was true he was jealous of Antonio but he would never hurt him or let anyone else hurt him for that matter. It was an unwritten law between them. Ever since they lost their family they were closer than ever and no one was going to interfere in that, especially not a woman, whoever they may be.

He phoned Honey in Manchester; they talked nonstop sex and all the things they were going to do to each other when they met up again. He promised that he would see her next week; he couldn't wait, she was insatiable, willing and eager to please. She was a cheap slut but he didn't really care about that, she was just an easy lay to him. Felicia was a good, honest, decent woman and he promised himself that one day he would be completely faithful to her, once they were married, that is. In the meantime he was going to sow his wild oats and have plenty of fun. Love-making with Felicia was slow and sensuous but his bit on the side was a filthy bitch and would do anything he asked of her. Indeed he never had to suggest anything, she always took control. His mind turned back to the last time they had been together, she had suggested a threesome. Gianni was adventurous and totally up for it. The thought of being with two women really turned him on. He could barely wait, he wished it was tonight, he was just in the mood for a raunchy session with two horny chicks.

Chapter Thirty Five

Antonio had constantly phoned to see how Katie was doing, she hadn't been out of bed for a couple of days. He was starting to get worried about her, maybe it was more serious than they were letting on. Lucy tried her best to reassure him that all she needed was complete rest. It was only a virus that was going around, nothing life-threatening, she had joked with him.

It was a busy time for Antonio attending many business meetings to raise his profile and propose several new business ventures. So, he stayed away from Katie's apartment as instructed by Lucy, and anyway the last thing he needed right now was to catch the virus himself. He continued to send the roses and cards to show that he was thinking about her. Gianni, surprisingly, had hung around with him the whole week. They had gone to all the meetings and spent a lot of time in Club La Pregheira and gambled into the early hours, sometimes winning big, sometimes losing big. Gianni decided it was time to put his foot down, Antonio was starting to get carried away and he was worried about the amount of money he was losing. In the past he had been a serious gambler and he didn't want him to go down that road again, it nearly finished him. Even Veronica had voiced her objections, but Antonio continued to ignore everyone, until of course he received a phone call from Katie to say that she was better.

Antonio's plans kicked into action. He talked incessantly to Gianni about his plans to take her out to the family vineyard in Umbria. It was a total shock to him when his younger brother announced that all the arrangements were already in place.

"It's all set for tomorrow, you and your lady friend will have a great time."

"I didn't realise you cared."

"Of course I do, I think the break will do you both good."

"What about the businesses?" Antonio demanded.

"Don't give them a second thought, all in good hands. Don't forget you are only a couple of hours away. If anything serious crops up I'll be right on the blower."

Antonio was bowled over by his brother's thoughtfulness, it wasn't often that he saw his brother's caring side. Just for a moment he wondered if there was some kind of catch, a reason why he wanted him out of the way. Had he gotten himself into trouble again?

As if reading his mind Gianni stated. "Hey, you'll only be gone for the weekend, what could possibly happen?"

"Anything could, knowing you!"

"Thanks for the vote of confidence."

"I know you, remember."

"Give me a break, bro, we've came through too much for me to mess up now."

"Ok, Gianni, you're my brother and I trust you." Antonio smiled.

"Glad to hear it. Now all you have to do is whisk your sweet little Katie off to the airstrip."

"Sounds good, but I want it to be a complete surprise."

"Leave it with me, bro, I'll get Stevo to talk to Lucy about it, they're together a lot lately."

"What, you telling me that Stevo and Lucy are an item now?"

"Yeah, where you been man, on another planet or what?"

"Ok, ok, I'll snap out of it real soon, no problems."

"Cool, just pack a case and be ready five o'clock sharp tomorrow. I've phoned on ahead so Francesca and Alfredo will have everything ready."

Antonio was looking forward to seeing the Carbones; he hadn't seen them for almost six years. It would be the first time he had been back to Italy since his parents and younger sister were killed, no, murdered, he knew that, but it was never proven.

He found his mind wandering on to the Calvis. Evil little bastards they were, they used to get a kick out of killing defenceless animals when they were just little kids. They moved on to bigger things, resorting to threats and blackmail, they had their own little protection racket going. But when they threatened Antonio's father the de Marcos decided to do something about it. They tried talking to Calvis' father, but he was a drunk and a wife-beater, who didn't give a shit. At least they had tried the easy route, approached the family first, but now they would have to think of something else. So Antonio and Gianni came up with a plan, they followed them one evening and beat them to a pulp, telling them to leave the town for good or next time they would end up in the morgue. Antonio was glad that they had finally got the message. The Calvi brothers vanished into thin air, job done. It was just a pity they didn't do it a bit sooner.

Everything was great, the locals adored them and brought presents to their house, home grown vegetables, meat, whisky, you name it, they brought it.

Antonio and Gianni had been away on a business trip to Rome, when they got the news about their family. It had to be down to the Calvis, they should have finished them off when they had the chance. They had to exact revenge and despite desperate attempts to locate them it had all been in vain. When the Calvis' younger brother Carlo and their father Alfonso had tried to take over from where they left off they knew that they couldn't let that happen. When the local baker's house and business went up in flames killing the baker and his pregnant wife, the Calvis sealed their own fate.

They had to pay for their heartless act. In retribution, they had tampered with their boat, making it look like an accident. The townsfolk knew it was down to the de

Marcos. The Police had been brought in from outside of La Pregheira but nobody would give them up. Frustrated, the official verdict was misadventure, case closed.

Antonio had yearned to visit his family's grave but hadn't dared to for fear of his own life. But he knew that the Calvis had moved out of the area and nobody had heard anything about them since; maybe they had pissed someone else off and met an horrific end, he could only hope that was true.

It would be strange going home; all those memories would come flooding back. But it was time to face his demons once and for all. He hoped that Katie would love La Pregheira; it was such a beautiful place, steeped in history and full of character.

Chapter Thirty Six

Stevo had a secret rendezvous with Lucy. She was all giggly and excited to see him. It was driving her crazy, wondering what all the urgency was.

"Listen, Lucy, you able to pack a weekend case ..."

Lucy cut in, "Sure, where are you taking me?"

"No, sorry, Lucy, I should have said, it's for Katie."

Lucy's faced dropped, what on earth was going on now, she pondered.

"Come on, baby, I'll whisk you away soon enough, don't you worry."

"I suppose so, what do you need?"

"Her passport and enough clothes to last the weekend, can you manage to do that without alerting her?"

"I think so, why, what's going on?"

"Antonio wants to take her off to Italy, to the family villa no less."

"When are they going?"

"Tomorrow."

"Tomorrow, you haven't given me much time!"

"Yeah, I just found out myself. Now can you do that for me, baby?"

"For you, sure, when do you want to get the stuff?"

"You need to try and get her out of the apartment tomorrow afternoon and I'll slip round once you give me the nod."

"Ok, she hasn't been out for ages so maybe I'll take her to the park for some fresh air. I'm sure she'll appreciate it."

"Fantastic, just ring me when you leave and I'll do the rest."

"So, how do we get her to the airport then?"

"That's easy, she thinks Antonio is taking her out for a romantic dinner."

"First I've heard about it."

"She'll get the invite tomorrow morning, with her single red rose, as usual."

"You have to hand it to Antonio, he seems to have thought of everything."

"Come here and give me a kiss."

"No, you better go before she gets out of the shower and rumbles us."

"Give me a kiss first," Stevo demanded. "God, you are so sexy when you pout like that."

"You smooth talker, you, how can I resist when you put it like that!"

They shared a long lingering kiss. Stevo hugged her tightly. "And while the boss is away," he winked at her.

Lucy giggled. "I can hardly wait."

"Until tomorrow evening then, my sweet."

He kissed her once more. Lucy waved to him out of the window and watched him climb into his car and speed off. Her heart was all of a flutter, maybe she too had found true love, who would believe it! The girl who said she would never fall in love, get married or have children. Now she was changing her mind, at least about the love bit anyway!

Stevo couldn't help becoming more and more fond of her. She was such a sweetheart, totally genuine and down to earth. She was like a breath of fresh air, bubbly and full of life. He didn't know how he had ever survived without her. There was definitely something special about her.

Chapter Thirty Seven

Katie was none too pleased to be bossed around by Lucy. She had just recovered from a crappy virus and the last thing she wanted was to go for a leisurely walk in the park. Fed up with Lucy's pleas she finally gave in.

"Oh, for goodness sake, if it makes you happy, let's go, but I want a cappuccino!"

"Yeah, me too, we'll need caffeine as soon as we get to the other side of the park."

The walk was beautiful, she had forgotten how pretty the park looked. The hum and chatter of the people as they made their way to work made her smile. The birds tweeting in the trees and the mothers rushing their children to school with freshly scrubbed, smiling cherub faces made her realise how much she missed this part of the day. Her early morning walks with Lucy were a real tonic for her. She linked Lucy. "Thanks, this is just what I needed."

"Hey, come on, girl, it's just a walk, same as usual!"

"No, it's much more than that, it's the steady throng of people going about their everyday life, it just makes me happy, that's all." Her voice was serious.

"Katie, you are strange at times!" Lucy exclaimed.

"What, you're my best mate and you've only just noticed!" Katie laughed, a whole hearted laugh, "Let's go to that lovely little coffee shop."

"Sounds like you are back to your normal self."

"I sure am."

"Good, then we'll have a full English breakfast, God knows you need fattening up girl."

"I don't know if I could eat it, but I'll give it a go."

"Looking forward to seeing Antonio then?"

"What do you think?" Katie tossed back her mane of shiny chestnut hair. "I was looking forward to getting to know him a whole lot better too, if you know what I mean."

"Too much information, Katie!"

"Well, if it hadn't been for that plastic Barbie doll anything could have happened between us that night!"

"Never mind, you'll have plenty of time for all that."

"I hope so."

"I hear he has been pining for you!"

"Really?"

"Yes, it's totally true. Now how about I help you get ready for this big date, it will be fun, I'll give you Lucy's special touch."

"What about Veronica, shouldn't you be back at work tonight?"

"Yep, it's all sorted, I've still got time to help do your hair and make-up, advise you on what to wear!"

"I want to look sexy, yet sophisticated. Not tarty, just stylish, I want Antonio to look at me and realise what he has been missing for the last week."

"I'm sure between us, we'll come up with the right look."

"Fabulous, then all I need to do is look beautiful."

They continued walking through the park, enjoying the fresh air and aroma of fresh coffee and croissants.

Chapter Thirty Eight

Gianni had been neglecting Felicia, he was going to have to make it up to her. She was the only woman that had came the closest to taming him and probably would be the only one that ever would. He admired her ability to keep him on the straight and narrow. If she ever found out about Honey she would have his guts for garters, that's why he had to be very careful. Antonio had been a great excuse to make a few trips to the club in Manchester. Honey had been as welcoming as he'd expected. She was just a fling he kept telling himself, there could never be any future with her, as far as he was concerned she was his latest conquest. Just a shag he thought, yet there was something dangerous about her that attracted him. He would have to let her down gently, but not yet. He was looking forward to the threesome she had promised him. She was a right little goer and sometimes that was just what he needed, no strings attached. He was marrying Felicia in a few months time, but for now he would continue having the best of both worlds. After the unfortunate Pete incident when he had defended Honey's honour he reckoned Antonio knew that there was still something going on between them. He shook his head, what was he on about 'honour', she had no idea what honour was. Oh, well, he resigned himself to the fact that Antonio would speak to him before the wedding to make sure it was well and truly over. One thing about his brother was that he was never unfaithful to his women and that counted for something; he wish he had the same control.

Unknown to Gianni, Felicia was very well aware of his shortcomings but decided she would let him get it out of his system, but God help him if he strayed once they were married, he would rue the day.

He did love Felicia in his own way and wasn't prepared to lose her for any old slapper that opened her legs at the drop of a hat. He was under no illusion about Honey. Harry told her that she would fuck anyone, as long as they were loaded. When the time came he would pay her off and if she couldn't or wouldn't accept it then he would find another way to rid himself of her. Whatever it took, he would do.

Chapter Thirty Nine

Antonio was waiting at five o'clock prompt in his limo outside of Katie's apartment block. He could hardly wait to see the look on her face when they turned up at his private airstrip. She would be ecstatic when he announced where they were going.

"How do I look then?" Katie asked her best friend.

"Totally sophisticated, that little black dress was a fabulous investment."

"Do you think Antonio will remember seeing me in this the first night in the club?"

"I expect so; he couldn't take his eyes off you!"

"Oh thanks, Luce, maybe I should have worn something else, have I got time to get changed?"

"Absolutely not, just wear your hair up, different jewellery and hey presto, a completely different look."

"Ok, I'll just have to do then."

The doorbell rang, it was Fred, Antonio's driver. "Good evening, Miss Saunders are you ready to go?"

"Hello, Fred, yes I am, but please, remember to call me Katie, I don't like all that formal stuff."

"Of course, Miss, er Katie I mean. Please follow me, your transport awaits."

"Where are we going?"

"I don't want to spoil the surprise so I'll let Antonio tell you."

Katie smiled at him and turned to Lucy. "Have a lovely, relaxing evening and I'll see you later."

"You too," Lucy grinned, wondering how Katie would react to being whisked off in a private jet to Italy, lucky thing. How romantic, if Stevo did something special like that for her she would be over the moon.

Fred opened the limo door and she was greeted by Antonio who produced a single red rose along with a huge smile.

"You must have spent a small fortune on all those roses."

"You're worth every penny, believe me. You look absolutely stunning. I must admit that I really have missed you." He remembered the dress well, it really flattered her slender figure. She wore her hair brushed back off her face and tied up high in a long sleek ponytail. She had a healthy glow about her and newly acquired confidence.

Katie blushed. "It's only been a week you know."

"Is that all, it seems like forever. Can I offer you a glass of champagne?"

"Why not, but I have to warn you it will probably go straight to my head. Actually the last time I had it was when you splashed out free champagne in the club."

"Oh, yes that's right, opening night. How did you like it?"

"I don't think that I could ever get used to it, just one glass and I'm away with the fairies!"

"Don't worry, I'll be completely honourable, I promise."

"I wouldn't expect anything less from you."

"Why, thank you, that's good to know!"

Katie secretly wanted the complete opposite. She had really missed him too, she didn't know what it was about him that excited her so much. "I really liked the cards you sent, it was really thoughtful."

"Thoughtful, it was supposed to be a romantic gesture," he teased.

"I suppose it was very romantic of you."

"My pleasure."

"Where are you taking me, it's a little early for dinner, or are we going on a magical, mystery tour?"

"Ah, patience, Katie, all will be revealed soon enough. Just sit back, relax and enjoy your champagne."

Why all the mystery, she wondered. He must be taking her somewhere really exclusive. She hoped she didn't look out of place in her little black dress.

Antonio noticed she looked a little bewildered. "Don't worry, you look beautiful, darling," he reassured her as he topped up her glass. He continued talking, filling her in on what had been going on in the club. Veronica and Nicholas had gone public with their relationship. Kyle had split up with his boyfriend and had been quite distressed, until a couple of days ago when he had pulled a toy boy. He was back to his usual bubbly self. Gianni and Felicia, or should he say, Felicia had been making the final preparations for their wedding.

"Oh, I didn't know they had fixed a date for the wedding."

"They've kept it relatively low key, as they are only having a small intimate wedding. I would be proud for you to be my date though."

"We'll see, anyway you haven't mentioned Sasha," Katie heard herself saying, she hadn't meant to bring her up, but the words had just popped out.

"She has gone back home, to Russia," he said simply.

"Why, what made her decide to leave, she was so intent on getting you back, are you sure she's gone?" Katie pushed him for an answer.

"There was nothing left here for her."

"But I thought she loved London and the lifestyle, I can't believe she went that easily."

"Let's just say that I used a little bit of friendly persuasion." He leaned over and tapped on the window in front.

Fred obediently wound down the window. "Yes, boss?"

"Are we here?"

"Yes, I'm just driving up towards the turn off now." And with that Fred put the window back up.

"What do you mean, friendly persuasion, did you threaten her?"

"Katie, I really don't want to waste this date on discussing that damn woman, please, let's just have fun. Tonight is about you and I, nothing else."

Katie knew that she had said enough and didn't want to push the subject. "Ok, you win," she smiled.

"Ok, close your eyes and promise not to open them until I tell you when."

"Why?"

"You do trust me, don't you?" Antonio asked her.

"Of course I do, oh, is this my surprise?"

"You bet it is, I hope you won't be disappointed."

She closed her eyes obediently and tried to count how many minutes had passed until the car came to a standstill.

"No peaking," Antonio ordered her. "Give me your arm and I'll help you." He led her slowly out of the limo. He took her arm and they walked several steps. Antonio gently turned her the opposite way. "Ok, you can open your eyes now."

"Where are we?" Katie was facing the limo, feeling a little dazed.

"No, this way." He pointed behind her head.

Katie gasped, they were on an airfield and Fred was standing, waiting at the bottom of the airplane steps.

"What's going on?" she stammered. "Is this yours?"

"How do you fancy taking a trip to Umbria?"

"Italy… right now, but, but…" she protested.

"Everything is sorted, we've got your weekend case packed and your passport, all courtesy of your good friend, and my partner in crime, Lucy."

"You're telling me she knew all about this and said nothing?" Katie couldn't believe Lucy could keep any secrets from her, especially one as big as this.

"So, what do you say?"

"Well, you've gone to so much trouble, how could I refuse?"

"Let's go then, Umbria awaits." He escorted her up the steps.

"Welcome aboard, Mr de Marco, Miss Saunders," the air hostess greeted them.

The interior took Katie's breath away, she had never seen anything like it in her life. The walls were a cream colour and the beige leather seats were huge. A sheepskin rug covered the middle of the aisle. All the glasses were crystal and the cutlery solid gold. There was an ice bucket containing a chilled magnum of champagne just waiting to be uncorked.

130

"Wow, this is amazing."

"Let me show you the cockpit and introduce you to the captain."

"It's so tiny in here," was all Katie could say.

"This is Philippe."

"Hello." Katie shook his hand, he looked so young, too young to be able to fly, God she hoped that he knew what he was doing.

"I'm the co-pilot," Philippe informed her.

"You are, then where is the pilot?"

"I'm right here."

Katie was gob smacked. "You're kidding me, you can really fly this?"

"Of course," he said matter-of-factly. "But I'm just going to take off and land, Philippe will do the rest, I wouldn't want you to get bored."

"Oh my God, I have never been on a plane before, never mind a private jet, it's just awesome."

"Just sit wherever you like, fasten your seatbelt and we'll prepare for takeoff, Michelle will take you through the procedures. Once I've checked the flight path and we're up in the air I'll be right back."

Katie was on cloud nine, this was an amazing experience, one that she would never forget. She marvelled at how she came to be here; of all people, why her, she had to pinch herself to make sure that she wasn't dreaming. Determined to make the best of it she fastened her seatbelt and looked dreamily out of the window. It was a wonderful view, breathtaking, she felt right at home, fit into the lifestyle with total ease as if she had been born into it. Through her short life she knew that something was missing and now she knew what it was. She was meant to have a life like this, she took it all in her stride and loved every minute of it, this was the start of something big. Antonio was the one and they were going to have a fantastic life together. Katie was daydreaming again, she remembered her mother's last words to her. "One day some lucky man will sweep you off your feet, he'll treat you like a princess and God knows you deserve it. Just be happy and live your life to the full, experience everything you can because you never know when it will be taken away from you." Her mother had spoken words of wisdom and she was going to follow her sound advice.

The more she knew about Antonio, the more she was convinced that he was indeed a man of many talents. It was going to be fun learning all about him; full of admiration she knew that he had already stolen her heart. But what was love she asked herself, excitement, the knot in her stomach every time she saw him or maybe it was the not knowing what was going to happen next, the thrill of adventure. Whatever it was it felt so right to her, this was the beginning of something special.

Antonio handed the controls over to Phillipe. "I'll be back for touchdown."

"No, don't worry about that, Antonio, enjoy some time with your lovely young lady, I'll do the honours."

"Thanks, Phillipe, you're very considerate."

"Hey, I love flying, it's my pleasure."

Antonio made his way back into the cabin. Katie looked a million miles away, she was so stunning, he could hardly believe how quickly things had moved between them. Although he hadn't made love to her yet he still had strong feelings for her, ones he had never felt before. It must be love, it had to be, he thought, so this is what it felt like. "So, tell me, are you having a good time so far?"

"I am so loving it, you wouldn't believe it," Katie gushed, genuinely impressed.

Antonio never had a woman who was so easily pleased; it was a totally new situation for him. "I'm so glad, this is just the beginning, Katie."

"This is so fantastic, I can't begin to tell you."

He leaned towards her and kissed her. "There'll be many more trips like this for us to enjoy, just wait and see."

Chapter Forty

Lucy had to work for a few hours in the club. She knew that Katie would be up in the air now, the lucky thing. If anyone deserved to be treated like a princess she did.

Tania snapped at her, "For goodness sake Lucy, get a grip and snap out of it, there are people waiting to be served. Jesus this is your first day back and don't you forget it!"

"What the hell do you mean by that?"

"Just get on with your work or you'll be out the friggin' door."

What a bitch, Lucy thought. Just because Veronica was off tonight didn't mean that she could treat her like shit. She had to bite her lip to stop her saying something she may regret, at least for the time being anyway.

Kyle was in extremely high spirits, he was telling all and sundry about his latest conquest, Richard, who was only sweet seventeen and still at school. He chattered incessantly to Lucy whenever he got the chance. He was like an excited schoolboy.

"You're such a case, Kyle, I'm sure you make all these stories up."

"As if, I could tell you some stories that would make your hair positively super curly!"

"Please, don't get him started," Colin piped up, cleaning the glasses behind him.

"Ooh, just because you haven't got a woman, no need to be jealous about my new relationship."

"Please, you don't know what you're talking about," Colin brushed his comments off.

"True, I'll give you that. Anyway," he turned back to Lucy, "so, come on, spill, spill, spill."

"What?"

"Oh, come on, Lucy, what's going on with those two lovebirds. Have they gone away to be married or something?"

"Don't be ridiculous, as if! They barely know each other."

"Come on, just a little bit of juicy gossip," Kyle persisted.

"No, it's really none of our business."

"Spoilsport, isn't she, Colin, all I want is a little tit bit." He put two of his fingers together. "Go on, just an incey wincey bit!"

"Ok, it's true they have gone off somewhere, but I'm sworn to secrecy."

"To get married?"

"No, don't be silly, it's too soon for anything like that."

"True, but I reckon it's love at first sight and it's only a matter of time before those wedding bells start ringing and I for one can't wait. Ooh, I so adore weddings."

Tania stomped over to them. "Less of the chit chat and get back to work, now!" she ordered.

"Just what is your problem, Tania?" Lucy was becoming extremely irritated with her bitchy attitude.

"You are, you're positively fucking bone idle."

"Oh, it was all my fault, Tania, please don't blame Lucy, you know what I'm like for chatting."

"Yes, I do and it's a good job everyone likes you, Kyle, but I warn you, if I catch you again I'm going to dock your bleeding wages."

"But… you can't do that, surely."

"I think you'll find that I can, dear."

"Ok, I'm sorry."

"Yeah, so you should be, don't let it happen again." Tania marched off to greet the next influx of customers.

"What the hell is wrong with her, she had a personality transplant or what?"

"Personally, I reckon she needs a good shagging, wonder if anyone would be up for it!"

Lucy was in fits of giggles. "Only if we paid them a handsome wedge of cash." She clocked Tania staring at her so smiled sweetly and waved over while she waited for Kyle finishing off the drinks order.

Stevo had the weekend off and was chuffed, he intended to spend as much time with Lucy as possible. He would pick her up tonight after her shift and take her to the late night movies or perhaps a quick bite to eat and then hopefully back to her place for dessert if he was lucky.

Brian also had his own ideas about Lucy. He had become quickly obsessed with her and was determined to make her go out with him. He had spoken to Colin, Kyle's brother, who had informed him in no uncertain terms that she was no longer on the market and that she was seeing Stevo. Brian was seething, what the fuck did she see in him? He couldn't believe it. Every woman he had ever wanted always rejected him or the relationship was very short lived. He had a love-hate relationship with all women, he thought of them as either whores or too far up their own arses for his liking. Lucy had given him a sexy smile and rubbed her body on to him the very first time she had came into the club and that he would never forget. Now she had betrayed him and he wasn't standing for it. The little slut would pay for winding him up, he would show her once he got her on her own.

Antonio and Katie had just touched down in Italy. She was thrilled to sit in the cockpit with him for the landing despite Phillipe's protests, who reluctantly went to sit in the cabin. Antonio was an excellent pilot and had handled the plane with complete ease and total control.

Chapter Forty One

Matthew was trawling through the de Marcos' past, hoping to find something on them. But what if he did find something shocking, as he suspected that he would? Would Katie even believe him if he did, what about his own sister, they were too close to these men to see sense? He knew the saying 'love is blind', but his gut feeling told him that both their relationships were doomed. He would try his best to be as discreet as possible as he wasn't sure who was in the de Marco's pay. He had been going to the local library after work looking through the microfiche. He pulled up an article from ten years previously about their parents, it read 'Carmine and his wife Carlotta along with their twelve year old daughter Adriano were all killed in a freak accident when their car suddenly spun out of control and veered over a cliff in their home town of Umbria. There have been unconfirmed reports that Carmine de Marco was in fact speeding. Anyone witnessing the incident should report to the local police station. Foul play cannot be ruled out, although there currently is no evidence to support this at this time'.

Matthew found another press release. 'It was noted that the de Marco sons had recently been involved in a feud with a local family involving extortion. The Calvi brothers had been seen violently arguing with the de Marcos. Despite the families' protests the police were satisfied that it had indeed been a tragic accident and have now closed the case. The triple funeral is to be held at La Pregheira Chapel on Tuesday June 17, 1979 at 9.30am'.

Matt had a funny feeling that there was more to this story than met the eye. He would do some research into the Calvi family. Something serious had gone down here and he had to find out what it was. The de Marcos were obviously a force to be reckoned with, but it seemed that their parents' and sister's early demise had indeed been a high price to pay for whatever they were involved in. All he was concerned about now was looking out for his little sister and Katie, what kind of people were they mixing with? He couldn't bear the thought of it. He still couldn't understand what it was she saw in this Antonio. Maybe it was his flashy lifestyle, no, he thought, Katie had never been materialistic, she always appreciated the simple things in life. She had changed virtually overnight and it shocked him. All of a sudden she had matured into a vibrant young woman with the world suddenly at her feet. He knew that it was over between them, yet he was still struggling to understand it. Accepting that there was nothing he could do to change the situation was hard to come to terms with. Lucy would look out for Katie and unwittingly keep him informed of what was happening in their lives. He hoped and prayed that they would be safe.

If it had been another couple of years time, he would have made enough money to buy the house Katie had always talked about and marriage surely would have followed and God willing a family of their own. But it wasn't meant to be, he reasoned, but he still couldn't stop loving her, and knew that he always would.

Chapter Forty Two

Lucy was so pissed off with Tania; it was really winding her up now. Kyle had been a sweetheart. "Don't worry, she's like that with all the new girls and you are no exception, just don't take it personally. Trust me, that's why the girls here don't last very long."

"She just drives me to the edge of insanity and beyond!"

"Remember she came from the Manchester Club, it's a northern girl thing, they obviously think they are better than the southerners. Tania thinks that she is special and in total control here, since Gianni gave her the head girl position."

"I don't know how you and Colin cope with her mood swings; you must have the patience of a saint!"

"Patience is nothing to do with it, the tips here are brilliant and the talent isn't bad either!" He eyed up the suited young business man walking past. "Nice bum."

"Kyle, shush, he'll hear you."

"Oh, good, let him, nothing wrong with admiring a fit bloke."

"But he might be straight."

"With an arse like that, I don't think so, and did you see the way he looked at me?"

"I think he was looking at me," Lucy teased him. "Fight you for him."

"You wouldn't stand a chance sweetie," Kyle waved his hand in her face.

"Whatever." Lucy waved her hand in his face copying his gesture.

They both laughed. "Oh, shit look out, she's clocked us again." Kyle mumbled getting the drinks tray ready. "Just act normally, you know as if we are actually working hard."

"God, what's her problem, someone rattled her cage or what? All I want to do right now is give her a good slap."

"No, don't even go there, sweetie, she seems to have a lot of clout in this club and God only knows why, believe me since she's been here the turnover over of bar staff has gone through the roof."

"And what does Veronica have to say about this?"

"Naturally she's not very happy, but remember she's on the payroll too. She's got her job to think about and that nice fat salary she's earning."

"Veronica seems very approachable, what if I just go and have a quiet word with her, when she's back in tomorrow?"

"No, don't even bother, you will just look like a trouble causer and then Tania will ensure that you are out the door quick smart!"

"Some of the management in here leaves a lot to be desired, does no one ever speak their mind?"

"The simple answer is no, they wouldn't dare put their jobs on the line, the tips are way too good."

"Damn it, so I should say nothing then, it's not in my nature to keep my mouth shut."

Colin listened in to the last part of the conversation and butted in. "Hey, Lucy, your friend Katie may be able to put a discreet word in. Trust me when I tell you that Antonio has never ever been smitten like this before and if that's anything to go by then your future here is one hundred per cent safe."

"I didn't realise you knew Antonio so well," mocked Lucy.

"Oh yes, Kyle and I along with Veronica all came from the old club, Pesaro's."

"Ooh, but it wasn't a patch on this, I mean it was like so tiny," Kyle emphasised. "Anyway its obvious Antonio will do anything to keep Katie and I mean anything!" he added.

"What kind of things do you mean?"

"Best left unsaid, just rumours really, idle gossip, nothing that anyone can pin point." He had heard things about the de Marcos and what they wanted they always got. He wished he had kept his mouth shut now, he couldn't repeat some of the things he'd been told as it was in strict confidence.

"And what about Stevo then, what can you tell me about him, would he do anything for me?"

"How on earth would I know something like that?"

"Well you seem to thrive on gossip, Kyle, you tell me."

"Now, now, ladies, let's not get carried away." This came from Colin as he tried to shut his dumb brother up; Lucy was right he loved a good gossip and enjoyed a bit of drama.

"Listen, seriously, I don't know much about Stevo, only that he is a lifelong friend of the de Marco brothers. I did hear that he once saved Antonio from drowning though when they were kids and that's why Antonio keeps him close. I guess he feels like he still owes him."

"I can understand why Antonio would feel like that, but what I really mean is what kind of a person is he, what are you not telling me?"

"I suppose he has his past, just like the rest of us, sweetie, just forget I said anything"

"Oh, Kyle, if you do know something just spill it!" Lucy was exasperated now.

The conversation was cut dead in its tracks when Gianni walked into the bar and walked towards them. "No one working here tonight or what? You look like a bunch of fish wives gossiping in the corner."

The brothers scurried back to the optics and carried on preparing the drinks.

"So, Lucy, you gonna serve me tonight or what?" Gianni asked.

"Sure, yes, no problem. What can I get you?" Lucy's head was in a whirl, she was sure Kyle was going to tell her more about their colourful history. It was just a shame Gianni turned up. She supposed it would have to wait for the time being. One thing was for sure, she had no intention of asking Stevo, he wasn't much of a talker regarding his past and kept his cards pretty much close to his chest.

"Cognac, Lucy, when you are ready!"

Tania Horrocks had been eavesdropping on part of their conversation. She had a soft spot for Stevo and always fell over herself to chat to him. But she wondered why Lucy was so interested in him. Maybe she should let him know she had been prying into his past. He was a private guy, he would be livid. Probably drop the stupid girl and with a bit of luck shut her up once and for all, leave the way open for her. After all Tania was very, very loyal to the de Marcos, she had proved that to them on more than one occasion. She would easily persuade the brothers that Lucy could soon become very dangerous to them, tell them about all these questions she had been asking. Maybe make it look like the little cow was some sort of plant.

Chapter Forty Three

Tania had had a checkered history herself. She got on in life because of her underhanded scheming ways. She barely had any friends, no surprise really the way she treated people. She was the type of woman who came across as though butter wouldn't melt in her mouth, at least to begin with. She'd reel in the weak and vulnerable, find out what she could and then stab them in the back. In the past she had been much more underhand, sneaky even, she loved gaining her victims' confidence especially in public. Then she revelled in giving them shit in privacy, denying all knowledge when questioned. It was because of her that some of the people she had become involved with had thought they were going out of their minds. No one could ever prove the evil streak that ran through her veins and nobody believed it of her. Tania just hated seeing anyone happy and getting on in life, it just really pissed her off, why should she not throw a spanner in the works every now and then? She was a complete bitch and she knew it, but that didn't faze her in the least. She was a bit on the plump side these days despite numerous new fangled diets, she had tried every one under the sun. Nothing had ever worked for her, perhaps it was because she could never stick to them, it just bored her. She didn't differentiate between men and women, they were all the same to her. Anyone showing a bit of happiness or power would automatically become her next target. She despised them and enjoyed putting the wheels in motion, being part of their downfall was a real buzz.

Tania had been married twice and they were the biggest mistakes of her life. She had screwed them both in and outside of the bedroom, taking them for every last penny she could get her hands on. Her first husband was poor pathetic Mark, who she could wrap around her little finger; he had a string of estate agencies, having built them up from scratch. She had ensured she got her cut after putting up with the boring bastard for five years.

Her second marriage was to a banker, another boring fucker, but he absolutely adored her. All he had wanted was several kids and a holiday home in the country. Tania knew how much he was worth and strung him along, even pretending to come off the pill to shut him up. He had been so desperate for kids that she even had to pretend to have a miscarriage. The poor bastard had been devastated. Tania had pretended to go into a deep depression, so Peter had let her loose with the credit cards as it was the only thing that seemed to make her happy. She spent as much as possible and stopped at nothing to get what she wanted and didn't give a damn who she hurt along the way. After her second divorce she went on holiday to Mauritius and bagged herself a local. The novelty had soon worn off and she became bored, like she always did. That's when she met the love of her life, a smooth talking Italian man. They had quite a lot in common, both cold, unfeeling and ruthless. Most of the holiday was spent in the bedroom, it had been amazing. Then she had wakened up one morning and he had vanished. Surprisingly he had left a note in reception, promising to meet up with her when he was next in the UK. Ripping it up she cursed, she might have fucking known it would turn out like this. Not one to wallow in self pity she decided it was time to move on. So she returned to England, determined to get her claws into some other unsuspecting weak, but wealthy man as the money was dwindling faster than she thought possible.

It hadn't taken long for the last of her cash to run out and she was forced to take a job as a cocktail waitress in a club in Manchester, owned by two wealthy brothers, to her delight. But unfortunately for her they were both in long-term relationships. Luckily for her that's where she had met Vince Fraser, he was really good to her, about twenty years her senior but that hadn't bothered her in the slightest. He enjoyed lavishing gifts on her, even setting her up in a luxury fully furnished apartment! Their affair had gone on for almost a year undetected and she had managed to save a little nest egg, courtesy of Vince's generous nature. But all good things must come to an end as Tania knew only too well. It was unfortunate that his dumpy, over protective, middle-aged wife had found out and threatened him with divorce, so he had wasted no time in telling Tania it was all over. Tania had to move into a crummy council flat on a run down estate. She had to do something fast, come up with a plan to blackmail Vince. Nobody got rid of her that easily, so she waited and waited, plotting an exacting revenge.

She had spent months sneaking around, listening at every corner, knowing that one day it would be worth it. Then, finally to her delight, the waiting had finally paid off! She accidentally overheard several disturbing conversations. This is it, she would show Vince fucking Fraser and have the final laugh if it was the last thing she did to the bald headed prat. The stupid arsehole had somehow gotten himself mixed up in drugs! Tania had cornered Vince and demanded cash to keep quiet, but there was no way he was having any of it. Tania wasn't listening to his whining, she wanted to be paid off or else! He pleaded with her, told her that the Driscoll gang had threatened to firebomb his house with his family in it, he was terrified of them. He had no choice in the matter, he had to do what he was told. Tania had other ideas, Vince would pay up one way or another, there was no way she was staying in that shit apartment any longer.

Tania immediately contacted the de Marcos. Antonio had been away on business in France, so it was Gianni she dealt with. She told him that she had been as discreet as possible and that Vince didn't suspect a thing. Pretending to be worried she told Gianni that she would be unable to work for Vince anymore and didn't know what she was going to do for work. Having a sick father to care for Gianni promised her a new job as head cocktail waitress in the London club. She had jumped at the chance and accepted it immediately, there would be plenty of wealthy men to choose from. It was time to move on and start again, with a new salary and more responsibility she would soon be pulling herself a new fella.

Tania was sick and tired of the way people treated her, all her life she had played second fiddle and she wasn't taking it any more.

Her mother had been the only one to fully understand her needs. As a child if Tania didn't get what she wanted she would throw a massive temper tantrum. They were that bad that her parents just gave in to her to keep the peace. But things changed dramatically when her mother died unexpectedly and then her father re-married soon after. Tania could not accept that her father had moved on so quickly, it was an insult to her mother's memory. The woman who replaced her mother was a bitch from hell and things changed for the worse. She made sure that Tania never got anything she wanted ever again, telling her father that it was so she could appreciate treats and not just expect them.

Tania wasn't going to take this lying down so had plotted revenge on her stepmother, hoping to get something on her. She had followed her several times until she caught her meeting with another man. She hoped and prayed it was a fling, it sure looked like it from where she was. Just to be sure Tania hired a private detective to take photos and tail her. She was very disappointed to find out that the mystery man was in fact her stepmother's long lost brother. Apparently he had been born when their mother was unmarried and she had been sent off to give birth and the baby was subsequently adopted. That was until his dying father made the shocking confession to him, so he had set out to find his real mother and discovered that he had a younger sister.

Tania had no intention of telling her father the truth, she was going to use the information to her advantage. She produced the photographic evidence and smirked to herself. Her father was deeply upset and asked her repeatedly if she could be mistaken. When Tania had told him absolutely not he had packed Patricia's bags and dumped them in the drive.

Patricia could hardly believe her eyes when she saw all her belongings strewn everywhere. She had banged on the door asking what was going on. Tania's father wouldn't listen and turned up the radio to drown out her pleas. Tania waved and smiled out of the window. Good riddance she thought, now things would finally return to normal.

Patricia never gave up on her husband and even brought her brother along with his wife and two kids. Eventually, realising the truth, he knew that his daughter was rotten to the core, even though it pained him to think it possible.

He called every private detective in the phone book, he needed to know his version of events, to see if his daughter was really that vindictive. The detective had confirmed his worst fears. He had told him that Tania knew who the man was all along. He had never felt so betrayed by her, his own flesh and blood, how could she do this to him? She had been hell bent on keeping him all to herself, she was nothing less than a complete spoilt brat. There was only one thing he could do, she would have to stand on her own two feet from now on. Reluctantly he disowned her, in his heart he knew that he was doing the right thing and hoped that maybe she was able to turn her life around for the better. Feeling a little guilty he gave her twenty thousand pounds to get out of his life for good; that, he decided, would be the last thing that he would ever do for her. And for good measure he told her that her mother would be turning in her grave if she could see what a bitter and twisted young woman she had turned into, never happy unless she was causing havoc for others, deliberately making them suffer. Tania was quite gutted by his cutting remarks but knew deep down that he had finally sussed her out, the game was up, so she packed her things and left.

So now she was on her own yet again and after her two miserable failed marriages she decided from now on they would have to be extremely wealthy. It would be nothing short of a miracle if she found someone wealthy and attractive too. Maybe the next relationship she had would have a chance of working out then, just for a change!

So she had her sights set firmly on one of the de Marco brothers, she didn't care which one, just wondered how she was going to worm her way into their good books. She preferred Gianni as he seemed to be more of a challenge but then again Antonio seemed to be a bit of a dark horse. But it seemed that was never going to happen now with Katie and Felicia on the scene. When she realised that she turned her sights to Stevo and really fancied the arse off him, all that muscle turned her on! And now she was too late, he only had eyes for the other new girl, that Lucy bitch! It wasn't fair, she felt like she was beginning to lose her touch.

And now she was looking for any excuse to get rid of Lucy and the sooner the better, nothing was going to stand in the way of her ambitions.

Chapter Forty Four

The driver had been waiting for Antonio and Katie to arrive for twenty minutes. He was becoming impatient and sighed with relief when he saw the plane in the distance. He wondered who this new woman was, he knew that Antonio was a bit of a ladies' man, but heard that there was something different about this one. The talk around the villa and vineyard staff was that it was pretty serious by all accounts. Alfredo was sure that it was, as Antonio had not been home for nearly six years and he had never brought any woman to his family home before.

He watched the plane touchdown and waited until they began descending the steps before he walked over. He greeted them warmly and gave Antonio a huge hug, patting him on the back as he did so. He had a tear in his eye, he was so pleased to see him. "Welcome, welcome home, it's so good to see you, Antonio. And who is this beautiful young woman?" He took her hand and kissed it.

"This is Katie Saunders. Katie this is Alfredo he has worked for my family for many years. Now Alfredo, don't be getting any ideas, she is way too young for you."

Alfredo gave a deep, throaty chuckle. "I am strictly honourable, you know that, Antonio, and of course my wife would not be too pleased."

"Good, I'm glad that's sorted, let's go home, I'm looking forward to Francesca's home cooking!"

"Tell me, how is your brother?"

"He told me to tell you that you better hadn't have any plans to sing at his wedding and to forget about the ukulele!"

"Fortunately he still has his sense of humour I see. Although I have to admit that I still can't believe that Felicia has managed to get him up the aisle, I thought that I would never see the day!"

"Me and you both Alfredo!"

"I can't believe that there is less than three months to go, everyone is so excited, it's going to be perfect."

"Excellent."

The vineyard was only a short drive away. Katie was immersed in the beautiful scenery. Antonio pointed out the local chapel where Gianni and Felicia had decided to get married. The brick faced chapel was set back off the road down a winding gravel path strewn with lavender. It was like going back in time, untouched by modern day.

"It's so peaceful, can we go and see inside it while we are here?"

"Of course we can, I'll introduce you to the local priest. He will tell you some tales about me and Gianni! But don't believe everything you hear, he does have a tendency to exaggerate."

"If you say so!"

"What do you mean?"

"Oh, I can imagine you and Gianni being a real handful when you were kids."

"Ah, we weren't that bad!"

Katie laughed, visualising them both causing havoc around the village.

The place was beautiful and had an air of tranquility about it. She wondered what it must have been like when Antonio was a child. She imagined that it would have been pretty much the same, unspoilt and unchanged for years. There was a peaceful feel around La Pregheira and she felt totally at ease in the surroundings. Away from the hustle and bustle of London city, smoke free and quiet, it was a different world to her. She was going to enjoy every moment here.

The drive through the vineyard was amazing; the grapes were sumptuous, ripe and ready for picking. Producing their own family wine had been a specialty of the de Marcos over the years. Katie began to understand the importance of this part of the business, it was how they were able to expand, try new ventures and all from this. She hoped that this would be the first of many visits to this little piece of Italy.

Chapter Forty Five

Lucy couldn't wait for her shift to end, she hadn't even had time for her break. Tania had been on her case all evening and she was at the end of her tether with her constant bitching. It was incredible why the de Marcos had made her the head girl, she was such a stroppy cow, she just couldn't understand it. She had a feeling that whatever the reason, there was more to her than met the eye!

The only thing keeping her going was her handsome Stevo, he was so manly and gorgeous! She had been annoyed with Katie and Antonio getting it on so quickly, but now she knew what it was like to fall head over heels for someone. The night seemed to never end, she was constantly watching the clock waiting for 2.30am to arrive. When Tania eventually told her that she could take her break she was incensed as her shift was nearly over. Little did she know that Tania had unwittingly done her a favour.

If she had taken her usual break it didn't bear thinking about. Brian had been waiting for her, hiding; he was intending to give her a nasty surprise! Touch her up a bit more and threaten her that if she didn't sleep with him willingly he would just take her whenever she least expected it, so she may as well just get it over with.

He was raging when that bitch Tania had insisted no one was having any breaks until it quietened down and if they did without permission they would be sacked on the spot! He could wait, he would have to, maybe he should follow her home one night. Yes, much less chance of being disturbed! Tutting to himself he reluctantly returned to work. There was no looking at him for the rest of the evening, he was short tempered and had a face like thunder!

Stevo had the entire weekend off thanks to the de Marco brothers. It was very rare for this to happen and he wanted to make the most of it. He was thinking that 2.30 am was a little bit late and no doubt Lucy would be exhausted after being on her feet all night. He had planned to take her to a little all night café that he knew where they could get to know each other better and perhaps have a couple of beers and a light snack. They would be able to talk without being disturbed.

He turned up fifteen minutes early and the first person he saw was Brian. "Hey Bri, how has it been tonight?"

"Ok, no problems, what you doing here anyway?"

"I'm picking up the girl of my dreams!"

"Who?" Brian already knew, but acted dumb.

"Little sexy Lucy of course."

"You better watch her, she's a bit of a tease!"

"What the fuck do you mean Bri? She is a good girl."

"I wouldn't be so sure."

"Watch your fucking mouth mate or you'll have me to deal with." Stevo was having none of Brian's nonsense, he was a strange fucker. True he was certainly good for muscle power but didn't have much in the brain department, a bit backward by all accounts.

Brian was worried now. "Sorry, Stevo, you know me, I always get it wrong mate, pay no attention, it's been a long night."

"Forget about it, Brian." Stevo walked past him, he didn't like the guy, he never did. There was something not quite right about him!

As soon as Lucy finished Stevo was there waiting for her. "How are your feet holding up, can you walk for another ten minutes?"

"Sure, I'm tougher than I look, I promise." She linked him as they exited the building, not noticing Brian watching their every move. "So, you going to tell me what you got in mind?"

"Just a little café I know, where they serve the best coffee in London and these little sticky buns."

"That sounds yum, but I could really murder an ice cold beer right now."

"Then a beer it will be!"

Chapter Forty Six

Gianni was thinking about his forthcoming trip to Manchester. He couldn't wait to visit Honey and her girlfriend, it was going to be one hell of a weekend.

He was just about to leave to check the club's takings when he received a disturbing phone call from Roberto Valetti. He had just been arrested for trying to smuggle drugs into the country via his Italian furniture business. His voice full of hysteria he assured Gianni that he wasn't involved in any way and begged him for his help.

"Look, Roberto, don't worry I'll send a lawyer over right away, we'll get to the bottom of this."

"I couldn't get hold of Antonio, you will contact him, won't you?"

"Sure, just calm down, everything's going to be ok, leave it with me."

Gianni sighed, bollocks that was his weekend totally screwed, all that pussy going to waste. He had a strange feeling that somehow it was the work of the Calvi brothers, but they wouldn't dare, surely, he reasoned to himself. One thing was for sure, if it was them they would almost certainly target their other business interests. He had to contact Antonio and the sooner the better.

He was just about to ring the villa in La Pregheira when his phone rang again. It was Henry Brookstein, at approximately 2.30am his art gallery had gone up in flames. Thankfully there was no one in the building at the time. Henry was distraught, his entire art collection had totally disintegrated, the building was absolutely gutted, he was ruined. He would have to start again, the insurance wouldn't cover the new collection he had recently purchased as he had wanted to check it personally before registering it with them.

Gianni was pacing the floor, wondering what the hell to do. He picked up the phone and dialled Stevo. Fuck it, where the hell was he when he was needed? His phone just rang out, damn him. He tried Lucy's number without any success.

"Is something wrong, I heard the phone ringing." Felicia, all bleary-eyed, was in her dressing gown, she had been asleep. She was so tired lately.

"No, it's nothing, just the club wondering where the hell I am. You know what Veronica is like when she wants to get home!"

"Ok, I'll see you later." She kissed him. "I do love you, you know."

"Me too, Mrs Gianni de Marco to be!" He playfully patted her bum. "Keep it warm for me sweetheart!"

"Cheeky, I'll be dead to the world by the time you get cashed up." She couldn't wait for her doctor's appointment tomorrow, then she would break the news to him. She hoped he would be thrilled with what she had to tell him! It had been difficult keeping it to herself, but she wanted to be absolutely sure.

She looked beautiful, Gianni thought to himself, even in her half-asleep state. He left the house and got into his car. He didn't see the man hiding in the shadows watching him drive off.

Felicia was just dozing off when she was disturbed by a bang just outside the bedroom door. "What did you forget?" There was no answer. "Gianni, is that you?"

She pulled on her dressing gown and stepped into her slippers. As she started to open the door she was knocked backwards. Before she had time to react Felicia took a fatal blow to her head and as she slipped into unconsciousness the last thing she saw was a gold protruding tooth and a familiar face. Eddie put his hands around her throat to finish the job, he had to make sure that she was dead. He then proceeded to rob the place and carefully cleaned away all traces of his presence, he couldn't take any chances. He half smiled to himself, it had been much easier than he thought. But it would remain his secret forever, no one could ever find out what he did. Gianni had been a bastard all his life and what he did to Veronica was the final straw! He wanted Gianni to pay for what he had done and had came up with the perfect way. He wiped his prints off the door handle as he left and slipped discreetly into the dark night. No one would ever suspect him, after all they thought he was a dumb mute! That was a job well done, he would sleep easier than he had in many years.

It would be a further two hours before Gianni heard of Felicia's brutal murder.

Chapter Forty Seven

Still unable to get hold of Stevo, Gianni contacted the family lawyer, Gerald Newman. He briefly explained what had happened. Gerald had a feeling that it was going to be a long night. These things always were, still the de Marcos were paying him handsomely so it would be worth it! Not that his wife would think so.

Gerald arrived at the police station and told the young woman on the desk that he was here to see his client Roberto Valetti. His wife Nina was sitting in the waiting area and rushed over to him.

"Oh thank God, I didn't know what to do, did the de Marcos send you?"

"Yes, yes, don't worry, Mrs Valetti, we'll have your husband out of here in no time."

The detective constable in charge of the case advised him that his client was in very serious trouble and unless he fully cooperated with them, would be going down for a long time.

Nina waited frantically outside saying over and over in her head 'this can't be happening, not to my husband, he would never be involved in anything to do with drugs, especially with our two little ones'. They were well off and didn't need profits from dealing in drugs. And anyway Roberto didn't move in those sorts of circles.

Gerald Newman introduced himself to Roberto. "Now the formalities are over, we don't have much time, tell me everything you know."

"I have a fine Italian furniture business. The goods come into my warehouse in Milan as usual and are then flown over to Gatwick airport, where the goods come through customs and are then sent on to my warehouse in Lovelock Street. Apparently the crates were seized by customs and excise and they recovered some three hundred kilos of cocaine with a street value of half a million pounds."

"Half a million, Jesus, you sure?"

"Of course I'm fucking sure. That's what the police told me!"

"Ok, Mr Valetti, please calm down."

"Calm down, fucking calm down, are you out of your mind, do you know what this means?"

"Please, Mr Valetti, if you want me to help you then I need to ask you some questions."

"I'll tell you whatever you want to know, but I am no fucking drug dealer!"

"Are you the sole owner of Valetti's handmade Italian furniture?"

"My wife has a twenty per cent share and Antonio has ten per cent, but ultimately yes I am, why do you ask?"

"Are you the manager and do you oversee the goods once they come into the country?"

"Yes, where is all this going?"

"Does anybody else have access?"

"No, why, what are you getting at?"

Before Gerald had time to answer the detective constable came back into the interview room. "We have just received further evidence, putting Mr Valetti well and truly in the frame," he announced.

"What evidence?"

"We have searched your property and found traces of cocaine. I suggest you make it easy on yourself and tell us who your contact is and your distributor here in the UK."

"I'm innocent I tell you, fucking innocent, I swear it." Roberto was petrified now, what was going to happen to him?

"You can swear it in a Court of Law, Mr Valetti."

"Whatever happened to innocent until proven guilty?"

"I will leave you with your lawyer, you've got ten minutes, but my advice is to tell us the truth, it may reduce your sentence." And with that the detective left the room.

"Someone must have planted it, but why, I don't have any enemies?"

"I'll be honest with you, Mr Valetti, this is not looking good. They are intent on charging you. Say nothing and I will speak to Mr de Marco. Try not to worry, I'll be back first thing in the morning."

"Have you seen my wife?"

"Yes, she's outside."

"Will you tell her I didn't do it, I could never do something like that, I swear on my kids' lives."

"You can tell her yourself in the morning." Gerald got up to leave. He felt sorry for Mr Valetti, he had heard of the man and knew that he certainly wasn't the type to be involved in something like this.

"Please, don't leave me in here, I'm begging you." Roberto pleaded with him. "I can't stand it!"

"Everything will be ok, you'll see."

Roberto slumped into his chair.

Gerald left, the poor bastard was in bits. Someone had stitched him up good and proper. He would need Antonio to contact his friend in the force, see if he could help, but somehow he doubted it.

Chapter Forty Eight

Gianni sent one of his bodyguards to locate Stevo; something was seriously wrong, he could feel it. He had rung the family villa in Umbria and left a message with Francesca for Antonio to contact him immediately on his return.

He was annoyed that Felicia wasn't picking up, she was usually a light sleeper. She was either ignoring it or was up to no good. No, he thought, get a grip, she was nothing like him.

Stevo had finally been tracked down, Don brought him up to speed. He had to cut his evening short with Lucy and she was none too pleased about it. He promised that he would make it up to her and that it was urgent business he had to attend to. He dropped her off at her flat and went in to ring Gianni.

"Where the fuck have you been Stevo, you're always supposed to be contactable, what happened to checking in every hour?" Gianni raged.

"I'm sorry, boss, but what can I do about Roberto?"

"You can fucking start by checking out the Calvi brothers' whereabouts!"

"Why, you think this is down to them after all this time? I mean it's been almost six years."

"Don't argue with me, Stevo, I have a real bad feeling about this. I'm still waiting for Antonio to make contact; he is in the best position to check it out."

"But the Calvis left the village and have never been back since!"

"Just fucking do something, Stevo, and stop babbling for fuck sake!"

"Ok, I'm on my way over to the club right now."

"Do me a favour and look in on Felicia on the way over, she ain't answering my calls." Gianni's voice was strangely quiet.

"Sure, I'll see you soon." Stevo was pissed off that his entire evening had been ruined. Felicia probably couldn't be arsed with Gianni. She gave him the silent treatment from time to time, it was nothing new, but he could sense the real fear in Gianni's voice.

Five minutes later he was ringing Felicia's doorbell and banging on the door to no avail.

Exasperated he rang Gianni from the phone booth just inside the building. "She isn't answering."

"Use the spare key and let yourself in, once you're in phone me and keep the line open."

153

Stevo pulled out his bunch of keys and searched for the right one. He and Don pulled out hidden hand guns and nodded to each other. They crept in, everything was in darkness. They sneaked warily around the house watching each other's backs as they did so. Trying not to make a sound they carefully checked out the kitchen. They found nothing, everything seemed normal. Stevo pointed to the stairs.

Don was the first one to enter the bedroom, he gasped and pointed to the bed.

"Jesus Christ, phone an ambulance!"

Stevo took one look at Felicia and knew immediately that she was dead, her face ashen, her eyes wide and lifeless just staring up at them. He checked for a pulse, nothing. How the fuck was he going to tell Gianni. Picking up the bedroom phone Stevo rang him. "It's me."

"Well, where is she, are you in?"

Stevo bit his lip, not knowing what to say.

"Answer me, you fucker, where is she?" In his heart Gianni knew something terrible had happened.

There was no easy way to break the news. "It's... it's Felicia, she's dead." Stevo struggled to get the words out.

Gianni barely understood the words, dropping the phone he signalled to Fred. "Get me home as quickly as possible, I don't care what you do, break every fucking speed limit if you have to, just get me there."

Fred was extremely worried, Gianni didn't tell him what was happening, he just knew that it was bad, really bad.

By the time they arrived the place was being sealed off. There was a police cordon of yellow and black tape saying "Crime Scene, Do Not Cross". Police swarmed the place.

Gianni was desperate to get into his home. "Let me in, you fuckers, she's my fiancée."

"Was your fiancée," Detective Constable Fearon corrected him.

"Why you fucking heartless bastard, I'll kill you." Gianni was held back by Stevo and Don, who were waiting for him.

"Come on, Gianni, don't let that son of a bitch get to you, there's nothing you can do here."

"That's right, listen to your buddies. We'll speak soon enough, don't worry about that."

"Just tell me what happened here." Gianni was desperate to get into the building.

"Best tell him, else he will fight his way inside." Stevo warned him.

Another detective butted in. "It looks like a burglary gone wrong sir and unfortunately Miss Carmine, er your fiancée, was in the wrong place at the wrong time."

"Maybe the intruder was expecting someone else to be home, after all it has been an eventful night for anyone connected to the de Marcos, surely no coincidence." This

154

came from Detective Constable Fearon, who was enjoying every minute of Gianni's obvious distress.

"What the fuck is that supposed to mean?" Gianni was going to wipe the smile off the prick's face once and for all; he lunged at him with his whole body.

Stevo and Don jumped in front of him and had to physically drag him down the drive and pushed him unceremoniously into the limo.

"Give me a fucking cigarette!"

"You've packed in, remember?" Don reminded him.

"Now's not the time, Don." Stevo pulled a pack of twenty out of his jacket and handed one to him. Gianni's hands were trembling as he struggled to work the lighter. Stevo took it off him and lit it.

"Let's go back to mine, you can stay with me as long as you like."

"No, I want to go back to the club."

Stevo nodded to a bewildered Fred. "It's ok, I'll go with him."

Fred hated seeing Gianni in this state, he felt so bad for him. Poor Felicia, she was just a young woman with all her life ahead of her.

It didn't take long for the news to reach the club. Nobody could believe it, everyone loved Felicia, she was very popular. She was the only one able to keep Gianni calm and level-headed, she had turned potentially volatile situations into peace itself, it was a knack only she had with Gianni. Everyone admired her for that.

Veronica was waiting for Gianni arriving and rushed to his office. "Oh, my poor Gianni, it's terrible, that lovely young woman, who could do such an horrendous thing."

Gianni hadn't spoken a word since he got into the limo. His head was in a spin, his hands still trembled as he took the double whisky Stevo passed to him. He gulped it down and grabbed the bottle, spilling it everywhere as he tried to get it into the glass.

"Everyone fuckoff," he snarled.

Stevo waved Veronica and Don towards the door.

"You too, I need to be on my own."

"I don't think you should be alone right now."

"I don't give a fuck what you or anyone else thinks, just go."

Stevo reluctantly left him. He pulled up a chair and sat outside the door, he wanted to be close in case Gianni needed him.

Gianni couldn't hold it in any longer and cried, he cried like a baby. He could barely believe it, his beautiful Felicia was dead. He lost control and smashed up everything in the office that was breakable. When he was finished he opened another bottle of whisky and drank himself into oblivion.

The last time Gianni was in this state was when his parents and sister were first killed, Stevo remembered. For a while he had been like a man possessed, but after their funerals were over he became calm and pulled himself together. Now he was a wreck of a man and when he was like this it was impossible to say what he might do. Stevo hoped and prayed that he would return to his normal self sooner rather than later. He prayed that Antonio would contact them soon before Gianni killed someone.

Chapter Forty Nine

Antonio and Katie were strolling through the vineyard when Alfredo signalled to him.

"Wait here," he told Katie. "I won't be a minute." Antonio knew that something was wrong.

"What is it?"

"It's Felicia Carmine, she's dead."

"Jesus Christ, what?"

"She was strangled, some sort of robbery gone wrong."

"My god, what about Gianni?"

"Gianni's at the club, he's ok."

"I can hardly take this in."

"There's something else, Roberto Valetti has been arrested."

"Arrested are you kidding me?"

"I wish I was."

"Shit, what is he supposed to have done?" Antonio knew full well that Roberto was straight as they come.

"I'm sorry to say that it was drug trafficking."

"Get me Gianni."

"I can't, apparently he has locked himself in his office, gone out of his mind and is inconsolable."

"Damn it, just get the jet ready as fast as you can, I need to go to him."

Katie was so immersed in her surroundings that she didn't notice their exchange.

"I need to get back to London; a close friend of mine is in trouble."

"Who, what's happened?"

"It's Roberto Valetti, he's been arrested, some kind of misunderstanding."

The look on his face told her there was more to this than he was telling her. "Antonio, you would tell me if there was something else?"

"It's Felicia, she's dead," he blurted out the news.

"My god, Gianni's fiancée?" Katie was dumbfounded she had only spoken to her a couple of days earlier. "Are you sure?"

"Yes, I'm sure. I need to go to my brother."

"It's a good job that we haven't unpacked yet."

"No, Katie, I want you to stay here. I'll be back tomorrow."

"But…"Katie tried to protest.

"Please, Katie. I just think it's better if I go alone, Gianni is in bits."

"It's ok, I understand."

He took her hand and looked into her startling blue eyes. "I promise I'll be back tomorrow, Francesca will look after you. I'll call you as soon as I can."

She nodded and gave him a half smile.

He leaned down and kissed her, it was a long lingering kiss that sent a shudder down Katie's spine. Her eyes were sparkling again now, the longing and need for him written all over her lovely face.

Antonio was totally mesmerised with her, but convinced that their relationship was cursed before it had barely begun. Twice now he had had to put it on hold, were they really doomed, he just didn't know, but things, events seemed to get in their way and it was becoming a regular occurrence. Right now he had to put Katie out of his mind and focus on Gianni and Roberto.

Once he was on the plane he called Frank, his dear friend in the police force. Frank told him that there was nothing he could do. Roberto had been set up and unless they found someone fast to take the rap he was going down for a long time.

Antonio cursed, wondering if it was anything to do with the Calvi brothers. They had always said they would exact revenge when they least expected it and could wait a lifetime if necessary. Then mysteriously they had disappeared off the face of the planet. Right now they could be anywhere and that seriously worried him.

Georgio Calvi followed Antonio to the airstrip and watched his plane take off. He smiled, a nasty little smile. He would find out what this woman meant to him and perhaps arrange a little accident of some sort!

158

Chapter Fifty

Antonio's flight seemed to take forever, he was becoming increasingly worried about Gianni, it was so unlike him to react in this way. Felicia had been remarkably good for him and now she was gone. God alone knew what he was capable of. He was racking his brains, wondering who else could be behind it, was it the Calvi brothers? Three things had happened and it was just their style, he needed to add extra security to the clubs, have his staff keep watchful eye out for anything odd.

Fred met him at the airstrip. "I'm sorry that you had to cut your weekend short, it's been a hell of a time."

"How is Gianni?"

"Still locked in his office, Stevo has tried everything to get him out of there."

"Jesus, anything happened in the club?"

"Nothing out of the ordinary, why?"

"No reason, just step on it."

Georgio's brother Ricardo was trying his luck in the casino with two of his henchman. They knew all the tricks of the trade and were determined to sting the de Marcos for a small fortune.

Veronica was watching these guys, they certainly looked legit, real pros. Gianni was in no fit state to discuss their limit. She decided she would allow them up to twenty five thousand and then take no more bets. The security tape was recording them the whole time so if there was a problem the de Marcos would track them down. One of the men received a phone call from reception. It appeared urgent, they cashed in their chips and hastily left the building, just a few minutes before Antonio arrived.

Veronica tried to speak with him as soon as he got through the door.

"Whatever it is, it will have to wait." He brushed her aside and made his way to Gianni's office. Stevo was outside the door.

"Is it still locked?"

Stevo nodded. "He's in a right state, do you want me to break down the door?"

"It's ok, I have a key." He said letting himself in. "Do me a favour, check if anything unusual has happened tonight. Go through all the tapes with a fine tooth comb."

"What exactly am I looking for?"

"You'll know it when you see it."

"Sure boss." Stevo was knackered, he hadn't been to bed, he was too worried about Gianni.

159

Gianni was slumped over his desk, with an empty bottle of whisky beside him. There were broken ornaments strewn everywhere and the security camera was smashed to smithereens. Antonio shook his head, he understood his brother's grief but hoped that he wasn't back on the slippery slope that in the past he had to constantly rescue him from.

"Gianni." He gently shook him.

"Get your fucking hands off me, I'll kill you, you bastard." He tried to make a swing for him.

"It's me, Antonio."

"No, Antonio is in Italy." He picked up the empty bottle and tried to hit him with it.

Antonio grabbed it from him. "Come on, you can't stay here on your own, you're coming home with me," he said firmly.

Gianni was struggling as Antonio pulled him from his chair. This was going to be harder than he thought. He pressed the intercom system. "I need some help here, guys, bring the limo around the back and be discreet."

"No problem, boss." Eddie was in his element. He had screwed Gianni up good and proper.

Don met him in the corridor. "Fred's waiting out the back."

Eddie simply nodded and quietly walked into the office. The place was like a bombsite. They carefully stepped over the broken furniture.

"I don't want anyone to know about this. Eddie, you get this place cleaned up, tonight."

"Yes."

"Don, give me a hand."

They half carried Gianni to the waiting limo. He was babbling, but his words were incoherent.

Ten minutes later they were at Antonio's apartment. They got him on to the bed and left him to sleep it off.

Antonio was pouring himself a stiff brandy. This was a fucking nightmare. Just then his phone started ringing. Stevo broke the news about three guys who had just walked away with twenty five thousand pounds.

"You'd better bring the tapes over right away, see if we can identify them." What the fuck else can possibly happen tonight.

Roberto Valetti was seriously claustrophobic, he couldn't bear being in the cell any longer. The thought of being sent down for twenty years was tipping him over the edge. He carefully removed his tie and pulled his bed under the light fixture. He tied it around the exposed wiring and brought his knees up to his chest. He closed his eyes, he could see his wife and children. Smiling to himself he kicked the bed away. His body would be discovered three hours later, when the new shift came on to duty.

160

Chapter Fifty One

Katie was trying her best to settle into the villa, but it was strange being there without Antonio. Francesca fussed around her making sure that she was alright. Katie couldn't help but warm to her. They immediately struck up a close friendship, one which would last for years to come.

"You must eat something," Francesca insisted. "You are a bag of bones girl, don't you eat in England?"

"Of course I do," Katie laughed. "I guess I'm just naturally thin."

"Well, we'll need to fatten you up a bit for all those little bambinos you're going to have running around."

"Don't be silly, we barely know each other," Katie exclaimed.

"I must say you make a very handsome couple and it's obvious you are in love."

"How can you tell, I don't even know that myself!"

"Ah, but I think you do, you see you can't fool me."

"Perhaps."

"Come to the kitchen and you can help me rustle up some pasta and meatballs."

Georgio was watching them through his binoculars. He would bide his time, he had waited long enough for this moment. He didn't know what the plan was, he would just play it by ear and see what happened. It would be a new challenge for him, she was a beautiful young woman, too nice for a de Marco. Maybe he would charm her away from Antonio, just like he did with Maria when they were teenagers. But once he had gotten her pregnant he dumped her, he had never loved her, just wanted to take her away from Antonio. It gave him a kick to get one over on him. Maria had left the village and had given birth to a baby boy, his son. But he didn't give a damn, he had more important things to think about.

Chapter Fifty Two

Gerald rang Antonio, it was six am. Roberto Valetti had been found hanging in his cell. No one had told his wife yet. Antonio decided to go and see Nina in person, it was the least he could do. Gianni was still out of it, so he left Stevo watching over him.

Nina hadn't slept most of the night and was in the process of making herself yet another cup of coffee. The children were still tucked up in bed, totally unaware of their father's predicament. How could she explain it to them, Carla was five and Roberto Junior two. She could barely understand it herself.

The doorbell rang, making her jump. She was surprised when her housekeeper announced that Mr de Marco was here.

"Show him in, Martha."

"I hope you are going to tell me that my husband is coming home, otherwise don't waste your breath."

"Nina, there's something I have to tell you, you'd better sit down."

"What is it, is Roberto ok?" Nina's face drained of all colour, all of a sudden she felt faint.

Antonio gently sat her down and held her hands. "There's no easy way of saying this."

"No, don't you tell me that he's going to prison, I couldn't bear it."

"Nina, listen to me, it's worse than that…"

"How could it possibly be any worse, Antonio, tell me."

"Roberto, he's dead."

Nina let out a high pitched scream. "No, no… it's not true, it can't be!"

"I'm so sorry, Nina, he took his own life."

"I don't believe you. Get out of my house, now."

"Please, Nina, is there anyone I can call for you?"

"Don't you think you've done enough, just get out, get out!" Nina was hysterical now. Martha came running into the kitchen to see what all the commotion was about.

"I don't know what's going on but I think you'd better leave now, Mr de Marco."

"I promise I'll find out who set him up."

"I don't care; I never want to see you again. You're not welcome in my house. I knew there was something about you de Marcos, I warned Roberto not to get involved with you," Nina was screaming at him.

"I'm so sorry; Roberto was a good friend of mine."

"I don't want your words of sympathy." She picked up her cup and aimed it at his head.

Antonio ducked; it struck the wall and shattered all over the kitchen. He was devastated; the Valettis were like a second family to him. He was godfather to Roberto junior and it hurt him that Nina had reacted this way. She was understandably distraught. She was in shock right now; maybe once she accepted his death she would reconsider her feelings towards him.

"You alright boss, you look a bit peaky?" Fred asked.

"I've had better days."

Fred knew not to push him, not when he was in such a dangerous mood. He had rarely seen him like this, but recognised the pain on his face. They drove along in silence, back to the penthouse.

Chapter Fifty Three

Katie couldn't sleep. She got dressed and slipped quietly out of the villa, hoping not to disturb anyone as it was still very early. As she walked through the vineyard she wondered what on earth she was doing here all alone. She wished that she had gone back to England with Antonio. He had called to say that he wouldn't be back for her until the next day.

She walked over to the stables and admired the palomino horses, they were magnificent creatures. She was going to have her first riding lesson later today and was really looking forward to it. The place was totally idyllic, it was just a pity that Antonio wasn't with her, so they could enjoy it together. The horse was paying her particular interest and she couldn't resist stroking its nose, it whinnied at her. This would be a fine horse to have her first lesson on, she decided.

Katie was unaware of Georgio Calvi watching her from behind the fence at the other side of the vineyard. Perhaps he would arrange for her to have a little accident. He looked at the stable door and focused on the plaque, "Pesaro".

Katie made her way back to the villa; she followed the smell of freshly ground coffee into the kitchen. "Good morning, Francesca."

"Good morning, dear, you're up and about early."

"I couldn't sleep and anyway it's a beautiful day."

"Oh, yes it is."

She passed Katie a mug of steaming coffee. "Here drink this and I'll make us some breakfast."

"Oh, don't go to any trouble on my account, I'll just have a bowl of muesli."

The phone started ringing, Francesca winked at her. "It's Antonio." She gestured for her to pick it up.

"Hello, the de Marco residence."

"Katie, it's so good to hear your voice."

"How is Gianni?" was the first thing she asked him.

"In a bad way, he hit the drink last night and is still sleeping it off."

"Poor Gianni, he must be devastated."

"I just need to talk to him once he sobers up."

"So when are you coming over?"

"I'll try and get back tonight, but it all really depends on Gianni. I don't want to leave him in such a state. Anyway, how are you?"

"I'm going for a riding lesson today, on Pesaro."

164

"Pesaro, he's a very spirited horse, sure you can handle him?"

"It's ok, Alfredo will look after me."

"He better had."

Katie laughed. "You worry too much."

"I'm sorry about the weekend, it's ruined."

"It's ok, Gianni is your brother, there'll be other times."

"Thanks for being understanding, I promise I'll be back soon, can you put Francesca on the phone?"

"Sure, just a minute." She held the receiver. "He wants to talk to you."

Francesca took the phone. Antonio told her to keep an eye on Katie at all times and to make sure a couple of bodyguards were nearby, just in case.

Katie was excited; she had never been on a horse before, it was going to be a wonderful experience. Francesca and Alfredo were going to follow in the horse and cart, they planned on meeting up by the river so that they could have a picnic.

One of the stable boys helped her mount the horse. "The reins go around your hands like this."

"Oh, I didn't realise there was a certain knack for holding them."

Gene smiled, she was a lovely young girl, Antonio had done well for himself. "I'll stay beside you until you get used to it."

Katie couldn't get Pesaro to move. "Come on, you silly horse."

"You need to tap him gently with your heels."

"Oops, silly me!"

Pesaro set off at a slow pace. "This is so cool," Katie gushed, thoroughly enjoying herself.

"You are handling him really well, do you want to pick up the pace yet?"

"Oh, can I?"

"Sure, just tap him a bit harder."

Katie was thrilled when Pesaro started to trot. It was amazing, she loved it!

"Are you sure you haven't done this before, you just seem like a natural to me."

"No, never." Katie didn't notice the two men in the distance, they were checking the way ahead to make sure there were no nasty surprises waiting for them.

Half an hour later and Katie wanted to go faster. Gene advised against it.

"Oh please," she begged him.

He reluctantly gave in and agreed. "Just for a little bit then."

Before he knew what was happening Katie was off. Hell, he'd better get after her and fast. She disappeared out of sight. He got his walkie talkie out. "It's me, Katie's galloped off and I can't see her!"

"You'd better hope nothing happens to her, Gene."

Gene was worried now, what if something did happen?

Katie pulled back on the reins to try and slow the horse down. She was heading straight for an overhanging tree branch. All of a sudden Pesaro kicked out with his hind legs which sent Katie hurtling over his head. Luckily she landed in a hay bale, she was winded and felt dizzy.

A concerned man appeared from nowhere and came over. "Are you alright?"

"Yes, I think so." The sun was behind him and she couldn't quite see his face.

"Let me help you up." She was beautiful, he thought. Those eyes were incredible.

"Thank you, I must look dreadful."

"No, you look beautiful."

Katie blushed as he helped her to her feet. "Thank you, Mr?"

"Calvi, Georgio Calvi."

"Thank you, Mr Calvi."

"And who are you?"

"I'm Katie Saunders."

"And are you on holiday here?"

"Yes, yes, I'm staying at the de Marco villa."

"So, you and Antonio are an item then?"

"You could say that, yes."

Georgio noticed the two men in the distance. "I must go, it was nice to meet you, Miss Saunders, but please be careful around the de Marcos they are not what they seem."

"Oh, what do you mean?" She paused, "And how did you know which de Marco brother I was seeing?"

But he ignored her and walked over to his motorbike. "Take care, Miss Katie Saunders." And with that he sped off.

Katie had to sit back down, she had had a nasty fright and still felt shaken up. She was alarmed to see two men coming towards her.

"Don't worry Miss Saunders, we work for Mr de Marco, are you ok?"

"Yes, just a bit dazed, is Pesaro alright?"

"Yes, he's fine." He didn't tell her that they had found some thorns under the saddle.

Francesca and Alfredo arrived shortly after in the horse and cart. "Are you alright?"

"Yes, yes, please everyone stop fussing."

"Come on, you can ride back with us."

"It was my fault, I shouldn't have got carried away." Katie sat in silence all the way back.

Francesca did not like it one bit, who wanted to harm her?

They arrived back at the villa. Katie was still in shock, she hadn't mentioned Georgio Calvi, it was all too weird. All she wanted was a long soak in a hot bath to ease her sore body.

166

Alfredo phoned Antonio. "There was some trouble today while Katie was out riding."

"Is she alright?" Christ that was all he needed.

"Yes, she's lucky she landed on a hay bale."

"Ok, I'll be over some time tonight, don't tell Katie, I'll surprise her." He hung up the phone and put a hand to his temple, he felt like his head was going to explode.

Antonio couldn't believe it, everything was going wrong. He felt torn, should he stay with Gianni or go to Katie?

Stevo had stayed over too and they had gone through the club tapes. Antonio was furious when he saw Ricardo Calvi. He had had the audacity to go into his club and pull a scam like that. The little bastard had some nerve. When Gianni found out he would kill him.

"You better go and get some sleep, Stevo."

"Ok, I'll send over some of the guys, just in case."

"I'll grab a couple of hours and then see if I can raise Gianni."

Stevo sighed, what a mess he thought, all the shit was well and truly hitting the fan.

Chapter Fifty Four

Antonio tried to sleep on the settee, but he couldn't, his mind was whirring! One thing was for sure they had to sort this out and sort it out fast before anybody else got hurt, or worse killed!

He was just nodding off when he heard a loud crash. "What the hell?"

Gianni was in the drinks cabinet, scrabbling around for the bottle of scotch which he had accidentally dropped.

"Jesus, Gianni, you frightened the hell out of me!" Antonio exclaimed.

Gianni ignored him and continued to open a bottle of brandy. He was a mess, drunk and scruffy looking.

Antonio jumped to his feet. "For Christ's sake, Gianni, pull yourself together!"

"Don't you tell me what to fucking do, it isn't your woman lying on a slab."

"This isn't helping."

Antonio took the glass off him. "Look, we need to talk, come and sit down. You need to sober up and fast." Antonio explained everything that had happened while he'd been out of it.

"I better make coffee then." Gianni got up to go to the kitchen.

"Listen, why don't you go and freshen up and I'll put the coffee on."

"Do I look that bad?" Gianni half laughed.

"Like shit, man!"

"I better get myself sorted out then."

Gianni realised how serious the situation was and he knew that Antonio would not be able to sort this mess out by himself.

Chapter Fifty Five

Katie sat down to some hot broth which Francesca had prepared accompanied by some freshly baked focaccia bread.

"I wish I could cook, this is beautiful."

"How about we open a nice bottle of wine to go with it?"

"Why not?"

Before long Katie found herself relaxing, enjoying this woman's company. She related stories of the brothers when they were young and all the trouble they got themselves into. It was only when Francesca mentioned the Calvi brothers that Katie remembered Georgio Calvi. 'The de Marcos are not what they seem', he had told her. It was imprinted on her brain now.

"I think I met one of them earlier today, in fact he came to help me when Pesaro threw me off." Katie studied Francesca's reaction.

She already knew about Georgio but tried to act surprised. "Really and what did he say to you?"

"Not a lot really, but he seemed to know about me and Antonio, yet I didn't tell him. How could he have known which brother I was seeing?"

"Well..." Francesca paused. "He must have known it was Antonio, as it's common knowledge that Gianni is getting married soon."

"But, how would he know what Felicia looked like, I mean for all he knew I was Felicia."

"Wait, I have a newspaper clipping." She reached into the kitchen drawer. "There."

Katie read the announcement of Gianni and Felicia's forthcoming marriage and their picture was next to it. "Oh, I see. But there was still something odd about this Georgio, there was no emotion in his voice, he was just, just..."

"There, there, he always was a strange one, take no notice."

Katie wasn't convinced, she was sure Fran was not telling her everything. "Why don't you explain to me why this Georgio Calver, or whatever his name is, insisted I should be careful around the de Marcos and that they were not what they seemed."

"Oh pay no attention, he's not all there, you know?" She pointed to her head.

"He was aloof, but seemed all there to me."

"Oh, my dear bambino, you worry too much."

"I suppose it was just a little strange at the time, perhaps I do worry too much."

"How would you like to go and see the little chapel, there is going to be a vigil tonight in memory of Felicia."

"Really, I only thought they did things like that for famous people."

Fran chuckled. "Well, the de Marcos are as famous as you can get in these parts. They have brought a lot of trade here and put La Pregheira on the map so to speak."

"I don't really know much do I? Why are they so famous to the locals?"

"They made their own fortune of course and are known and respected in the business world! They have won awards, everyone hereabouts think it's fantastic!"

"Self-made millionaires, I'll drink to that!" Katie laughed.

"So, would you like to light a candle for Felicia?"

"I'll pass if you don't mind, I mean I didn't really know her that well."

Francesca nodded, perhaps it was just as well, she would be safer here, where they could keep an eye on her.

Chapter Fifty Six

Veronica rounded up the staff. "Ok, listen up, we are not opening up tonight so you can all go home."

"Are you serious, what about all the bookings?" Tania had a few choice clientele booked in and she was looking forward to making some serious money tonight.

"Do you know anything about respect, Tania?" Veronica shot her a dark look.

"Of course, I was just thinking about the de Marcos how they always carry on no matter what. It just isn't their style to close and lose money."

"And how do you know what their style is, you've only been here five minutes!"

"I know them better than you think," Tania persisted.

"Oh, really, why don't you grow up and get a life dear." Veronica was having none of it.

Tania was blazing, how could Veronica embarrass her in front of the staff like this. "But I was only saying life goes on."

"How dare you, get out of this club right now and never let me hear you speak about Felicia like that!"

"But I didn't mean anything against Felicia, you know how much I liked and respected her!"

"Just get out, Tania." Veronica was sick of this selfish bitch's attitude, today of all days. All that woman thought about was money and one day it would be her downfall.

Colin and Lucy looked at each other and smirked, about time the bitch got a public dressing down! They were pretty sure that the rest of the staff were thinking the same thing too.

Tania tried to keep her cool as she walked towards the door with her head held high.

"That uptight bitch, maybe if someone gave her a good seeing to she might loosen up a bit!"

The fits of laughter echoed around the room and Tania knew that it was at her expense. Veronica would regret her actions of today, she would see to that. Nobody treated her like shit and got away with it.

"So, as I was saying, we'll resume work tomorrow as usual. Does anyone else have a problem?"

Nobody answered. "Good, then you can all leave."

Some of the staff decided to make the most of it and go out on the town, they never got the chance to socialise in their line of work. It would be a good bonding session.

Colin suggested that it would be fun if they went to Bar Exotica.

"Where's that, I never heard of it?" Lucy asked innocently.

"Really, well you haven't lived, girl, come on, get your skates on!" Colin exclaimed. He would show her a thing or two!

Kyle was pulling faces, why couldn't they have gone to a gay bar instead, open their eyes to his world just for a change.

Colin whispered in Lucy's ear. "Kyle is in for a big surprise, I hear they have got this gorgeous gay working as a bouncer there now, but for goodness sake don't tell him!"

"What you two whispering about?" Kyle demanded.

"Never you mind. The first round is on me!"

They made their way into the bar and were greeted by a buxom brunette called Liliana. "Welcome to Bar Exotica, how about some shots to get you started, on the house of course."

"Sounds good, we need, errm, how many of us are there?" Colin started a head count. "Fifteen."

"No problem, you can sit over there." Liliana nodded her head to the centre of the room.

"Wow, this is lush!" Alice was impressed.

They sat in high backed pink velvet chairs around a long wooden table. Another waitress came over carrying a silver tray with little shot glasses balanced on it. She set it down and began to pour straight shots of the house speciality.

When everyone was ready Colin stood up. "To little Felicia, bless her heart, she will be missed."

Lucy gulped back the burning liquid, which took her breath away. "Wow, what the hell is this!" She coughed.

Colin patted her on the back and laughed. "I know, why don't we have tequila slammers!" He nodded to the waitress.

The shot girls were wearing black hot pants and sequined bras, finished off with white knee length fluffy boots. They looked incredible, all of them young and gorgeous.

"I didn't know you came to a place like this," Lucy smiled at Colin.

"You'd be surprised the places he goes to!" Kyle said in a serious voice.

"Hey, stop giving away my secrets." Colin was intent on enjoying himself.

Just then a young lady approached Lucy. "You got a quid sweetie?"

Lucy was unsure, so Alice passed the girl the money. She promptly lifted her bra and flashed her boobs and with that she walked off.

"What the hell?"

The raucous laughter of the friends echoed around the bar. Lucy laughed with them, that had never happened to her before and she was quite shocked.

Kyle had to admit that he had asked the girl to do it as he wanted to see the look on Lucy's face.

"You, little shit, I was petrified."

"The look on your face was priceless!"

The tequila shots arrived. "Hey, just leave the bottle and can we get some salt and slices of lime?"

"Sure, baby, anything else you need?" Liliana flirted shamelessly with him.

"How about your phone number?"

Liliana winked at him and obediently handed her number over, which she had already written down when she saw him arrive.

"You've scored, I didn't know that you were such a super stud, Colin!" Lucy was well impressed.

They lined up the shots and passed the salt around. "Ok, pour a little salt on the back of your hand, lick it, sink the tequila and suck on the lime."

"After three, one, two, three!"

Lucy was having an absolute blast, the shots going right to her head.

The gang continued drinking different shots and partying hard. Some of the customers complained as the drunken group started singing loudly and began dancing on the table. Alice strutted her stuff and ended her routine by doing the splits!

Some of the shot girls were jealous and told the bouncer that they were losing money because this girl was putting on a free show.

"Sorry, folks, but it's time to leave," the bouncer ordered them.

"But we haven't done anything."

"You're disturbing the rest of the customers."

"Actually I thought that they rather enjoyed my performance." Alice drawled in that rich husky voice of hers. "Maybe I should give them a song instead."

"Sorry, love, but you must leave."

"Oh, what's it worth?" hiccupped Kyle, trying his luck.

The bouncer leaned over and whispered in his ear. He put his card into Kyle's hand and patted his backside. Kyle was jumping with glee, he had pulled and this guy was hot, hot, hot.

Liliana waved at Colin and he promptly waved back, miming that he would call her.

Once outside Colin questioned his brother. "Jesus, was he one of your sort then, cos he looked straight as a dime to me?"

"Ooh yes, lucky me, I have to give him a call sometime. Do you think I should take him up on it?" Kyle knew that whatever his brother said he would call him no matter what.

"What a waste, he was rather hunky, who would have thought it!" Sarah sighed. "All the best ones are either gay or married, hell what's a girl to do, maybe I should think about becoming a lesbian!"

Roaring with laughter they staggered down the street and began singing Sinitta's 'So Macho'.

Alice and some of the other girls jumped into a taxi. "We had a great time, we should do it again!"

"Oh, don't go," pleaded Kyle. "I was hoping you would sing to us tonight."

"Sorry, Kyle, I need my beauty sleep!"

"No you don't, that's just an excuse!"

"Goodnight all," the girls shouted out of the window.

From then on the gang dwindled until there was only Colin, Kyle, Lucy and Sarah left.

"Ok, what should we do now?"

"Let's go to the park and go on all the kids' rides!" Kyle shouted.

They made a drunken dash to the park, fighting over the swings. The boys won leaving Lucy and Sarah a choice of the seesaw, climbing frame or the roundabout.

"Well, what's it to be?" Sarah hiccupped.

"Ooh, I don't think that I could face the roundabout, do you?"

"If we don't spin it, we'll be fine."

Lucy clambered on to the roundabout. "God, I feel like I'm back in my childhood!"

"Some of us are still in our childhood!" Sarah pointed at the twins who were trying to see who could swing the highest.

"What are they like!"

"So, what do you really think happened to Felicia then?" Sarah had been dying to ask her.

"How would I know?"

"Aw, you are seeing Stevo, I just thought he might have said something to you."

"Why on earth would he tell me anything? Anyway I haven't seen him since it happened," Lucy sighed.

"It all seems rather strange though doesn't it?" insisted Sarah.

"It's a robbery that went wrong."

"Have you spoken to Katie yet, maybe she knows the whole story?"

"Why, do you think there was more to it than a simple robbery, poor Felicia was in the way and that's why she ended up dead?"

"I just have a feeling; I mean I wouldn't want to get on the wrong side of the de Marcos!"

"What is it about them?" Lucy sighed.

"Hey, girls, come on we're going back to the club to make a few cocktails!"

"Do you want to go?" Sarah asked.

Lucy nodded. "Why not?"

Veronica was still in the club when they arrived. She was sitting with Nicholas sipping a bottle of fine wine. They had been trying to put the world to rights discussing the premature death of Felicia.

Veronica shook her head. "Hey, what are you guys up to, I gave you the night off, remember, you shouldn't be here!"

"Oh, sorry, Veronica, we just wanted to toast Felicia, and what better way than in the club?"

"Come over," Veronica beckoned them.

Sarah hesitated, this was a side to Veronica that she had never seen.

"Nicholas, go and get some more wine, darling, the most expensive one that you can find."

Nicholas obediently left the table and came back a few minutes later with two bottles of wine. "Will this do?"

"Sure." Veronica was red-eyed, it was obvious that she had been crying. "I just can't believe it!" Her voice was quiet.

Nicholas patted her arm. "Come on, I think I'd better take you home."

"Jush one more drink then." Veronica slurred her words, she'd obviously had a few already.

Colin opened the bottle and topped up Veronica's glass. When everybody had a drink in their hand, he stood up. "To Felicia, we will really miss her."

Veronica gulped back the wine. "Take the bottles with you." She got to her feet and Nicholas put a protective arm around her.

"You heard the lady, time to leave." Nicholas helped Veronica with her coat.

Veronica cursed under her breath. "Shit, what did I do with the keys?"

Nicholas rattled them. "I'll lock up tonight, come on, guys."

"Goodnight, Veronica."

"Gudnight."

As they walked down the street Kyle said. "Jesus she was a bit bladdered wasn't she?"

"Was she close to Felicia then?" Lucy asked.

"She had a bit of a soft spot for her, I think she admired how well she could handle Gianni and now that she's gone who'll keep Gianni in his place?"

"Is Gianni really that bad?"

"He has got a foul temper that's for sure," Sarah agreed.

"What should we do now then, you want to come back to mine to finish the wine?" Colin asked tapping the bottles together.

"Sorry, guys, I gotta go, I'm knackered." Lucy could hardly stand up.

"Oh, darling, I agree, you are in no fit state at all," Kyle shrieked. "All the more for us then!"

Hailing a taxi Lucy waved to her friends. "See you tomorrow then."

Chapter Fifty Seven

"See if you can find out where Ricardo Calvi is." Antonio put the phone down.

Gianni came into the room, looking much fresher. "I'm going to break the fucker's legs, then I'm going to gut him like a pig!"

Antonio walked over to him. "No, you've got to stay out of this, I've got some of the guys on it, they know what to do."

"But it was me they came after, I need retribution."

"You'll get it, I promise you. We don't want to bring attention to ourselves, the police already think that we were involved in Vince's murder, we can't take any chances."

Gianni's face changed. "No, I've got to do it my way."

Antonio shook his head. "No, you can't be caught up with this, you know it makes sense, listen to me Gianni."

"Ok, you win!" Gianni slumped into the chair. "What do you want me to do here?"

"Just carry on as normal, don't go anywhere alone until we find the fuckers. Are you going to be ok, I need to go and see what's been going on back home?"

"What do you mean?"

"Looks like the Calvis organised a little accident for Katie."

"What, is she ok?"

"Yes, she's fine. I'm going to the airstrip now but I'll be back as soon as I can."

"Ok." The brothers hugged each other.

"Be careful." Gianni said.

"You too, bro."

Chapter Fifty Eight

Katie was looking through some old photographs with Fran when Antonio walked into the kitchen.

"Hey, how are you?"

"I'm fine, but how is Gianni doing?"

"He's bearing up, how about you after your accident?"

"Oh, just a few bruises, I'm ok, Fran has really looked after me, fussed around me like a mother hen!" she laughed.

"Thanks Fran." Antonio hugged her.

"Are you hungry?" Fran asked.

Antonio hadn't eaten all day and his stomach was rumbling. "I guess so," he said, patting his toned stomach.

Fran scuttled over to the hob. "I'll knock up some pasta."

"Sounds good."

"Have the police caught anyone yet?" enquired Katie, genuinely concerned.

Antonio shook his head. "Let's go for a walk."

"Don't be long, the food will be ready in thirty minutes."

"Don't worry I wouldn't want to miss your home cooking that's for sure."

They went outside, Antonio pulled Katie to him and kissed her passionately. "I want you so much, Katie," he murmured into her ear.

She could feel his heart beating faster through his shirt as he pressed her to him. "We always seem to get interrupted, but not tonight darling."

They strolled hand in hand through the vineyard as if they didn't have a care in the world. It was so peaceful here and it helped soothe his aching head. He had an idea. "After what happened to Felicia I don't want to let you out of my sight. Let's get married!"

"W… what?" Katie thought she was hearing things. "Are you being serious?"

"Yes, why not. It just feels right, we feel right, don't you agree?"

Katie didn't know what to say, she struggled for an answer.

"I understand that it's a bit of a shock. Promise me you will at least think about it, it's not such a crazy idea. Lots of people meet and fall in love and get married straight away, we are no different to them."

Katie was trembling. "Antonio I don't know what to say."

"Then don't say anything, my darling. I'll ask you again when we get back to the UK, only I promise I will do it properly, let's take this as the practice proposal."

Katie was elated, what on earth did he see in her? He had all these women falling over themselves to be with him. She didn't feel his equal, he was a millionaire and she was virtually penniless.

"We'll have a wonderful life together you and I, I can feel it. We'll be the happiest couple in the world," he laughed. "I'll take you anywhere you want, buy you anything you want!"

He drew her close once more and kissed her lightly on her cheek. "Come on, Fran will be wondering where we are!"

"I really like her and her quaint ways!"

"I'm pleased to hear it! And I have a funny feeling she feels the same way about you!"

They strolled slowly back to the house arm in arm, looking the perfect couple. Georgio Calvi smirked, he would make Antonio suffer slowly. Sneaking into the barn he threw down his still smouldering cigarette. Hopefully a couple of the horses would perish along with his precious barn. He had done a little bit of damage to the de Marcos and for now that would be enough. Luckily he had a few people on the inside that were close to the brothers and he would use this to his advantage at a later date. The Calvis had to stay out of the way, let the dust settle at least for the immediate future. There would be police and bodyguards all over them, they would be virtually untouchable; it was far too risky for further action. So for now he and his brother Ricardo would disappear once more until the time was right for the next move. Hit them hard when they least expect it and where they least expect it.

Chapter Fifty Nine

Stevo received a call from one of the boys. "What is it?"

"We found Ricardo, he's staying at the Plaza, what do you want us to do?"

"Nothing for now, just watch his every move and for fuck's sake don't screw this one up or there'll be hell to pay." Thank God for that, now he would have to let Gianni know. He was in a sticky situation as Antonio had given him strict instructions not to let Gianni be involved in any way. He was torn between the two, he wanted to obey Antonio but if he was Gianni he would want to personally sort this one out. He took a deep breath as he got into his car and headed for Antonio's pad. He delayed contacting Antonio as he knew that he would talk him out of what he was just about to do.

"I hope you've got some news for me Stevo," Gianni was calm, too calm. His voice was firm and emotionless.

"Gianni, we found one of them."

"Which one?"

"Ricardo, but we'll have to be extremely careful. I haven't told Antonio yet."

"Good, let's keep it that way."

"We need a plan, one that has got absolutely no chance of coming back on any of us."

"The police don't know anything about the Calvis involvement so they won't be watching the Plaza." Gianni's brain was on overload trying to come up with a plan of action.

"One thing is for sure though ... you cannot leave the house, it's too risky."

"Are those fuckers still out there?"

Stevo peered out of the window and waved. "Yeah, they are watching the apartment and have both ends of the road covered, so there's nowhere to go without being spotted."

"Fuck it, I want to torture that little bastard, rip him from limb to limb for what he has done!" Gianni was shaking with rage. "I need a drink."

Stevo poured them both a straight brandy. "What about Frank?"

"What about him?"

"Can't we set the bastard up for something and tip off Frank?"

"Like what, murder of my fiancée?" he said through gritted teeth. "We'll never be able to legitimately prove that."

"I'm not sure yet, but between us we'll come up with something."

"We haven't got much time, Stevo, the bastard is probably getting ready to move on as we speak and we can't allow that to happen."

"Ok, what about a car bomb, the fucker won't be expecting anything like that?"

"Now you're talking, where's his vehicle, is it accessible?"

"Parked in the underground car park, it should be easy to plant one."

"Ok, sounds good. Who we got in the vicinity?"

"Two of our most trusted guys, freelancers, worked for us before, very discreet. If the price is right they'll do anything and then disappear out of the country until things quieten down."

"Set the wheels in motion, Stevo, I want this finished!"

Stevo nodded. He made the call. Now all they had to do was wait until the bastard got into his vehicle and then kaboom!!!

Chapter Sixty

Fran's cooking was superb as usual and Katie was definitely going to miss being looked after. She had actually enjoyed the short time she had spent in La Pregheira and had felt quite at home. Perhaps if they came back, when they came back, she told herself, he would show her the little chapel and the market Fran had raved about.

Just then Alfredo burst through the door gasping for breath. He pointed outside. "It's the barn, hurry, it's on fire!"

"Oh, my God, we need to get the horses out!" Antonio rushed towards the stables, which were right next to the burning barn. The clouds of smoke were thick and heavy as he fought his way through, desperate to reach the horses and praying they were alive!

Francesca rang the fire brigade. "Yes, yes the de Marco vineyard, please be as quick as you can."

Katie and Francesca watched all the commotion from the doorway. The yard was full of the workers frantically attaching hoses to the water supply.

The horses were going wild and Pesaro was kicking at the stable door with his hind legs in a frantic bid to get out. The choking smoke made Antonio's eyes water. He hauled the door open and the horses bolted out just missing him. He managed to jump out of the way and fell on to the cobble stones. One of the vineyard workers pulled Antonio to his feet. He dusted himself down and looked around.

The fire was burning out of control and the flames were engulfing the two buildings. Despite the workers desperately hosing the buildings down there wasn't much chance of saving either building. Part of the stable roof had collapsed and Antonio yelled for some of the men to concentrate on putting the fire out.

"Are the horses ok?" Antonio coughed.

"I'll call in the vet to give them a once over but I think they'll be ok. What happened?"

"I have no idea!"

The fire brigade's siren could be heard in the distance. "There's not much they can do now." Antonio was just glad that the horses were unscathed. "Alfredo will you take care of this?"

"Yes, of course."

Antonio returned to the main house. His clothes reeked of smoke and his face and clothes were black.

"My God, are you alright?" Fran was worried.

181

"Just a little smoke inhalation, I'll be fine. I just need to get cleaned up and I'll be right as rain."

"You look a little worse for wear," Katie said as she noticed the cut on his face.

"I promise you, I'm fine, everything is under control, there's nothing for you to worry about."

Katie squeezed his hand and smiled at him. "And Pesaro?"

"Pesaro is very high spirited, he nearly had the door burst open before I even got there!" he laughed. "He's a strong old brute, make no mistake about that!"

"I know, he threw me off, remember!"

"Do you know how the fire started?" Fran asked him.

"Probably one of the workers smoking!"

"Don't you worry, Antonio, Alfredo will find out and sack the incompetent idiot!"

"I have every confidence in him." Antonio wondered if it had been deliberate or if it had simply been a discarded cigarette. The outcome could have been much worse though, that was for certain.

"I'm going to go and take a shower." Antonio told Katie.

"I think I'm going to have an early night if that's ok, I feel really exhausted. Goodnight Fran," Katie half smiled at her. "See you in the morning."

"Goodnight, my dear." Fran kissed her on the cheek. She seemed such a young fragile thing. How on earth was she going to cope in the de Marco world, she wondered.

"I'll see you in the morning."

Antonio followed her up the stairs. "Is it ok if I pop in after my shower, I just want to make sure that you are alright and of course to say goodnight!" His voice was sexy and mischievous.

"It's your house, Antonio, you can do whatever you like!"

He gave her a long lingering look before vanishing into his quarters.

He was so goddamn sexy she sighed. Even covered in soot and grime, he still oozed that incredible charm of his.

She looked out of the bedroom window. The firemen were still hosing the building down, although the main fire had been put out by Antonio and his men. The horses were in the field happily grazing. She saw the vet pull up and go over to Alfredo. What a nightmare it would have been if anything had happened to those poor horses, she thought. Antonio had been marvellous rescuing them like that without a thought for his own safety. That's what she loved about him, always putting others first. He was one in a million and she decided from that moment on she never wanted to let him go.

Her mind wandered back to a couple of hours earlier to Antonio's proposal. She couldn't wait to tell Lucy, she would be absolutely gob smacked, not that she had even said yes to him, not yet anyway. She knew that she was in love with him, but he

182

hadn't actually told her that he loved her. He must though, she reasoned, if he asked her to get married. It was a funny kind of proposal though, maybe he was still in shock about Felicia. Maybe once they returned to the UK things would be different, perhaps he wouldn't even mention it again. She hoped and prayed that he was being serious and would indeed propose more appropriately as he said he would.

She brushed her long dark hair and stared at her complexion. She wasn't bad-looking, she was quite pretty in a girly sort of way. These days there was an inner glow around her and everyone had passed comment on how confident she had become. Who would have thought that she would become a cocktail waitress in one of the most prestigious clubs in London. And even better, become involved with a multi millionaire who genuinely cared for her. The knock on the bedroom door brought her back to her senses.

"Yes?"

"It's me Antonio, can I come in?"

Katie hesitated, she was only wearing her robe. "Err, yes of course." It's his home after all she thought.

Antonio's gaze lingered as he watched her brush her hair. He brought two glasses and a bottle of wine with him. Placing them gently on the bedside table he took the brush from her hand. "Here let me." Slowly he gently brushed her hair easing it to one side. He run the back of his hand down her face and rested it on her neck.

"Antonio…" Katie's heart was pounding so hard she thought it was going to explode.

Antonio started to cover her in kisses, on her neck, her shoulder, her back.

Katie was lost in the moment, enjoying, savouring every moment. His touch was electric, she was aching for him. She turned her head towards him, their lips met. Hungrily she kissed him back, her hands were in his hair pulling him towards her. She had never felt passion like this before, it overpowered her, the neediness in her began to show as she started to unfasten Antonio's shirt. She let out a little cry as he lifted her up with ease and carried her to the bed.

"Oh, my darling, you are so beautiful." With one rapid movement he expertly removed her robe.

Their bodies entwined as they began their urgent lovemaking. Totally oblivious to the outside world they gasped and moaned as they reached the heights of ecstasy. Finally when they were spent they lay lovingly in each other's arms.

"How about that glass of wine now?" Antonio got out of bed.

Katie watched him, admiring his muscular body, he was perfect, like a God, she thought.

He felt her eyes on him and spun around. "Ok, the wine can wait." He jumped back on to the bed and began to make love to her once more. This time it was slow and more sensuous; he explored every inch of her body until she couldn't stand it any longer.

"Antonio…" She gasped.

"My darling, you are so demanding."

They couldn't get enough of each other and their love making carried on through the night until they were so exhausted they finally fell asleep tight in each other's arms.

Chapter Sixty One

Tania was in Ricardo's hotel room. "So, what really brings you here then, surely not me?"

"You always said to look you up if ever I was in England!"

"I know, but it was just one of those things you say when you're on holiday. You don't expect it to ever happen!"

"Then you don't have much faith in men!"

"I just couldn't believe it when you called me, Ricardo. I never thought I would see you again!" She remembered back to their holiday fling in Mauritius; he had been a wild lover and she had enjoyed his company.

"So, tell me what really brings you here?" Tania demanded to know.

"Business darling, I popped into your place last night, but you were nowhere to be seen, in fact it was all shut up."

"My place, you mean the club?"

"Of course I mean the club, where else?"

"We were all given the night off as Felicia Carmine was murdered."

"Who is she?"

"She is," Tania corrected herself, "I should say that she was the owner's fiancée, they were due to get married soon."

"Really, who was she engaged to?" Ricardo wasn't really interested, he had his own agenda to think about.

"Gianni de Marco the co-owner of the club."

"What happened to her?" Ricardo's ears pricked up, now he was genuinely interested in what she had to say.

"A robbery gone wrong is what everyone is saying, but I'm not so sure."

"What do you mean, you think something more sinister happened to her?"

"I wouldn't be surprised, I mean the de Marcos do have a dark side."

Ricardo knew exactly what she meant, he had experienced their rage first hand. He smiled to himself, someone had beaten him to it, what a stroke of luck. That was one less job for him to worry about. "What makes you say that about them?"

"The club manager up in Manchester was involved with a seriously heavy drug gang. It was getting out of hand and I contacted the de Marcos, I was frightened of what was going to happen next!"

"You frightened, I don't believe it!"

"I really was scared at the time. Anyway the de Marcos sorted it out all right, they killed him!"

"Why didn't you call the police?" It seemed the de Marcos hadn't changed their ways then! It may prove harder to deal with them than he thought. They obviously still had that vicious streak hidden away, which rarely came to the surface.

"I can't prove it and anyway I'm not a grass. Apart from that I believe they have friends high up in the police. So you see they'll never be able to pin anything on them with connections like that."

"Why do you still work for them, Tania?"

"I don't really know," she sighed. "Anyway enough about me, what kind of business are you into?"

"Just looking to make a base in London, you know, check out a few offices, property, see who my competition is!"

"The de Marcos are fierce competition in this area!"

"So they own a couple of clubs, so what." Ricardo smiled inwardly and waited for her answer.

"A couple of clubs, are you kidding me? They own much more than that. They were only recently voted the most fucking successful businessmen in the whole of London!"

"Very impressive, tell me more!"

"They have lots of business interests, art, furniture, property here and abroad. They are minted!"

Ricardo already knew all this but kept up the pretence. "Jesus, suppose they pay you pretty well then!"

"Not as much as I would like, naturally!" Tania smiled at him wondering how the conversation had turned to the de Marcos.

"Come here!" Ricardo ordered her.

"What's it worth?" Tania teased him.

"Whatever you want."

"I want to know why you are really here, you seem strangely interested in the de Marcos."

"Just weighing up the competition that's all!" he assured her.

"You wouldn't want to cross them, take it from me or you'll wind up dead somewhere!"

"I don't intend to cross them, Tania, I told you I am here to weigh up the business prospects."

"So, how long are you intending to stay for?"

"I'm not sure yet, I'm waiting for a business call."

"So, not long then, by the sound of that!" Tania was annoyed she still hadn't grasped what he was doing here.

"Did the de Marcos pay you off then?" Ricardo asked her.

186

"Pay me off, whatever do you mean?" Tania laughed. "Nobody pays me off!"

"You are a clever girl, I can see that. The de Marcos don't recognise that you are an asset to them. They do not respect you, isn't that true?" He studied her intently, he could see that she despised them, he just needed to get her to open up to him.

"Yes, you're right, after everything I did for those greedy bastards and all they could do was move me from the Manchester club into a shitty head waitress job at La Pregheira and a couple of grand for my trouble!"

"What? After all you did for them and they give you a measly couple of grand, what an insult. The drugs and money going through their business could have ruined them. The way I see it is that they owe you big time!"

"You know, Ricardo, you're absolutely right, I should have been offered more, especially after they murdered poor old Vince!"

"Ok, then this is what we are going to do about it. We'll wipe the smiles off the faces of those ungrateful shitheads once and for all!" Ricardo had her attention now, he could see the cogs moving, her green eyes wide and alert.

"What, you would do that for little old me?" Tania was impressed. "No one has ever done anything for me in my entire life!"

"Hey, I don't let no-one walk over my woman." Ricardo was loving it, she would be on the inside and he could pull all the strings. Make things happen, ruin the fuckers once and for all.

"But I thought we were just a holiday romance!" Tania was flattered, so flattered that she didn't stop to think why someone like him would want to help a waster and sponger like her. She didn't care; she just wanted what was rightfully hers. A few more grand would sort it; she had been a push over, but not anymore. She would teach those bastards, she would blackmail them. Threaten to tell the police, but she would have to be smart. Tell them that someone else knew and if anything happened to her they would go straight to the police. Gianni had been in Manchester when Vince had gone missing, she knew that for a fact!

"We're still a holiday romance, darling, I am on holiday!" Ricardo was playing with her and she was lapping up all the attention, it felt good.

"So, what were you thinking of then?" Tania was intrigued, there was more to this guy than she had anticipated. Her judgement all of a sudden became clouded and all she could focus on were the pound signs dancing in front of her greedy little eyes.

Ricardo had studied Tania's past and knew that she would stop at nothing if she thought that she was going to make anything out of it. Now all he had to do was sow the seeds and hopefully she would do the rest. They would make an excellent team. And he wouldn't stop until he had he succeeded in arranging the de Marcos downfall. He could feel it, this was the nearest they had ever been to being in total control. Fate it would seem was finally smiling down on the Calvi brothers.

187

Chapter Sixty Two

Katie burst into the apartment. "Lucy, you home, girlfriend?"

"Sure am, how are you after your jet set weekend?"

"Fabulous, just fabulous!" Katie was glowing from head to foot, and her eyes sparkled.

"Oh, my God you haven't!" Lucy exclaimed.

"Haven't what?!" Katie said indignantly.

"Come on, spill the beans!"

"We did and it was absolutely amazing, he was incredible, totally wow, and I mean wow!"

"Katie, I'm shocked!" Lucy giggled. "I want details!"

"And that's not all!" Katie looked all dreamy.

"Oh, oh, always a bad sign when you look like that." Lucy braced herself for what Katie was about to reveal.

"He's asked me to marry him!"

"You what? I thought that was just a rumour going around! Wait a minute did he ask you in the throes of passion, I mean when you were in bed together?"

"No, he asked me long before that!"

"Was it romantic, how did he ask you?"

"In a weird sort of way, he just said that we were meant for each other and that we would have a great life together!"

Lucy could tell that she was holding something back. "Well, spit it out, I know there's something else on your mind!"

"Sometimes you just know me too well! He didn't actually say that he loved me, not directly anyway!"

"That's kind of strange, did you accept?"

"No, not yet, he's asked me to think about it and said that he will propose officially, then I can give him my answer!"

"Jesus, Katie, isn't it all a bit too quick? Anyone would think you were up the spout or something. Oh my God, you're not are you?"

"Lucy, stop getting carried away, that was the first time we slept together! And for your information I would have a hard job getting pregnant seeing as how I am still on the pill!"

"But it's still too soon." Lucy was concerned, fast, hot romances usually ended as quickly as they started. It was rare indeed for this kind of relationships to last, and she wondered if Katie was in the minority.

"No, not really. I know that he's the one for me so you see it doesn't matter how long I wait, I will still feel the same way about him five years on as I do today."

"I must admit that I have never seen you so happy, you're positively radiant!"

"It's true I am ecstatic!" Katie paused. "But you can't tell anyone yet, we have to keep it secret until he asks me again!"

"Don't worry; your secret is safe with me!" Lucy couldn't help thinking that it was all going to end in tears.

"I knew that I could rely on you."

"What are friends for?" Lucy hugged her.

"Anyway tell me what's been happening here Luce? Poor Gianni must be absolutely devastated. I can't believe that Felicia is dead!"

"Murdered in her bed, the poor thing!"

"What a waste, she wasn't very old, was she?"

"I think she was about twenty-four, but she dressed and acted older. I mean she was sensible for her age."

"My God, you're not even safe in your own house these days."

"I know, it's scary isn't it, especially as his house is apparently like Fort Knox, I mean how did the intruder manage to get in?"

Katie shuddered. "Oh, please I don't want to think about it any more. Let's change the subject shall we?"

Lucy obliged. "Would you believe that Veronica gave everyone the night off yesterday!"

"Veronica? Is this the same 'what time do you call this, time is money, your wages will be docked' Veronica Lamont?" Katie stood in a Veronica style pose tip tapping on her wrist watch.

Lucy giggled. "You been practising that or what?"

"Moi, never my girl, now get on with it!"

"Yeah, well, she was really upset, crying into her wine glass and slobbering all over Nicholas. And to top it all she even gave us a couple of free bottles of wine and I mean really expensive wine from the de Marco vineyard no less!"

"My God, was she pissed up or something?"

"As a matter of fact, yes she was!"

"I can't imagine her gattered, I bet it was hilarious!"

"Well put it this way, we were all flabbergasted. I mean we couldn't just burst out laughing in case she sacked us all, so we just held it all in!"

"It's a shame I missed that one!"

"Nicholas had to take her home, she was totally legless, I mean he had to half carry her out of the club!"

189

"Shit, she must have been in a right old state!"

"Oh, yeah I nearly forgot, earlier on when she told us that we could have the evening off her and Tania had a stand off!"

"Really, what happened?"

"You know what that Tania can be like, a gob on a stick! Just being her usual cold-hearted self!"

"I don't know why she works there, everyone hates her!" She was the first person Katie had despised as soon as she had met her. Usually she saw the good in people, but something about Tania frightened her, even more so than Sasha.

"Well, just think, when you become Mrs Antonio de Marco, your first job will be to sack the horrible cow!"

"I can't make any promises but I'll see what I can do!"

Just then Stevo came out of the bathroom.

Katie jumped. "Jesus Stevo what a fright, I didn't realise that we had company!"

"Err, hello, Katie, I was just taking a shower, I hope you don't mind."

"Of course not, you're welcome here anytime, you know that."

"I have to go now, Lucy, Gianni is expecting me."

"How is Gianni?" Katie asked him.

"He's Gianni, what can I say?" Stevo shrugged his shoulders. "I gotta go, I'll see you later tonight then?" He looked at Lucy as he headed towards the door.

Lucy followed him and pulled the door behind her. "Don't say anything but Antonio has asked Katie to marry him!" she whispered.

Stevo was stunned. "You absolutely sure about this?"

"Shh, or she'll hear. Yes I'm sure, just don't tell anyone, it's not official yet!"

"I don't think this will go down too well with Gianni, it's real bad timing to say the least!"

"Oh, I never thought of that! Of course that would explain why Antonio wants to keep it quiet for now!"

"Well, Gianni isn't going to like it much, there'll be fireworks. I can't believe Antonio has popped the question, he must be insane!"

"They do seem to be genuinely mad about each other!"

"Just like us eh?" He kissed her hand. "My lady!"

Lucy blushed. "I guess so."

"I really have to go, Luce, I'll catch up with you later after work!"

"I can hardly wait, remember not a word to anyone."

He blew her a kiss as he left and pulled an imaginary zip across his lips.

"So, I'm not the only one smitten then!" Katie smiled.

"Well, he hasn't proposed yet!"

"Give him time."

"What's his surname anyway?"

"I have no idea!" Lucy giggled.

190

"You're kidding right?"

"No, I'm not!"

"Lucy what are you like, you've been sleeping with this guy and you don't even know his surname!"

"I know, it's crazy isn't it!"

"Yes, but that's just typical of you!"

"Oh, please! Why don't you tell me all about this beautiful old vineyard you've been to, I'm so jealous!"

"I can't believe that you knew all about it and never said a word, that must have been one hell of a secret to keep!"

"See, I can keep secrets when I need to!" Lucy stuck out her tongue.

"Cheek of it!"

"So, you gonna tell me about it or what?"

"It was as if I had stepped back in time, it was a lovely quaint, rustic old place. It's steeped in history you know, the land of poets, saints and painters!"

"Sounds very romantic, darling, do carry on!"

"I've taken some photos, so I'll show you when I get them developed!"

"I can hardly wait!"

You'll just have to be patient!"

"Stevo said that you had been involved in some kind of riding accident or something, is that right?"

"Yes, I did, but thankfully I only had a few bruises and stiff joints."

"You should have rung me, instead of letting me hear it from Stevo, you silly thing."

"I didn't want to worry you and anyway there was enough going on back here without chit chatting about my little accident, it pales in comparison."

"I suppose you're right, the murder has been hot gossip."

"I bet it has, I still can't get over it though."

"So, what happened, your accident I mean?"

"I'm not sure, something really upset the horse and he just threw me off. I was very lucky to have a soft landing. Then this strange guy came out of nowhere, his name was Georgio something, er Calver I think. Right after I fell off the horse he came over to help me up. There was something quite odd about him, he warned me off the de Marcos and said that they weren't what they seemed."

"What did he mean by that?"

"I don't know, I'm still trying to figure it out. Why would he say such a thing and to me?"

"God, he didn't hurt you, did he?"

"No, he just disappeared rather quickly when he saw some of Antonio's guys coming to my rescue!"

"So who do you think he is, an enemy of the de Marcos?"

"I have no idea, it was a bit creepy."

"Did you tell Antonio?"

"No, but I did mention it to Fran, the housekeeper."

"What did she say?"

"She knew the name alright and said that there was history between the two families, but it was all a long time ago. She did say that I shouldn't pay any attention as he wasn't altogether there!"

"Did you think that he was a full shilling then?"

"He seemed a bit odd, but I didn't get the impression that he was a few sandwiches short of a picnic, if you know what I mean!"

"Seriously, Katie, promise me that you'll be careful, I'm worried about what's going on with the de Marcos right now."

"Oh, come on Luce, the guy was just helping me out, that's all."

"The more I hear about the de Marco's the more I worry about you. Poor Felicia has been murdered and I heard that Roberto Valetti has committed suicide!"

"Oh God, poor Nina and their kids. Why would he want to kill himself? They adored each other."

"Something to do with drug smuggling, the police raided his warehouse and arrested him after they found a massive amount of heroine. Stevo said that he was going down for a long time and couldn't bear the thought of it, so he topped himself!"

"I'm going to go and see Nina, see if I can do anything to help."

"Do you think that's a good idea, you don't really know her after all?"

"I only want to give her my condolences in person."

"You're always the good Samaritan, remember when Ella's boyfriend died? She would have killed herself if you hadn't persuaded her to go to counselling!"

"Don't forget the old dear who was robbed and shoved to the ground!" Katie smiled as she remembered taking her into the nearest store and waiting until the ambulance arrived. The police managed to arrest a man because of her description. Thankfully it didn't go to court as the robber confessed.

"Sure I do, and the injured cat you took to the vets and paid all the bills! Pity the owner came back to claim it. You never did get the money back did you?"

"It doesn't matter, I'm just glad that the cat survived."

"You have this manner with people in these sorts of situations, maybe you should have been a nurse or something!"

"Ooh, no, you know what I'm like with the first sign of blood, I just keel over!"

"Do you want me to come with you, to Nina's?"

"No thanks, it's ok, I know where she lives. I'm just going to freshen up and I'll head over."

Lucy shook her head, what the hell were the de Marcos mixed up in. She would ring her brother once Katie left and tell him everything that had been going on. Perhaps with his newly established connections he may be able to find out!

Chapter Sixty Three

Nina was surprised to see Katie on her doorstep. "I hope you don't mind me just turning up like this. I just wanted to tell you in person how sorry I am for your loss."

"You'd better come in, Katie."

Nina looked pale and exhausted. "Can I get you a cup of tea, something stronger maybe?"

"Tea will be fine, thanks."

"Please, sit down. Do you take milk and sugar?"

"Just milk please."

Nina busied herself in the kitchen, the whole place was gleaming and smelled strongly of disinfectant. Katie noticed that her hands looked very red as if she had been scrubbing them non stop. She got the anti bacterial spray out of the cupboard and started wiping down the units.

"This place is driving me insane, I just can't seem to keep it clean."

"Nina, this place is spotless, it's like a show home." Katie was concerned for her well being. "Why don't you sit down and I'll make the tea."

"No, no you're a guest, I'll do it." Nina suddenly dropped the spray. "Damn it, look what I've done, its burst all over the floor, I'll have to get the mop out, Roberto will go spare!"

"Please, Nina, sit down, I'll clean it up, where do you keep the mop?"

Nina dropped to the floor and began sobbing, her whole body was shaking uncontrollably.

"Oh, Nina tell me what I can do to help, you shouldn't be on your own."

"Can you bring my Roberto back, can you, well can you?"

Katie put her arms around her. "I wish I could, I really do."

"It all seems like a bad dream, I keep hoping that I'll wake up soon and see him coming in through that door, all happy and jolly with a big bunch of flowers. I just can't take it!" she cried.

"Oh, Nina, you're trembling, let me help you up."

"Why did this happen to me, what did I do to deserve this, what did the children do to deserve losing their devoted father? Life was good, brilliant and all that's gone in the blink of an eye! Make sure you enjoy your life, Katie, while you can because you never know when it will end!"

The house seemed rather quiet. "Where's the children, Nina?"

"My mother has them, I couldn't cope. I've smashed all the cut glass crystal in a terrible rage and frightened them! I was screaming at the poor things and God knows that they don't deserve that!"

"I know, you've had a terrible shock, it's understandable that your emotions are all over the place. You need to focus on doing something, but certainly not cleaning!"

Nina laughed hysterically.

"Have you thought about making the funeral arrangements yet?" Katie held her breath and waited for a barrage of insults.

"I spoke to the vicar this morning, he wants me to go and see him later today." Nina's voice was quiet and calm.

"Do you have someone to go with you?"

"I haven't asked anyone, would you come with me, Katie?"

"Of course I will. Roberto seemed such a lovely man."

"Yes, he was a lovely man, he would never hurt a fly let alone dabble in drugs. You don't think that I have misjudged him do you, I mean do you think that everyone thinks him guilty of such a thing?"

"No, I don't believe that your husband would ever be mixed up in something like that."

"Thank you, Katie, you are the only one who has said that to me. But I suspect people will have already drawn their own conclusions."

"People are just in shock, that's all. Once they think about it, they'll realise he would never have done anything like that. The police will prove that it was all a mistake, you'll see."

"Thank you for your kind words but it doesn't mean anything to me. It just means that my poor Roberto died for nothing!"

"I'm so sorry, Nina, I don't know what to say, I wish I could make you feel better."

"Just being here shows that you care and I appreciate that. You have such a caring nature, not many people have that quality."

"So have you, Nina, your children need you now more than ever, you've got to be strong for them."

"You talk a lot of sense for someone your age."

"No, I just know what it's like to lose someone close, it's like your whole world falls apart."

"Who did you lose?"

"I lost my mother; she had a heart attack, totally out of the blue. I was only seventeen at the time, just when I needed her the most."

"I'm so sorry, that must have been really tough for you and your father."

"It was, there isn't a day goes by without me thinking about her, wishing she was still here."

"What about your father, I take it he's still around?"

194

"In a fashion, he moved to Australia recently, his sister lives there. I haven't seen him for months and now he's off on a world cruise. He never got over her and vowed to do all the things she wanted to do when they both retired."

"You poor thing, how are you managing without any parents around you? I don't know what I would do without my mother to help with the children."

"I have my best friend, Lucy, and now I have Antonio too."

"Just be careful around him, he's not what he seems." Nina said bitterly.

That was the second time Katie had heard those words. Why did everyone have it in for him? Was he that bad? No, she had never seen a dark side to him and couldn't believe he would hurt anyone deliberately. She had seen the soft, loving side to him and she would not believe that he had any maliciousness inside him. "Don't worry about me, I can take care of myself." Katie changed the subject. "Right now you need to focus on your children, that's what Roberto would have wanted."

"Yes, you're right, the children will help keep me focused."

Katie poured the tea and passed the china cup and saucer to Nina. Nina gratefully gulped the hot liquid. She felt like she was in some kind of bad dream and that she would awaken up any moment to find that it had all been some huge mistake. But in her heart she knew that it was all true, Roberto really was dead. Her brain ached as she struggled to keep back the tears once more. "We should be making tracks soon, I better put on my war paint before I leave the house, I must look absolutely dreadful."

Katie carefully washed up the cups and placed them on the draining board. She didn't know what she would do if anything ever happened to Antonio, her life would never be the same again, that was a certainty.

Nina re-appeared, you couldn't tell that she had been sobbing less than ten minutes earlier, her skin was absolutely flawless. Nina noticed her looking. "Yes, it's amazing what a bit of make-up can do, isn't it?"

"You don't need make-up, you have a beautiful complexion."

"I always made an effort for my husband and I wouldn't want to let him down now. He always appreciated the effort I made for him and I don't want that to change. You'll think I'm mad but even a little thing like that makes me think that life is still worth living."

She sounded much more calm and relaxed, even a little positive. Katie knew that it was all a front, albeit a necessary front, but once reality hit home her real loss would bring out all those held-back emotions she was struggling to come to terms with. But for now Katie said nothing, she was determined to help her get through the funeral arrangements before she fell to pieces again.

"The church is only around the corner but I think I'll drive, I don't think that I could face any of the neighbours right now."

"Whatever you want to do, Nina, is fine with me."

The door from the kitchen led into the garage. Nina climbed into her Mercedes and picked up the remote control. "I never thought that I would be so grateful for a little thing like an electronic door, it was a good investment."

Katie couldn't help but think that Nina was delaying the inevitable, she would have to face the outside world sooner or later.

A few minutes later they arrived at the vicarage. They were greeted by a matronly woman and shown into the parlour.

Everything passed in a bit of a haze as Katie couldn't help but remember her own mother's funeral. It had been the worst day of her life, watching her coffin lowered into the ground. She had been inconsolable, yet her father remained aloof, showing no emotion whatsoever. At her lowest point Katie had told him that he never cared about his own wife, she had regretted it as soon as the words had came out. But like a loving father does he forgave her harsh words, telling her grief was a funny thing and we all deal with it in our own ways. The words were ingrained in her brain, words that had helped her through the worst of it.

As Nina flicked through the service to check on the details she was unaware of the feelings of loss flowing through Katie, taking her back to that horrendous time of her life.

Nina's voice broke into her thoughts. "I wanted to pick out hymns that Roberto would have liked, I hope I've made the right choices."

"You have chosen well, Mrs Valetti." The vicar entered the room and shook her hand. "And who is this young lady?"

"Oh, this is a friend of mine, Katie Saunders."

"It's a shame that we had to meet at such a sad time."

Katie nodded in agreement.

The vicar turned his attention back to Nina. "I'm sorry to press you on this but have you decided whether you want to say anything?"

"There's lots of things I would like to say but I don't know if I'll be able to do it on the day."

"Don't worry about that, if you like you can write them down and I'll read them at the service."

"Oh, thank you, Vicar, I would appreciate that."

"Not at all, Mrs Valetti, that's what I'm here for. If I can help in any way, perhaps if you need to talk I am a good listener."

"I am very grateful but that won't be necessary."

The vicar nodded politely. "Please follow me so that I can show you the burial plot." He led them into the cemetery. "Your husband was very organised; the plot is already paid for." He paused. "It's a double plot that your husband asked for." He waited for the usual reaction and pulled a handkerchief from his pocket.

Nina couldn't hold back the tears any longer. The plot was next to a lilac tree and Roberto knew how much she loved the smell of lilac. Even in death he had

196

thought of everything. The vicar passed her the handkerchief and put a comforting hand on her shoulder. "I know that this is a difficult time for you and your family, Mrs Valetti, but please come to church more often, it will help you."

"Thank you, Vicar, I may take you up on that."

Katie took Nina's arm and led her to the car. "Come on, Nina, let's get you home."

Chapter Sixty Four

Gianni was becoming extremely impatient, all he wanted to hear was that the Calvi bastard had been blown to smithereens. Then at least he could take some comfort from it, try and move on as best he could. "Antonio, you're back!" He hugged his brother. "What's the news back home?"

"One of the Calvis must have been watching the house, but they obviously didn't have time to plan much, if setting fire to the barn was all they could come up with."

"Anything else I should know about?"

"I think Georgio got lucky spotting Katie, he somehow fiddled with the saddle causing her accident. Then he apparently turned up just after Pesaro threw her off, then to add insult to injury he had the audacity to warn her off the de Marcos and introduce himself."

"That fucking punk, where is he now, did you nail the bastard?"

"No, he's vanished off the face of the earth, crawled back into the woodwork!"

"Is your woman alright?"

"Yes, she's fine. But for some reason she didn't even mention Georgio Calvi, not to me anyway, although she did confide in Fran."

"Well if she didn't tell you then that means she wasn't worried for her safety."

"I suppose so, but we shouldn't underestimate her, she's not as gullible as what you think."

"Whatever you say."

"Give me an update on what's been happening here."

"We've managed to locate Ricardo, he's in the Plaza hotel. A couple of our guys have managed to plant a bomb in his car. I'm just waiting for the news coming through, should be any time now." Gianni was pacing the floor again. "My only regret is that it's too quick for him and I ain't even gonna be there to see it happen. I still think that I should have kidnapped the fucker and tortured him!"

He had that wild look in his eyes and Antonio knew that given the chance he would be off to do the job himself. "Gianni, we have been through this and it's not possible, my apartment is under surveillance, we daren't put a foot wrong. We have to be whiter than white, do you get my drift?"

"That some kind of fucking joke, white, drift!" Gianni threw his head back and laughed hysterically.

Antonio put his hand on his brother's shoulder. "Do you fancy a brandy?"

"I thought you'd never ask, all this fucking hanging around is doing my head in!"

Antonio took the key out of his pocket and unlocked the drinks cabinet.

"So, that's where it was, if I had wanted a drink I would have smashed it in, you know that!"

Antonio turned to him. "I know that you'll get your revenge, brother, of that I am absolutely certain."

Tania couldn't wait to show those bitches back at the club who was boss, once she got rid of Veronica things would change. Once more the world was her oyster, she could have whatever she wanted and Ricardo was the icing on the cake.

"So, you know how to play it?" Ricardo asked her.

"What do you think I am, stupid or something?"

Tania was a liability, a very dangerous one, once she did what he wanted she would be history. Hopefully the de Marcos would take care of that side of things, once the damage was done he would slip out of the country leaving Tania to take the rap. The stupid fat whore, how could she think he would want a woman like her, a predator and a leech.

"Let's go." Ricardo put on his sweetest voice, he really wanted to vomit. If he had to shag her one more time he would kill her himself.

They left the hotel at 10.30am. "So, where do you want dropped off at?"

"You better drop me off at home so that I can get changed."

"No problem, my sweet, you'll have to give me the directions."

Ricardo continued to play it smooth and politely opened the car door for her.

"Why thank you, kind sir."

"You're welcome, Tania." Ricardo closed the door and gritted his teeth, she was doing his head in, the stupid old tart. If she hadn't proved useful to him he would gladly have snapped her neck. She was good in the sack but all that flab suffocated him, her horrible sweaty tits swinging in his face disgusted him. Her arse was like the back end of a jumbo jet. Her mannerisms left a lot to be desired, she strutted around with her nose in the air as if everyone were beneath her. No wonder everyone hated this self-obsessed fat fucking witch! Well once he was finished with her, he would drop her like a hot brick, preferably off the top of a fucking mountain.

As he opened the door she smiled a sickly horrible smile, it made his stomach turn. He knew he had to keep up the façade, but was finding it extremely difficult to keep his hands from shooting around her throat!

"You know, this is the happiest I've been in ages," Tania sighed breathlessly, she was well and truly hooked.

"Me too, hang on I just need to use the phone." He pointed to the phone booth.

"Well, don't be long."

"I won't." Ricardo dialled his brother. "It's me, how did it go?"

"Good, what about you?"

"Great, all went like clockwork." He paused. "With an added bonus you wouldn't believe."

"Forget about the added bonus, I want you back home, out of harm's way. I think that it's time you come back, the de Marcos will be on to us now."

"Oh, I'm having way too much fun for that, besides I told you I've got another plan lined up."

"Never mind another plan, you stung him for twenty five thousand, remember!"

"That's just a drop in the ocean to them!" Ricardo fiddled with his keys, impatient to get going. "Trust me, I know what I'm doing." His voice was full of confidence.

"No, Ricardo, it's much too dangerous, just pull out, are you listening to me?"

Ricardo was watching Tania fiddling in the glove box. Dropping the phone he rushed over to the hire car. "Are you ok, Tania?" He smiled through gritted teeth as he fastened his seat belt, thankful that she didn't find the revolver.

"Of course, let's go."

Ricardo was putting the key in the ignition. "Look, we are going to be cool, trust me..." He turned the key and the car exploded.

"Ricardo, can you hear me?" His brother had left the phone off the hook for a few seconds then it seemed to go dead. "Fuck, fuck, fuck, Ricardo, answer me." The silence sent a chill down his spine, he had a horrible feeling something or someone had just taken his brother out.

When the news came through Gianni whooped with joy. "Get me a fucking celebratory drink, one fucker down and one more to go!"

It was Antonio who had received the call and was told that a young woman had been in the car with Ricardo and had also been killed. He hated an innocent person being killed for no reason, even if she was just some goddamn prostitute he had picked up. But they had no choice, they had to get Ricardo out of the way fast before he did any more damage. He didn't want to mention the woman to Gianni just yet, he had enough to deal with right now.

"Have the plod been around yet?"

"No, not yet. Felicia's mother is still waiting for the coroner to complete the autopsy."

"I spoke with Gerald, he's going to see what the delay is. The sooner her body is released the better." One thing about Gerald Newman was that he had a good rapport both with the police and likeminded lawyers. He was extremely meticulous in everything he was involved in leaving no stone unturned. They respected him for that, he was one of the best at what he did.

"So what about Georgio, he's got away with it hasn't he?"

200

"We'll catch up with him sooner or later but I'm afraid that there's not much else we can do right now. We've got all the business interests covered and our houses, the men are on standby until we tell them different. Georgio will not be able to sneak up on us again without us knowing about it."

"We'll have our time with him, you'll see, what goes around comes around."

"Yeah, you're right about that. Anyway I was planning on going into the club later, see how business is, are you up to coming?"

"Sure, I can't hide in here forever can I? The sooner I get back into a routine the better, it's gonna be tough but I'll ride it through."

"Good, then we'll go in together, have some of Nicholas' fabulous home made cooking and perhaps wash it down with a bottle of 'de Marco' wine, 1978 red perhaps. What do you say?"

"My mouth's watering already, what are we waiting for?"

"Thank God you said that, you look like you could do with a good feed, we can't have you wasting away, bro!" His brother was finally talking sense, this was the Gianni he knew so well.

"Me waste away, not a chance, I love my grub too much, especially the renowned chef Nicholas Carlotti's cuisine!" Gianni grinned as he patted his stomach. "Sounds like a good idea, Antonio, and at the same time we can kill two birds with one stone and show everyone nothing will keep the de Marcos down for long!"

"That's the spirit." The best thing for Gianni was keeping him occupied, he would give him some extra responsibility, give him a new challenge of some sort, although he wasn't quite sure what yet. All he knew was that he had to do something to prevent him from going over the edge. He would talk to Veronica, maybe she would have some ideas. A new challenge was just what Gianni needed.

Gerald Newman had just finished speaking to the Coroner, Felicia Carmine had been two months pregnant. He was told to contact Antonio as soon as the report came in. Gerald was grateful to be dealing directly with Antonio, breaking the news to him wouldn't be so bad. Antonio had a coolness about him and whatever emotion he felt he would keep it in check and never publicly reveal his true feelings. It was a quality he appreciated. He was glad that it was Gianni's own brother that would be the one to tell him. Gianni's reaction would be explosive to say the least. Thank God he was going on holiday at the end of the week with his family and for three whole weeks of glorious sunshine. Hopefully everything would have calmed down by the time he returned, but somehow he doubted it.

Chapter Sixty Five

DC Fearon was at the scene soon after the explosion, what the hell had gone down here? That was two murder cases and a suicide all in the space of a few days, was this also somehow connected to the de Marco's too, he wondered. They were a force to be reckoned with alright and they needed to be stopped and he was the man for the job. No one messed around on his patch and got off scot free.

"Do we have any idea who was in the car yet?"

"No sir, we believe that it was a guest at the Plaza!"

"You don't say, of course it fucking was! Find out who the car was registered to and I'll go and speak to the hotel manager!"

The young copper was extremely offended by DC Fearon's attitude, he was only trying to help, this was his first murder case and he wanted to show his boss that he knew what he was doing. "I've already taken the liberty of checking the hotel register. We," he corrected himself, "I believe that the man in the car was on business here for a few days, his name is Richard Gomez, the young woman hasn't been identified yet but the hotel has security footage which may show them leaving together."

"Well, don't just stand there, man, get on to it. Take Robinson with you and let me know immediately when you have any news."

"Yes sir." PC Cooper couldn't stand this pompous old fool, it was about time that he retired. How he had managed to stay in a job like this for so long amazed him.

DC Fearon was talking to the bomb expert. "It's a miracle that nobody else was killed."

"It was a homemade device, nothing like I've ever seen before, there are no prints and as you can see not much of the bodies left to examine."

DC Fearon's stomach turned as he neared the scene, the smell of charred skin made him queasy. "Jesus Christ, what a fucking mess, better put up a tarpaulin screen, we don't want the public seeing this!" He took out a cigarette and was just about to light it.

"Stop, stop, Jesus Christ, there's still flammable liquid on the ground, do you want to cause another explosion?"

"Er, no, no, I wasn't going to light it, just habit." DC Fearon tried to cover up his hideous mistake.

"Just leave this to the bomb expert's, sir, and we'll get the report to you as quickly as possible."

DC Fearon kindly obliged, he didn't want to make more of an arse of himself.

The two police officers were in the security room trawling through the video footage of earlier that morning. Andrew Moore, the hotel manager, and his assistant were in a state of shock, this sort of thing had never happened to them before. What kind of people had been frequenting his hotel? This was very bad publicity and he didn't know how they were going to recover from it.

"So, this Mr Gomez, he left with a young woman about ten minutes before the blast occurred?"

Andrew Moore nodded. "Yes, Liz checked him out, he paid for everything in cash."

"Was there anything unusual about that?"

"Yes, we charge £1000 per night for the suite he used and most of our customers pay by charge card."

"I see, so you never saw any identification then?"

"No, we didn't, he paid cash up front." Liz was shaking. "He was such a polite young man, always had a spring in his step."

"Was he local then or did he have an accent of some sort?"

"He, er, he was definitely foreign, Spanish perhaps, he had that sort of colouring."

"Spanish you say, hm, when did he check in?"

"Three days ago."

"Did he have any visitors, make any phone calls?"

"No, he never used the phone in his suite and I only seen him with that woman this morning." Liz started crying.

"There, there, come on, love, sit down. I don't mean to upset you, we're just trying to find out who could have done something like this."

"Yes, I know that and I'll help you any way I can." Liz blew her nose unceremoniously into a scrumpled up handkerchief supplied by the hotel manager.

"Stop, stop, that's them."

PC Cooper rewound the tape. He saw a smart young man leaving the hotel with a petite redhead. He kept winding it back until he was able to freeze the frame. "I'd better get DC Fearon."

DC Fearon was outside the hotel lobby sucking hard on his cigarette. He was mopping his brow and the sweat was running down his red bloated face.

"Sir, we got footage of a young couple leaving the hotel, it's got to be the blast victims."

"Good job, lad, let's go and see it."

After he was satisfied that the footage proved it must have been those poor buggers who were murdered he ordered the young PC to take statements. "No, no, not you, Cooper, you can drive me back to the station once we are done here, see what we can come up with, get George to have a look at it, see if this guy had a record of any sort, try and figure out who he pissed off, cos he must have really hacked somebody off, good and proper. Robinson what are you waiting for man!"

"Yes, sir." Robinson jumped. "I'm on it."

"Mr Moore, we need the room sealed off, no-one comes in and no-one goes out until forensics have had a good look around. Do you understand?" DC Fearon informed him.

"Yes, yes, of course I do." What did he think he was, some kind of blithering idiot?

"Good, the team should be here any second, may I have the key please?"

"Sure, follow me." Andrew handed DC Fearon the key and gave him directions to the suite.

"When is the maid due?"

"Any minute, why?"

"Fucking hell, forensics of course." He immediately got on his radio. "Has anyone seen the maid"?

"No, sir." The team came back with the same response.

"But the maids don't come through reception, they come up the back stairs."

"What, fucking hell, come on, man, which way?"

Andrew tried to tell him again.

"No, no, I need you to come with me, we better get a fucking pace on, if that maid gets there before us and cleans it we are fucked!"

PC Cooper couldn't help but think that his boss had finally lost it.

The lift was taking an age to reach the tenth floor. As the lift doors opened they saw the maid disappear around the corner. Darting up the corridor DC Fearon shouted, "Police, stand still."

The poor woman nearly fainted. "Please, please, don't shoot I haven't done anything." She dropped her cleaning paraphernalia on to the corridor floor and froze.

The hotel manager was livid, he couldn't believe this idiot of a man had a gun pointed at her.

"It's ok, Maria, no harm done, it's not you he is after. Please just take the rest of the day off, I insist."

"Oh, Mr Moore, I thought he was going to shoot me!"

"I can assure you that he was going to do no such thing, isn't that correct DC Fearon?"

"I'm sorry, madam, it's just that there may be important evidence in that hotel room connected with the car that exploded."

"I understand."

But Mr Moore did not understand and he was going to report this oaf of a man to the Chief Superintendent as soon as he left his hotel.

DC Fearon sat outside the door waiting impatiently for forensics to turn up. He wondered how the bomb expert was doing with the remains of the car. They would be extremely lucky to find anything left still in one piece.

Several hours later Antonio received an urgent phone call from his friend Frank.

"The girl has been identified as one Tania Horrocks, an employee of yours I believe, I don't know what the connection is with Ricardo Calvi, but it's only a matter of time before Fearon finds out his real name. I'll do whatever I can, but be careful and be prepared for another visit." Frank replaced the receiver, he had to get Howard Fearon off the case as soon as possible. And with the complaint he had just received from Andrew Moore from the Plaza Hotel it would be much easier.

Antonio's face went white.

"What's happened?"

"There was someone else in the car with Calvi when it exploded, a woman."

"And?"

"It was Tania Horrocks!"

Gianni couldn't get his head around it. "Tania, our Tania? How did she know Calvi? That bitch, has she been working for him all this time, spying on us? That would certainly explain a lot of things. That fucking whore, if she wasn't already dead I would fucking kill her myself!" he ranted.

"I don't know how she was involved with him, but we have got to be smart. Fearon knows about Vince Fraser, once he checks Tania's background he'll soon find out she worked up in the club too! Fuck, we'll have to be very careful."

"They can't pin anything on us, don't worry, it's just some kind of weird coincidence that's all, and that's the story we will stick to."

"What if Fearon starts digging into Calvis' past?"

"What if he does, nothing was ever proved one way or another it, was all hearsay."

"Yeah, you're right, no need to panic. Fearon's that thick he may never find out who Calvi was, the name he was using was Richard Gomez."

"Richard, Richard Gomez, isn't that Ritchie?"

"Yeah, it was." The Calvis were responsible for Ritchie drowning when they were all kids.

"Fucking drowned by that prick Ricardo." Gianni spat the words out.

Antonio had happy memories of Ritchie, all four of them did everything together. But this particular day Gianni and Stevo had been meeting their girlfriends and had arranged to meet Antonio and Ritchie later on. They had gotten into a fight with the Calvi brothers and things had turned really nasty. He remembered back to that fatal day at the riverbank. Ritchie had been knocked unconscious by Ricardo and had somehow got lodged underneath a branch. Antonio had desperately tried to dislodge him when he banged his head and also lost consciousness. If it hadn't been for Stevo he too would have lost his life that day. He had never forgotten Ritchie and he would be forever grateful to his long time friend Stevo. Of course the local police had investigated and had ruled that boys would be boys and that it was a case of misadventure. But deep down the de Marcos knew it had been planned but had never been able to prove it. Over the years they had many incidents with the Calvis until finally it had all came to a head and the Calvis had disappeared, until now that is.

Stevo was shocked when he heard the news. "I can't believe the audacity of that little punk, using Ritchie's name like that. But what the fuck was Tania doing mixed up in all of this?"

"It doesn't matter now, forget about them!" Antonio couldn't get his head around it. "I wonder if anyone at the club has heard the news yet."

"I don't think that anyone will really give a shit, it wasn't as though Tania was number one in the popularity stakes!" Stevo announced. "She won't be missed that's for sure."

"You still coming to the club, Gianni?"

"You bet that I am!"

"I'll send for Fred."

Chapter Sixty Six

Eddie burst into Veronica's office. "Dear God, Eddie what is the emergency?"

"It's Gianni and Antonio they're here!" he gasped, sweat pouring down his face, he had run all the way from the foyer.

Veronica glanced up from her desk. "What, why didn't anybody tell me that they were coming?"

"I'm sorry, nobody knew."

"You'd better warn the staff!"

"I'm afraid that it's too late for that, they are already going into the bar!"

"Then I'd better get over there and fast." Veronica shoved her chair back and checked her famous pout. She quickly renewed her lipstick and straightened her clothes. "How do I look, will I pass?"

"You look beautiful, a beautiful oriental lady." Eddie half grimaced showing his gold protruding tooth.

"Good, now out of my way, man." She brushed past him. Eddie made sure he was close enough to feel her body next to his just for a split second. He lived for moments like this, that's what kept him going.

As she left the office, she threw him the key. "Lock up, Eddie, and give the key to Tania, that's if she ever turns up. She's thirty minutes late already."

Eddie nodded and sank into Veronica's soft leather chair. He rubbed his hands all over it, he could smell her musky perfume, it filled him with desire for her. Looking quickly through her drawer he spotted a small bottle of her distinct perfume. Slipping it into his pocket he envisaged spraying it on to his pillow that night and holding it tight to him, a little piece of her in his bed. He actually looked forward to going to bed that evening, his room would be filled with her aroma and her photograph would be on his bedside table.

It was unusual for Tania not to turn up, or to even bother ringing in. As Tania hadn't showed it was left to Lucy to greet the brothers and Stevo. "Good evening, your usual table?" She gave Stevo a sexy smile.

Gianni ignored her; he marched past the aghast staff and sat down in the middle of the room. It wasn't his usual table, he sat as close to the centre of the room as possible in full view of anyone coming or going.

Lucy looked a little awkward.

"Don't worry, just bring us a bottle over when you're ready." Stevo rubbed her arm.

"Sure." Lucy summoned Kyle over.

"Do you think he should be here?" Kyle enquired.

"It's just his way of dealing with it I suppose. Just get me his usual and please tell everyone to get back to work. All this staring will make Gianni snap if we are not careful and then God knows how he will react."

Kyle looked a little worried and quickly obeyed her. It was a very odd situation, he could feel the tension in the air. Tonight could turn out to be very interesting indeed.

Veronica waved over to the de Marcos and marched over to the waiting Lucy. "Where the devil is Tania?"

"Nobody knows and she hasn't called in either. Sarah suggested that I should take her place."

"Ok, I'll take the wine over." Veronica headed towards their table. "It's so nice to see you both, although I must admit that I am a little surprised."

"Surprised?" Gianni looked directly at her.

"I'm sorry, Gianni, I'm just saying what everyone is thinking."

Antonio was annoyed and it showed. Gianni put a hand on his arm. "No, it's alright, Veronica is right, it's human nature to wonder why I am here. You tell the staff that I will always mourn Felicia and that she was the love of my life, nothing will ever change that. Felicia was always the first one to tell me that life is for living and that we are only here for a short time and to enjoy every precious moment while we can."

"I'll be sure to convey your wishes." Veronica wasn't used to seeing this much softer, caring side to Gianni. She wished that he would be like this all the time, but she guessed it would be short-lived, he liked playing the hard man too much.

"So, it looks like no one knows about Tania then? What do you want to do?" Stevo aimed the question at Gianni.

"Let's eat first, then we'll tell Veronica, she can break the news to the staff when they knock off. I don't want to spoil my appetite."

"Whatever you say." Stevo knew he was a man on the edge and right now he was capable of anything.

Chapter Sixty Seven

Katie returned home feeling drained after the few hours she had spent with Nina. She felt so sorry for her and the children, it must be like a nightmare for the poor woman. Still she had left her with Lorraine Anderson and Diana Brookstein, the three of them had been friends for years. Nina had insisted that Katie stay but she felt a little awkward and made her excuses and left. Nina had her contact number and Katie told her that she was welcome to ring her anytime.

Just before Katie left her apartment she rang Antonio, he was at the club. "I've been to see Nina Valetti."

"You have, how was she?"

"How do you expect, she's just been widowed, left with two children to bring up on her own."

"I'm sorry, Katie, things are a bit frazzled at the moment, I'm with Gianni."

"Do you need me to come over?"

"No, it's alright, why don't you unpack and chill out tonight, I'll call you tomorrow." He put the phone down.

Jesus, what's with the cold shoulder? I see, she thought, he's had his wicked way and now he's dumping me. Katie was upset to say the least. Damn you then.

In her rage she took her shoes off and threw them across the room, nearly smashing the crystal vase as she did so. What the hell is up with that man? His mood swings drove her crazy. She switched on the radio as she rubbed her aching feet. Checking the fridge she found half a bottle of wine, good that will do.

She caught the end of the news... the woman has been named as Tania Horrocks. The police are appealing for witnesses, the bomb exploded at approximately 10.35am this morning in the Plaza underground car park.

Tania, Tania Horrocks, killed in a bomb explosion. Katie could scarcely believe it, if she hadn't heard it on the radio she would have thought she had imagined it! She hated the woman, it was true, but she wouldn't wish this on her worst enemy. She supposed that everyone in the club would know.

She picked up the phone and then put it down again. What would she say? Maybe it was better to go over in person. Having second thoughts she rang Antonio's office but it went straight on to his answer machine. She tried Veronica's number, no answer. Where the hell was everyone? Left with no choice she decided to go over in person. Dialling a cab she grabbed her coat and house keys.

"Club La Pregheira please," she told the driver as she fastened her seat belt. It seemed to take an age before she finally arrived. She thrust some cash into the cabbie's hand telling him to keep the change. She didn't really want to see Antonio in case he thought that she was stalking him or something and quite frankly she wasn't that desperate.

"Good evening, Miss Saunders, we weren't expecting you," Brian grinned at her.

"Can you get Veronica for me, but please be discreet, I don't want anyone to know that I'm here."

"Sure, no problem. Eddie can you locate Ms Lamont please and tell her to meet Miss Saunders at her office?" He spoke into the walkie talkie.

Eddie's distinctive voice came over. "I'll go and get her."

He had one of those bland voices, totally void of emotion. It was a weird high pitched unnatural sounding voice that gave her the shivers.

"Go ahead, miss, she'll be right with you."

"Ok, thanks, Brian."

"You're welcome." Now why couldn't Lucy speak to him like this, with respect. It was a pity he didn't fancy Katie, she was far too prim and proper for him. He always went after the unattainable ones. Well one day, not far from now, he would have his way with whomever took his fancy and right now Lucy was top of his list.

Katie was sitting outside Veronica's office when she finally arrived. "Evening, Katie, I wasn't expecting you, is everything alright?"

"Yes, no, I mean, no, not really."

"Explain, darling, explain." Veronica shooed her into the office.

"Well, I didn't want to bother Antonio and Gianni, I figured they needed time on their own and of course poor Gianni has enough to deal with."

"Katie, I haven't got the foggiest idea what you are trying to say to me."

"I'm sorry."

"Sorry, sorry about what?"

"Have you heard about Tania?"

"No, what has she done now?"

"She's dead!"

"What, what happened?"

"I just heard it on the radio, well the tail end of it that is!"

"Stop talking in riddles, Tania is dead?"

"Yes, some kind of bomb explosion."

Veronica switched the TV on and flicked through the channels until she found the news. It was true, Tania had been killed by a car bomb, it was showing her picture and not a very flattering one. The police were asking for any witnesses to come forward and the owner of the Plaza Hotel had offered a substantial reward. He obviously was concerned about losing potential customers.

"I always knew that there was something about that girl, but I could never quite put my finger on it. I told the de Marcos I thought she was trouble from the day she set foot in this place, but would they listen? No. Do they ever listen? No!"

"You know, I never liked her much either!"

"I'm sorry, Katie, I shouldn't really say that, I mean I wouldn't want you telling Antonio what I said."

"Don't worry about it, I would never say anything to get you into trouble."

"I don't think the de Marcos can know anything about Tania as they didn't mention anything to me, although they were all in a strange mood. I just put it down to the recent events."

"Maybe they know and just don't want to say anything in the middle of the club."

"No, they would have taken me to one side and told me, surely." Who was she kidding? The de Marcos kept their cards close to their chest and sometimes it was hard to know what any of them were thinking.

"So, is there anything I can do to help out?"

"Are you kidding me, Antonio would have my guts for garters if I made you work!"

"Oh, come on, Veronica, let me do something to help, you know I'm an excellent worker."

"Oh, I'm not sure."

"But you could do with the help, right?" Katie persisted.

"Yes, I could, but I don't want to upset Antonio!"

"Listen Veronica, I can handle Antonio, trust me." Katie wanted to show Antonio that she could stand on her own two feet. She wasn't going to be told what she could and couldn't do, she wasn't a child any more.

"Ok, you win, but I would prefer if you go into the restaurant out of the way."

"Are they eating tonight?"

"I don't think so, they haven't mentioned it, usually they phone ahead to let us know."

"Well, I think our secret will be safe then!"

"Have you done silver service before?"

"Er, sorry no!"

"Ok, you can meet the guests, show them to their table, give out the menus and then one of the other girls will take their order. How does that sound?"

"Sounds too easy. Why don't I take the orders too?"

"No, but you can go back to the tables and ask how the clients' meals were."

"You sure that's all I can do?"

"Yes, now what are you wearing under that coat?"

"Oh, a T-shirt and jeans."

"Oh, dear, come on let's go and see if we can find something more suitable." Veronica dragged her into the dancers' changing rooms. "Where's Alice at?" she asked one of the girls.

"Not here yet, she's not on until eight tonight."

"You're about the same size as Alice, we'll just have to help ourselves, I'm sure she won't mind if we borrow something."

"I think all her stuff may be a bit too fancy."

"Don't be silly, dear, come on let's have a rummage through her things."

Katie didn't really think that any of the clothes were suitable for hostessing. Veronica was piling garments into her hands.

"There must be something you like!" Veronica was becoming more and more exasperated, maybe the whole thing was a bad idea.

Katie spotted a black sequined dress on the rack. "Now, maybe this? What do you think?" She held it up to herself.

"Looking good, try it on, we've got thirty minutes until the first guests arrive in the restaurant."

Two minutes later Katie reappeared. The dress was like a second skin and fit her like a glove, it was long sleeved and a flattering knee length creation. As she walked the sequins dazzled in the light.

"Beautiful, shows your legs off to perfection. I think you better wear some stockings though." Alice walked in.

"Oops, Alice, sorry, I hope you don't mind!"

"It's alright, Katie, you actually suit it quite well." Alice came over to her. "What's the occasion?"

"Just going to help out in the restaurant for the evening."

"Oh? I thought Mr de Marco wouldn't allow you to?"

"God, news travels fast, just for the record I'm my own boss Alice and I'm only helping out."

"I hope you know what you are doing then!"

"I'm not frightened of Antonio." Katie was defiant. "I can please myself."

"He won't be happy if he sees you, mark my words. He doesn't like his women working."

"We'll I'm just about to change his way of thinking, but thanks for the warning."

Alice liked Katie, she was so different to Antonio's other girlfriends, maybe this is just what he needed.

"When are you going to tell the staff about Tania?" Katie whispered.

"I'll tell them later when they all knock off. Right now her name is mud as they are running around like blue arsed flies trying to keep up with the customers' orders!" Veronica laughed.

"Oh well, that's too bad!" Katie smiled.

Alice couldn't help but overhear. "What's all this then, Tania done a runner?"

212

"Oh shit, Alice, you weren't supposed to hear that." Veronica pulled a face. "I was going to tell everyone together."

"Well, you may as well tell me now that I'm here, I can keep a secret, trust me."

"I'm not doubting how trustworthy you are, Alice, it's just kind of delicate that's all."

"She hasn't robbed the tills has she?" Alice knew that Tania was the type of girl to do anything if there was money involved. "Or run off with one of our millionaire customers?"

"No, nothing like that, if only it were that simple."

"I think we should just tell her, Veronica." She would find out soon enough, no point in pretending nothing had happened.

"Yes, I have to admit, Katie, you're right. Ok, she was killed in that explosion this morning."

"What, you are joking aren't you?!"

"I wish I was, I'm afraid it is true."

"Oh, my God, how awful. I heard about that car bomb, but I don't understand she couldn't even drive."

"Yes, someone else was driving."

"Who? I didn't think she had any friends."

"Oh, I don't know, do you remember the guys name, Katie?"

"Ritchie somebody, I don't recall his surname."

"Ok girls, enough chit chat, we'll discuss this properly later. For now let's keep this between ourselves."

There was something about this young girl that Veronica liked and if Antonio was serious about her she wanted to keep her on side.

As Veronica watched Katie greeting the steady stream of customers she was amazed at how quickly she picked things up, she was a fast learner that was for sure. A clever young thing, she would be a real asset to the club, providing she didn't find out about her sideline! It seemed that Gianni had forgotten all about it, at least for the time being anyway. When he asked she would tell him that it was over and that would be the end of that! No money was passing hands in the club, it was all done privately. It was actually much better, the girls were paid by the clients and Veronica received her cut in the mail. It was nice and easy does it! Her retirement plan was back up and running.

Back in the bar the de Marcos and Stevo were relaxing and having a few drinks. It made a change for Stevo to be off duty, although he knew that he still had to keep an eye out for any potential situations that may arise.

"Gerald Newman's on the line, Antonio, can you have a word with him?" Veronica interrupted them.

"What? Is it urgent?" Gianni was not amused.

"He said so."

"Can't you see that we are trying to chill out here." Stevo could see that Gianni was getting wound up and was trying desperately to diffuse the situation.

Antonio followed her with Gianni in hot pursuit.

"Here, pass it to me." Antonio reached for the phone, but Gianni was too quick for him and snatched it out of Veronica's hand.

"What is it, man, and it better be worth disturbing our social evening."

Gerald didn't expect to hear Gianni's voice and tried to think of what to say. "I, I just wanted to remind you that I am off on holiday tomorrow, so if you need anything my stand in is Matthew Carmichael."

"Fuck me, is that all you're ringing for?"

"Er, yes, sorry to disturb you." Gerald rang off. He would get his trainee Matthew to break the news tomorrow after he had left the country. He felt a little bad about it, but it was better that Matthew told Antonio the news, maybe he would be easier on him as he was just the messenger.

"No more disturbances tonight, Veronica darling, hold all calls unless it is a dire emergency."

"Certainly Gianni." Veronica hated the bastard sometimes, even after the beating he gave her she still forgave him. He wasn't all bad, she kind of felt sorry for him, he'd been through hell lately. She continued to make allowances for his behaviour and accepted that he would be like this for some time to come. She would keep her head down, after all she had no intention of losing her status in this club. It was her lifeline and she was very important to the de Marcos as they were to her; they appreciated her excellent work and respected the way she handled any situation that occurred.

In the restaurant Katie was an instant hit. She went out of her way to strike up conversations with all the customers she met. Her confidence had grown and she felt totally at ease.

"Good evening, er Mr Breschnevsky? I hope I pronounced that correctly."

"Yes, that was perfect. And who are you then?" the silver haired gentleman asked her.

"My name is, Katie, and I am here to make sure that your evening is as enjoyable as possible. If you have any questions, please feel free to ask me."

"You are much too beautiful to be a hostess."

"You are very kind, Mr Breschnevsky, but I enjoy doing this."

"Yes, you look very much at home."

"Are you dining alone, sir?"

"No, I am expecting a young lady any time now."

"Oh, that's no problem, you booked ahead so we have a nice intimate table for you."

Sergio Breschnevsky chortled. "Oh, it is not what you think!"

"I'm sure it isn't, sir, let me show you to your table." Alarm bells were ringing in Katie's head.

So this was the girl Antonio had dumped his daughter for? She seemed so delicate, so sincere, it was no surprise really. Sasha was very highly strung, she was in fact more suited to Gianni. He hoped that they would get back together, that was the plan anyway. The sooner he got Sasha off his hands the better, he was getting older and it was becoming more difficult to deal with her these days. Anything for a quiet life, that's all he wanted. Sasha had been to see a counsellor and it seemed to be helping her, she had calmed down after several expensive sessions.

Katie was so busy she barely had time to catch her breath. Meeting and greeting was much more involved than she had anticipated. She was flitting from table to table with the chef's recommendations of the day and advising which was the best wine to have. Of course that was easy, it would have to be the de Marco label. Katie excelled, her manner was so endearing that the wine sales went through the roof.

The restaurant was heaving. Katie noticed that the silver haired gentleman was still on his own. "Would you like to order now, sir?"

"No, not yet, I'll give it another ten minutes or so," he insisted.

Katie nodded politely and made her way back to the greeting area.

"Boy, I'm hungry now, did you book a table, Antonio?" Gianni asked him.

"No, I need to go the gents so I'll check and see how busy it is on the way back." Antonio wasn't really very hungry, but he would make an effort if it meant that his brother was finally going to get a good solid meal inside him.

As he was taking a pee he recognised a voice in the background.

"Good to see you, Antonio." Sergio's distinctive Russian accent filled the air.

"Sergio? Why didn't you tell me you were coming?" Antonio pulled up his zip and began washing his hands.

"I wanted to surprise you of course."

"Well you have, how is Sasha?"

"She's better, she's been getting professional help."

"I'm glad to hear it."

"I just met Katie, she's some lady."

"Met her? Met her where, here?"

"Yes, she is doing a wonderful job in the restaurant. I'm afraid my date didn't show, so I must leave. But please thank her for the hospitality. She is a definite hit, hold on to her, Antonio."

"I intend to." Antonio was livid, what the hell was she doing here? He told her that he didn't want her working here anymore, what was she playing at, embarrassing him like this. "Are you staying long?"

"I wanted to stay for Felicia's funeral if Gianni will allow me."

"I think under the circumstances you should keep away."

Sergio sighed. "If that's what you wish." He shook his hand and left.

Antonio marched up the stairs to the restaurant. He was so angry he wanted to drag Katie right out of the building. As he got to the top of the stairs he saw her and all the anger drained from him. She was radiant and smiling, there was something special about her. Everyone just seemed to love her, her quiet nature, the way she presented herself. He was one lucky man that was for sure. Peter Hika was all over her; he was not impressed. The little shit may own a multi billion pound airline but that didn't give him automatic rights to his woman.

"Katie, darling." He pulled her to him. "How are you, Peter?"

"I was just saying what a wonderful job Katie was doing for you." Peter's voice trembled as he suddenly realised that she was more than just a hostess to Antonio. "Why don't you join me?"

"Maybe some other time, Peter, I'm with company tonight." Antonio was enjoying the look of discomfort on his face.

"I hope that I haven't offended you, Katie." Peter was panicking, hoping that he hadn't overstepped the mark.

"No, of course not, please enjoy your meal, you've made an excellent choice."

"Now, if you don't mind I need a word with my fiancée." Antonio blurted out the words, he couldn't help himself. He put an arm around her and whisked her off to the top of the stairs. "What are you doing?"

"Fiancée? How dare you, I haven't even accepted, just who do you think you are? You're not my keeper!" Katie was really annoyed with him.

"Katie, please don't cause a scene, sweetheart."

"Me, cause a scene, I would say that you are doing pretty well on your own."

"Why are you being like this?" Antonio was frustrated.

"You were a different person in Italy and now since we have came back you've been cold towards me."

"Darling, I'm sorry if you think that but it's just not true, there's things going on that you don't know about."

"What, like Tania?"

"What do you know about that?"

"It's all over the news, Antonio!"

"Is it?"

"So, you already knew then?" She looked into his steely blue eyes. "What the hell is going on here?"

"I don't know what you mean, Katie."

"What do you take me for, some kind of idiot?"

"Please, Katie, it's complicated."

"Complicated, just what are you mixed up in?"

"That's enough, Katie, people are looking." He was trying to stay calm, but she was really getting to him.

"I don't really give a damn, Antonio. Can't you see that I am working?"

216

"I'm sorry Katie I don't mean to upset you." He genuinely felt bad. "I do love you, you know that don't you."

Katie was dumbstruck, he had actually said the word, she didn't think he was capable. "Really? Then stop treating me like a child."

"There's nothing childlike about you, I can assure you." Antonio pushed open the side door and dragged her through it. He cupped her face in his hands and kissed her. "You've got to know that I would do anything for you, believe me."

"I do." Katie murmured as her lips parted allowing his tongue to explore. She arched her back and their bodies were entwined around each other. "Oh, Antonio, I have to get back, everyone will be wondering where I am!" She gently pushed him away.

"I want you." Antonio's husky voice sent shivers through her, the effect he had on her was scary. She had to resist him, there was no way she would let him make love to her on the stairs, anyone could walk in on them.

"Please, Antonio, not here, not now." She was half serious, half of her not really caring if they did make love there and then.

"You're right, I just can't resist you, you're so gorgeous and sexy."

"I don't understand you sometimes, when we are alone you're so different. It's like there is only me and you in the world."

"Ssh my darling." Antonio kissed her once more, he slipped his hand up her dress, feeling her smooth, pert buttocks. He lifted her up. "My God, stockings really turn me on."

"Antonio, please stop!" Katie protested. "Later!"

"Whatever you say, darling." Antonio gently put her down. He ran the back of his hand down her cheek. "I want you to stay with me tonight." His voice sounded so needing, so full of desire, how could she refuse him?

Katie couldn't believe the power she had over him, it was incredible to think that a man like him could be remotely interested in someone like her, love certainly was a strange thing.

"Let's get out of here before anyone notices we've gone missing."

"I have a better idea, stuff them all and come home with me right now."

Katie was seriously tempted to take him up on his offer. "Your priority is to look after Gianni, you know that. We've got all the time in the world."

Antonio sighed. "You're right, what am I thinking of?"

"Ok, let's be sensible then, at least for tonight."

Katie's cheeky grin was sending Antonio into overdrive, no one had ever affected him in this way. "But, baby, I hate being sensible."

"Bye, Antonio." And with that Katie slipped back into the restaurant hoping that no one had noticed her disappearing act.

Antonio laughed, she was something else, his Katie, and he wasn't ever going to lose her.

217

Two minutes later Antonio appeared and made his way back to his table.

Veronica had seen everything, dear God, she thought they can't keep their hands off each other. And she had to admit that they made a very fine couple indeed.

"Sasha, where were you? I was so disappointed that you never turned up." Sergio Breschnevsky was not in the least bit amused.

"Oh, Nana, I am sorry, really I am. I couldn't face it, seeing them together, I really messed up, didn't I?"

"My dear, you are coping really well, your therapist said that facing this head on will help you move on."

"Nana, have you been talking to my therapist?"

"Only in passing, my dear."

"You want me to grow up, yet you continue to smother me. I can't stand it, I don't need you to tell me what to do!"

Sergio was relieved, this was the Sasha he knew and loved so well, her fighting talk was back. "I saw Antonio, very briefly."

"Oh, yes, and?"

"I think we should stay away from the funeral."

"But Felicia was a friend of mine!"

"I don't care, just send a card to Gianni, he will appreciate that."

"Ok, whatever you say."

"Good, that's settled then. If you play your cards right Gianni will take you back, he is very vulnerable at the moment and affection is what he needs."

Sasha smiled. "Of course Nana, I know him remember."

"Of course." Sergio agreed with her. "But you have to be very sincere in everything you do, your future depends upon it."

"Don't worry Nana, I know how to play it."

"We've had an exceptional night of wine sales thanks to you, Katie!" Veronica was very impressed, the takings were much higher than usual.

"I actually enjoyed myself."

"I noticed! You were a complete natural! I saw Antonio come in."

"Oh, did you?" Katie went crimson.

"I suppose he told you not to work here any more?"

"As a matter of fact he did. But I told him I'll do what I want!"

Veronica laughed. "Good for you, my girl, Antonio needs someone to stand up to him!"

"Did I hear my name mentioned?" Antonio sneaked up behind them.

"I'm just congratulating Katie on the massive sales of the de Marco wine we sold tonight."

"Oh, yes, I didn't know that we had a wine connoisseur in the house, apart from me of course!"

"I'm sure that Katie could give you a run for your money."

"Perhaps, but don't get too used to it, she won't be here much longer!"

"What do you mean?" Katie hated it when he treated her like a possession. "You don't own me, Antonio, and you never will."

Antonio was shocked that Katie had spoken to him like that in front of Veronica, of all people. He was lost for words.

"I'm just going to get changed, Veronica, what time do you want me tomorrow?" Katie was defiant.

"Er, I'll check the bookings and let you know before you leave."

"You'll do no such thing!" Antonio put his foot down. "I'll decide what's best for my staff and Katie, you know that you shouldn't be working, I won't allow it!"

"Won't allow it? Who the hell do you think you are?" Katie was becoming more annoyed. "I've got to go!" God he was so irritating, sometimes she could just slap him, at times he was so old fashioned. Being a perfect gentleman was part of his charm, but not when he treated her in this way and not when they had an audience.

Veronica didn't know where to look, it was so embarrassing watching them at each other's throats. "I need to cash up, so if you don't mind I'll leave you to it." She made a quick exit, there was no way she wanted to be involved in a lovers' spat.

"Katie." Antonio tried to hold her hand but she pulled away from him.

"I've got to go!"

"But what about tonight?"

"What about it, Antonio," Katie stormed off. She was sick of his goddamn attitude, if this is what he was going to be like then he could stick it. What an arrogant pig of a man he was, marriage, marriage to him, he must be joking. No wonder he couldn't keep hold of a woman. Sasha may have enjoyed spending his hard-earned cash, but she wasn't going to live off anyone!

As she entered the changing room Lucy was coming out.

"Everything ok?"

"Yes, fine."

"You don't look it and you don't sound it either, what's wrong?"

"Oh nothing much, just met Sasha's father in the restaurant and then had a fall out with the lord and master!"

"Jesus, are you ok?" Lucy was concerned to hear the anger in Katie's voice.

"I'm ok, just annoyed with bloody Antonio, he's a pain in the arse sometimes!"

"You ready, Miss Saunders?" Fred stuck his head around the door.

"Ready, ready for what?" she snapped back at him.

"I've got the car waiting for you."

Poor Fred, she was taking it out on him. "I'll be there in a minute, sorry, Fred."

He smiled at her and tipped his hat. "No problem."

"What are you doing?" Lucy couldn't understand what she was playing at.

"The lord and master beckons, but he hasn't counted on my reaction!"

"What are you going to do?"

"Give him a great big piece of my mind, that's what!"

"Oh, God, please be careful, you don't know what he will do!"

"Jesus, Lucy, he's only a man, he's not indestructible."

Lucy took a deep breath and shook her head, she hoped that Katie hadn't misjudged Antonio. The de Marcos were very dangerous and they were capable of anything. They didn't take shit from anyone, especially not a woman.

Antonio was already in the limo. Gianni and Stevo had decided to go crazy in the casino and spend the night in the hotel down the street. Perfect, he could have Katie and the apartment all to himself.

The door opened and Katie got in. She was wearing blue faded denim jeans and a white t shirt, but still looked a picture of elegance. "You would look fabulous in a bin bag!"

"What? Antonio, I am so mad with you!"

"I just mean, that you look beautiful no matter what you wear."

"Stop changing the subject." Katie was exasperated with him.

"What is it?"

"Are you seriously telling me that you don't know?" Katie tapped on the window in front of her. The electric window came down.

"Yes?"

"I would like to go home now, please, Fred."

"It's ok, Fred, I'll sort this out, just carry on."

Fred immediately put the window back up and headed for Antonio's apartment. Oh dear, this must be their first row he thought, he hoped that it wasn't serious as he had become attached to Katie. It would be a shame if it was over before it really started.

"Antonio, please stop trying to control me, I won't have it!"

"Ok, calm down, darling. Whatever makes you happy is fine with me." Antonio had to backtrack, she certainly was a feisty little thing and much more than he had bargained for.

"So, you'll tell Veronica to re-hire me?"

"Of course, there now, all sorted."

"What, just like that?"

"Yes, just like that." He reached over to her and cupped her face in his hands. "Now, bella, let's not fight anymore." He kissed her and she tried to push him away, but she didn't resist him for long.

They were going to have an uninterrupted night of passion and he was looking forward to every intimate moment of pleasure.

Chapter Sixty Eight

"Can we place any of these fuckers at the crime scene?" DC Fearon had just been told that the male victim was Ricardo Calvi, originally from La Pregheira in Italy, the same place as the de Marcos; surely this was no coincidence.

"Ok, what do we have? Everything seems to be connected to the de Marcos. Number one, Vince Fraser is found murdered and dumped, allegedly because he was mixed up in some local drug racket. Number two, Felicia Carmine is asphyxiated after a burglary gone wrong or was it something more sinister? Number three, Roberto Valetti is arrested on suspicion of drug smuggling through his import, export business. Later on that day he commits suicide in his cell, does that make him guilty or a very worried man? Number four, Henry Brookstein's art gallery is mysteriously burnt to the ground, was it arson or faulty electricals? Number five, Tania Horrocks is blown to smithereens in the same car as Ricardo Calvi, what's the connection?"

DC Fearon had the names of the victims written on to the whiteboard. He reached for the black marker and began drawing lines on the board.

"Ok, for those of you not listening, pay attention now. Vince Fraser was the manager of La Piacenza in Manchester, owned by, yes you guessed it, the de Marcos." He quickly drew the line between Fraser and the de Marcos.

"Felica Carmine, fiancée of, yes you guessed it, Gianni de Marco." Again he swiftly drew the line between the connections.

"Roberto Valetti is a known business associate of, yes the de Marcos." DC Fearon was like a man possessed. He pulled his handkerchief from his pocket and mopped his brow. "Henry Brookstein, another business associate." DC Fearon was pink and breathless. "Tania…" He couldn't get his words out, clutching his chest he fell to the floor.

DS McAllister had been watching and listening intently, Fearon had really lost it, what was he trying to prove? It was a well known fact that he detested the de Marcos. He was old school and believed that the de Marcos had taken over part of his beloved town. The whole station had listened to his ramblings for years and it was now wearing a bit thin. He had come to tell Fearon that he was taking him off the case, but unfortunately for Fearon nature had taken him off it. He would report back to Chief Superintendent Frank Mason. There were no real resources to go traipsing off to Italy to dig up the de Marcos' past and no resources to bring every member of the de Marcos' staff and known associates in for questioning. The money would be better spent on a new police station in another borough where he would be the next Chief Superintendent.

The ambulance arrived. DC Fearon never made it to the hospital and was pronounced dead on route.

Chapter Sixty Nine

Matthew Carmichael reluctantly made his way to the apartment, he was dreading this meeting. He had tried to ring ahead but to no avail, it was only nine in the morning but he knew that Antonio would not have left home yet. He rang the intercom button.

"Yes?" The voice boomed back.

"Er, I'm here on behalf of Gerald Newman, I have some news."

"Ok, come on up." Antonio buzzed the door open for him.

Katie had just got out of the shower and was wearing one of his dressing gowns, she looked good enough to eat.

"Have you got any juice?"

"Sure, help yourself, I'll put the coffee on."

"I'm kind of hungry, where's your bread at?"

"Me too, we certainly worked up an appetite, that's for sure."

Katie blushed remembering every single caress and her moans of pleasure.

"You shouldn't be embarrassed, my darling, you were amazing." He passed her the bread out of the cupboard.

Katie popped it into the toaster and waited patiently. She was in the middle of buttering it when Antonio grabbed a slice. "Hey, that was mine."

The doorbell was ringing. "Aren't you going to get that?" Katie pulled the toast out of his mouth and started chomping on it, the butter was dripping on to her face. Antonio kissed her.

"The door, Antonio."

They were giggling at one another, they had melted butter and crumbs all down their faces. As Antonio opened the door he began to wipe the tell tale marks from his lips.

"Good morning, Mr de Marco, I'm here regarding the results of Felicia Carmine's autopsy."

Katie nearly fainted, she recognised that voice.

"And you are?"

"Matthew Carmichael." He shook Antonio's hand.

Oh God, he was going to see her, there was no way she could get to the bedroom without being spotted, what a nightmare. Katie braced herself for Matt's reaction.

"Please, come in."

Matt was shocked to see Katie, especially in an oversized dressing gown, that was obviously not hers. Antonio noticed him looking at her. "This is my beautiful girlfriend, Katie."

Matt could barely look at her. "Er, yes I know."

"Oh, have you two met before?"

"Antonio, this is Lucy's brother." Katie heard herself say the words, she didn't say he was also her ex-boyfriend.

"I'll leave you to it then." She didn't want to hang around, it was so embarrassing. She felt that she was betraying him all over again.

"Do you usually have an effect like that on women?" Antonio laughed.

"I think you better sit down, Gerald wanted me to tell you this in person." His hands were sweating as he tried to explain.

Antonio didn't like this one little bit, there was something about Felicia's death that he wasn't sure he wanted to know about.

"The cause of death was asphyxiation as we were already aware of." Matt paused. "I'm just going to come out and say this, Felicia was pregnant, the Coroner estimates six weeks."

Antonio was so stunned he couldn't speak.

"I'm sorry to put it so bluntly, if there's nothing else, I'll see myself out."

"Wait, who else knows about this?"

"The Coroner, Gerald, me and now you. The report hasn't been typed up yet, why?"

"I need to speak to the Coroner immediately, come on."

Antonio scribbled a note and left it on the table for Katie. "Had to nip out on urgent business, back asap. Love you, Antonio".

Matt felt sick to the pit of his stomach, what was Katie doing falling for this man? And what did he want from the Coroner. He didn't want to be involved in this, it was bound to be something illegal. Why had he been assigned to Gerald Newman, wasn't he suffering enough? Now he was too close for comfort, it broke his heart all over again.

They arrived at the Coroner's office unannounced. The girl on reception was filing her nails. Antonio banged his fists on the desk making her jump with fright. "I need to speak with the Coroner right now."

"Do you have an appointment?"

Matthew stepped in, being angry wouldn't get them into the office. He flashed the girl a big smile. "Please, it is very important that we speak with him."

The girl smiled back at him. "Let me see what I can do, seeing you asked so nicely." She shot Antonio a disgusted look.

"Who shall I say?"

Matt passed his business card.

"I have a Matthew Carmichael here from Jacksons Solicitors, he says that it's urgent." The girl nodded as she listened to the response. "He can only spare literally five minutes, he's a very busy man you know." She showed them to Mr Edward's office. She carefully put the business card in her purse and planned to call this handsome young solicitor.

Antonio was trying to appeal to the Coroner. "All I'm asking for you to do, is just to miss out the pregnant part."

"I cannot do that, I can't withhold any information from the police." Mr Edwards was adamant. "Do you realise what you are asking me to do?"

"Mr Carmichael, would you mind giving us a minute here?"

Matt nodded his head, grateful that he didn't have to listen to whatever they said, he wanted no part of it. He waited patiently outside, the young girl from the front desk waved over to him and he waved back.

Antonio emerged ten minutes later. He and Mr Edwards were laughing and joking as if they had known each other for years. As they shook hands Antonio passed his business card to him. "Just ring ahead and I'll arrange one of the best tables for you and your wife."

"Certainly, it was a pleasure doing business."

"How did you manage to change his mind so quickly?" Matt wondered if they did a secret handshake or something in there, maybe that's why he wanted him to wait outside.

"I convinced him it was for the best." Antonio stopped on the steps outside. "How good are you at keeping secrets, Mr Carmichael?"

Matt didn't like his tone, it was quietly threatening. "I signed a clause for the law firm which prevents me from discussing anything outside the office other than with the clients of course."

"Of course, I'm glad that we understand each other." He went to shake Matt's hand, his grip was tight. "Gianni must never know about this, ever."

There were no words needed, Matt knew that he would keep his mouth firmly shut.

"Can I give you a lift back to your car?"

"I'll pick it up later, I have a few things to do." Matt had seen and heard enough of this man, he didn't like him one little bit. Who did he think he was, God, or something? He just thought he could click his fingers and get whatever he wanted from people.

"Suit yourself." And with that Antonio vanished around the corner.

Matt was left standing on the steps. Why couldn't he just tell his brother the truth, surely he deserved to know? He would want to know if it was him! Would he, he asked himself, if the woman he loved was murdered then it would kill him all over again if he was told that she had been pregnant too? Perhaps Antonio's heart was in the right place, it was possible that just maybe he was trying to protect his brother. He had to admit that if he was in the same situation he would probably do exactly the same thing.

Chapter Seventy

There were three funerals that week all very different. The first one was Tania Horrocks; her father came for her remains and had her swiftly cremated. There was no announcement of her death in the newspapers and there was only him and his wife in attendance.

Roberto's funeral was all over the press and the paparazzi were desperate for photos of the event. The service took place in a private chapel and the hearse was driven into the family grounds which were surrounded by security fences away from prying eyes. Nina had broken down and collapsed in the church, unable to finish her husband's eulogy; the vicar took over. Katie had rushed to her aid and together with Diana Brookstein and Lorraine Anderson's help they managed to get through that horrendous day. Antonio had noticed Katie's way with people and how they respected it, especially at a time like this. He didn't hang around for fear of upsetting Nina, she was angry with him and still wouldn't take any of his calls. He had made a considerable private donation and hoped that in some way it would make up for her loss.

Then came the day of Felicia's funeral. It was all rather bizarre. Gianni had insisted on everything being in white. The announcement in the paper had said that anybody not wearing white would be turned away. This was Gianni's way of saying goodbye to his beloved wife to be. Felicia was buried in her wedding dress, which nobody would get to see apart from the undertakers. The flowers were white lilies and at the graveside two white doves were released. Throughout the whole ordeal Gianni stared into space, he couldn't speak to anyone. The whole day was far from a typical funeral, whatever that was, Katie thought.

At the wake, there was a three-tiered wedding cake. Gianni stood up. "Please can I have a bit of hush, we are going to cut the cake now."

The room fell deathly silent. Nobody dared utter a word, Gianni must have totally flipped, yet he was acting so calm.

"The lovely Mrs Carmine will cut the cake with me, I want you all to enjoy, it was made especially by our cake maker and close family member, Francesca, who has came all the way from Italy!"

Antonio began to clap loudly and everyone followed suit. Katie nudged him. "Is he going to be ok?"

"Yes, he'll be fine, he just needs to get this day over with."

Katie glanced over to Lucy and shrugged her shoulders. Antonio had not told her quite what to expect, but it was the most bizarre thing she had ever witnessed in her entire life.

The music began to play and the tune was 'Nights in White Satin'. The lights were dimmed and Gianni took to the dance floor with Felicia's mother. The record seemed to go on for an age.

All of a sudden Billy Idol blared out. The song was familiar to Katie, it was a punky sounding song called 'It's a nice day for a white wedding'.

Katie couldn't bear it any longer and feigned a headache. Antonio summoned Fred and asked him to take Katie home and then to take the rest of the night off.

Lucy too made her excuses and left. This suited the guys as all they wanted to do was get pissed and reminisce about the good times.

Once safely inside their apartment the girls burst out laughing. "God, I feel bad, I shouldn't be laughing."

"I know what you mean, but it was so surreal, I mean I was cringing the whole time. I had to keep pinching myself to see if I was dreaming!" Katie cracked open a bottle of wine.

"My feet are killing me in these stupid stilettos!"

"I'll have to introduce you to Fran and Alfredo, they are lovely people, you will really like them."

"Yeah, but it's a real shame to meet them under these circumstances."

"Do you think they will ever get anyone for Felicia's murder?" Katie was pensive.

"I doubt it, crimes like that are usually solved within forty eight hours, any longer and there isn't much of a chance," Lucy informed her.

"Oh, yeah and how would you know?"

"Matt of course, we do talk from time to time you know!"

"Matt? How is he doing?"

"Great he's got his first murder case starting next week. He's defending some rich bitch who's been accused of bumping off her husband for his fortune."

"Wow, he must be thrilled. What's his chances of winning, did she do it?"

"He assures me that she is innocent and therefore he has an excellent chance of getting her off, pity we couldn't go and watch! It's a family affair and they have asked for it to remain out of the public domain!"

"I'm sure he will do brilliantly!"

"Hey, when I pop my clogs I'll just have a regular funeral please!" Lucy began to giggle, she couldn't stop thinking about Felicia's bizarre send off.

"Yeah, me too."

Chapter Seventy One

It was New Years Eve and the party was in full swing. The de Marcos had pulled out all the stops to make it the best night that the city had ever seen. They were determined to get over the past few months of hell that they had all endured, especially Gianni and Nina Valetti. It had taken a while for Katie to persuade her to attend the event but she was like a new woman since they had gone into business together courtesy of Antonio. He had Gerald Newman on the case and had managed to overturn the ruling of the freeze of Roberto's assets. The share of the business was an engagement gift to Katie; she had surprised Nina with her keen interest in Italian handmade furniture and the business was ticking over nicely.

Gianni had long since forgotten about Honey but somehow she had managed to obtain a ticket for the night's event, she was really looking forward to seeing how he was and hoping that now he was a free agent she could move in for the kill.

Sergio had persuaded Antonio that Sasha had attacked Katie after she had suffered some kind of breakdown and promised that she wanted to make amends. He had told Katie all about it and with her forgiving nature she had agreed to let her attend. She was the happiest woman alive right now and nothing was going to spoil her moment.

Katie was delighted to see Alfredo and Fran Carbone, it had been a total surprise.

"My little bambino, it has only been four months and you look absolutely radiant, come, let us go and talk and catch up with everything that has been happening since I last saw you." And with that Fran pulled her to the other side of the room.

"I'm so glad that you are here, it's really made my evening."

"Ah, but it has only just begun, maybe there will be a few more surprises in store for you. Antonio has done wonders for you." Fran's voice was full of joy. Antonio was like a son to her and now Katie would be her daughter-in-law. "So, tell me how did he propose to you?"

Katie giggled. "Well, you know how impulsive he can be."

"Yes, yes, please put me out of my misery."

"I can't believe you haven't heard, no one can stop talking about it!"

"My dear, I have only been in the country for less than an hour!"

"Well, yesterday he dragged me out on to the balcony, it was freezing and I only had my dressing gown on!"

"Oh, please get on with it!" Fran was so excited.

"He pointed up at the sky and a small airplane was flying over with this huge banner attached to it. It said, 'Katie Saunders marry me' with a huge red heart next to it." She sighed remembering how she felt at that exact moment. He had promised that he would propose to her officially but she had never dreamt that it would be like that.

"How fantastically romantic, then what?" Fran was all ears.

"Then he pulled out this whopping diamond ring, got down on one knee and asked me." Katie flashed the ring. It was encrusted with fifty diamonds, set on a gold and platinum band.

"Yes?"

"Oh, Fran, you really do want all the details don't you? Do you know how many times I have told this story?" Katie loved relating the events of the previous morning.

"Ooh, it just makes me feel so jealous."

"I couldn't possibly tell you the rest!" Antonio had scooped her up into his arms and threw her on the bed and they had sealed their betrothal with fast, hard love making. She could still smell him on her, even though they had gotten into the Jacuzzi and filled it with bubbles. They had washed each other down and slowly made love, savouring every inch of each other.

Fran hugged her. "Antonio is an extremely lucky man, you will be wonderful together of that I am totally sure."

"Do you mind if I sneak my fiancée away now?" Antonio cut in. He was wearing a sharp Italian designer suit and was beaming from head to toe.

"My, you look very dashing, Antonio, you should have met Katie a long time ago!"

"Ah, but then I would have been called a cradle snatcher." He was ten years her senior.

"I will go and mingle with your other guests."

"I suppose she grilled you for all the little details," he laughed. "We must go to our table now, my little brother is going to give a speech before the meal."

Oh dear, she hoped that Gianni wasn't drunk for once. She cringed at the thought of what he would say, he was extremely outspoken and no doubt his speech would be straight to the point. It was a shame that she hadn't been able to get hold of her father, despite leaving messages all over the place. His cruise should have been finished over a week ago, but still nothing.

"You aren't worried about Gianni?"

"Don't be silly, I know he loves you and would never embarrass you." Who I am kidding she thought, Gianni wouldn't care these days.

"Antonio, the press are here, are you ready?" Stevo asked him, he hated the press with a vengeance.

"Yes, is it Adrian Carter?" Antonio liked him, he always wrote very favourably about his family and the businesses.

"He's waiting in the foyer for you, he wants a few shots of you and Katie."

230

Antonio looked around to see where she had disappeared to. His heart sank when he saw her talking to Sasha. He hoped she wasn't going to pull any stunts, especially today.

"Do you want me to go and get her?"

"No, I'll go." Damn it, what the hell was she saying to his fiancée.

"Oh, Antonio, I was just telling Katie how wonderful she looks and of course I have apologised profusely for that horrendous incident." Sasha smiled sweetly.

He knew that tone and mannerism, she hadn't changed at all, he should never have listened to Sergio. "Come, we have an important meeting."

"It's so nice to see you, Antonio, you look as dashing as ever."

Antonio took a glass of champagne from the waitress and passed it to Sasha. "Then you won't mind if we have to leave you, enjoy."

He took Katie's arm and whisked her down the stairs to the waiting press officer. "Adrian, good to see you." Antonio shook his hand. "This is Katie."

"You are much more beautiful than he described you." Adrian shook her hand. "Now, I would like to take a couple of photos before the party gets into full swing."

"Sure, how about one on the stairs?"

They stood at the foot of the stairs. Katie was wearing a red off the shoulder satin dress and Antonio wore a suit with a red tie. They complemented each other, both dark haired and immaculately groomed. "Katie can you put your hand on Antonio's chest, so that we can see the ring."

Katie obliged and smiled up into Antonio's eyes. "Perfect don't move." Adrian snapped away. "Now, I would love to take one of you in front of the fountain if it's not too cold for you."

Veronica handed Katie a black velvet stole. "This will help keep the cold out."

"Oh, thank you, Veronica."

"You're welcome."

It was bitter outside and it was starting to snow. Antonio rubbed Katie's shoulders and kissed her on the cheek. "I love you."

"I love you too."

"Come on you two young love birds before we freeze to death!" Adrian laughed as he snapped away. "Perfect, that's all I need."

"Good."

"Have you set a date for the wedding yet?"

"We are thinking next summer, in La Pregheira." Antonio informed him.

"Can I quote that?"

"Sure, why not. Now, I really must get my fiancée back inside."

"Don't you think we should discuss the wedding venue together?" Katie asked him once they were back inside the building.

"It's perfect for us my darling. Anyway lets go and enjoy ourselves, we'll talk about it later."

It was exhausting chatting to everyone; all Katie wanted to do was blend into the background. She hated being the centre of attention, it overwhelmed her.

"There's a phone call for you, Katie," Lucy told her. "In the office."

"A phone call for me? Are you sure?"

Lucy nodded. "Yes, I'm sure."

"Who is it?"

"I don't know, Veronica just asked me to tell you."

It all sounded a bit mysterious to Katie, who could possibly be phoning her? "Veronica's office you say?"

Lucy was becoming a little bit frustrated by all the questions, it was as if Katie knew something was going on.

Katie waved over to Antonio and made her way to Veronica's office. She knocked on the door and waited for Veronica to answer.

"Come in."

It was a man's voice, which sounded very familiar. Katie slowly opened the office door and popped her head around the corner. She recognised those broad shoulders and silver receding hair. She put her hand to her mouth and gasped in astonishment. "Is… Is it really you?"

"Yes, it's really me, come here and give your old dad a hug."

She ran into his arms, trying to hold back the tears.

"Don't cry, you silly thing." He pushed her gently from him. "Here let me have a look at you. You look wonderful, Antonio must be doing you the world of good."

"Antonio, what do you know about him?"

"I know that he loves you immensely and can't wait to marry you."

"But, I don't understand."

"He contacted me and invited me here as your special guest."

"But, Dad, I left you all sorts of messages and nothing."

"I know, I felt really bad about that but Antonio persuaded me to turn up unexpectedly, he said that it would make your day even more perfect. Now show me this fabulous engagement ring of yours."

Katie proudly showed him the dazzling ring.

"Beautiful, just like you."

"Oh, Dad, I'm so glad that you are here, it's a brilliant surprise." Katie paused. "But what about your lady friend?"

"Don't worry about that just now, I'm here for you. All I ever wanted was for you to settle down and be happy, I always thought that it would have been with Matt though."

Katie still felt a little guilty about him. "So did I, but Antonio has changed my life."

"Yes, I can see that."

"You must tell me all about your cruise and all the wonderful places that you have visited."

"All in good time, now let's go and join your guests." He took her arm and they headed back to the function room.

Lucy ran over. "Mr Saunders, my God you look very well, that tan suits you."

"Lucy, my dear girl, come and give me a hug."

Lucy obliged and linked his other arm. "So, this was the surprise guest," she giggled.

Antonio saw them all together and could see that he had made both girls very happy, it pleased him.

"Mr Saunders, come and meet my brother, but first let me get you a glass of champagne." He whisked him off towards the waiter.

"I can't believe it," Lucy told her.

"Me neither, I wonder how long he will stay for."

"Don't worry about that, just be glad that he made it."

"Oh, I am Lucy, I am."

The atmosphere was filled with joy and laughter, the music played and the drink flowed, it was a perfect evening.

Gianni was knocking back the champagne, preparing to give his little speech. Stevo was trying to find out what he intended to say as per Antonio's instructions, but so far had been unable to sneak the paper out of his inside jacket.

"You better slow down, Gianni, you don't want to be incoherent when you come to read the speech."

"I'm ok," Gianni hiccupped.

"Come on, let me get you some coffee."

Gianni reluctantly agreed with Stevo. He was a good mate, a mate for life and he relied upon him a lot these days.

Time was getting on and Antonio decided to say a few words. He asked the DJ to turn off the music and put the lights up. "Can I have everyone's attention."

The room fell silent. "Now, where is she?" Antonio but his hand over his eyes and searched the room. "Ah, there you are, come up here."

Oh God, she hated these moments, at least she didn't feel so nervous after a few glasses of bubbly.

"I would just like to say a few words, if I may." He put his arm around her tiny waist. "Katie has decided that she can never love another and will be at my beck and call for the rest of her life."

Raucous laughter filled the room.

"Seriously, I am delighted she accepted and promise to treat her like a princess for the rest of her life. To the future Mrs Antonio de Marco." He raised his glass. "Katie."

"To the future Mrs Antonio de Marco, Katie." Voices boomed around the entire room and glasses clinked. The guests were all on their feet applauding their newfound happiness.

"I would also like to say a few words," Katie's father announced. "I have only met Antonio briefly and he has certainly impressed me with his finesse and of course his choice in women, namely my beautiful daughter Katie. I wish them every happiness. To Katie and Antonio."

Once more the crowded room applauded and raised their glasses in another toast. Everyone was having a marvellous time and admiring the handsome couple in front of them.

"Are you sure you want to say something, Gianni," Stevo whispered to him as he followed him, pushing their way through the crowd.

Before he had a chance to stop him Gianni was on the stage alongside his brother. "Now I think it is time I said something." He pulled the scrumpled piece of paper from his jacket pocket and cleared his throat.

"No need for an essay, Gianni," Antonio laughed.

The room fell silent not, sure whether to join in the laughter as Gianni was unpredictable especially when he had had a few drinks.

Gianni laughed. "Ok, then, bro, I will give you the short version." He tore the piece of paper up and threw it on the floor. "I am delighted in my brother's choice and wish them all the luck, love and happiness in the world. I have grown fond of Katie and wouldn't mind her as my own wife." He paused waiting for the reaction.

There were a few gasps and shocked faces in the room.

"Naah, just kidding, no offence but she ain't really my type! To the beautiful Katie and of course my gorgeous brother, who I might add gets his good looks off me! To Antonio and Katie."

Stevo was relieved, he was piecing together the discarded speech. Jesus if Antonio had seen exactly what his brother had planned to say he would have thrown him out on his ear. He stuffed it into his pocket.

A gong echoed loudly. "Dinner is ready to be served if everyone would like to make their way into the restaurant please," Veronica announced, pleased that so far everything was going to plan. It was nine pm and she hoped that the meal would be over before eleven pm. That would give her staff time to clean up and join everyone to bring in the New Year.

Sitting around the table were Antonio and Katie, her father James, Gianni and Sasha, Stevo and Lucy, Ralph and Lorraine Anderson, Diana and Henry Brookstein and Fran and Alfredo Carbone and Nina Valetti. She had only turned up because Katie had pleaded with her and as they were now business partners, thanks to Antonio, Nina was prepared to make the small sacrifice.

Sasha was all over Gianni and he appeared to be loving the attention, hopefully it would be fleeting, Antonio thought. If this was the new refined Sasha then you could bet your life it wouldn't last long and together she and his brother were dangerous. They definitely brought out the worst in each other.

"Penny for them," Katie leaned over.

"Just happy."

After Antonio had introduced Katie's father to his closest friends he settled down to the sumptuous meal. Nicholas had surpassed himself this time, the food was exquisite, broccoli and stilton soup for starters with freshly baked rolls.

He liked Katie's father, he was the down to earth type, not short of a bob or two either, which always impressed him.

The restaurant was buzzing and Nicholas was in his element, he was always at his happiest when he was in the kitchen. He was rushed off his feet, there were one hundred guests to feed that evening and everything was perfect.

"So, Nina, you are in business with my daughter, Italian furniture no less."

"Yes, she's quite the natural. It is a new partnership but with our connections we are doing just fine. Everything is handmade and comes over from Milan…"

Sasha was draped all over Gianni, rubbing his hand and whispering into his ear. "Darling, we need to somehow celebrate the New Year, do you have any suggestions?"

"I could think of a few!"

Fran was in deep conversation with Katie. "You must let me help you with all the wedding arrangements, I know this dressmaker…"

"Trust Fran, anyone would think that it was her getting married!" Alfredo laughed. "Now, Antonio, tell me what is this Sasha woman doing back on the scene?"

"It's a long story…" Antonio began.

"Are you having fun?" Stevo asked Lucy.

"Oh, yes, I sure am, and this dress you bought me was a great choice, it really suits me don't you think?"

"It does, but you'll look even better out of it later!"

Ralph and Henry were discussing business as usual, while their wives chatted about holidays and designer clothes.

It was a superb evening, the best New Year ever, Katie thought as she glanced around her. She felt extremely privileged to be in such company.

The waitresses scurried around like little ants quickly removing plates and topping up empty glasses. Dessert was being served and the dishwashers were working like the clappers in the kitchen.

Nicholas was pleased to see clean plates coming back, these people appreciated good food that was for sure.

"Well done darling, you are an absolute hit in the restaurant. Antonio has promised a fat bonus for all your hard work and the day off tomorrow. We should do something nice."

"Veronica, I would go to the ends of the earth for you, my darling, but nothing would suit me better than cooking us an intimate dinner at your place, followed by a dip in your Jacuzzi."

"Ooh, Nicholas, you do say the nicest of things."

It was almost midnight and the guests were all assembled in the bar area, all ready with their glasses.

"Ten, nine, eight, seven, six, five, four, three, two, one... Happy New Year!"

Streamers and balloons were released from a net attached to the ceiling above the restaurant and poppers went off simultaneously all across the room. Voices in unison began to sing Auld Lang Syne. "May old acquaintance be forgot..."

A couple of days later and Katie's father returned to Sydney. It was a tearful farewell, but he assured her that he would be back for the wedding and hoped that they would spend part of the honeymoon with him.

Sasha was well and truly under Gianni's skin, he couldn't keep his hands off her. Now all she had to do was persuade him to talk to her father. Gianni liked danger and it would make him the man he once was, full of fight and determination.

Chapter Seventy Two

"And where do you think you are going, il mio te soro?"

"To the store, where else?"

"Can Nina not manage by herself today?"

"No, Antonio. You gave me a share in the business and I want to do my bit. I don't want to be a sleeping partner, I want to play an active part, besides I have some ideas I want to run past Nina."

"Oh, yes?"

"Never you mind. What are you up to today?" Katie changed the subject.

"I have a meeting with Ralph and some business associates."

"Oh, what will you be discussing?"

"Why?" Antonio was inquisitive, wondering why she wanted to know.

"No reason, just trying to show an interest in your business, that's all."

"We are going to discuss plans for building a new hotel."

"Hmm, what kind of hotel?"

"Obviously it is going to have an Italian influence, but other than that I don't know."

Katie's head was full of ideas, but she had to speak with Nina first and seek her approval. She was determined to expand the business and make Antonio proud of her.

"What's going around in that pretty little head of yours?"

"Have a little bit of patience and you'll find out soon enough."

"Now you have me totally intrigued, tell me more."

"No. If you behave, I may tell you later," Katie laughed.

"Are you keeping secrets from me?" Antonio put on his downtrodden expression.

A car horn was tooting outside. "I have to go, darling, I'll talk to you tonight." She kissed him and grabbed her coat and handbag, not giving him a chance to say anything else.

She was a law unto herself, Antonio thought, wondering what she was up to. Whatever it was, it made her happy and a happy woman was definitely a good thing.

"Good morning, Nina." Katie got into the passenger seat.

"My, you're happy and jolly this morning."

"I sure am, I've been thinking about the business and wanted to suggest a few things."

"Look Katie, I know that since, since my husband died things haven't been the same, but I don't want to change anything. Roberto had a good business head and we were doing perfectly fine, before all the trouble that is."

Oh dear, she was going to have to try and convince Nina to at least consider her ideas. "Well, it won't do any harm just to listen to what I have to say, and of course I will honour your wishes, you know that. And I certainly don't want you to think that I am trying to undermine Roberto in any way."

"I know you're not. Ok, we'll have a coffee in the office and you can tell me all about it, does that sound fair?"

"Yes, very fair."

Nina drove up to the huge glass fronted building.

The sign on the far right of the walled area still read "Villa Valetti", that too needed to be changed. Nina had lost valuable customers because of the drug situation and it was time they announced it was under new management. Perhaps they could come up with a new name for the place. They were beginning to break even financially, but they could be doing so much better.

Simon Fitzgerald was waiting at the door for them. He was their accountant and he had come to do the books. "Good morning, ladies, how are we today?"

"Yes, fine." Nina snapped at him.

Simon looked a little uncomfortable. "Err, have I come at a bad time?"

"Yes, no, oh I am sorry, Simon."

"That's ok, Mrs Valetti, how are the children?"

"The children are fine." Nina disarmed the alarm system and let them in. She locked it behind them. "Our first appointment is 10.30am, so that gives us plenty of time to talk." She turned to Simon. "Why don't you make a start and use my office, everything you need is in there." She handed him the key to the filing cabinets.

"Very well."

"I'll make us all some coffee." Katie went into the kitchen. Nina was in a strange old mood today, she had her good days, but when she was like this it was hard work. Maybe it wasn't a good idea to make any suggestions, it was perhaps better left to another time.

She took three cups out of the cupboard above her head. One of the cups had Roberto's name etched on to it, sighing she put it back.

"I'll have his mug."

Katie turned around. "Nina, you gave me a start!"

"Just because he's dead doesn't mean to say that he was never here."

"I know."

Nina was really feeling the loss of her husband today, it would have been his fortieth birthday.

"Do you want to talk?"

"No, let's talk business and hopefully it will take my mind off it."

238

They went into the board room and sat on the rich mahogany chairs. "It seems a waste this huge room."

"What do you mean, Katie?"

"I think we could utilise it better."

"How?"

"Ok, please hear me out first and then if you disagree let me know."

Nina nodded her head, wondering what all this was about.

"I am thinking of the future of the business and of course your children's and hopefully one day my own. Firstly I have been looking at our advertising." Katie pulled the papers out of her bag. She handed her the original advert and the new one she had devised. "I have changed a few things, what do you think?"

Nina looked at the paper in front of her, my, my Katie had been a busy girl. It read:

'Experience creativity and innovation with a fresh and exciting approach to providing a unique opportunity to view our classic Italian range of designer furniture, exquisitely handmade and crafted in the city of Milan. We offer a level of service and attention way beyond anything customers would experience in any other store worldwide. We welcome visitors to our showroom to view representative displays from each of our renowned collections. As we are specialists in this field of business it is essential for our potential clients to book an appointment. This will ensure necessary time and assistance is given on a one to one basis by our expert team of interior designers'.

Wow, Nina thought, this advert was far better than the original one, much bolder and welcoming. "I am lost for words, did you come up with this yourself?"

"Of course I did, I just want to help us succeed even more. It's just a case of selling the business a bit more, giving that personal touch. I also thought that if clients were unable to visit the store we could go to their homes with brochures and swatches."

"I must say, Katie, I am extremely impressed."

"So, you are happy with the advert?"

"Yes, I am, and this other idea of visiting people in their own homes is fabulous, but we will need more staff if it takes off."

"I also think that we should stress that the business is under new management and branch out a bit more."

"Branch out?"

"Yes, we deal only in Italian furniture at the moment, what if we also supplied curtains, carpets, bed linen, crockery even down to table cloths? You must admit it would be a very strong selling point if we could provide everything and I mean absolutely everything!" Katie was on a roll now.

"You have really thought this through haven't you and with my contacts in Italy I am sure we can manage that. But we may have a problem with finance, we are only

239

just managing with the furniture business and can't really afford any more retainers for other specialists."

"Don't take this the wrong way, Nina, but I can ask Antonio for a loan."

"No, I would prefer not to."

"But we'll pay him back once the money starts coming in."

"But what if it doesn't?"

"Trust me, it will." Katie was confident and she had something else up her sleeve. "I have another alternative if you don't wish to borrow from Antonio."

"I'm listening." Nina was very curious.

"What if we involved Ralph and Henry?"

Nina was alert now. "My God, you have thought of everything haven't you?"

"It makes sense, we can all help each other out and pass on our business contacts. So, should I set up a business meeting?"

"You really have me convinced now. Yes, let's go for it, why not, after all we have nothing to lose!"

"Let's shake on it!" Katie offered her hand.

Nina shook it. "You're one hell of a girl, I'll say that for you."

"We are going to be multi millionaires, mark my words!"

"I think this calls for a celebratory drink." Nina opened the drinks cabinet. "What do you fancy?"

"Do you think it wise, we have a customer in forty minutes."

"Sod it, let's have a small glass of wine, we can do the real celebrating once you reel in Ralph and Henry." Nina popped the cork and poured the wine into crystal glasses. "To expanding our business."

"Cheers." Katie was really pleased that Nina could see the potential in her plans, they had the contacts, so why not make use of them?

Chapter Seventy Three

The working lunch was arranged by Nina, it was in a private function room in the Dorchester Hotel. She did not tell the business men anything about their plans, she hoped that they would be tempted to turn up out of curiosity. All she had told their secretaries was that the meeting was with a Mr Tognerelli, giving them first choice to invest in a new money venture, guaranteed to turn over a million in the first year, followed by many more millions the next. An idea that had not happened in the UK yet, theirs would be the first business to launch this unique service.

"Are you nervous, because I am!" Nina announced totally out of the blue.

"Not at all, I think it was a good idea of yours to meet on neutral ground though, less pressure."

"Why thank you, partner."

"You're welcome."

Ralph Anderson was the first to arrive, he had spoken to Henry Brookstein who had also been invited to this meeting which was shrouded in secrecy. He waited patiently in the hotel foyer.

"Ah, my good man, where have you been?"

"I was with Antonio and had to make an excuse to get away, I don't think that he was very happy with me."

"No, I wasn't, I knew you were up to something, now what's going on. You keeping me out of something?" Antonio demanded. "Well?"

"Er, it isn't what you think," Ralph said quietly.

"It's a business meeting, a new venture," Henry said putting his hand on Antonio's shoulder. "Nothing for you to bother about."

"What kind of business venture, new you say? Then why was I not approached? I am known for my interest in new ventures."

"Antonio, we were asked to keep this as discreet as possible."

"Fine, I can be discreet, what suite are you using?"

"The Emperor suite, why?"

"I'll leave you to it then!" Antonio stormed off. How dare someone miss him out of the loop, he hadn't heard anything on the grapevine which had surprised him. Who was this person who had the audacity to ignore the most prestigious person in the business world. He had won Business Man of the Year for Christ's sake. He was just about to step into the revolving door. No, damn it, he wanted to know what was going on and he wanted to know now. He marched back towards the front desk.

"Where is the Emperor suite?"

"It's on the twelfth floor, sir, can I help you?"

"Yes as a matter of fact you can." Antonio pulled the receptionist to one side and explained that he had to listen in to the meeting that was taking place.

The receptionist was having none of it. "I'm sorry, sir, I can't help you."

"But it's a matter of life and death." Antonio turned on the charm and the mature receptionist fell for it. "A lady of your integrity would realise, that it really is urgent, I'm not here to cause any trouble, it's just vital that you help me, I beg of you, please."

The pleading in his voice and those handsome good looks really played on her heart strings. "There is a room adjacent to it where we bring the refreshments in by, but they didn't require use of that room. I suppose I could let you have the key, but you must realise that my job is on the line here, sir."

"Yes, yes, I appreciate that." He pulled out his wallet and peeled off a wad of notes. "Here, for your trouble."

"I couldn't possibly, sir." Violet Hilderburn blushed, there was something about this man that excited her and she couldn't remember the last time she had any kind of attention from a man such as him.

"I insist."

"No, not here," Violet whispered. "Meet me around the corner in a couple of minutes."

Antonio winked at her. "I understand." Jesus he hated buttering up old hags, and this one definitely thought she was in with a chance. Maybe he had laid it on too thick, his sweet talking had gotten him into trouble many times in the past. But he was an engaged man now and couldn't promise any other women anything other than a flashing smile.

Two minutes later and true to her word Violet appeared. She slipped the key into his hand and let it linger there a little longer than she should have. "If there's anything else I can do, you only have to ask me." She winked at him. "And please remember to return the key once you are finished."

"I appreciate your help." Antonio pushed the lift button, it couldn't come fast enough for him. The woman's perfume was overpowering and when she smiled he noticed all her black fillings, urgh, as if he could fancy a bit of that.

It seemed to take an eternity before he reached the twelfth floor. The corridor was huge and he didn't have a clue which way to go. Oh well, it will have to be pot luck then he thought, fingers crossed. He walked down the never ending blue carpeted corridor carefully stopping to check the rooms. Shit the Emperor Suite must be at the other end, trust him to go the wrong way. Now, he was running, if he didn't hurry he would miss the entire meeting.

"I must say I am quite surprised to see you, Nina, and of course you, Katie, does Antonio know about this?" Ralph questioned them.

242

"Just because I am engaged to him does not mean that we live in each other's pockets, Ralph."

"Please take a seat and we will explain everything to you." Nina's voice was commanding.

"I must say you have us both intrigued." You could hear the admiration in Henry's voice. "I can't wait to hear what you have to say."

"Well, I am going to let Katie do all the talking as it was all her idea and I can't take any of the credit for it. But what I will say is that I am very impressed with her business sense and Roberto would have been too."

"That's good to know, I respected your husband so much," Henry stated, remembering Roberto's sunny disposition, he enjoyed life, it was such a waste.

"Please, allow Katie to put the proposal over."

Ralph and Henry looked at each other.

"All I ask is that you hear me out, we will all benefit from what I am about to suggest. I'll be as brief as I can and give you a general overview of our plans," Katie began. "Basically we are all interested in making money, so therefore we already have something in common."

Ralph was wondering where all this was going, he had cancelled a meeting with the art gallery to come here and hoped it was going to be worth it.

"I know what you are thinking, yes, I've only been on the scene for five minutes and yes I am very young and you don't expect me to know very much, but I have been doing some research." It was as if Katie had been reading his mind. "As you are aware Nina's business supplies the richest people in the country with hand made Italian furniture, we would like to branch out into furnishing an entire house, hotel, restaurant, anything basically."

"Yes, but what does that have to do with us?" Ralph was slightly agitated.

"All in good time Ralph," Nina shot daggers at him.

"Yes, Ralph, do let the young lady continue." Henry told him.

"Ok, we specialise in interior decorating, able to supply the most unique and exquisite furniture along with whatever the client desires. What Nina and I aim to do is to be able to provide architects, art dealers, competent workers and assemblers all specialists in their own particular fields. Our service will be second to none. Our team of workers will pay remarkable attention to detail and ensure that all our customers' expectations will be fulfilled to their satisfaction." Katie took a breath. "So you see together we will be able to provide everything in one complete package."

Nina bit her lip and watched the expressions on the men's faces, had they bought it? It was certainly presented clearly and concisely, she crossed her fingers under the table.

"So, therefore our customers will be your customers and vice versa, that way it is win, win for all of us."

Henry stood up. "Bravo, little Katie, you have this quality about you, something that has convinced me." He started to clap.

"I have to say that you are one smart young lady, Katie, it's a pity there wasn't more of your kind in the world, I applaud you." Ralph was astonished that no-one had thought of this before.

"Does that mean we can count on your support?" Katie pushed them.

"Yes, why not, it is a fantastic opportunity, one not to be missed." Henry loved making money and this was going to make them plenty.

"I agree with Henry, let's shake on it." Ralph shook Katie's hand and then Nina's.

"This calls for the champagne, I'll just get it."

Antonio had heard the gist of Katie's proposition and couldn't believe his ears, this young woman of his continued to surprise him. He glanced towards the champagne on ice, shit he had to get out of here and fast before he was discovered. He made it outside of the door just before Nina came in.

Everyone thought Antonio was choosing a young inexperienced woman so that he could control her and keep her at home bringing up babies and keeping the house in order. Wow, what a woman, she amazed and stunned him. She was going to make them millions and the prospect of that impressed him.

"So, we need to set up a meeting with our lawyers, draw up a contract that we all agree on and discuss our investment, I assume you require a substantial investment?" Henry always had his financial head on.

Ralph laughed. "Yes, we'll discuss the final details."

"Sorry to sound so corny, but here's to a beautiful working relationship and the start of fabulous new project." Nina felt like life was worth living again and she had a new positiveness around her.

"I also think we should rename the business, what do you think Nina?"

"Yes perhaps you're right, let's see what we can come up with."

Brilliant, everything was falling into place and Katie was thrilled, it was an exciting time for them all. She could hardly wait to tell Antonio the news, he would be so proud of her.

Antonio handed the key back into reception. "Thank you."

"Did you hear what you needed to?"

"Yes, I sure did."

"If ever you are back, please look me up, I would like that."

"Thank you, my dear, but I am engaged."

It was as if Violet's eyes had turned black in a violent rage. "I'm calling security." She shrieked picking up the phone. "Yes, there is a man, he is causing a scene, please send someone quickly."

Before she had finished speaking Antonio was out of the hotel and into his waiting car. "Step on it, Fred." The woman was completely neurotic!

Fred obediently obliged. What had his boss been up to now? He watched him in the rear view mirror, he was smiling triumphantly to himself. Well it must be something good and he could only be thankful for that after the previous year's dramas.

"I think we ought to get a cab back to the office." The champagne had gone to Nina's head.

"Please, allow my driver to drop you off, it's the least I can do." Henry also wanted to have a look at their current collections.

"Why don't we all go together, it will give us a chance to look around?" Ralph was also keen to see exactly what he had agreed to.

"Sure, I'll just ring reception to tell them that we have finished." Nina picked up the phone.

"You're not having second thoughts are you?" Katie was troubled.

"Not at all, we know Valetti had an outstanding reputation and only ever sold the best lines," Ralph assured her.

Katie smiled. "Good, let's go then."

They all clambered into the waiting limousine. Ralph arranged for his yellow sports car to be kept overnight at the hotel.

"I'm interested to know how you came up with this idea," Henry was inquisitive.

"Nina has taught me a lot in a short time and I have the utmost respect for what each of you do. I know that Antonio has invested in your businesses and has done very well, I thought that you both would be perfect for this project. It was perfectly simple really, with Nina's contacts and your own we can't possibly fail!"

They pulled up outside the huge, eye catching building. One side was half brick and the other glass, it certainly looked the business. The location was ideal, set back from the main road, quite private really. Henry's gut instinct was that this was going to work, it was a great shame that Roberto was not here to see his empire expand.

Katie took them into the store to have a look around. "This is the Occasional Selection, inlaid wine and coffee tables, chaises longues, chairs, lamps etc."

"This is the dining range, the lacquered finish gives the collection a resilience to knocks and scrapes." Nina was enjoying herself.

"And the bedroom range is just over here, this is our newest collection, classically designed. The furniture is hand finished and is available in a wide choice of vibrant colours, with generous use of gold leaf." For emphasis Katie ran her hand over the headboard.

"Of course all that you see here is just the tip of the iceberg really. We have brochures for our customers and we are also able to make furniture to meet any specific requirements." Nina handed them a brochure each.

"And we have samples of the material over here, it is mainly all silk." Katie showed them the swatches.

"The furniture we sell comes in a variety of materials, we can do marble, porcelain, durmast, walnut and red cherry," Nina informed him.

"Don't forget that it is all hand crafted and hand finished," Katie and Nina spoke at the same time. They began giggling.

"You know, you make a great team." Henry was truly impressed.

"I am happy to make the investment and watch the money start rolling in." Ralph couldn't wait to tell Lorraine, she'll be thrilled, more cash for her to waste, he thought. Still he didn't mind, she was always there for him and always would be and of course he loved her expensive taste in her outfits, always the picture of perfection.

"I think we have seen everything we need to for now, however I'll need my accountant to go through your books if that is ok with you." Henry was being sensible as usual.

"Of course, that's not a problem." Nina knew Henry would insist on seeing the accounts, they were in profit but could be doing so much better and that is hopefully where they would come in.

"We'll see ourselves out and meet up next week to sign the documents."

"It's been a pleasure doing business with you." Nina shook their hands.

"Likewise, bye for now."

After they left the two women collapsed into the chairs. "My god I feel positively exhausted."

"Me too, I could do with a good pampering session."

"How about we go to Palmeiras Pampering Studio?"

"I would love to, but isn't it one of those exclusive places you have to book well in advance? And I've heard that it is very expensive!"

"Ah, do not fret, I am a member and I have contacts and money to burn, so this is my treat!"

Nina disappeared into her office and came back a few minutes later. "Whenever you're ready!"

"What about this place?"

"It's ok, I've cancelled the rest of today's appointments"

"Oh, but I thought we were going to look at those new designs and decide on a new collection."

"You are so keen, we'll do that tomorrow in between our appointments!"

"Ok, you've convinced me."

Chapter Seventy Four

The studio was in Soho, on the outside it looked quite ugly, the building was dark and reminiscent of Victorian times with traditional architecture. The sign on the door read '*Welcome to Palmeiras Pampering Studio, an experience never to forget, we are one of the most luxurious and relaxing health spas in the country. A peaceful atmosphere awaits you. So come and enjoy the ambience*'.

Nina and Katie walked into the converted house. The studio's wooden floors were freshly polished, the walls were cream and there were a few pictures of the countryside. Katie looked up, there were wooden beams and the lights ran down the centre of them. The furniture was cream too and placed around the outside of the room close to the walls.

"Wow, this looks fab!" Katie whispered.

"Mrs Valetti, there you are, it is so nice to see you, how are you?"

"Anneka, you look wonderful as ever."

"Oh, stop flattering me! Who is your friend, no, wait I've seen you in the paper recently. Oh my God, it's Katie Saunders isn't it, the future Mrs de Marco?"

The girl hugged her. "You're much prettier in real life. You certainly don't need much help with your looks, darling."

Katie was taken aback, my God people actually knew who she was! How freaky was that she thought!

"I hope you come to me for your pre-wedding package, I'll do you a deal. I'll get you our brochure before you leave, now don't let me forget will you?"

"Anneka, leave the poor girl alone, we have just cut an important business deal and need some serious pampering, what can you fit us in for?"

"Well, unfortunately with it being such short notice we can only manage a manicure, pedicure and a facial, I do hope that's ok."

"Yes, that's perfect."

"Do take a seat, would you like a glass of wine while you wait?"

"Yes that would be nice."

"Very well, Mrs Valetti, I shan't be long, Valerie can you take the ladies' coats please."

"Whoa I am exhausted just listening to her!" Katie shook her head.

"She can talk for England you know, but she is harmless. I don't know who our appointments are with, but Anneka doesn't talk much while she is actually working!"

Katie giggled. "Thank God for that or it wouldn't be very relaxing would it!"

"You can say that again!" Nina laughed, she felt good for the first time in ages. Katie certainly brought out the real her, the woman she was before her husband's tragic death.

"It smells gorgeous in here."

"That will be all those super lotions and potions we are going to experience." Nina wondered if Katie had ever been to a health spa before. "Is this your first time?"

"Yes, does it show? I wouldn't want to embarrass you." She felt somebody's eyes on her. "Look at that woman over there staring at us."

"She probably recognises you from the newspaper." Nina giggled as she waved over to her.

"Stop it, oh my God, she's coming over now!"

"I am Mrs Farnworth Campbell the third." She extended her hand to Nina.

"How do you do."

"I would like to talk with you about making a substantial purchase from your store my dear."

"Let me introduce you to my new business partner, Katie Saunders."

She turned to Katie. "Oh, the Katie Saunders, the de Marco fiancée, that will be a nice inheritance for you."

"Er yes, the very one, but I'm not marrying him for his money."

"Hmm, yes whatever, charmed to make your acquaintance I'm sure." She brushed Katie off and turned to Nina. "I would prefer to deal direct with yourself Mrs Valetti."

"Listen, lady, I don't like your tone."

"I beg your pardon, do you know who I am!"

"I don't give a damn if you're the thirteenth cousin, seventh in line to the throne, nobody speaks to my business partner like that!"

"Nina, it's ok, really it doesn't matter." Katie was trying to save the situation, before it got totally out of hand. People were starting to look at them.

"Well if you don't want my business, that's up to you, but I hear that you're not doing very well since your husband's suicide, so it doesn't make any sense to throw away good money!" The woman was a pompous ass.

"How dare you!" Nina was shocked at the woman's cold mannerism towards her.

Just then Anneka was walking back through the waiting area with a silver tray and two glasses of wine. Before she could even think about what she was doing Nina grabbed a glass and threw it in the woman's face.

Anneka went white not knowing who to comfort. Mrs Farnworth Campbell the third was one of her best customers, but she liked Nina. "Oh, Freda, Freda take Mrs Farnworth Campbell the third into the other room, quickly."

"Forget it, Anneka, as long as this woman and her so-called business associate are using this salon I will never cross the threshold again!" She pulled her handkerchief out of her designer bag and mopped her face. "Get me my coat now!" She shrieked at Anneka.

"Oh, please I'm sure we can sort this out, can't we, Mrs Valetti?" Anneka didn't want to lose the business, she didn't really like the woman but she was a regular customer and spent quite a bit of money there.

Nina didn't answer.

Mrs Farnworth Campbell the third grabbed her fur coat and hurriedly left the salon.

"Oh, Nina, are you alright?" Katie was concerned.

"I'm fine, ready for our treatment more than ever."

"Yes, the room is ready now, I have got you a double room so that you can chat during the treatments if you like."

"Thanks, that's ok with us." Nina's voice was steady, she wasn't going to let that snob get to her, no way.

As soon as they entered the room, the smell of essential oils and dimmed lighting along with the burning candles and the soothing sound of the ocean in the background completely changed the mood.

Nina felt her anger disappear and she relaxed.

"We have Susie and Wanda today, they are very experienced. If you wouldn't mind removing your shoes and hopping into the chair."

The sound of waves crashing and birds singing was calming and soothing. The beauticians had a special treat for Katie and Nina.

"Now," Wanda began. "We wanted you to be one of the first to experience our deluxe chocolate pedicure and manicure."

"Chocolate?" Katie giggled.

"Yes, we are going to start with a warm milk soak followed by a sumptuous hot vanilla and brown sugar scrub."

"Wow, that sounds divine."

"And then we will do a warm cocoa butter masque for super hydration, your feet will never be the same again!"

"How cool is that!" Katie was impressed.

Wanda got to work, first she soaked Katie's feet in the foot spa. Ten minutes later she set about massaging her feet and in between her toes. Katie started laughing hysterically. "Oh, I'm sorry, I didn't realise my feet were so ticklish!"

Nina began to laugh, she laughed so much she began to cry. The therapists also began to laugh, Katie's laugh was so infectious!

There was a knock on the door. Anneka came into the room. "What on earth is going on, you're having way too much fun in here, what's the joke?" She passed mugs of steaming hot chocolate to Nina and Katie.

"It's all my fault," Katie laughed. "I'm just very ticklish, I can't bear it!"

"Oh my goodness, you are supposed to be relaxing!" Anneka took her job very seriously. "Does your fiancé know about this ticklish area!"

"No, but he soon will!" Nina burst out laughing once more.

"Oh, don't you dare!" Katie protested.

"It will be interesting in the bedroom then won't it!" Anneka joined in the laughter.

"Oh, please, stop I can't take it anymore!"

"Ok, shall I do your manicure now?" Wanda asked.

"Please."

"Wow, your ring is very beautiful." Wanda had never seen anything like it in her life. "It must have cost a fortune, he must really love you!" she exclaimed.

"Yes, he does." Katie had that dreamy look of a woman in love.

"You're very lucky," Susie sighed, wishing her boyfriend would propose to her.

"Yes, I am," Katie admitted.

"And of course, Antonio is an extremely lucky man." Nina knew that Katie adored him and would do anything for him, she didn't want everyone to think that Katie was the only lucky one in their relationship.

"I'll leave you to it, ladies." Anneka returned to the waiting room and her next client. She really wanted to be sitting in that room getting all the gossip. Next time they come, she thought I'll have them booked in personally with me.

Chapter Seventy Five

Lucy had left her purse at the club, damn it she would have to go and pick it up. She only lived a short distance away so decided to walk as it was such a nice day. She opened the window and looked out, it was a frosty morning but the sun was shining and she was feeling really happy with the world. Everything was going so well, Stevo was wonderful, her job was wonderful and well her life was just wonderful too. She loved working in the club and meeting new people was great, it was an added bonus. Lucy was definitely a people person and she did her job well, everyone enjoyed her company and that showed in the huge tips that she got.

Lucy was just getting ready to leave when the phone rang. "Hello."

"Hi, Lucy, it's me do you want to meet up later?" Katie felt like she hadn't had a girly chat with her for ages.

"Sure, I thought you'd forgotten about me!" Lucy hadn't seen much of her since she had virtually moved in with Antonio, although most of her clothes were still in her wardrobe.

"As if! What are you up to?"

"I'm just about to go over to the club, I left my purse there! I'm such an idiot!"

"What are you like, no wonder you're a blonde chick!"

"Hey watch it, you!"

"Just kidding, hun! Do you want to come over to mine? I'll get Fred to pick you up."

"Sounds good."

"Why don't you bring Stevo with you, say around seven and I'll cook something nice."

"Let me guess, Italian?"

"What else!" Katie had been practising and she was confident that she was more than capable of making spaghetti bolognese.

"Can't wait, I'll see you later then."

"Ok, bye, chick."

"Bye, hun."

Lucy arrived at the club and punched the code in and walked into the back room. Where was her purse at?

She was alarmed to hear raised voices coming from outside the room.

"What is your problem Gianni, you didn't mind dealing with my father before?" Sasha shrieked at him.

251

"I told you, I'm out of it now!"

"You're not out until he tells you, Gianni, just think of the money!"

"I don't give a fuck about the money!"

"But we'll make a fortune, cocaine will make us wealthy!"

"You forget, Sasha, I am wealthy!" Gianni was pissed off with her, he didn't like to be told what he could and couldn't do, especially by a woman.

"At least think about it. If you don't do it then someone else will!"

"I swore after what happened to Roberto I wasn't going there again!"

"Don't tell me that you're starting to develop a conscience."

They were startled by a bang in the changing room. Lucy's heart was pounding, oh my God, Gianni was somehow responsible for Roberto Valetti's arrest and ultimately his death. She looked for an escape route, where could she go! She was panicking, if they found her she dreaded to think what they would do to her!

"Ssh, Gianni, there's someone in there." Sasha pointed to the door.

"You stay here, I'll check it out." Gianni pulled out a small hand gun. "Just go I'll deal with this."

"Be careful."

Gianni threw the door open. "Who's there, you better show yourself. I've got a gun and I'm not afraid to use it."

Lucy was scrambling out of the window in the ladies toilets. She was so scared that she could hardly breathe, God knows what Gianni was going to do, but one thing was for sure, she wasn't hanging around to find out.

Gianni spotted the purse, picking it up, he opened it. Fuck it, Lucy Carmichael, of all people, he could do without this! Shit, if she told Katie and Katie told Antonio he would cut him out of the business for good and then he would be destitute. He had to do something and do it fast.

"Is it safe to come in?" Sasha appeared in the doorway.

"It was Lucy, Lucy Carmichael, blackmail her, threaten her, do whatever you have to do, but make sure she doesn't talk to anyone." Gianni told Sasha.

"Yes, yes I understand, I'll try my best."

Lucy went to the phone box and dialled her brother's number. "Matt, I've got to meet you, something's happened... I... I don't know what to do."

Matt couldn't make head nor tail of what she was saying. "Calm down, Lucy, I'll come over now where are you?"

"I'll be home in about ten minutes, meet me there!" Lucy's nerves were in shreds, her head was spinning. "I'm worried for Katie... hello, Matt, are you still there?" The phone went dead and she didn't have any more change on her.

Sasha spotted Lucy, hurrying down the road. She slowly drove towards her. Whatever happened Gianni would owe her one after this, he would have to continue working for her father whether he wanted to or not.

252

Lucy was miles away, unaware of the imminent danger she was in. Poor Katie, she didn't know what she was getting mixed up in. If Gianni was dealing in drugs then Antonio must be too, what cold heartless bastards, how could they continue on in their lives without any guilt or remorse for what they had done to Nina's husband? And what about Felicia, God, maybe it wasn't a robbery gone wrong after all, Jesus just what were the de Marcos involved in!

Sasha wound the window down. "Lucy, get in."

"What? What do you want?"

"I just want to help you, please just get in." Sasha was becoming frustrated.

"No, you were at the club just now, I know what you're up to! Just stay away from me!" The words spewed out.

"Look, Lucy, just get in the goddamn car, we'll talk, see if we can sort this thing out!"

"How are you going to do that, I know about Roberto, how could you!" Lucy screamed at her.

They were in the lane behind the club, the place was deserted at this time of day, good, no witnesses thought Sasha.

"Lucy, wait, do you want money, maybe a promotion, I can make it happen for you."

Lucy suddenly stopped. "What, are you crazy, I don't care about any of that, I've got a conscience even if you lot haven't."

"What are you going to do?"

"You'll find out soon enough!" Lucy started walking faster.

"What proof do you have? No one will believe you, you stupid girl!"

"Katie will believe me and so will my brother."

Sasha didn't know what to do, she sat in her car watching her walk away. Then suddenly without thinking about it she went after her. As she turned the corner, she mounted the pavement and hit Lucy head on, she hit the bonnet and the force tossed her up in the air like a rag doll. She stopped the car and looked in her rear view mirror, Lucy wasn't moving.

She ran over to the phone box. "Gianni, you've got to help me, I've done something terrible, but I had to do it, I did it for you."

"Sasha, what have you done?"

She blurted out the awful truth.

"Ok, this is what you have to do." Stevo would be after someone's blood for this, he was really taken with her. Gianni put his face in his hands, he wished he had never let Sasha back into his life, wherever she was, there was always trouble.

Sasha sped off towards the warehouse Gianni told her to go to. Once there someone would dump the car and burn it out, all she had to do was report it missing to the police. There would be no evidence of any crime having been committed and she would be home free. She scrabbled around in the glove box and prepared a line of cocaine, she desperately needed a hit. She lay back in the seat and waited for Gianni's men to come and fix everything, just like they always did.

She tip-tapped her acrylic nails on the steering wheel. Jesus they should be here by now, where the hell are they? She lit a cigarette and inhaled on it deeply. That Lucy was a meddling little bitch and got what she deserved, snooping around, what the hell was she playing at? Her only regret was that it wasn't that simpering bitch Katie, but one day she'll get her comeuppance. And that day couldn't come soon enough for her.

Two cars pulled up behind her. At last she thought, she needed to get back to the hotel as soon as possible before she was missed. Gianni had organised for a masseur to go over, one that Sasha could use as an alibi.

Two men came over and knocked on the window. "The other car will take you wherever you want to go."

"Ok, thank you."

"Don't thank me, lady, I'm doing this for Gianni, not for you."

Sasha got out of the car.

"No, leave your handbag."

"I couldn't possibly."

"It's a small price to pay for taking someone's life don't you think?" He grabbed the bag from her.

A passing motorist spotted a body in the road, he jumped out and ran over. It was a young woman and she was in a really bad way. He felt her pulse, it was very faint. "Don't worry, I'll call an ambulance, you're going to be ok." But he didn't think she was going to make it. He put his jacket over her and made the call.

It was fifteen minutes later when the paramedics finally arrived. They put Lucy's limp body on the stretcher and put her into the ambulance. The police were interviewing Mr O'Neil, but he couldn't tell them anything about what had happened to her.

Lucy went into cardiac arrest and there was nothing anyone could do to save her despite all attempts.

One of the paramedics got out of the ambulance and went over to the policeman. "I'm sorry to say that the young lady's dead."

"I can't believe someone just left her in the road to die. Does she have any identification on her?"

"No, there's nothing."

"We need to find out who she is. Mr O'Neil, we may need to speak to you again, but for now, please just go home."

Mr O'Neil was in shock. "I…"

"Just take a few deep breaths, Mr O'Neil," the policeman advised.

He sat down on the roadside, he couldn't get the dead girl's image out of his head, it was just too horrible for words.

Chapter Seventy Six

Katie was in the middle of preparing the food when Antonio came home. "Ciao, bella."

Just the sound of his voice sent shivers down her spine. He came up behind her and put his arms around her. "Mmm, something smells good, are you cooking for the five thousand?"

"We're having guests over."

"Are we?"

"Yes, you don't mind do you?"

"Well, I did want you all to myself tonight," Antonio joked. "I hate having to share you!"

"Oh, Antonio, behave!"

He kissed her neck. "Mmm you smell good enough to eat!" His hands started wandering.

"Antonio, stop it, I'll burn the food if you don't, then you'll go hungry!"

Antonio put his hands up. "Ok, ok, I'll just go and have a quick shower then."

"Don't you want to know who's coming for dinner then?"

"No, surprise me." As he walked towards the bathroom he smiled to himself, it was probably Nina, they were obviously going to tell him about their business plans. He would have to pretend that he didn't know anything!

Katie tasted the bolognese sauce, hmm not bad she thought, especially for an amateur chef. She chopped the basil and tossed it into the pan, there nearly done. She glanced at the clock, 6.30pm, just enough time to get changed. She turned the gas down to let the food simmer gently.

Antonio was just drying himself off. Katie stood in the doorway and watched him, he was so handsome and his body well defined. As if sensing her Antonio turned around. She immediately turned red.

"Venuto qui."

Katie hadn't got a clue what he had just said, she instinctively ran into his arms. He frantically tore her clothes off and made passionate love to her on the bathroom floor. "Il mio tesoro."

"I love it when you speak to me in Italian, it is so romantic, but what did you just say?"

"My darling."

Katie was still trembling and her heart was racing. "I need to get dressed before Lucy and Stevo arrive."

Antonio raised an eyebrow. "Oh yes?"

"Yes, I want to offer Lucy a job in my business."

"But I thought you were only just breaking even?"

"That's true, il me tesora, but not for long."

"Il mio tesoro, but good attempt!"

"Cheeky, now release me so that I can check on the food before it burns."

Antonio held her tight. "But I don't want to let go of you."

"Is that your stomach I can hear rumbling?"

Antonio grinned. "Ok you win, but I'll be thinking about you all tonight. Every time I look at you I'll be mentally undressing you."

"Oh, don't do that I won't be able to concentrate!"

"Exactly, only you and I know what each other will be thinking."

"Ooh, you are terrible, Antonio, but I love it!"

Antonio playfully patted her bum. "Better hurry I can smell the bolognese burning away!"

"Oh, don't say that!" Katie quickly pulled on her dress and piled her hair up. She rushed into the kitchen. Antonio, he was such a tease, the food was fine. Tutting she boiled up a pan of water and added the spaghetti.

It was ten to seven, where are they, she thought? It's not like Lucy to be late, especially where food was concerned.

The phone rang and Katie smiled, that's probably her now, telling me she's going to be late.

It was Fred. "I'm at the flat, there doesn't seem to be anyone at home though."

"That's strange, wonder where she's got to."

"What do you want me to do?"

"Just wait there, I'll get back to you."

"Problem?" Antonio asked her.

"Fred went to pick Lucy up but she isn't at home and I keep getting her answer machine."

"Don't worry I'll ring Stevo."

"Stevo, where the hell are you?"

"I thought you didn't need me tonight."

"I don't! But you are late and Katie has spent ages cooking, you better have a good excuse!"

"Antonio, what are you on about?"

"Give me the phone, Antonio, I'll talk to him. Stevo, I spoke to Lucy earlier on and she was supposed to invite you over her for a meal tonight," she explained.

"It's the first I've heard of it!"

"Oh, when did you last speak to her?"

"This morning."

"I'm getting worried now, where can she be?"

"Leave it to me, I'll go and look for her!"

"Ok." Katie passed the phone back to Antonio.

Chapter Seventy Seven

The police knocked on Matthew's door. "Yes, officer?"

"Can we come in?"

Matthew looked puzzled. "What's this about?"

"Look, sir, it would be better if we could just come in," the officer insisted.

Matt reluctantly let them in and directed them into the living room. "What is it?"

"I'm sorry, sir, but there's no other way of telling you."

"Telling me what?"

"I'm afraid that there's been a fatal accident, sir."

"Fatal? Who, oh my God, not Katie, tell me it isn't Katie."

"No, I'm afraid that it's your sister Lucy."

Matt went ashen and grabbed the chair in front of him. His head pounded. "What... what happened?"

"It was a hit and run, I'm so sorry, sir. We need you to identify the body."

"Identify her body? You mean to say that it might not even be her?" Matt was aghast.

"She had your business card on her." The officer held up a clear plastic bag.

Matt nodded, he could barely stand up.

"Do you need some time?"

"No, I'll come with you now." Matt put his coat on and followed the officers to the police car, he was in a daze. Surely this couldn't be happening, it was some kind of bad dream, his little sister, dead. She can't be, he thought, she just can't.

The drive to the mortuary seemed to take forever. As they entered the building Matt stumbled and leaned on the corridor wall to regain his balance.

"Are you ok, sir?"

Matt nodded his head. "I'll be ok."

The police woman led the way down the twisting dark corridor, he could smell death all around him. "Please wait here, Mr Carmichael."

The police woman hated this part of her job, she would never get used to telling families that they had lost a loved one.

A few minutes later she returned. "We're ready for you now."

Matt followed her into the room, the body was covered over in a white sheet. The mortuary attendant slowly pulled back the cover revealing Lucy's battered face and bloodied hair.

"Oh, no, my poor Lucy, it's her!" he sobbed. "I can't believe it."

"Thank you, please come with me, sir." The police woman led him out of the room and sat him down on the chair. "Can I get you a cup of tea or something."

"No." His voice was empty, devoid of all emotion.

The police woman's heart went out to him. "Is there anyone you would like me to call?"

He shook his head, he would have to break the news to the family and to Katie. She would be devastated, they were the best of friends.

"A hit and run you say?"

"Yes, it happened near La Pregheira, I believe she worked there?"

"Yes, yes she did, have you got anybody for this?"

"I'm sorry, sir, not yet but you'll be the first to know when we do."

"Do you have a phone I could use, I need to make a phone call."

"Certainly, follow me."

Matt punched the number in the phone.

Antonio answered. "Hello."

"This is Matthew Carmichael, I need to speak to Katie, it's personal business."

"Whatever it is you can tell me, we have no secrets between us."

"Please, I need to speak to her personally, Mr de Marco."

Sensing the urgency in his voice he obliged. "Katie, it's for you."

"Me, who is it, Lucy?"

"No, her brother."

Katie had an awful feeling in the pit of her stomach. "Matt, what is it, has something happened?"

Antonio watched Katie's face, she went white and dropped the phone.

"Katie, Katie, are you still there?" Matt was shouting down the phone.

"She's in bits here, what's going on?"

Matt relayed the story of his sister's death, trying to keep himself together. His voice trembled. "They haven't got anybody yet, but it's only a matter of time."

"If there's anything we can do to help, Mr Carmichael," Antonio offered.

"There's nothing you can do, just ask Katie to call me when she's up to it."

"I will." Antonio replaced the phone.

Katie couldn't speak, she was in shock. She wrapped her arms around herself and swayed in a rocking motion, shaking her head.

"Come here, my darling." He pulled her to him and held her tight. "It's ok, just let it out."

Katie was trying to speak, but she could barely get the words out. "S... s... Stevo, you must..."

"Ssh, my darling, I'll tell him. You need to have a lie down." He gave her some sleeping pills and a glass of water. "Here this will help."

Katie held them tightly in her hand and went to lie down. Antonio pulled the covers over her and kissed her on the forehead. "Try and get some rest."

She saw his lips moving but never heard a word he said, her brain was numb.

Closing the bedroom door he called Frank. "What do you know about this hit and run business?"

"There are no witnesses, Antonio, no leads, nothing. It's going to be nearly impossible to find out who did this."

"Then I will have to get some of my guys looking into it."

"I have to advise against this after all your recent troubles."

"This doesn't make any sense, things like this don't just happen. I need to know who did this and why."

"So, you don't think it was a simple accident then?"

"No, I don't."

"Who was this girl to you?"

"She was an employee of mine and also the best friend of my fiancée. You can imagine how devastated she is, and then there's Stevo. If you don't get someone for this fast then he will be out for blood, he won't care what happens to himself."

"Stevo?"

"Yes, Lucy was his girlfriend and he was in love with her."

"Don't let him do anything stupid, Antonio."

"Once I tell him, I'm afraid it's out of my hands," Antonio sighed, trouble was always at their door these days.

"I can't keep bailing you out. We have a new replacement for Fearon and trust me he's out to make a name for himself. I don't know if I will be able to help you any more, I may be taking early retirement."

"I'm sorry to hear that, Frank." Antonio put the phone down and prayed for the end of this run of bad luck.

Chapter Seventy Eight

Gianni met Sasha at the hotel. He could barely look at her.

"What?" she asked him. "There is nothing to worry about, your guys have seen to that."

"You really are a heartless bastard aren't you?"

"Whatever, darling, you should be thanking me for this!"

"You are fucking nuts do you know that, you should be in a fucking loony bin!"

"Yes and so should you. Don't pretend that you didn't know what I was going to do because I don't believe it for a second. I will do anything to protect the de Marcos."

"The de Marcos? You stupid fucking airhead, you were supposed to buy her off not fucking kill her in broad daylight!"

"She could not be bought off, I had to do something. It was too dangerous to let her go, Gianni, surely you can see that?"

"We could have found a way, Stevo would have talked to her!"

"Ah, but you forget my darling, her brother is a lawyer and we all know how inquisitive they are. She would have told him and then what would have happened!"

"Yes, maybe that's true, but we own that fucking firm. There's fucking ways and means, no need to murder anyone!"

"Well, it is done now, so deal with it!"

"You evil bitch."

Sasha shrieked with laughter. "You really are starting to get a conscience these days, what is wrong with you?"

Gianni grabbed her by the hair and dragged her writhing and kicking along the floor. "I'll show you my fucking conscience."

He threw her on the bed and yanked at her underwear, he was like a man possessed. Sasha was really turned on, she liked a bit of rough sex every now and then. "Yes, do whatever you want, darling, punish me, I have been a bad, bad girl!"

He turned her over and thrust himself into her. He pulled at her hair as he took her. It was all over in seconds, all the hate he felt for her now gone. Gianni quickly got dressed. "Tidy yourself up, your fucking hair is coming out." He threw the chunk of hair at her. "What the fuck is this?"

"It's ok, it's just my hair extensions," she purred. "I'll get them fixed tomorrow."

"I'm going out!"

"Out, out where, darling?"

"Anywhere, away from you, just don't expect me back tonight."

After he left Sasha laughed, she liked this new side of Gianni, she must make him angry more often if this was her reward. Now, he wouldn't be able to get enough of her, she quite enjoyed being submissive just for a change.

Chapter Seventy Nine

Antonio called Nina and explained what had happened to Lucy. "So, you see, Nina, I wouldn't ask you if there was someone else, you're the closest thing to family she has."

"I would do anything for her, Antonio, you know that. Luckily the children are on holiday with their grandparents, so it isn't a problem."

"Thanks, Nina."

Antonio had tried to get hold of his brother with no success, it was always the same with him, he was probably with some piece of arse, namely Sasha Breschnevsky.

He rang Stevo. "I need you to come over right now."

"Why, what's going on?"

"Look Stevo, I'm asking you to please come over."

Stevo knew by Antonio's voice that something serious had happened, so he jumped into his car and drove like a maniac. The lift wasn't coming quick enough so he took the stairs two at a time. He banged on the apartment door.

Antonio let him in, he was dreading his reaction. He poured them a large whisky and shoved one into Stevo's hand. "You better drink this."

"Just tell me what the fuck is going on, we've all been looking for Lucy so where is she? This is about her isn't it?"

"I'm so sorry, Stevo, Lucy was killed in a hit and run about two hours ago." Antonio steeled himself for his friend's response.

Stevo didn't speak, he couldn't, he was choking back the tears. He held his chest, it was as if his heart was about to explode.

Antonio put his hand on Stevo's shoulder. Stevo glared at him. "This better hadn't be down to you or Gianni."

"Why would you think that?"

"Why? Are you fucking kidding me, lately all things point back to you and yours!"

"Come on, Stevo, you're not thinking clearly."

"It's simple really, trouble follows you around, I thought we left all that in the past."

"This was an accident, Stevo, it's just that the bastard didn't stop."

"Where is Gianni?"

The doorbell rang interrupting their conversation. Stevo got to the door first, he was like a mad man. He grabbed Gianni by the throat. "I swear to God if I find out you had anything to do with this, I'll fucking kill you."

Antonio was trying in vain to separate them. "Let go of him, Stevo."

Stevo knocked Antonio to the ground with one punch. He was so angry he was capable of murder. He had Gianni on the ground now, he was kicking and punching him.

Katie heard the commotion and came to see what was going on. "Stevo, please stop, what are you doing?" she screamed at him. "You're going to kill him."

Stevo let go of Gianni. "You're not worth it!"

Antonio was sitting on the floor rubbing his chin; shit, that was like being kicked by a mule. Katie rushed over to him. "Oh, God are you alright?"

"Yes, yes I'm ok, what about Gianni?"

"I'm ok, man." He looked at Stevo. "You've got one hell of a punch!"

"Is somebody going to tell me what is going on here?" Katie demanded.

"Nothing, just a misunderstanding that got out of hand." Antonio told her. "I thought you were having a lie down."

"I was."

"But you took the sleeping tablets?"

"No, I couldn't face them, I didn't want to block out the pain of losing my best friend!"

"I'm sorry, Katie."

Katie walked over to Stevo and put her arms around him. "I can't believe that she's gone and we'll never see her ever again!" Katie was struggling with her emotions.

Stevo held her. "She was a wonderful bright young woman, she had everything to live for, who could do such a thing?"

"She truly loved you, Stevo, all she wanted was for you to marry her and then she was going to have loads of babies!"

"I loved her too, Katie, but I never had a chance to tell her. I don't think I'll ever be the same without her." At that moment Stevo swore to himself that he would never let anything happen to Katie. There had been enough deaths to deal with.

Antonio watched them, he felt a twinge of jealousy, why had she not opened up to him like that? Was he not approachable? He knew that she loved him, but he doubted it was completely. Did she not trust him?

"Look tensions are a bit high, why don't we open a bottle of wine and talk?" Antonio suggested, interrupting them.

"I don't want to talk to you right now Antonio." Stevo told him. "Gianni, I'm sorry if I hurt you."

"Don't worry about it, I've had worse!" he laughed, but not too hard as his ribs hurt.

"I'm going to ring Matt and arrange to meet him at the flat. Do you want to come with me, Stevo?" Katie asked him.

"Yes, I'd like to see him."

"I just need to get straightened up, give me five minutes."

Antonio felt helpless. "I'll drive you."

"I'll take her in my car," Stevo insisted. "Don't worry she'll be safe with me."

"Katie?" Antonio looked at her.

"That's fine with me." Katie couldn't be around the de Marcos right now, there was something that wasn't quite right here, they had all been fighting and it was definitely something to do with Lucy.

After Katie left the room Antonio tried to talk to Stevo. "I promise you, Stevo, we'll find out who did this."

"Yes, we'll do everything we can," Gianni spoke up.

"I know you will."

"Bring Katie back safely."

"Hey, it's only a ten minute drive from here, what could possibly happen?"

Katie came back into the room. "I think I'm going to stay over at the flat tonight, you know. I just want to be on my own."

"You don't have to do that, baby."

"I do."

"Then I'll come with you, you shouldn't be on your own at a time like this."

"I won't be, Stevo and Matt will be there."

Antonio didn't like the idea of Katie being on her own with Matt, she was so vulnerable right now, anything could happen. "I called Nina she's on her way over, I thought you would appreciate some female company."

"You shouldn't be bothering her, God knows she's had enough to deal with."

"Yes, I know that, but you get on with her really well and I thought if you talked to her it might help," Antonio paused. "She lost someone she loved too."

"Didn't you lose your parents and your sister?"

That hurt, thought Antonio, he gritted his teeth. "Yes, but I thought female company was what you needed right now."

"Don't patronise me!"

Antonio could feel anger surging through his entire body. He tightened his fists. "I'm only trying to help."

"Jesus, Antonio, put your own house in order first!"

"Katie, you can't possibly think that this is somehow connected to me?"

"I can't talk to you right now." She picked up her overnight bag.

"Come on, Antonio, Katie's upset, she doesn't know what she is saying." Gianni could see the sweat dripping off his brother's brow, he looked like he was going to explode at any minute.

266

"I beg to differ, Gianni, what the hell was I thinking getting mixed up in your family." Katie looked right through him, she was so angry, she hated them both right now and didn't know if she would ever recover from the devastating death of her best friend.

"Come on, Stevo, let's go." Katie couldn't look at Antonio, there was more to this than any of them were saying.

Antonio was livid, he wanted to grab her by the scruff of her pretty little neck and give her a goddamn shake, bring her to her senses. Gianni held his brother's arm.

"Let her go, Antonio."

Reluctantly Antonio did as he said, but he was far from happy. "Call me, Katie." His words fell on deaf ears as she slammed the door behind her.

"I can't fucking believe this, what the hell am I supposed to have done?"

"She's just reacting in anger, don't worry she'll calm down." Gianni tried to reassure him.

"I hope so, I can't lose her, not now, everything was going so goddamn well. I knew that it was too good to be true."

"Come on, man, you're totally overreacting."

"Am I? I wonder."

Katie and Stevo left the building just as Nina was pulling up. Katie was relieved to see her.

"Oh, Nina, this is one of the worst days of my entire life."

Nina put her arms around her. "Dear God, Katie, what's going on here?"

"I don't know what to think, just get me the hell away from here." Katie's voice was full of anguish.

"Where are you going?"

"Stevo and I are meeting Matt at the flat."

"Do you want me to come along?"

"Please, Nina, I would really appreciate that."

Stevo nodded, he desperately wanted to get to the bottom of the days events, somebody would pay for taking Lucy's life and he didn't give a shit if he got a life sentence for it.

Chapter Eighty

Matt arrived first, he still had a key and let himself in. He smiled to himself when he saw his sister's stilettos and remembered how excited she was getting ready for her birthday, it only felt like yesterday to him. He picked them up, Jesus, she would never have fun again, her life was over. Those bastards would pay for this, it had to be down to them, he just knew it. He was going to tell Katie everything he knew and then it was up to her what she did with that information. He hoped and prayed it would be the right thing and that she would see sense.

He heard the key in the door and was surprised when Katie turned up with Stevo and Nina in tow, that was the last thing he expected. He couldn't talk to her in front of Stevo, that was for sure, he was loyal to the de Marcos and nothing would change that. His first reaction was to hug Katie and kiss her. "I can barely believe it, Lucy dead."

"Oh, Matt, I can't put into words how I feel right now, she rang me you know, earlier today."

"I'll make some coffee, or would you prefer tea?"

"I think we need something stronger pal," Stevo was feeling it now, his brain felt like it was going to explode.

"Whatever you want Stevo," Matt's voice was soothing. "Lucy talked about you all the time you know, she thought the world of you."

"I can't get my head around this, was it definitely her or could they have made a mistake."

Matt put a comforting hand on Stevo's shoulder. "I truly wish it was all some kind of huge mistake, but I identified her body less than two hours ago, I'm so sorry. I can't help thinking that if I was there for her more she would still be here."

"It's not your fault, she looked up to you, you were a great brother to her."

"Thanks, Stevo, that means a lot to me."

Nina's mind flashed back to her husband's death, just briefly. She knew that she had to try and keep these guys together.

"Katie and I will make a pot of tea, do you have any whisky?"

"Sure, Lucy liked a tipple every now and then, Katie will show you where it is."

Nina remembered that they were once an item. This guy seemed so nice, so down to earth, so genuine, she couldn't help but feel that Katie should be with him. The de Marcos were bad news, she knew that more than anyone. If she could get her away from him then she would. After all this heartache this young girl deserved better.

Katie led her to the kitchen. She saw a picture of Matt, Lucy and her when they were all on a night out together, they looked so happy. She picked it up and ran her finger over Lucy's image. "She was so full of life, so bubbly, I don't know what I will do without her to confide in."

"I understand how you feel, Katie, it is a horrible feeling to think that you will never see her again. It's like a big gaping hole that will never be filled, always a small part of you missing." She had a distant look in her eyes.

"You are so brave, Nina, you've been through hell and back. I don't know how you managed to keep it together."

"If it wasn't for you and your kindness I don't think I would be here right now myself."

"Oh, please don't say things like that, I can't bear it."

"I mean it, Katie, you have no idea what you did for me and the kids, you gave me something worth living for again, brought me back to my senses. If Roberto is looking down now, he would be so proud of me."

Katie couldn't take it anymore, she collapsed and fell on the kitchen floor and sobbed. It was a heart wrenching sob. "Why, why her, what did she do to deserve that?"

Nina's heart went out to the poor girl. "Shh, Katie, I'm here." She held her tight as Katie rocked back and forth in her arms.

She was trembling and shaking her head. "I just don't get it."

In the living room Matt and Stevo felt slightly awkward, the last thing they wanted was to show their emotions. Matt was unsure of what to say to this guy that Lucy was mad about, but there were many questions that he wanted answers to.

"Can I ask you something?"

Stevo looked a little disturbed. "You're going to ask me about the de Marcos aren't you?"

"Yes, but you don't have to answer anything you don't want to, I know that you are loyal to them."

"I was, but I'm not so sure now."

"Can I trust you?"

"You can trust me implicitly, I want to find the bastard that did this more than anyone, I worshipped the ground your sister walked on, she was everything to me. I wish I had never let her out of my sight, she was a special person."

Matt held his breath, unsure of whether he should say what he really thought. "I can't understand what has happened to my sister, but somehow I think it's connected with the de Marcos." He waited for Stevo's response.

269

"If it makes you feel any better, I feel exactly the same, but I can't prove anything, they are well protected. So you see if they were somehow involved it will never be pinned on them."

"Well protected you say, what do you mean, someone on the inside?"

"They have protection, high up in the police force."

"I need help to bring them down Stevo, they took Lucy's life."

"I can't help you, they'll kill me!"

"But what about justice for the woman you loved?"

"I know what you are saying, but I can't do it."

"Do it for Lucy, the love you lost, that bouncing personality who had so much life in her."

"I wish I could, but you don't mess with these guys."

"Stevo, no one is closer to them than you are, you are in a prime position. Help me bring them down." He was almost begging him now.

"Whoa, wait a minute man, you don't know what you are asking of me."

"I do."

"I gotta go man, this is doing my head in."

"Promise me you will think about what I said."

Stevo shook his hand. "I will." He left the apartment and headed for the nearest bar, right now all he wanted to do was to drink himself into oblivion.

Matt went into the kitchen. He saw Katie distraught on the floor. "It's ok, Nina, I'll look after her now, we need to talk."

"Katie?"

Katie nodded her head. "Thanks, Nina, but I'll be ok with Matt."

Nina was frightened for them both, Antonio would be crazy if he knew they were here alone together. "If you're sure, I just want you to be alright."

"Thanks Nina, but nobody knows me better than Matt, it's ok, you go and I'll call you tomorrow."

Nina kissed her. "You know where I am if you need me."

"I know, thank you for being here for me, but you have been through enough."

Nina knew in her heart that Katie was right, she just worried about the repercussions. "Ok, we'll talk tomorrow."

Matt saw Nina to her car. "Thanks, Nina, I know you care about her, so do I."

"You still love her don't you?"

"Yes, and I always will no matter what."

"Good luck to you both, I hope she stays with you."

"Me too, I need her as much as she needs me right now."

"Just promise me you'll move on, forget about the de Marcos, it's too dangerous."

"Right now, I can't promise you anything."

270

"She's in safe hands, I know that, I can see how much you care about her. But if I were you, after the funeral I would get as far away from here as possible. Antonio will fight you tooth and nail for Katie, believe me."

Matt didn't react. "It was good to meet you Nina, I'll keep her safe, don't worry." His voice was cool and steady.

Peter Hammond was in the phone box, he dialled Antonio's number. "Stevo left ten minutes ago and Nina Valetti is just getting in her car."

Antonio was seething, he had to get Katie away from Lucy's brother. He knew about Felicia's baby and if he didn't do something that son of a bitch would blurt everything out.

Matt sat Katie down on the sofa and placed a cup of strong tea, laced with whisky into her still trembling hands.

"So, you said that Lucy phoned you?"

"Yes, she was at the club."

"At the club? What would she be doing there mid afternoon?"

"She was looking for her purse."

"Did you hear from her after that?"

Katie shook her head. "No, I didn't, I just told her not to be late. I was making a meal for us, I wanted to impress her with my cooking."

Matt took the tea out of her hands and sat down beside her. He tilted her chin towards him and looked into her eyes. The blueness of them still amazed him. He took a tissue from the box on the table and gently wiped her tears away. She was so beautiful for one so sad, he felt his old feelings rush to the surface and planted a kiss on her lips. Caught up in the moment Katie kissed him back.

"What the hell are we doing Matt," she whispered.

"I'm sorry, I shouldn't have done that, it was wrong of me." He stood up. "I'd better go, we'll talk tomorrow."

"Matt, please don't feel guilty, I was as much to blame, I shouldn't have kissed you back."

"It's ok, let's pretend it didn't happen, nobody needs to know."

Katie knew what he meant, if Antonio knew he would go mental. "Ok, I'm going to stay here tonight."

"Will you be ok?"

"Yes, I need some space, you know?"

"I understand, I'll let you know if the police come up with anything."

She walked to the door with him. "Take care, Matt."

Chapter Eighty One

Matt was just about to get into his car when somebody pulled him by the arm. "Mr de Marco would like a word." The man pointed to the limo.

"Mr de Marco can go to fucking hell."

"I like your bravado, Mr Carmichael, but my boss ain't taking no for an answer," Jed barked at him.

"I told you, go to fucking hell."

"Look we can do this the easy way or the hard way." The man opened his jacket pocket and revealed a gun.

"Ok, ok, where are we going?"

"Just get in your car and follow the limo."

Matt did as he was told, he was frightened now, very frightened. Was his time up too? Would he be murdered and his body never found. He heard about this kind of thing happening all the time. There were no witnesses, this was a quiet area that Lucy lived in and everyone kept themselves to themselves. "Look what's this all about?"

The man said nothing and pointed the gun at him. Matt stayed silent, he pulled on to the waste ground, beads of sweat were dripping off his brow and his heart was racing.

"Get out."

Matt thought about grabbing the gun from him, just for a split second. He wouldn't stand a chance, this guy wasn't messing around. He walked over to the waiting limo, he was shaking now, he didn't want to die. He took a deep breath as he opened the door.

Antonio de Marco smiled at him, that dazzling smile that annoyed him, who did he think he was. "What can I do for you?"

"It's more about what I can do for you."

"What do you mean?"

"I want to help you."

"How, my sister is dead?"

"I have contacts, we'll find out who did this and bring them to justice, trust me."

"Why have you brought me out here, in the middle of nowhere." Matt stammered. "And with a gun pointed at me for Christ sakes!"

"It was a bit heavy handed, please excuse my associate."

"Jesus I thought…" his voice trailed off.

Antonio de Marco laughed at him suddenly realising that Matt was a very worried man. "Oh my God, you actually thought I was going to have you killed, what kind of man do you take me for?" He could hardly believe it. "I have no intention of harming you in any way."

"What can you do that the police aren't doing already?"

"I told you I have contacts."

"And I suppose you want something in return?"

"Ok, I'll cut to the chase shall I?" Before Matt had time to answer Antonio continued. "I love Katie very deeply and I am going to marry her, I don't want anything getting in the way."

"You have nothing to worry about, she's in love with you, not me."

"She's very vulnerable right now and I wouldn't want you to let something slip, something that might hurt my brother."

"If I was going to say something I would have done it by now."

"I'm glad to hear that."

"Is that it?"

"Just one more thing, Mr Carmichael, do me a favour and stop digging into my past, you won't find anything."

Matt gulped. "I don't know what you mean."

"I'm not a fool, please don't treat me like one."

"I was just looking out for Katie, that's all," Matt admitted, it was no use lying to him.

"That's not your job any more."

"Are you finished, Mr de Marco?"

"Yes, thank you for your time."

Matt couldn't believe the arrogance of the man, what the hell did Katie see in this jumped up arse in his designer suits?

"By the way there may be a new position coming up in Jacksons, I'll put in a word for you."

"No, thank you." Matt left the car. Taking a hanky out of his pocket he wiped his brow as he watched the limo drive off. This was a fucking nightmare, he didn't want to be mixed up in whatever the hell was going on. He had to stay away from Katie and the only way to be safe was to move out of the area, go abroad or something. He would decide after his sister's funeral.

Chapter Eighty Two

Gianni was waiting for Antonio, he was dreading telling him about Sasha's car being found burnt out. His brother wasn't stupid, he was bound to click on that it was involved in the hit and run.

"Everything ok?"

"There's been some news."

"Good news I hope."

"Not really, Sasha's car was stolen earlier on today and the police have just found it burnt out."

"Joyriders?"

"Probably."

"Burnt out you say?"

"Yes."

"How convenient."

"How's that?"

"Well, strange that Sasha's car is stolen the same day Lucy Carmichael is killed in a hit and run."

"So what."

"It just seems an odd coincidence that's all."

"You can't seriously think that Sasha had anything to do with this?"

"Did I say she did Gianni?"

"Look I want to find out who the fuck did this as much as you do."

"Then you better find out and fast."

"I'm already on to it. We got a couple of suspects, there was a bank robbery two streets away, right scum bags they are, dregs of society."

"Get it sorted out then, send a few of the guys over."

"Already in hand."

Stuart Canavan was pissed up as usual, he was looking for a fight and he didn't mind who with. He had pulled off a big bank job and nobody was any the wiser, he thought he was the dog's bollocks.

"What the fuck are you looking at?" He stared at the young lad next to him.

"Er… Nothing I'm just getting a drink."

"A fucking drink you tosser, you're barely out of nappies, lad. I suggest you fuck off."

"Look what's the problem?"

"Come on, Stuart, behave will you or I'll have to put you out." The landlord didn't want his pub smashed up again.

"That little shit is annoying me, not showing any respect like."

"Prick," the young lad whispered as he walked past Canavan. His job done he left the pub.

Stevo was waiting for him and shoved a wad of money in his hand.

"Did you fucking hear that, the little son of a bitch, who's he calling a prick?" Canavan kicked his chair back and staggered out of the pub. He saw the young lad waving at him, that made him even more angry. "Come here you little bastard, I'll fucking kill you."

The lad disappeared around the corner, Canavan was running now. Gasping for breath he leaned against the wall. "Little fucker."

He saw the glinting blade but it was too late to do anything about it. Stevo shoved the knife into him. "Die you murdering bastard." He twisted the knife deeper into his gut.

As he pulled the blade out, Canavan dropped to the ground, a look of total disbelief on his face. Stevo watched as the scumbag's life ebbed away, a crimson tide of blood seeping into the gutter. He leaned over him as he gasped his last breath and smiled into his face. "A little farewell present for you." He left a small trace of heroin in his jacket pocket, removing the wad of notes. He would burn the money, it was blood money as far as he was concerned and already marked. The police would think Canavan had been robbed of his drugs and killed for them, they wouldn't bat an eyelid for the likes of him, they would be pleased for one less scumbag on the streets, end of story. It was all too frequent these days, Stevo sighed, he was sick and tired of this shit.

"You should have consulted me first," Antonio sighed.

"Too late for that now, bro."

"So, which mastermind have you got on the job?" Antonio asked, dreading his response.

"Stevo."

"You what, are you crazy?" Antonio was livid. "He's not in a fit state, what if he makes a mistake?"

"You worry too much, man, he's got help, nothing will go wrong."

"I hope for your sake that you're right about that."

"Jesus, they're professionals, all our guys are, remember."

"I just don't like being out of the loop, that's all."

"What? You think I need your advice for something like this. Christ we've dealt with this sort of thing all our lives, it's no big deal."

"I've got enough going on with Katie right now, she's the one I'm worried about."

"Don't be, nobody's interested in harming one hair on her head, they wouldn't dare and anyway she's so likeable and cute."

Antonio laughed. "Yeah, she's definitely not like that chick Sasha that's for sure."

"Oh, come on man, don't bring Sasha up again. I'm just having a bit of harmless fun with her that's all, she's a good shag after all."

"Yeah, she sure knows how to please."

"Hey, I don't want to get into details, but how was she on blow jobs!" he joked.

Antonio threw a cushion at him. "Enough."

"I'm going over the club, are you coming?"

"I may as well, I got nothing better to do."

"The lovely Katie will be back to her normal self tomorrow morning and she'll regret being off with you."

"I hope you're right, Gianni."

"Fancy a turn on the roulette wheel?"

"The wheel of fortune, yeah why not, I'm going to whoop your arse tonight."

"In your dreams."

Antonio felt so much better, his brother had a knack of making him feel at ease in times of crisis.

Chapter Eighty Three

Stevo was watching Luke Henderson, he was trying to tap up a tom. Whatever he was suggesting wasn't going down too well.

"Filthy bastard." The prostitute couldn't believe what he was asking her to do.

Henderson had been up at court a couple of times for serious assault. He was a woman hater, the police knew it and the locals knew it. He blamed the assaults on his drug addiction and that he didn't know what he was doing. As none of the women would testify against him the judge had no option but to give him a light sentence.

The woman was trying to get away from him, but Henderson had a vice-like grip on her arm. "Let go, you're hurting me."

Henderson laughed cruelly. "Good, you goddamn bitch, you'll do what I tell you."

"This man bothering you?" Keith asked.

"Yes, I just want to go."

"You heard the lady, let her go."

"Lady, I don't see no fucking lady, why don't you fuck off and mind your own business."

"I said, let the lady go, I may have a business proposition for you." Keith pressed a handful of cash into the woman's hand. "For your wasted time."

"Ok man, no problem." Henderson loosened his grip.

The woman ran off clenching the cash in her fist glad to be away from that sick bastard.

"Just out of interest, what did you ask her to do?"

"You wouldn't understand, pal."

"Try me." Keith couldn't be shocked; he'd heard about Henderson and his bag of instruments he liked to use to inflict pain on his victims.

Henderson opened his jacket pocket and showed him. "I was going to give her five hundred for letting me stick this up her arse." The syringe was ready to go.

Keith felt the bile rise in his throat and it was all he could to do contain himself. Swallowing the vomit back. "Is that it?" He forced out a loud laugh, Henderson certainly was a sick fuck, it would be his pleasure to remove him from this life.

"So, maybe we could pick up a couple of toms and watch them do each other, they're all druggies anyway, what difference would it make?" Henderson's eyes were on stalks, he was high as a kite and still floating.

"Let's take a little walk." Keith had seen some things in his life but nothing like this, it was beyond even his comprehension.

"Why?" Henderson was bricking it. "Have I offended you in some way?"

"Nah, I couldn't give a fuck about the toms, they're in this for the money, mainly for drugs, so what the hell, they get what they deserve don't they." Keith although cringing inside put his arm around Henderson as if they were best buddies.

"Finally, somebody who agrees with me, fan fucking tastic, that's what I say."

"How about we talk a bit of business then, see if we can help each other out like."

"Oh yeah, what you got in mind?"

Good, he had Henderson's interest now. "I got this nice deal coming up and need a distributor, I thought you were the guy for the job seeing as how your name keeps cropping up as the man in the know." Keith was playing on his ego and hoped that he had him.

Henderson was lapping it up, finally he was recognised as being a useful contact. "Sure, what you got?"

Christ, Stevo was right, how easy was it to reel this punk in. "Why don't you come to mine and I'll let you have a sample, a freebie of course, and then you can decide for yourself if it's any good."

"Hey man, cool, where's your place at?" Henderson was rubbing his hands, he was the big man now, nobody, but nobody would mess with him, he would be able to do whatever he wanted. Life was going to be one long party and he couldn't wait.

"Not far." The dumb arse didn't even ask his name, he was so smacked up that he didn't have a clue what was going to happen next, everything was going to plan.

They arrived at the dingy bedsit. Keith could see that Henderson was extremely disappointed. "Hey man, I'm keeping a low profile, once this shit hits the streets we will be fucking Gods, trust me," he reassured him.

"Low profile huh?"

"Yep, I don't want the likes of the Fishers and Tattersills getting a whiff of this, or we'll be snuffed out like that." Keith clicked his fingers for ultimate effect, and it worked a treat.

"Ok, ok where is it?" Henderson was like a kid in a candy shop, excited and ready for his sweetener, all courtesy of Stevo.

Keith unlocked the cabinet door, it was the only piece of furniture in the entire room. "This is going to blow your mind, you're going to get a feeling like you never had before." He produced the bag of white powder.

Henderson was like a pig in shit, he couldn't get enough. "Wow, man, this is good stuff, what the fuck is it?" He stuck his finger back in the bag and sniffed it up his nostril.

"Hey, if I told you man, I would have to kill you."

Henderson stuck his finger in the plastic bag once more. "You're so fucking funny."

"Yeah, yeah, just enjoy it." Keith excused himself as he pretended he needed a slash. He made the call and two minutes later Stevo and Jed appeared.

"Hey what the fuck is going on, we avin a party man?" Everything was a bit of a haze now and his limbs were stiff, he felt paralysed, unable to move. Was this part of the hit or was something else happening? His mind became clogged and he suddenly realised that anything could happen to him now and there would be absolutely nothing that he could do about it.

"Hold him down." The two men obediently obliged. "And take off his belt."

Stevo rolled up Henderson's sleeve and produced a needle. "This will be the best hit you ever had, you deserve it."

"Hang on a minute." Keith whispered into Stevo's ear, Stevo had a massive smile on his face, he was going to enjoy every minute of this.

"Get his fucking trousers off and turn him over."

"What, I'm not fucking gay, you monster!" Henderson was trying to shout but his voice was all mumbled.

"What's that? You'd love a gay monster!" Stevo laughed. "I'm glad to oblige. I hope that you enjoy this as much as I am going to."

"You gay fuck, get off me." Henderson's words went unnoticed.

Stevo pulled on some rubber gloves and opened the jar of Vaseline. He rammed two fingers up Henderson's arsehole as hard as he could, he'd make the fucker squirm. This was the ultimate, shameful insult that you could ever do to a man. As much as it disgusted Stevo, he knew that he had to go through with it, all he could think about was his poor Lucy, in the wrong place at the wrong time. Taking a deep breath he pulled Henderson's cheeks wide apart and rammed the needle as far up his anus as was possible. Blood and pus, along with the contents of the needle, spurted out all over the place, just missing his face. "Again, again, we need to do it again."

Keith looked at him incredulously, was Stevo for real? Looking at his face he knew not to argue or that syringe would end up in his eye.

He nodded to Jed and as he pushed his face into the rotten carpet, Henderson began to vomit.

Stevo once again shoved the syringe up his shitty arse, it looked like he hadn't washed in the nether regions for months, the filthy bastard.

"Hey, you need to get a vein man, that ain't going to kill him!" Keith said, he couldn't bear to watch much more of this torture.

"You don't say!"

Keith and Jed picked him up and threw him on to the floor. They pulled up his sleeve and wrapped the belt around tight.

Stevo winked at him as he emptied the contents of the syringe into his rotten body. He watched as his body squirmed and shuddered violently, standing back well

279

out of the way in case of any more unexpected eruptions. He laughed, enjoying the horrific sight in front of him. "If it's good enough for a tom, then it's good enough for you, pal. Good night, scumbag."

"He deserved that," Jed smirked.

Keith couldn't hold back any longer and spewed up.

"If it's any consolation, he wasn't gay, his arse was too tight for that, must have stung like fuck." It was all over in the blink of an eye, more's the pity Stevo thought, still the fuckers had paid their dues, retribution for his poor sweet Lucy.

"Let's get out of here."

"What about the landlord?"

"No probs, he was happy with the grand I gave him, Henderson will be discovered tomorrow morning."

Stevo pulled off his gloves and shoved them into the plastic carrier bag, along with the syringe. The police would think that Henderson had brought a tom back, tried it on with her and she had got the better of him, another case closed. Stevo was proud of himself.

Chapter Eighty Four

Katie was trying her best to sleep, but finding it impossible she rang Matt. It went straight onto the answer machine. "Oh, God, Matt, where are you, I need you, please call me back as soon as you get this message."

Matt was sitting in the dark in his sitting room, he so desperately wanted to go to her. His heart ached, but he knew that he couldn't answer her call, Antonio had made it clear to him that he wanted him nowhere near her. Poor Katie, she wanted a link to Lucy and who better than Matt, he was the only one who truly knew her. He visualised Lucy's rigid body, the life taken so abruptly from her.

The phone rang again interrupting his terrible vision of his sister. It was Antonio de Marco. "What we discussed earlier, just to let you know that everything is ok." The phone went dead.

Shit, it was too late to stop the paper going to print, too late to retract his reward!

Right now he didn't know whether to laugh or cry. Justice had apparently been served, his sister's killer had been disposed of, of that he was sure. Now he would stay for the funeral and move on, get out of this insane situation while he still breathed. Should he take Katie with him, would she listen? He doubted it, he had to lay it to rest along with Lucy, Katie had been the love of his life and he would never love anyone like that ever again. Katie had chosen her own path, a dangerous path, but if ever she needed him then he would drop everything for her. He had been dealt a devastating blow and now had to be a man and deal with it. Coward was not in his vocabulary, but some situations you just had to step back from and this was one of them. He hoped that he would never regret it.

In complete desperation Katie called Antonio, there was no answer. Cursing she phoned Nina. "It's me, can you come over, I know I said that I wanted to be alone, but I can't stand it any longer."

"Oh, Katie, I'll be right there, honey, it's ok."

"I'm so sorry to bother you."

"It's no problem, I can be with you in thirty minutes."

"Thanks, Nina." Katie replaced the receiver and began to sob, she still couldn't believe the events of the day. In her short life she had been to too many funerals and she didn't know how she would handle this one. Lucy had always been the life and soul of the party and life would never be the same without her.

Chapter Eighty Five

Nursing a bit of a hangover from the previous night's drinking with Gianni, Antonio poured himself a fresh cup of coffee. He opened the patio door and stepped out on to the balcony, breathing in the fresh air. His luxury penthouse was on the twelfth floor of the building overlooking Regents Park. The early morning rush hour and the hustle and bustle of the city always amazed him, it was days like this that he really enjoyed waking up to. Although the sun shone it was still a chilly morning, he sipped at his hot coffee and flicked through the morning newspapers just as he did religiously every morning. It was an item in the local newspaper that grabbed his attention.

Gianni had stayed over, although he couldn't exactly remember getting here, he must have been well plastered. The smell of fresh coffee hit him and he went into the kitchen and helped himself to a huge mug. "Hey, what about breakfast?"

Antonio was engrossed in the newspaper. "Er... No thanks, not hungry, help yourself."

"Not hungry, that's not like you, you coming down with something?"

Antonio ignored him as he continued reading.

Gianni was getting annoyed now, he hated the silent treatment. He marched over to the balcony. "What's up?"

Antonio handed him the newspaper. "This."

Gianni cast his eye over it and flung it back. "So?"

"So, we don't need this, every fucker will be crawling out of the woodwork."

"But we got them didn't we?"

"Yeah, but has anyone told her brother?"

"Yes, I phoned him last night, he must have gone to the press yesterday morning."

"The stupid fuck."

A ten thousand pound reward had been offered to anyone who could provide any information leading up to the arrest and conviction of the hit and run driver. He had guts after all, Antonio thought. "Ring Frank and get him to send someone over to Matthew Carmichael's house, sooner he's told the whole story the better."

"This could be the perfect opportunity to go and speak with Katie, tell her the police have evidence connecting Henderson and Canavan to the hit and run," Gianni advised him.

"Sure, sounds like a good idea, but how would I tell her that I knew?"

"She knows you have connections right, knows that you have friends in high places?"

Antonio nodded.

"Good, now get your coat and go and tell her before she hears it on the local bloody news and think yourself lucky that it hasn't hit the mornings papers."

"Only because it was too late to print it."

"Just go, bro, I'll contact Frank and meet you at the club, we have got a big night tonight."

"Big night?"

"Yeah, only the Businessman of The Year awards, last year's winner is this year's host!"

"Shit, I can do without it."

"Just be grateful. You've got the best manageress and a top class chef, it's going to be amazing."

"I can't be arsed going."

"Listen, I'll oversee the setting up of the cameras, Veronica's employed extra staff and the menus were devised over two months ago. All you have to do is be there tonight, see if you can win it for the third year on the trot, now that would be something worth celebrating"

"If I cared, probably."

"You have to be there, you've waited all year for this."

"And this year, I really don't care." He wanted Katie on his arm, but he would be lucky if she was even speaking to him. Remembering the pampering session he had booked as a surprise he smiled.

"Brainwave?"

"I hope so." He switched on his answer machine and checked his messages. "Even better."

"What's that?"

"I have a missed call from Katie, early this morning."

"Sounds promising." Thank God, Gianni thought.

Chapter Eighty Six

Katie was still lounging around in her dressing gown when Antonio arrived. Nina opened the door for him. "She doesn't want to see you."

"She'll see me." He pushed her out of the way. "I have some news."

"What news?" Katie looked directly at him. "Nothing you say will bring Lucy back though will it?"

"I'm so sorry about Lucy, she was a lovely young woman." Antonio went over to her and sat next to her on the sofa he held her hand. "They've got two men."

"Who were they?"

"I don't have their names, but apparently they were involved in a bank robbery a couple of streets away. They were making a fast getaway."

"And they ploughed straight into her?"

"Yes." Antonio omitted to tell her that it was Sasha's car, it was for the best that she didn't know, he decided. It wouldn't come out in court as there would be no court case due to the fact that both men were dead.

"Has anyone told Matt yet?"

"The police should have told him by now."

"I need to call him." Katie jumped to her feet.

"Why don't you get dressed and I'll drive you over to his place?"

"Are you sure?"

"Yes." Antonio was stalling for time, knowing full well that Matt was being picked up by the police as he spoke. They were taking him down to the station to give him a full briefing.

Once Katie was out of the room Nina turned to him. "Why are you being so nice, I thought you didn't want her near him."

"I want whatever she wants, he's merely a friend to her."

"Who are you trying to convince, me or yourself?"

"She's in love with me and that's all I need to know."

"Be careful, Antonio, one day she'll be on to you."

"Come on, Nina, don't be like that."

"Like what, I'm only civil to you for Katie's sake, but I haven't forgotten my husband's death even if you have." She shot him a cold dark look. "I can't bear to be around you, tell Katie I had to go and pick up the children."

284

He wished he could change Nina's mind about him, but he realised that he never would. One thing he knew was that Nina had not discussed her concerns with Katie, if she had then he would have known about it.

Katie reappeared dressed in her skinny jeans and a canary yellow t shirt, her hair in a pony tail. She looked fresh faced, you couldn't tell that she had barely slept all night. She was a picture of perfect health as usual. He wanted to tell her how beautiful she looked but now certainly wasn't the right time.

"Oh, where's Nina?"

"She had to go and pick up the kids. She apologised, I guess she'll call you later. Are you ready to go?"

"Do you think I should call him first?"

"Do you really want to tell him over the phone?"

"You're right, I'd rather tell him in person." She picked up the house keys. "I better give him these too."

"So, have you finally decided to move in with me officially?" Antonio smiled.

"Yes, why not, I've got nothing to lose have I?"

Katie was banging on the door with sheer frustration.

"He obviously isn't home."

"Then where is he, his car's here."

"Bathroom?"

Katie shot him an annoyed look. "This is strange, you don't think he's done anything stupid do you?"

"No, of course not, he's not the type."

"Are you looking for Mr Carmichael?" a robust balding man enquired.

"Yes? Why do you know where he is?"

"The police came for him about twenty minutes ago." The middle-aged man seemed to be enjoying all the drama. "Perhaps he was mixed up in his sister's murder."

"Don't be so goddamn ridiculous." Antonio got hold of Katie's arm and led her back to the car. "Pay no attention, silly old fool."

"We'd better go and find out what's happening."

"Do you think that's wise?"

"I don't know and I don't really care." Katie was insistent.

"Ok, ok, I'll get Fred to take you, I've got some business I need to attend to."

"I'll get a cab."

"How about I drop you off and Fred picks you up when you're ready?"

"Whatever." Katie felt totally drained now, in fact she was rather unsteady on her feet. Everything went black, the next thing she remembered was coming around in hospital.

"Wh... what am I doing here?"

"You passed out, you were out for some time. It's nothing to worry about, your blood pressure is a little low. Rest and recuperation is what you need now dear," the little dumpy nurse tutted. Girls these days, a little bit of excitement and they couldn't handle it. She'd better go and tell that charming young man his girlfriend was awake.

"Mr de Marco, your lady friend is awake, she's just suffering from nerves and exhaustion. I would suggest a nice holiday, a stress free one."

"Hmm thank you nurse, I'll see what I can do." Walking back into the sideroom in the Accident and Emergency department he looked at Katie's pale and pasty face. "The nurse said we have to wait until your blood pressure comes back to normal. A cup of tea and biscuit should do it."

"I'm sorry, Antonio."

"Ssh my, darling, it's ok, I'm just glad that you are ok." He sat on the bed next to her and pulled her into his arms. The smell of jasmine and hyacinth hit his nostrils, he was familiar with the smell of her hair now. "You know, Katie, you really are the best thing that ever happened to me."

Katie buried her head in his chest and sighed. "Why do things keep happening? It makes no sense."

"No sense at all my darling." He kissed her head and held her tight. "I called the police station while you were in here. Matt has just been told about the men responsible for Lucy's death."

"They took him down the police station for that?"

"Yes, I guess they thought it was for the best."

"Bastards, I hope they rot in hell."

Antonio was shocked, he had never heard her swear before. "They'll get what's coming don't you worry." He wasn't about to tell her that he knew they were both dead, murdered by Stevo. "Why don't we go home, you can get some rest and speak to Matt later."

Katie nodded, she had no energy to argue, she hadn't eaten since she got the news about her best friend, or had much sleep.

He picked up her coat and helped her off the bed.

"Hold your horses, the doctor hasn't said she could go." The young nurse tried in vain to stop them.

"She's ok and that's all I need to know, but thanks for your help."

Once back at Antonio's apartment he insisted on Katie having a nap.

"I'll try but I don't know if I'll be able to sleep much."

"Do you want a sleeping tablet?"

"No, I'll be ok, but you won't let me sleep for more than a couple of hours?"

"Whatever you want, sweetheart."

"Promise?"

"I promise."

After she was sound asleep he phoned Gianni. "Did you find Stevo?"

"Stevo's gone home for a few days to see his mum."

"Probably a good idea."

"Is everything ok?"

"Yes." Antonio replaced the receiver. He had to go and meet Ralph Anderson and Henry Brookstein, see how they were getting on with Nina Valetti. He had checked Katie's diary, she wasn't in a fit state to discuss business, it was the least he could do, he told himself.

Nina was none too pleased to see him. "What are you doing here, shouldn't you be at home with Katie, or do you not care?"

"Come on, Nina, give the man a break, he's merely looking after Katie's business interests." Ralph couldn't be bothered with this pettiness.

"Yes come on, Nina, give the man a break." Henry put his two penny worth in.

"Jesus Christ, what is it, pick on Nina day, how about we all have some coffee before we begin?" Nina looked at all three of them with total disdain.

"Sounds like a good idea."

Nina left the room, she hated Antonio and it showed. She would have to remain businesslike for her own sake, if they thought she wasn't capable of running this business then they would pull the rug out from under her feet in a flash. And that was one thing she couldn't afford to happen.

Melissa smiled at her boss. "Are you ok, Mrs Valetti?"

"Thank you, yes. I just need some coffee."

"Allow me, that's my job, remember."

"I just need five minutes on my own."

Melissa knew when to keep her mouth shut, Nina had a very fiery nature and she had had a tongue lashing off her on more than one occasion.

After a few deep breaths Nina resumed her composure. Lifting the carefully prepared tray she went back into the meeting room and placed it on to the table.

"Help yourself, gentleman." Once more she was in control. "Now, did you all have a chance to flick through the business proposals?"

"Very impressive, it looks much better than I could ever have imagined."

"Katie came up with the original idea as you know, but with our connections it's going to explode. The orders are coming in thick and fast, we need more experienced staff and the sooner the better," Nina informed them.

"I have a few connections abroad, what if I made some enquiries?"

"For a small fee I suppose?"

Antonio laughed. "Well of course, it is a business after all."

"Did you all bring a list of your contacts, that would be a great start? We want to have an opening evening with our latest range, the last one went down really well. And if we could add to our existing client list then we would have achieved something exceptional. The way it's going we will need bigger premises!"

"Fabulous, then I could look into the design of it." Ralph was excited, another new project, one that he would personally benefit from. It would be fun to see if he could come up with something special to keep all of them interested.

"That would be wonderful Ralph, your name alone precedes you, as do all of ours in our own way. It would be an absolute masterpiece, of that I have no doubt, with your talent it will be world class."

"Hear! Hear!" Henry clapped.

"Now take the proposals home and guard them with your life!"

"So serious, Nina," Antonio chuckled.

"You better believe it, we already have Dobson's sniffing around trying to find out our prices and contacts. It's only a matter of time before someone tries to undercut us."

"I agree, but by the time anybody does we will be well established." Antonio's words were welcomed. "Then it will be too late, as it will be sacrilege to go anywhere else."

"Well that's the meeting over, how about this time next week to finalise?"

"Sounds good."

Antonio left with Henry and Ralph. "So, are you coming to the business awards this evening?"

"Would we miss it?"

"Good, I'll reserve you a table."

"Good man, see you tonight then."

Henry got into his car and sped off. Ralph turned to Antonio. "I see you have had a bit of trouble, real shame about this Lucy girl."

"Yes, it is. Did you meet her?"

"Yes, just the once in the club you know, seemed like a nice enough girl."

"She was."

"What about Katie, how's she taking it?"

"Pretty badly as you would expect."

"I hope to see her with you tonight."

"I very much doubt that she'll be up to it, I left her sleeping, she was utterly exhausted."

"You seem to have had a lot of bad luck lately, my friend." Ralph patted his arm.

"Yeah, you gotta take the rough with the smooth."

"I admire your strength, Antonio."

"I admire your frankness, Ralph."

"See you later then."

Antonio had just got into the car when Nina shouted to him, "I've got Stevo on the phone."

He went back into the building. "Stevo, where the hell are you?"

288

"Just arrived in La Pregheira, just wanted to touch base with you. Sorry I can't be there tonight."

"Hey, that's the least of your problems, take as long as you need."

"Thanks, I will." Stevo put the phone down. He couldn't wait to see his family, live a quiet life for a while. Maybe he would stay, take over his father's farm, find a pretty young local girl to take as his wife. He was sick of the fast life he led in London, maybe now was the time to get out. His mamma would be pleased to see him, he hadn't phoned ahead, he wanted to turn up out of the blue, surprise her, and he knew how she loved surprises.

Chapter Eighty Seven

The club was a hive of activity; Gianni and Veronica were overseeing the whole operation. They were working well together just for a change, that was until Sasha turned up.

"Christ, Gianni, what is that bitch doing here? You know she just winds everybody up, she's so negative!" Veronica looked over at Eddie.

He knew that he ought to do something but he wasn't quite sure what, not yet anyway.

"Gianni, darling."

That Russian accent grated on Veronica's nerves.

"Is there something you would like me to do? I'll go and make sure the tables are set up correctly."

Before Gianni could speak Sasha was off towards the young waitresses. "No, no not like that you stupid idiot, here let me show you." She snatched the napkins out of the young girl's hands.

Gianni couldn't be arsed with Sasha right now, all she was to him was a means to an end. Sergio had promised him that if he looked after his daughter then he would be set for life. That he could have easily endured, but after the Lucy incident he didn't know what to do. He was well and truly in bed with her now, what the fuck could he do to get shot of her? Nothing, he thought, Sergio would come after him and he would be a dead man. He was stuck with her now, unless he could find her an even richer man than him. He would have to think about that one, it would certainly take a brave man and he didn't think anyone was up for the job.

Colin and Kyle were busy ensuring that the glasses were all immaculate. "Poor Lucy, do you think Katie will be here tonight?"

"Knowing Antonio, yes."

"Don't be so cynical, Kyle." Colin was really disturbed about what had happened, he loved Lucy, she was such a sweet girl.

"You know the boss, life goes on, nothing keeps him from business," Kyle stressed.

"Kyle, don't let Gianni hear you or there'll be hell to pay," Veronica warned him.

Kyle shrieked, "Oh my God, Ms Lamont, I nearly had a heart attack."

"Just be careful what you say, you never know who is listening."

"She's right, Kyle, we don't want to start world war three do we?"

Kyle put his hands on his hips. "Sometimes life is such a drama, I feel like I'm in a movie I have no control over." He wiped a tear away.

"Pull yourself together, Kyle." Veronica handed him some napkins.

"Oh, thank you, you are so kind." He pulled one out of the package and blew his nose.

"Those are for the tables, darling."

"Oh, no, what have I done." Kyle broke down.

"Oh for goodness sake, get him out of here before somebody sees him." Veronica pulled the rest of the napkins out of his hands. "I'll do it myself." Bracing herself she walked over to Sasha. I see you are supervising the table setting." She shoved the napkins into Sasha's hands.

"How dare you treat me like a mere servant," Sasha squealed.

"How dare you, I am the manager of this club, one more word, woman, and I'll have you thrown out."

"I think you'll find it will be you, sweetie, who'll be removed and not me."

"Want to try me, darling?"

Sasha saw her beckon Brian, he was a huge man and she definitely didn't want to be shown up in front of all the press who were in the process of setting up the cameras for the evening. She didn't need any bad publicity right now. "Ok, you're the boss, darling, carry on."

"Good, I'm glad we understand each other. I need to check on the kitchen, Brian will be around in case you, shall we say, need some help in leaving."

"I have it under control." Sasha smiled sweetly. Veronica may have won this round, but she certainly hadn't won the battle.

That was easy, thought Veronica, not like that bitch to back down so easily. No doubt she would get her own back when she least expected it, but she would be ready for her.

"Nicholas, darling, something smells absolutely divine, mind if I have a sample?" Before he had time to answer she tasted his latest creation. "Wow, that's so good, you're so clever."

"Now I've told you not to do the taste test, it doesn't need it, it is total perfection even if I say so myself."

"I can't help it, you know how much I love your cooking, one day you will make a wonderful house husband."

Nicholas raised an eyebrow. "You proposing to me?"

"Er, no, whatever gave you that idea? Although I am open to offers, whenever you're ready."

"I'm not really the marrying kind, been there, done that, end of story."

"You forget, Nicholas, so have I, it just wasn't meant to be. We would be a perfect match, don't you think." It was a statement not a question.

"Perhaps, but I am happy as we are."

"I'm just letting you know, darling, that if you were to pop the question I would seriously consider my answer." She kissed him on the cheek. "I'd better let you get on."

"You are a strange lady, Veronica, but I do care for you very deeply."

"I know you do."

Nicholas carried on preparing the banquet, smiling to himself. He would never re-marry, not in a million years. He hoped that would be the last time the subject was ever raised. If Veronica wanted to get married then she was definitely looking in the wrong direction.

Gianni was talking to the local press officer when Sasha spotted him. She'd had enough of table setting, it seemed like a good idea at the time, but now that Veronica wasn't there any more there was no point.

"Gianni, darling, aren't you going to introduce me?"

"Sasha Breschnevsky, this is Lionel Reed, he's organising the pictures."

"Oh, perfect, why don't you discuss your ideas with me?" She put her arm through his and walked off with him. Turning around she blew Gianni a kiss.

Gianni laughed, she had a cheek, he thought. He really didn't mind leaving her to it, that was fine by him, after all it wasn't really his scene.

Antonio had Fred pick up their suits for tonight's event and he was just on his way into the club with them. If he left it to Gianni they would be wearing any old clobber.

"You been splashing out on new gear?"

"Pure Italian suits, complete with silk shirt and tie, one for you and one for me. Mine is the blue one."

"What do I get?" Gianni was like an excited child, trying to look into the holders.

"What do you think this is, Christmas or something?" Antonio laughed. "It's black with a green shirt."

"Cool, green suits me, good choice."

"Eddie," Antonio shouted noticing him just down the corridor. "Can you do me a favour and hang these up in the office."

"Yes of course, Mr de Marco, do you want me to take them out of the bags?"

"That would be a good idea, thanks." Antonio gave him the key to his office. "I'll be in the function room for a while, just bring it on over when you're done."

Eddie nodded and scuttled off towards the office. He'd only been in it once before and was curious to have a good look around. He looked at the key, perfect opportunity.

"What's Sasha up to?"

"Oh, she's alright, just sorting out what pictures we need for the Business Express issue, due out day after tomorrow. That's one thing she is good at organising."

"That's ok then. Stevo called me earlier, he's gone home for a while to try and sort himself out."

"Yeah I know, I suggested it, figured he needed a break."

"Is there much left to do?" Antonio asked changing the subject.

"No, Veronica's sorted everything."

"I just wanted to go over the table plans with her one last time."

"Something changed?"

"No, just want to remind myself who I put together, make sure there's no awkward situations, I want everything to run smoothly."

"Stop worrying, you'll win the award again tonight."

Chapter Eighty Eight

Matt left the police station in a total daze, he couldn't believe it. The men responsible had both been found dead, it felt strange, almost as if he had been cheated out of justice. He had wanted his day in court, wanted to see their murdering faces, see what kind of scum they were. He couldn't bring himself to feel elated, it didn't seem right. He shuddered recalling de Marcos words, "we'll do what it takes, we all want the same thing, 'justice for your sister'. He couldn't help but wonder if they had anything to do with these men's deaths.

Pulling his coat around him he walked towards a coffee bar, picking a newspaper up on the way. His reward money was no good now. He needed to sort out the funeral and contact the rest of the family and Lucy's friends. Maybe he should put an ad in the paper just in case he missed anyone out, he would hate that.

The waitress came over to his table. "What can I get you?"

"Just a coffee please."

"You look a bit down, love, are you ok?"

"Thanks, I'm fine." Deep down he wanted to scream, no my sister is dead, the woman I love is mixed up with gangsters and I fear what will happen to her, apart from that everything is hunky dory.

"Do you have a phone in here?" he asked the waitress.

"Just outside the toilets, over there, love," she pointed.

"Thanks." He rang the de Marcos number and hoped that Katie would answer, he had to speak with her.

"Hello."

"It's me, can you meet me?"

"Yes, where are you?"

"Bella Coffee House, on the corner of West Street."

"Ok, I'll be there in ten." Katie yanked on her clothes and splashed cold water over her face. Ordering a cab she tied her hair up and applied a little make-up.

She took a deep breath as she walked into the coffee house. Matt was sitting in the corner looking a million miles away, but smiled as soon as she caught his eye. Pulling out a chair she sat down opposite him.

"What can I get you, miss?"

"Cappuccino please."

"He's been a bit down in the dumps, but his face lit up when you come in. He's a lucky man." The waitress went back towards the kitchen.

"Sorry about that."

"Oh, don't worry it's not your fault, people do like to gossip, I guess its part of their job trying to put the world to rights." Katie took her jacket off.

"I wanted to talk to you about Lucy, have you heard, they caught the two men?"

"Yes, I know it's a dreadful business."

"I just wanted to see them in court, find out what kind of scum they were. Now thanks to your fiancé I won't get that chance."

"What do you mean?"

"Oh, didn't he tell you? What a surprise!" Matt's voice was full of sarcasm.

"Tell me what?"

"The men who did it were murdered, brutally murdered."

"What happened?" Katie couldn't believe her ears, was Matt trying to tell her that Antonio had put out some kind of contract on them?

"One was stabbed to death, the other had a heroin overdose, after he was injected up his anus."

"What...?" Katie nearly choked on her cappuccino.

"Yes, this is the man you are sleeping with. You see what he is capable of? Doesn't it frighten you? Because I tell you it absolutely scares the shit out of me."

"You're just making assumptions, you hate Antonio anyway."

"Katie, listen to what I am telling you, what I've been trying to tell you."

"Matt, I love you dearly, you're like the brother I never had, but you have got to get a grip."

"No, it's true, if you don't listen then you'll end up in the ground too!" His voice was raised and a few heads turned to see what was going on.

"Ssh, you're making a scene, you're upset I know, but this is the wrong way to deal with it."

"Did you know that Felicia was pregnant when she was murdered and I helped cover that fact up so that Gianni would never find out?"

"Listen, Matt, you need help." She reached over the table and held his hand. "I suggest you go and see someone."

"Did you also know that the reason I finished with you is because Gianni threatened me and my sister?"

"What, why would you say such a terrible thing?"

"Because it's totally true!"

"You're not making any sense, Matt, calm down."

"I'm not having some kind of breakdown, I've got evidence that he is a crook."

"My God, you'll stop at absolutely nothing to split us up, you're incredible." Katie grabbed her jacket.

"Wait, do you know anything about his past?"

"I know enough. Call me when you come to your senses."

"Katie, the last thing I want to do is upset you, I care about you, what happens to you. Mark my words if you keep this relationship going then you will regret it. Everything around them turns to shit eventually."

"You really are bitter, I feel sorry for you." And with that she stormed out of the café and walked quickly around the corner out of sight. Feeling faint she stopped and leaned her back against the wall, clutching her jacket she slid to the ground. Antonio was not a violent man, never had she seen any signs to alert her that he was a vicious thug. It couldn't be true, she wouldn't believe Matt's lies. He had always been jealous, but this was sinking to new depths. Matt had changed, he was angry and rightly so, he had just lost his only sister. She was angry too, but not to the extent that she would make up vicious lies to make herself feel better.

Her immediate instinct was to ring Nina, she needed to talk to someone, try and figure out what to do. Maybe she should just approach Antonio, confront him, see what he said. Yes, that's it, she would keep him happy and go to the goddamn stupid business event, wait until he had a few drinks and then question him. Yes, maybe that was the best thing to do she decided.

Chapter Eighty Nine

When Antonio got home he was genuinely surprised to see Katie getting ready.

"Sweetheart, what are you doing?"

"Did you think that I forgot?"

"Well, I didn't like to mention it, I thought you would prefer to stay home. The press will be there and they are filming the award ceremony. I just thought it would be too much for you to handle right now."

"I'm alright, I know how important it is to you. I just think as your fiancée I should be there for support."

"You don't have to, I understand."

"Really, I'm fine about it." Katie was putting on a brave face, she had an agenda and she wanted to stick to it, keep him sweet.

"I wish I had known, I had you booked for some beauty treatments, not that you need it of course. I just thought it would get you in the mood."

"Oh, yes what kind of mood?" Katie said suggestively.

"Are you trying to seduce me?"

They didn't need any words as Antonio led her into the bedroom. It felt like ages since they last made love, and every time they did it felt different, more enjoyable than the last.

"I've missed you," Antonio whispered in her ear.

"Don't be silly, you'd think we hadn't been together for weeks, it's only been a couple of days."

"Is that all?" Antonio pulled her back into his arms.

Katie remembering the real reason she wanted to keep him in an exceptionally good mood, wriggled out of his arms. "Look at the time, we don't want to be late."

Antonio sighed. "Yes, you're right. We'll finish this later!"

"I can hardly wait." Katie got out of bed and slipped on her robe. "I'll have to have a quick shower now."

"Want me to join you?"

"No, I'll be quicker by myself."

"Spoilsport."

As Katie stood under the shower she couldn't help but feel totally loved, totally wanted. She loved him, she admitted, but what if he was this monster that Matt had made him out to be. What then, would she leave him? Or was she too weak? Either way it was one hell of a revelation to digest. She was beginning to think that it was a bad idea to confront him, what if he said he had done those things? She would be forced to make a decision then. It would break her heart, maybe it was better to leave it well alone; least said soonest mended, that was one of her gran's sayings.

Fred drove them to the club, Katie was a changed woman. There was something about her mannerism, she seemed to have this barrier around her, keeping her emotions in check. Fred couldn't quite put his finger on it, he wasn't sure he liked this new woman Katie had suddenly become. She didn't seem as fragile anymore, in fact her character had changed almost overnight. Maybe it was losing her best friend that had toughened her up. Fred wished that the old Katie would return, the kind sweet girl he had first met and remembered well. What had happened to her? Probably the de Marcos, he sighed. He loved them dearly but lately they had been hard to deal with. And it seemed Katie had been seriously affected. He just wanted to scoop her up in his arms and tell her everything would be ok.

As they stepped out of the car, the press were in their faces, flashing cameras seemed to be everywhere. Katie forced a smile, she looked stunning as usual, wearing an elegant black evening dress, it clung to her accentuating her stunning figure. Antonio was dressed immaculately in his Italian designer suit. He put a protective arm around her waist.

"So, when is the wedding, Mr de Marco?"

"We haven't set a date yet."

"You're keeping him waiting then, Katie."

Katie smiled, she couldn't respond to these cold people. They didn't give a damn about Lucy, just wanted headlines for their bloody paper, it was incredible.

As they entered the club the waitresses stood in a line with trays of champagne. Taking one she made an excuse and went to the ladies toilets. Holding back tears she gulped the champagne down. The bubbles went up her nose making her sneeze.

Nina was watching her from the doorway. "Katie, what's wrong?"

Startled by her presence Katie jumped. "God, you gave me such a fright, where did you spring from?"

"I arrived just after you."

"I didn't think you would be coming."

"I nearly didn't! But with our new business I thought we may be in with a chance of winning something."

"Seriously?"

"I'm quietly confident, we are up and coming after all."

"It never really entered my mind. It's obvious Antonio will win it again!"

"We'll win it next year, mark my words."

They both laughed. "We'll be the first female business to win such a prestigious award in this part of the country." Nina was trying to get through to her.

"If I'm still here next year."

"What, surely you're not thinking of leaving."

"No, just ignore me."

"Katie, is there anything I can do?" She put her hand on her shoulder.

"No, it's something I have to deal with by myself."

"I'm worried about you, you seem so distant."

"I'm fine, honestly. Let's get back to the party, whose table are you on?"

"Yours of course."

"Oh, brilliant, I don't think that I could cope with Sasha by myself."

"No need to worry, between us we'll give her a run for her money."

Giggling they headed back into the function room. All eyes were on them, Katie felt like a caged animal. She hated being stared at, being judged by these people who didn't know anything about her. It was crazy, she was an ordinary girl, yet this publicity had catapulted her on to the front cover of every magazine and national newspaper. Anyone would think that she was royalty, that's how they treated her and it was becoming increasingly difficult to bear.

"Miss Saunders, how do you feel about Lucy Carmichael's death?"

Katie could feel the blood surging through her body, she was going to lose it at any moment.

"You insensitive prick, fuck off." Nina was taking no prisoners, she summoned Fats. "Get this piece of shit out of here."

"I'm sorry, Mrs Valetti, I'm just doing my job," the reporter protested. "No offence, Miss Saunders."

"I want you out, now!"

Fats eyeballed the reporter, waiting for him to move. "Well, you heard the lady, we can do this the easy way or the hard way." He folded his arms across his chest which made him look even more threatening.

The reporter certainly didn't want to be manhandled by this huge muscular man. "Ok, I'm going, again I'm sorry if I upset you." He would be well and truly in the shit with his boss. He just couldn't resist asking the question on everyone's lips.

A major scoop and he'd blown it, what an idiot he had been.

Veronica was chatting to Antonio, trying in vain to get some information out of him.

"Thanks for your concern, I really do appreciate it, but we're fine." He wasn't giving anything away.

Katie saved him from any further questions as she stepped in. "Hi, Veronica, you did a great job, Antonio should be very proud of you."

"Oh, I am, marvellous job, Veronica, you deserve a bonus."

"Next payslip it is then." Katie sat down. "We better let you get back to work, I'm sure you still have plenty to do." She dismissed her just like that.

299

Veronica was astonished, she wasn't sure if she liked Katie's attitude. She seemed cold and distant, not the quiet, naive and charming Katie she had employed. What had happened to her? Influence of the de Marcos no doubt.

Gianni arrived with Sasha on his arm, she was wearing a low cut black dress, her huge cannonball breasts were straining against the material and looked as though they were going burst out of the skimpy attire at any given moment. Her bleached blonde hair extensions flowed down to her waist. She was perfect and all eyes were on her. The women looked on in jealousy and the men drooled with lust.

Katie observed Antonio, but he didn't bat an eyelid, he wasn't in the least bit interested in his ex. He could have any woman, but she still wondered why he had chosen her. She had asked herself that question many times, but had never understood it and probably never would.

Sasha went straight over to Antonio and kissed him on both cheeks. "It's going to be a fabulous evening, darling, I can feel it." Her breasts brushed against him.

God she was so obvious, she almost threw herself at him, it was embarrassing. Antonio took a step back, he felt slightly uncomfortable. Katie was amazed that they had let this neurotic woman back into their lives, what was Gianni thinking of? He must be nuts. The woman may have apologised to her but there wasn't an ounce of sincerity in her voice.

Henry and Diana Brookstein made their entrance along with Ralph and Lorraine Anderson. The cameras loved Ralph and his wife, they were well matched. Both gorgeous and charming, they knew how to handle the press, posing and laughing with the photographers.

As they came over to the table Gianni stood up and shook their hands, kissing their wives on the cheek and remarking on how wonderful they looked.

Sasha wasn't too happy. "Frightened he may drop you, darling?" Katie whispered to her.

"What did you say?"

"You heard me, you bitch."

Sasha couldn't speak, she was shocked at what she had just heard from this little cow, how dare she? Smiling sweetly she turned to Katie. "Just worry about your own relationship, darling, Antonio will get sick of you sooner or later and come back to me, mark my words."

"You're living in cloud cuckoo land, darling," Katie mimicked her voice.

Nina nudged Katie, what the hell was she doing antagonising Sasha? It didn't take much to set her off, she was a loose cannon and was liable to explode at any moment.

"Ouch what was that for?"

"As if you didn't know, behave yourself. This isn't like you, what's came over you?"

"Nothing, just sticking up for myself, I'm nobody's doormat."

"What's happened to you, I don't like it?"

Katie sipped her champagne and smiled sweetly. "I just want her to know that she can't intimidate me any more."

Nina placed a hand on hers. "Ok, let's say no more about it then." She had a funny feeling that it was going to be an explosive night.

Gianni cringed when he saw Honey come in, she was with Simon Henshall. He was smartly dressed with a cigar hanging from his mouth; he was in the real estate business and was very successful. Simon headed straight for their table, damn it what was he going to do now? If Honey said something there would be trouble. He decided to face it head on.

"Simon, my man, how are you?" Gianni shook his hand.

"Very well, Gianni, I would like to introduce you to my lovely date, Honey."

"Er... How do you do?"

"Long time no see, Gianni." Honey smiled at him, she was enjoying making him squirm.

"Do you two know each other?"

"Yes, she works in our Manchester club."

"Oh, you know me a bit better than that, Gianni," Honey said suggestively as she eyed him up.

"What is that little tart inferring?" Sasha's ears pricked up, she knew something had gone on between them.

"Me a tart?" Honey pointed to herself and then pointed to her. "Take a look at yourself, Sasha."

"How dare you, you little bitch, nobody speaks to me like that."

"Ladies, please, let's all calm down." Antonio tried to diffuse the situation.

Gianni didn't know where to look, whatever he said now would only make the matter worse. "Sasha, darling, pay no attention I haven't got a clue what she's talking about."

"It wasn't that when you were fucking me day and night, you couldn't get enough of me." Honey was letting rip into him, after Felicia she thought that he would have brought her to London and looked after her properly. Instead she found out he was back with psycho Barbie.

A couple of the photographers were snapping away, hoping for something explosive to happen. And they didn't have to wait long.

"Gianni, say something."

Gianni shrugged. "What can I do?"

"Right then, if you won't do anything, I'll do it my fucking self." Sasha grabbed the champagne bottle and launched herself at Honey. The next thing they were on the floor, the bottle smashed as they writhed around. The press were loving it, they were trying to scratch each other's eyes out.

"Bloody hell, someone stop them before they kill each other." Simon shouted.

Katie looked at the ice bucket and then over at the two women who were now yanking each other's hair out. She picked it up and before anyone realised what she intended to do, promptly threw the ice bucket over them.

"Christ, you bitch." Sasha stood up she was fuming. "What gives you the right to do that to me," she gasped.

"Just returning the favour, darling, I did owe you one after all." Katie sat back down and calmly sipped her champagne.

Antonio laughed, followed by Gianni, it became infectious and soon everyone was laughing, apart from the two drenched women.

"I think you better go and get dried off before the ceremony begins."

"Fuck you, Gianni." Honey scrambled to her feet and slapped him hard across his face.

"There was no need for that, Honey," Simon told her. "I'm sorry about this, if I'd have known I wouldn't have brought her."

"Don't apologise to him on my behalf, he's an arrogant pig." She turned to Sasha. "You're welcome to him."

Gianni grabbed Sasha's hand. "Here, let me help you."

"Get off me, you son of a bitch, you have some explaining to do."

"There's nothing to explain."

"Bullshit, I'm going home. Antonio can I use your driver?"

"Of course, no problem."

Katie struggled to keep a straight face. Nina kicked her under the table, what the hell was she playing at?

After they both left Antonio pulled his brother to one side. "Jesus, do you ever learn?"

"Oh, come on, bro, it was just a harmless piece of fun."

"You know what Sasha is like, she'll be on the warpath now."

"Not being funny, man, but don't you think you should keep an eye on your own woman."

"Don't bring Katie into this."

"Hey, she brought herself into this by chucking that ice over them."

"I'm glad she did, someone had to, they were like wild cats!"

"No harm done then, eh?"

They returned to the table and carried on as if nothing had happened. The champagne flowed and the food was exquisite as usual.

It came as no surprise that Antonio won Businessman of The Year award for the third year running. He accepted the award and made a short speech thanking his business associates and staff. The entire room cheered him and clapped, he had them eating out the palms of his hands.

By the end of the evening Katie was a little drunk and ready for anything. Fred picked them up and drove them back to Antonio's apartment.

Katie curled up on the sofa. "Get me a drink."

"Don't you think you've had enough," he said softly.

"No, not nearly enough."

"Look, this is obviously about Lucy, but getting drunk won't change anything."

"It will block out the pain."

"Maybe, but it will all come flooding back when you sober up."

Katie staggered into the kitchen and took a bottle of wine out of the fridge.

Antonio followed her. "I think you better go to bed, we'll talk in the morning." He tried to prise the bottle out of her hands.

"L… let go of me." Her words were slurred.

"I'm only trying to help."

Katie went back into the sitting room and sat on the sofa, the wine now forgotten about. "Ok, you win."

"Are you coming to bed?"

"Yes." Getting to her feet, Katie stumbled into the bedroom and collapsed on the bed. "You are a bad man, Antonio, do you know that?" she mumbled.

"Just go to sleep." Antonio undressed her and put her to bed. He kissed her on the forehead and brushed her hair from her face. She looked so peaceful and beautiful, he was a lucky man. But he was a little bit worried about her behaviour, he hoped it was a one off and put it down to the fact that her best friend had just died.

Chapter Ninety

Gianni was knocking at the door, it was 7.30am.

"What the hell is it?"

Gianni shoved the newspaper in his hand. "Guess who didn't make the front page."

Antonio howled. "Is that all?"

"It's not funny, man, my reputation has gone right down the pan, it's humiliating."

"Stop overreacting there's no such thing as bad publicity."

"It's alright for you, you haven't been made to look like an idiot."

Antonio looked at the picture, Sasha and Honey brawling in the middle of the club, it wasn't a pretty sight.

"There's more inside, a spectacular one of Katie throwing ice over them."

"Christ, is there?" He turned the page and sure enough there was Katie with the ice bucket, looking pleased with herself.

"What you got to say now then?"

"It's no big deal."

"Who you trying to convince? They even wrote a piece on her."

"What, where?"

"Turn the page."

"Katie Saunders, the recent fiancée of Antonio de Marco, shows her true colours. Normally a quiet, pleasant young woman she lost it when Gianni's two lovers came to blows. She calmly took the champagne bucket from the table and emptied the ice over the two women who were fighting on the floor. Miss Saunders definitely looked like she enjoyed it. Is this another side to the young business woman, one that she didn't want the public to see? It makes one wonder if she still holds a grudge against Antonio's ex fiancée, the beautiful Sasha Breschnevsky. Is this the end of the newly engaged couple's romance?' He scanned the rest of the article. 'Antonio was seen half carrying his drunken fiancée to the waiting limo, looking none too pleased with her. Congratulations to Antonio de Marco on winning Businessman of The Year for the third year running and we wish him all the best both in his businesses and personal life."

"Fucking hell, they've made her out to be some kind of nut job!"

"I told you, what are you going to do about it, dump her?"

"Certainly not."

"So, you're just going to let her get away with it then?"

"So, she got a bit drunk, threw ice on Sasha and that scrubber. It's not as bad as what Sasha did to her."

"It is when it's the goddamn headlines."

"Jesus, what's all the shouting about." Katie appeared in her dressing gown, her hair all over the place.

Gianni grabbed the newspaper from Antonio and threw it at her. "I hope that you're proud of yourself."

"Please keep the volume down, my head hurts," Katie whimpered, putting her hand to her aching head.

"I'll see you later." Gianni left, slamming the door behind him.

Katie picked up the newspaper and read the article, cringing she felt herself turning red with total embarrassment. "Oh, no, what have I done?"

Antonio didn't speak, he just walked past her and into the kitchen. He filled the kettle and switched it on. "How about a nice cup of tea?" He opened the cupboard and reached for the headache tablets. Taking two out of the packet he poured a glass of water and passed them to Katie. "This might help." He had never seen her in such a state, it was so out of character.

"I'm sorry, about last night I mean."

"I know you haven't been yourself lately and I don't blame you at all. I totally understand why you did what you did. But it was a one off, wasn't it, I mean you can't carry on like this. I want the old Katie back, the one I fell in love with."

"Oh, please don't compare me to that goddamn Barbie doll you were once engaged to, she would rub anyone up the wrong way, you know that. Jesus, I've never been that type of person and never would be, it just isn't who I am."

He put his arms around her. "It's ok, I'm just worried that you're losing it and that's the last thing we want."

"I think I just needed to let my grief out, vent my anger and when she showed up shouting the odds and making a scene, I, well, I just saw red."

"Sssh, my love, it's ok."

"It was nothing to do with revenge, I don't hold grudges, but I don't ever forget when someone does something bad to me. I'm not the revenge type, I prefer a peaceful life, I hate confrontation of any sort," Katie was babbling.

Antonio didn't want her to become obsessed with this so-called incident. The press had a bad habit of making a mountain out of a mole hill, and he knew that, more than Katie did. He felt terrible now, making her feel worse than she already did, she had suffered enough.

Katie nuzzled into his warm chest, enjoying the smell of his aftershave, she loved him so much and the last thing she wanted was to hurt him.

"It'll be ok," he reassured her.

"I just feel bad that's all."

"I must admit it was rather funny, the best laugh I've had in a while. Sasha's face was a picture!" Antonio turned the mood around in seconds.

They both laughed, as they looked at the photo of Sasha dripping wet, her designer dress clung to her body, emphasising her huge, indestructible, mountain like breasts.

Antonio pointed out the paragraph. "Leaving little to the imagination and rushing out of the club in total despair one had to wonder amid all the countless rumours if this Amazon woman actually even knew what under garments were, ah Sasha Breschnevsky strikes another fashion faux pas!"

Chapter Ninety One

Katie contacted her father, but he was too busy with his new woman to fly over for her best friend's funeral; busy was beginning to be the norm with him now. She was upset that he couldn't make the effort and annoyed that another woman seemed to have taken her mother's place, just like that. In a way she was glad that he was moving on, but he just wasn't a part of her life anymore. She wanted him to be happy but not to the detriment of their relationship, which was fast fading. Sad though it was she concentrated all her efforts on Antonio and the business; that gave her the strength to carry on, God knows that she needed something to focus on. If she thought about Lucy too much she really would go off the handle, it would be so easy to go out and get drunk out of her skull. But at the end of the day she knew that it would solve nothing, the pain of loss would come surging back, just like Antonio told her. Better that she accepted Lucy's death and tried to live her life the way her best friend would have wanted her to. She felt sad for Stevo, he hadn't been able to show his face since the night at Lucy's flat, he had vanished off the face of the earth. If she lost the love of her life, she would just want to die, follow him to the grave, because without him she was nothing.

The next few days were a complete blur, she painted on a false smile and dressed immaculately. She had a different way about her, everything was all a front, her defence mechanism had set in and she was taking no prisoners.

Nina remarked on the change in her, she had all of a sudden become this astute young business woman, everyone hung on her every word, she had become even more persuasive if that was possible. She had a cool determination about her and when she was in a room she commanded it. The clients loved her, in fact they always insisted on Katie being present during any sale. Her advice was second to none, Nina swore that she could sell ice to the Eskimos. She had definitely found her niche, but Nina held her breath, knowing full well that after Lucy's interment the following week, things could drastically change and not for the better either.

Matt had tried to contact Katie on many occasions, but she would not return his calls. Somebody or other always covered for her, saying she was in a business meeting or with a customer. He regretted what he had said but the damage was done. He knew in his heart that she would never forgive him and that pained him. He wished that he had handled things differently, but he hadn't, she didn't believe him. According to her, he was blind with jealousy and would say anything to split her and

Antonio up. That's true he would, but never, ever had he lied to her and one day, probably when it was too late, she would realise that he was just trying to warn her.

They never met again until the funeral. Katie dutifully went over to him and gave him a hug, there didn't seem to be a need for any words, she was grateful for that, as it would have been difficult to know exactly what to say.

Antonio stayed close to her, he didn't want her to be there alone, he wanted everyone to know that he supported her and would be there for her no matter what. Realising that it could just as easily have been Katie who lost her life that fateful day instead of Lucy, he swore that he would protect her and keep her safe. Time was precious as he knew from past history. He had dreaded this day, but also couldn't wait to get it over with, move on, look after her. Katie may come across as being assertive and cool, but he knew her inside and out. She was still vulnerable underneath and he had to do all he could to make sure she come through this as unscathed as possible. He kept his distance from the Carmichael family, not wanting to antagonise Matthew, as he knew he was capable of verbally exploding at any given moment. He stood back and watched as everyone exchanged hugs, kisses and tears.

The church was packed out, mostly with young people, what a waste. Still the scum who did it were no longer on this earth, thank God, Antonio thought. Stevo had seen to that and who could blame him, if he were in his shoes he would have done exactly the same thing. But he thanked God that he wasn't at Katie's funeral, because she was under his skin and he didn't think he could live without her. The sooner they were married the better, he couldn't wait for the day they had little bambinos running around the house. A miniature version of him, he couldn't wait to see what his son would look like. He would have his father's dark and brooding good looks and probably his mother's sense of propriety. He could live with that, but was growing impatient. He wanted Katie to set a date, but since Lucy's death she was reluctant to discuss any marriage plans. It pissed him off, but he couldn't force her to move on, when she wasn't ready. He resigned himself to wait, as long as it would take, she was worth it.

Lucy's mother was wailing hysterically. Her husband desperately tried to keep her volume down, whilst trying to keep his own emotions in check. Spotting Katie, she grabbed her and hugged her tight. Katie felt like she was going to suffocate, she was squeezing her so tight that she was finding it difficult to breathe. "Oh, Katie, I can scarcely believe it, my daughter dead before her time, what's wrong with this society today?"

"I don't know," was all that Katie could manage to say. She was trying to wriggle out of Mrs Carmichael's grip, but with little success.

Antonio looked on, wanting to rescue her but knew that he daren't, not with Matt watching his every move. He was certain to kick off if he tried to intervene.

"Come now, Mary." Mr Carmichael was a little frustrated, he had a funny feeling that his wife was trying to latch on to Lucy's best friend. She was looking for a substitute for her lost daughter and Katie unfortunately was the one she had chosen. He gently removed her arms from Katie. Half smiling at her he pulled Mary towards him.

"I'm really going to miss her, she was such a good friend," Katie sighed. "I keep expecting her to burst in at any moment with yet another pair of shoes."

"Yes, she definitely had a thing for shoes." Mrs Carmichael blew her nose. "Who is that man that's looking over?"

Katie looked behind her. "Oh, that's Antonio de Marco, he was Lucy's boss."

"Then I must say thank you to him for showing his respect and organising the wake." She made her way over to him.

"Oh, you're Mr de Marco, it's so nice to meet you, it's such a shame that it's under such a tragedy." She started crying again.

Antonio shook Mr Carmichael's hand. "I'm so sorry for your loss."

Matt watched in horror as this man had the audacity to befriend his parents, how dare he? He was just about to march over when he noticed Katie looking at him. That was enough to stop him in his tracks. It was his sister's funeral and he didn't want the day to be remembered for bickering, especially with de Marco.

His mother waved at him to come over, reluctantly he did so.

Antonio offered his hand to Matthew, he hesitated and then decided he'd better shake it, he didn't want any trouble. The touch of his hand sent shudders through him, he was capable of murder, of that he was one hundred per cent certain. Lucy's image flashed through his mind and it was all he could do to stop himself from punching this man out, he despised him and everything he stood for.

"Let's go and sit down." Katie could feel the tension between them and wanted to separate them before anything happened.

As they walked away Antonio looked back and saw Matthew staring at him. Christ, he really despised him, he could feel the vibes from where he was standing. He just hoped that they would get through the day without any trouble. The press were outside, and they were probably waiting for something to kick off.

Most of the staff from the club came to pay their respects, as did Veronica and Nicholas. Veronica had liked Lucy very much, she could see potential in her and had hoped that she would train her up to become her personal assistant. It was a dreadful shame that her life had been snuffed out, just like that. She held Nicholas's hand and put her head on his shoulder. Life indeed was too short, you never knew what was around the corner, so she intended to make the most of it.

Katie was looking around the church to see if she recognised everyone. She was surprised however when she noticed that Stevo wasn't around. Where was he, still in Italy? He should be here, maybe he just couldn't face it, she thought. Turning to Antonio she whispered, "Where's Stevo?"

"He thought it best to stay away, he's working at the villa, helping with the renovations and it seems to be keeping him busy. Maybe it's the best thing for him right now. It's nothing personal; he just has this thing about funerals."

They took their seats and waited for the vicar to begin. The service was beautiful and was followed by a heart wrenching eulogy that Matt had devised.

Tears welled up in Katie's eyes. Antonio squeezed her hand as the tears slowly trickled down her face.

After the burial they all went back to the club, courtesy of Antonio and Katie. Lucy had loved working there and it was the least they could do, to give her a good send off. If she was looking down on them she would be loving every minute of it.

Matt amazingly had agreed to let them foot the bill and allow Lucy's final farewell in Club La Pregheira. All she did was talk incessantly about the place and which famous people had been there and who was coming next. It was sad to think that she would never marry, never have a family. Her career was over before it had barely begun.

Antonio thanked Nicholas for providing the buffet, it was another one of his masterpieces.

"At least nobody will starve to death." The words popped out before Katie knew what she was saying. Putting her hand over her mouth she looked around to see if anybody had heard her.

"It's ok, I don't think anyone heard you," Nicholas whispered, not realising Matthew was standing right next to them.

"That was in poor taste, Katie, even for someone like you."

"Matt, I'm sorry I don't know what I was thinking."

"Come on, Matthew don't start anything, nobody loved Lucy more than she did. It was a genuine mistake said in grief, surely you must understand that," Antonio intervened.

He hated to admit that Antonio was right and apologised to Katie.

"Can we go now?" Katie had had enough; she just wanted to get out of here. She was sick of listening to Mrs Carmichael wailing like a banshee, her throbbing head couldn't take any more.

"Whatever you want, where do you want to go?"

"Anywhere, just out of here."

As they left the club Antonio summoned the limo.

"No, I want to walk."

He told Fred to take the rest of the day off.

Chapter Ninety Two

It was hard to believe that four years had passed since Lucy's death. Katie placed a bouquet of sunflowers on the grave, she smiled as she remembered Lucy's exuberant personality. The flowers reminded her of Lucy's sunny character. She wiped a tear from her face and was startled when someone passed her a handkerchief.

"It's a clean one, honestly."

She recognised that voice, spinning round she saw Matt in front of her. Not knowing what to say she dabbed her eyes and looked down.

"I didn't think you visited her grave."

"I wasn't here for her birthday last year, I was in Italy, so I'm afraid I was a couple of days late."

Matt placed a bunch of white lilies on the grave. "These were one of her favourites too."

There was an awkward silence between them, neither of them wanting to leave without finding out about the other. It was Matt who spoke first. "So, he still hasn't made an honest woman out of you." It wasn't a question, it was a remark.

"Er, no we put it back, I wasn't ready."

"Do you think you'll ever marry him then?" Matt asked gently.

"Yes, of course. We're getting married in La Pregheira next summer, it's all sorted."

"La Pregheira ?"

"Yes, we want a quiet ceremony with no press, it's ideal, there's this perfect little chapel, it's so quaint, you would love it." Katie's voice broke off, she could see the pain in his eyes. "I'm sorry, Matt, I should be asking how you are doing, it's ages since I last saw you."

"Life is good, I'm a partner in Carter, Nicholson & Carmichael."

"Oh yes, I've heard of them, but I thought you were content working for Jackson's."

"I didn't like some of the people they represented."

"I see, how's your family?"

"My mum died last year, she had a heart attack, my father reckons she had a broken heart and it never really healed after losing Lucy."

"Oh, why didn't you tell me?"

"Because we have different lives now and I've got a family of my own."

"What, you're married?"

"Yes, her name is Carla, I met her at Jackson's, she was the receptionist there."

"My God, that's wonderful and you say you have a family?"

"Yes, my daughter has just turned three, she's called Letitia."

"That's a beautiful name, I'm so happy for you."

"You know I would give it all up, for you, right now if you asked me to."

"Matt, don't say things like that, it's wrong of you."

"Yes, I know it is, but I can't help it, I see you and it just brings everything flooding back."

"I'd better go, I've got a business meeting."

"I hear your business has been nominated for Business man or should I say Business woman of the Year, that would be funny if you knocked Mr de Marco off the top of his perch."

"Hmm, we'll see."

"How's the house coming along?"

"My house is doing fine, how do you know about that?"

"The press of course, you guys can't make a move without it being in the papers."

"I try not to read them these days, they are so depressing, don't you think?"

"I suppose, but I wouldn't know anything about you without the press."

Katie stiffled a laugh. "Matt, you're so funny."

"I was being serious," he half joked.

"It was good to see you, Matt."

"You too." Matt brushed the hair from her face. "You get better looking every day, Antonio has certainly made you bloom."

Katie backed away. "I've got to go."

"Here." Matt pushed his business card into her hand. "Just in case you ever need me."

"Matt, let's hope that I never do, murder isn't part of my life and never will be." Shaking her head she popped it into her handbag. "But if you don't mind I would like to pass your name on to this poor woman I know, who accidentally killed her abusive husband."

"Oh, the Bannerman case?"

"Yes, that's the one, her name is Wendy Bannerman. Her solicitor is useless and she is due to stand trial in less than two months. She is beside herself with worry, and she has a little five month old baby girl to look after. I'll give her your card."

"I'm glad to be of service. Just out of interest who is representing her?"

"Er... not sure Benjamin Cas... something Claskey."

"Benjamin Colquoshki?"

"Yes, I think so."

"I'll have a word with him, see if I can persuade him to let me take the case on."

"But you don't know the details yet."

312

"Is she innocent?"

"Yes, I'm absolutely one hundred per cent sure."

"Then that's all I need to know."

"Good luck with the family, Matt."

"Have a nice life Katie," he whispered as he watched her walk away. She definitely improved with age he thought, she had an air of refinement about her. No doubt she could mix with royalty and nobody would be able to spot the odd one out. It was amazing how she had come on in life.

Wiping Lucy's headstone he wondered what she would have been doing now. Would she have been married to Stevo, if so she would have been living in Manchester with him. He heard Stevo was running the club now, although it was more famous for the casino. He had expanded it, every new game that came in, he would install it into the club, make it a huge success. Matt made a point of reading any and every article he could get his hands on, and he kept all the clippings. They were all locked away in a big silver box which he kept in the safe in his office. One day something in there might come in useful, but right now he wasn't sure what that was.

Chapter Ninety Three

"You're late," Nina scolded Katie as soon as she came through the door.

"I'm sorry that I'm late everyone, I bumped into an old friend."

Candice Danesh hated to be kept waiting. She tapped on her watch. "Time is money, darling, I'm sure you're aware of that, now what is this new collection, I'm dying to see it."

"You will adore it, I assure you, you won't have wasted your time here."

"You say that it is inspired by Greece."

"Yes, the Prestigio collection is detailed with the Greek Key design and the Medusa head. It is a range of classically designed furniture specific to your requirements with a marble effect finish."

"But what about all the parties I hold? It will be knocked to hell."

"Ah, but we have solved that problem for you. This collection is unique, the lacquered finish gives this collection a resilience to knocks and scrapes."

"Wow, do you have any pieces in the showroom?"

"As a matter of fact we had some imported specifically with yourself in mind. A woman of your calibre expects first class treatment."

"Yes, I'm glad you agree."

Nina watched in sheer admiration. Mrs Danesh was a formidable character, yet Katie had her eating out the palm of her hand. Now all she had to do was make the sale.

Mrs Danesh was more than pleasantly surprised, the sight took her breath away. "My God, this is fabulous." She ran her hand over the dining table. When you have finished my dining room, I would like you to advise on the bedroom."

"Certainly, it would be our pleasure."

"It's a deal then?" Candice shook her hand and then Nina's. "Nice doing business with you."

"We just need to go through the paperwork and agree the prices and of course I think a discount would be appropriate."

Candice waved a hand. "I do not care how much it costs, just bill me."

"But, it is customary to share a glass of wine once the deal has been sealed." Nina pointed out.

"I trust you, now I must go. I have an important appointment." And with that Candice put her sunglasses on and left the store.

"God, you're getting better at this, but wasn't that Frank Gianelli's order?"

"It was, but I persuaded him that the Empiro range was better suited to his requirements."

"I nearly shit a brick when you told Mrs Danesh she could view the range, I honestly thought that we had blown it."

"Nina, you underestimate me, darling!"

"I promise that I never will again, now how about that glass of wine?"

"Sure, then we need to go through our client list, see what jobs are ongoing and what bookings we have."

After sifting through the books they both came to the conclusion that the business had exploded. It was time to either relocate to larger premises or open another store.

Nina could tell Katie was thinking up another plan, it was written all over her face. "Ok, what have you got in mind?"

"I'm thinking, another store in an entirely new location, expand the business."

"Tell me more."

"I'm afraid I will have to involve Antonio, what with his connections and already having a footing in Manchester so to speak, he would be ideal to approach."

"Er... as long as it doesn't mean asking him for more money." Nina was adamant about that.

"No money will pass hands, I promise."

"What about Henry and Ralph?"

"I'll call Henry, you call Ralph, see what they think."

"Oh, Katie, I think that you should call Ralph, you know what he's like, he'll want to design the new store."

"No, he won't, he's too busy overseeing the building of my house, remember?"

"Yes I know, but we all know that he loves a challenge. He'll be flying back and forward now he's got his helicopter licence!"

"Oh, I didn't know. Mmm, maybe he can fly us up there and we can have a look at prospective properties."

"It's not in the bag yet, you know."

"It soon will be."

"Here." Nina passed her a glass of wine. She was just about to take a sip of her own when Katie stopped her.

"No, not yet, let's wait for confirmation that it's a go."

Twenty minutes letter, it was all sorted. "Now, let's do a toast. To a successful and thriving business, long may it continue."

They chinked glasses and sipped the wine, it was a dry woody wine, one of Antonio's expensive bottles she had taken from his huge collection. "Whoa, this is powerful stuff, isn't it?"

"Absolutely."

"So, have you decided whether to come to the big meal tonight, and not forgetting the casino?"

"Yes, but I won't have a clue what to do."

"That's funny, because neither do I. It will be fun, what do you say?"

"Would you mind if I brought a friend?"

"Anyone I know?" Katie teased her.

"Just Steven, we are just friends," Nina stressed.

"Of course I don't mind, he's a lovely man. You make a very attractive couple, although not as attractive as Antonio and I," Katie giggled.

"You're such a little rotter at times! Good job that I love you like a sister!"

"That reminds me, I would like you to be my bridesmaid and would love for Roberto Junior and Carla to be my page boy and flower girl."

"Oh, I don't know Katie, I am getting on a bit," she said seriously.

"Don't be silly, you are only in your thirties!"

"I'm not sure."

"Look, I'm asking you to do this for me, not for Antonio. You're my closest friend and it wouldn't be the same without you."

Nina was in a quandary, she still couldn't accept Antonio and probably never would. She had hoped that their romance would fizzle out and now she realised that their love was stronger than ever. "Ok, I'll do it for you."

"Oh, thank you." Katie hugged her. "You don't know what that means to me."

"I'd much rather you had married Matthew Carmichael."

"Funny you should mention him, he was the old friend that I ran into today at Lucy's grave."

"Oh?"

"Yes, he's married now and has a three-year-old daughter."

"Really, I am surprised, I mean he was always hung up on you. You don't have any regrets do you?"

"Absolutely none. Matt's moved on, got a life for himself, I'm happy for him."

"But?" Nina knew her well enough to know that she was holding something back.

"Ok, but this must never go any further. He told me that he would leave everything, his wife and daughter, if I would take him back."

"Shit, he said that." Nina was finding it hard to digest this piece of news.

"Then he said he knew that we were having a house built, he read about it in the newspaper."

"Well, he probably did, these days, you and Antonio are never out of the papers!!"

"True, but it was kind of weird seeing him again, I mean he said some terrible things about Antonio the last time we spoke."

"Oh? You never told me."

316

"It's all water under the bridge now, it doesn't matter."

"Katie, it must still be bothering you, Matt's stirred up all these memories that you have tried so hard to block out. What did he say to you?"

"Nina, I really don't want to discuss this right now. I'm getting married next year and I don't want the past raked up."

"Ok, but if ever you want to talk to me you know where I am."

"Thanks, Nina, now I really must go and so must you."

"What, clocking off early, again?"

"Well, now that we have a team of experts on hand and our sales advisors, we can easily do that."

"What about Wendy's position, should we advertise?"

"No, I have a feeling that she will be back before we know it." Katie remembered Matt's business card, she would call her later and pass on his details. If anyone could help her then Matt would, even if it really was just to impress her and not specifically get Wendy off the murder charge.

Chapter Ninety Four

After the meal was finished they made their way into the casino. Antonio handed some notes into the cashier's booth in exchange for chips. He handed Katie a big stack.

"What am I supposed to do with this?" she joked.

"Darling, I'll show you, we'll have some fun tonight." He kissed her. "Thanks for persuading Nina to come."

"She deserves a good night."

"What do you make of this Steven character then?"

"I like him, I think he's good for her, what about you?"

"I checked him out and he seems like an ok kinda guy."

"Antonio, what did you do that for?"

"I'm just looking out for her, that's all."

"If she found out she would go crazy, you know that don't you?"

"I won't tell if you don't," Antonio shrugged.

He did it for all the right reasons and she agreed that Nina didn't need to know.

"Ok, what are we going to try first?"

"Are you feeling lucky?"

"No, I'm feeling sexy," she whispered.

"You're looking sexy and hot tonight, you better watch out later."

"Ssh, someone might hear."

"So what if they do, we are engaged, remember?" Antonio's voice was husky and filled with longing for her.

"Stop it, you're making me want to go home and make mad passionate love to you!"

"Good, do you want to have an early night?"

Katie looked around her, how could they cut the night short and leave the others. "I would love to, but right now we are the hosts, it would be rather ignorant don't you think?"

"At times you're way too sensible, and of course that's why I love you so much." He kissed her hand.

He was playing her and she knew it, a shiver went down her spine, imagining the feel of his warm skin on her.

"So, you ready to try the roulette wheel?" Antonio's voice interrupted her wicked thoughts, bringing her back to her senses.

318

"Yes, tell me what it's all about first, I don't want to look like an idiot!"

"An idiot, never, my darling. So, do you want the history of the roulette wheel?" Antonio asked the group.

"Ooh yes please." This came from Ralph's wife, Lorraine. She was like a big kid.

"Ok, roulette means 'small wheel' in French. The history is a bit vague but what I do know is that this is the oldest and one of the best casino games around, especially for a novice like yourself," he teased her.

The waitress passed them all a complimentary glass of champagne. Antonio was so charming the women hung on his every word.

He continued. "Some stories say that ancient Romans tilted their chariots to play the game with their wheels."

"Really?" Diana Brookstein was intrigued.

"Yes, another story is that the Dominican Monks were the ones who introduced it into Europe."

"Are you making all this up?" Nina wasn't sure that he was telling the truth, it sounded like a totally made up story.

"Another theory is that Blaise Pascal invented it in 1657, whilst conducting an experiment."

"Who is that?" Katie asked him.

"He was a mathematical genius, he's in the history books, you can go and look it up, Nina."

"Ok, Mr clever, how do we play it then?" Diana was raring to go.

"The wheel is numbered 0 to 36, numbered in black and red, and the grid," Antonio pointed, "shows the colours."

"And?" Lorraine was really inquisitive now.

"The numbers are arranged in a numerical way and divided into three columns. Each number is colored red or black, which corresponds to the wheel."

"Please place your bets," the croupier instructed them.

"What do we do then?" Katie asked him.

"Just pick a number or colour that you think the roller ball will end up in, you can choose even or odd, whatever you like."

"So, really it's a game of chance." Nina was not impressed, what kind of fun was this, they wouldn't make a penny. It was some kind of lottery with really poor odds.

"Just remember, it's just a bit of fun."

"Ok, black thirty four." Nina put her chips down.

"Red, number twelve." Katie was loving the excitement.

"Any more bets please?"

"Sure, black number eighteen." Ralph placed his bet.

"Rcd, thirty three." Antonio put all his chips down.

"What are you doing?"

"It's ok, no problem, I can afford to lose a little."

The croupier spun the wheel and they all waited with baited breath. "It's red, number twelve."

"Oh, that's my number," Katie whooped with joy. "This is so cool, I'm a winner." The croupier passed her chips back and tripled the size of her pile.

"Beginners luck," Nina observed and dragged Steven over to the slot machines. "I have really had enough of this crap, do you want to go?"

"Why are you so hung up on Mr de Marco?" Steven adored her but couldn't understand her insecurities.

"Best that you don't even know about that, trust me, he is not a man you want to get close to, he screws people up."

"I don't think that you should have any more to drink." He attempted to remove the glass from her hand with little success. "You seem so bitter towards him and it's not like you hide the fact. You make your feelings so blatantly obvious."

"What can I say, I'm an open book, Steven." She grabbed another glass of champagne from the waitress. "Are you telling me that you prefer the de Marcos over me?"

"Not at all, I think the world of you, you know that. I'm just not a man for trouble, all I want is an easy, peaceful life."

"So, you're a coward then?" Nina was a little bit drunk.

"I think I should leave now, just call me tomorrow, when you are back to your normal self."

"I am fucking normal, Steven." She pulled the slot machine and hit the jackpot. "Oh my God, I just won one thousand pounds, can you believe it?!" When she looked up, Steven had gone. The shithouse had left her on her own, how dare he do that? That convinced her that if he couldn't understand her then she was better off without him. She just thanked God that she hadn't slept with him yet. He didn't deserve her love, not that she had any left to give.

Katie left the roulette table and went to see Nina. "Are you ok?"

"I'm fine." The staff were milling around her, congratulating her on her winnings.

"Please, just cash in her chips and I'll sort the rest out." They knew who she was and obediently went back to the booths. A couple of minutes later Sarah returned with her winnings.

"Sarah, I told you to leave it in the booth, I'll get it to Mrs Valetti tomorrow."

Sarah was embarrassed to be dismissed just like that by Katie bloody Saunders, who did she think she was these days, obviously thought she was a cut above her. Katie didn't notice the black look she gave her as she took the tray of cash back to her booth. Her co worker Amy noticed she seemed a bit agitated to say the least.

"What, the future Mrs de Marco giving you shit then?" she half mocked.

"Shut it, Amy, and stash this for Mrs Valetti."

Amy knew when she had said enough, better not rub her up anymore now that she was in a stinking foul mood.

"I better go home now," Nina said half falling off the stool.

"Where did Steven go, the restroom?"

"Huh, no he could see right through your precious fiancé and decided that enough was enough."

"Don't start again, Nina, Jesus you really need to sort yourself out, getting slaughtered doesn't solve anything, believe me."

"And what would you know, Antonio's got blood on his hands."

"Shh, someone will hear you."

"Good, let them, it's about time everyone knew what they were really like."

"Nina please, I'll get Fred, he'll take you home."

Nina was slugging back the rest of her glass of champagne and was barely able to stand upright. "Don't do me any favours Katie," Nina was so drunk, she was almost incoherent.

"I think you've had enough." Katie tried to prise the glass out of her hands.

"Waiter, waiter, get me some more." She thrust the glass into the young waiter's hands, he didn't know what to do.

"It's ok, I'll take care of this, just carry on serving the rest of the guests." She summoned Eddie who was lurking in the corner watching with interest.

"Can you help Mrs Valetti down to the office and have Fred drive the limo around the back, we want to avoid the press if we can."

"Yes, Miss Saunders, no problem. This way, Mrs Valetti." By this time Nina was quiet and submissive.

"Ok, where did I leave my coat?"

"I'll get it for you, just come with me." Eddie led her by the elbow out of the casino.

Katie went back over to see Antonio. "I'm sorry, babe, I need to make sure that Nina gets home alright, do you mind?"

"It's ok, I understand, she's a bit worse for wear. Are you coming back, I'm just going to have a few more tries on the roulette and head to the blackjack table with the guys for something a little more serious."

"No, but do me a favour." She passed him the rest of her chips. "Just put this on black twenty five for me, ok?"

"That's a lot of chips, you sure?"

"I'm sure."

"Why that particular number?"

"It would have been Lucy's birthday today."

"You never told me."

"Why would I, it wouldn't interest you."

"Whatever interests you, interests me, you know that."

"It doesn't matter, forget about it, I'll call you later."

"I hate when you can't confide in me, has something happened?"

"Antonio, we have been together for four years now, trust me, you know everything there is to know about me."

"Exactly, so why don't you tell me what else is bugging you?"

"Er, it would have been my best friend's birthday today, if she was still alive that is. What else could be bugging me, isn't that enough?" Katie was short with him and becoming more and more exasperated.

"Katie, I don't want a row, let's talk later." He followed her out into the foyer and pulled her into his arms. "Whatever is bothering you we can sort it out, I love you." He tried to kiss her but she ducked out of his reach.

"You know, Antonio, sometimes I wish that I had never met you!"

"Don't be so harsh, Katie, things happen, outside of our control."

"What really happened to Lucy?"

"I don't know what you mean."

"Oh come off it, either you or Gianni know the whole truth, that is one thing that I am sure of."

"It was an accident, you already know that."

"An accident? Stop taking the piss. I am not as dumb as you think." In sheer frustration she stomped her foot like a little child.

"I don't underestimate you, I never have and never will. You are the woman for me, there is absolutely no doubt about that. We both deserve to be happy, that much I know, just leave the past where it belongs."

"I'm sorry, you're right, we shouldn't be fighting, not after everything that's happened."

"I know, when we walk down that aisle and I finally make you my wife, I'll be the happiest man alive."

"Antonio I adore you, but there are things that worry me, that have worried me for some time now."

"So, what are you saying, you don't want to marry me?" Antonio was shocked.

"Don't be silly, I want that more than anything, we've waited long enough."

"Exactly and I waited out of respect for Lucy's memory. You said it was too early, you were right, but she would want you to be happy now."

"I know that."

Antonio had won her over again, he hoped that he wouldn't have to keep doing this as one day it would wear him down. These past few months it was like a constant battle and he was inclined to blame that on Nina, she was beginning to become a bad influence, it must be all the time they were spending together. God knows when Nina started drinking but it wasn't doing her any favours, or the business for that matter. Maybe he should suggest to her that she should go and run the new business in Manchester for a while, get it up and running. No, better still he would put the idea into Ralph and Frank's head, make Nina think that they thought it was an excellent idea. "Come here."

They kissed and held each other tight. "I won't be too late, il mio te soro."

"See that you're not, because I'll be damned if I'm keeping your side of the bed warm," Katie laughed.

"See, that's better, bella."

She looked up into those sexy brown eyes of his and melted just like she always did; she still found him totally irresistible.

Chapter Ninety Five

Katie and Nina took the helicopter flight, courtesy of Ralph, to Manchester to view potential properties. They couldn't find anything remotely suitable and had almost given it up as a bad idea when the estate agent told them about a former nightclub that was in serious disrepair and if they went in with an offer now the owner would probably bite their hand off. Apparently the guy was in the middle of a messy divorce and all he wanted was to cut and run.

"Oh, I don't know, what about his wife?" The last thing Katie wanted to do was ruin the woman's chances of getting her payout.

"And do they have children?" Nina asked.

"Ladies, please one at a time. The wife took off with a much older and much wealthier man, she doesn't have any children and she doesn't need the money. If you can come up with the cash, say, in twenty four hours then he'll be on the next flight out of here and she'll get nothing."

"Just give us a minute, Peter."

"Why don't you go and have a bite to eat and we'll meet back here in say, two hours?"

"It won't do any harm to discuss it," Katie reassured Nina. "We don't have to do anything we don't feel is right, we're in this together."

"Ok, ok, let's go and have something to eat then."

"Can you recommend somewhere, Peter?"

"Sure, there's a little pasta place, does whatever you like, salad, pizza, huge dish of pasta, really friendly place. I'll drop you off there if you like."

"Yes, that sounds good."

"What about you, Ralph?"

"I'll go with Peter and go over all the details, see if it's right for us."

After Peter and Ralph left and they were sitting alone, Katie had an idea. "Why don't I call Stevo, kill two birds with one stone? I haven't seen him for a couple of years and it will be nice to catch up see how he's getting on and ask what he thinks of the property. After all he knows the area, better than us anyway."

Nina shrugged. "As you say, it won't do any harm to talk to him."

Twenty minutes later Stevo arrived, Katie recognised him immediately. He hadn't really changed, just bulked up a little bit.

"Katie, you look bloody fabulous, and Nina you never age."

"Aren't you full of compliments." Nina held out her hand and Stevo kissed it.

"So good to see you, ladies."

"You too, Stevo, you look really well, Manchester obviously suits you."

"Let me look at you, wow you really look the part."

"What part is that?"

"The powerful, yet enchanting young businesswoman, takes no bullshit and is honest and straight down the line."

"Really, all that from my designer suit and Italian sunglasses?" Katie laughed. "Please take a seat before you embarrass me."

"Waiter, could we have some more coffee please?"

The waiter smiled sweetly at the women, it wasn't every day that two stunning young women came into the café and he was tripping over himself to serve them. "Do you want me to set another place?"

"Not for me, I have to be careful what I eat." Stevo raised a hand.

Katie giggled. "What do you mean, you should be keeping your strength up."

"I do body building as you can probably tell, I only eat certain types of food, it helps me build muscle."

"Well, you look very well, now tell me what you think of Silvers Nightclub."

"Mmm, used to be our strong competition when I first started working at La Piacenza. Mr Silver was a decent bloke, but he had some dealings with a bad crowd and things went downhill from there really. His wife left him and he was devastated, that's why he wants a quick sale."

"And, do you think the location is suitable?"

"If I get to see more of you two lovely young women, then yes." Stevo was half joking.

"You're such a flirt, Stevo." Nina was enjoying the attention.

"Seriously if you don't snap it up then someone else will.

"We can't have that, Nina, can we?"

"No, we can't, but it means that we have to move fast."

"I want to see what Ralph has to say first."

"Well, why don't you stay over tonight, I'll book you a room in the Thistle Hotel. You can come and see how La Piacenza compares to La Pregheira, what do you say?"

"Ok, why not, it will give Ralph time to see if the building is worth salvaging or if we should just flatten it and do a complete rebuild."

"It makes sense to me," Nina agreed.

"Ok, give me five minutes, I need to speak with Antonio." Katie pushed her chair back.

"Leaving already?" the owner of the restaurant enquired.

"Oh, no, I'm just going to make an important call, by the way the food was wonderful."

"You're very welcome. Can I ask you something, I seem to recognise your face from somewhere, are you famous?"

"Good God, no," she laughed. "I'm just here on business, that's all."

The day before they arrived Peter Driscoll's body was found and the gang were out for revenge. They had pulled Harry from the club to see what he knew. They had brutally tortured him in a warehouse they saved for interrogations just like this. They beat him to a pulp and opened a tool bag. Harry was horrified, he didn't expect to die like this. Charlie Driscoll waved the pliers in his victim's face. "Fancy, losing a few teeth, how about a finger or toe?"

"Please, God, no, I'll tell you whatever you want to know," Harry pleaded. "There's no need to kill me."

"About fucking time, pal." And just for the hell of it Charlie snipped off his little finger, the blood spattered on to his jeans. He laughed. "I'm waiting, or do you want me to take another?"

Harry could hardly breathe, the pain was excruciating. "It…it was Antonio de Marco."

"See, that was easy wasn't it?" He looked over to Nigel. "Shoot the fucker." And with that he left.

As soon as Katie finished talking to Antonio, George Driscoll got straight on the phone.

"You'll never believe this, guess who's in my cafe right now?" He was so excited he couldn't contain himself. "Only the future Mrs Antonio de Marco." He whistled. "She's even better looking in the flesh, trust me on that one, what I wouldn't give to have a woman like that."

Charlie Driscoll's ears pricked up. "You're kidding right?"

"No, really it's her and that Valetti woman, I overheard they were looking for property to expand that furniture business they've got."

"Whatever happens, keep them there, fuck me this is an opportunity not to be missed."

"Just remember, wait until they leave, I don't want any trouble in the cafe."

"Sure, no problem, pop." Charlie rubbed his hands thinking what he was going to do to her. Maybe give her the same treatment as his brother, knife her to death. No, he smirked, maybe he would have a bit of fun with her first.

Nina and Stevo were chatting away, anyone would think that they were a couple, Katie thought. "Perhaps, I should go to the hotel and leave you to it."

"No, its ok, I'm just about to head off anyway," Stevo announced.

Overhearing the exchange, the owner came over. "No, no you can't go yet," he insisted. Seeing the strange look on Katie's face he quickly said, "No, no what I mean is you really must try our dessert, our chef has specially prepared it and he will be in trouble if anything goes to waste."

"I'm quite full actually, I don't think that I can manage anything else," Katie smiled at him.

"Please, you will really offend the chef if you do not try his dessert, he is a traditional Italian man, you understand don't you?"

Katie wasn't unaccustomed to the strange and wonderful Italian traditions and nodded. "Ok, you win."

Looking up Nina smiled at her. "I hope it's something simple, like a sorbet."

"You two seem to be getting on like a house on fire," Katie commented.

"Well, we are old friends." Stevo spoke up. "We have a lot to catch up on."

"The owner was quite insistent, wasn't he?" Katie remarked.

"Yes, a little bit too insistent for my liking," Stevo noted.

"Darling, you can afford to eat dessert, I can't," Nina laughed.

"Just have a little bit, we don't want to get the chef into trouble because we refused to even try it."

"You are a big softie, Katie," Stevo laughed. "And Nina, don't put yourself down, you have a fantastic figure."

Nina blushed. "Oh behave yourself, Stevo, people will talk!"

"Hey if I can't give a beautiful woman a compliment she deserves, then…." He broke off, noticing the motorcyclist pull up outside the window, complete with camera. Shit the fucking press were here. "Come on let's get out of here."

"Why, what's going on, what about dessert."

"Fuck dessert." He jumped up from the table and shoved some cash into the waiter's hand. "Here this should cover it, you got a back way out of here?"

The young lad look bewildered. "Er, yes, go through the 'Staff Only' door and through the kitchen, there's a back door you can use."

Stevo shoved the two women through the door. "Hurry up, come on, move it."

"Jesus, Stevo, what's the problem?"

"Excuse us please, we need to get out of here and quickly, if anyone can help there's five hundred quid here."

The chef looked up in total surprise. "What the fuck are you doing in my kitchen, get out, get out."

Stevo shoved the money in his hand. "Exit, where is it?"

The chef pointed to the rear of the kitchen and quickly put the cash in his pocket, giving a black look to his assistant.

Once outside the back door Stevo turned to them. "Can you both run?"

"Not in these heels," Nina exclaimed.

"Take them off, come on, do it, both of you, now!"

Obediently the two women removed their shoes. "Now what?" Katie asked.

"Just run, follow me quickly."

Ten minutes later Stevo found a phone box. "Just wait here." He picked up the phone. "Antonio, it's me, the Driscolls just tried to make a move on Katie."

327

"What, is she alright?"

"Yes, but I should tell you that H disappeared last night, I'm afraid that they are on to you."

"What have you told Katie?"

"She just thinks it was the press, he had a camera."

"Good, I want her back here now."

"Ok, I'll arrange it with Ralph."

"Don't tell him anything."

"I won't. What do you want me to do about the Driscolls?"

"They obviously know about me, which means poor H is almost certainly dead. Try and reason with them, Stevo, tell them it was an unforeseeable accident, see if we can buy them off."

"I don't think they can be bought off, Antonio."

"The last thing I want is any more murders, I'm getting married in a couple of months."

"I understand." Stevo phoned his associate.

Five minutes later they were all in the car.

"Ok, what the hell was all that about?" Katie was still breathless.

"It was the press."

"You've got to be kidding, all this drama for the press, Christ, Stevo."

"Antonio told me to look after you and that is what I have just done. You've got a high profile business, a high profile wedding coming up and you don't need this uninvited attention."

"He's right, Katie, the press are just vultures on the make, not bothered about your feelings, a quick snap, intruding in your private space."

"I suppose, but you would think a hitman was after us," Katie laughed hysterically.

She wasn't too far off the mark, Stevo thought, she was exposed to the criminal element now and the Driscolls were hard core. If they had got her then they could have raped and tortured her, just for the fun of it.

"Don't be so dramatic, Katie," Nina scoffed. "Stevo was just looking out for us that's all."

"I'm sorry, Stevo, I should be thanking you, but right now I feel like I am going to throw up."

"That's ok, just not in the Porsche," he joked.

"I must phone the estate agent." Katie paused. "Oh no, do you think it was him who tipped the press off?"

"No, he wouldn't risk the deal falling through, trust me, he knows he's on to a good deal and wouldn't do anything to hinder that."

Chapter Ninety Six

Matt couldn't stop thinking about Katie and the imminent wedding, once more splashed all over the press. He was like a tortured man since he last saw her.

He was interrupted by his little girl, who had just turned four. Letitia was the spitting image of her mother, the same brown eyes smiling up at him.

"Daddy, Daddy, I want a clown, my friends all had clowns. Jessica had one remember, but I want a better one." She stamped her foot.

"Why can't you have an ordinary birthday party, for goodness sake. You don't need a clown to have the best party ever."

"I want a clown now, Daddy."

"Letitia, I just haven't had time, sweetheart, to organise one."

"Mummy said that she would get one anyway."

Matt sighed, she was becoming more and more spoilt and his damn wife didn't help matters, she totally smothered her and gave her anything she wanted.

"Oh, Carla, where are you?" he shouted.

His wife entered the room dressed to the nines. "Yes, what is it now, Matthew?" she tutted at him.

"Letitia, why don't you go and get ready, tell the nanny to help you."

"Ok, Daddy." She ran out of the room yelling for Eloise.

"You've booked a clown?"

"I took the liberty, seeing as how you are always busy, I didn't think you would mind."

"Well, I wanted to get a magician, a really good one, and a bouncy castle."

"What does it matter, I've sorted it out now."

"Jesus, Carla." He looked at her, she had totally changed from the quiet woman he had met in the office, all she did was spend as fast as he earned. Thanks to the Wendy Bannerman trial Katie had given him, he was now on the road to success, he had proved it was self defence. Now, he had cases coming out of his ears.

"Christ, Matthew, you're never here, what do you want me to do? If I left it to you there would be no party for your daughter."

He knew that she was right of course, he avoided her as much as possible these days. And although he totally adored his little girl she was becoming more and more like her materialistic mother and he just didn't know what to do about it. "You spoil her too much."

"She's only young once, Matthew, I'm making the most of it."

"Well, she just expects everything on a plate and one day when she grows up she'll get a real shock."

"She will be well educated, marry a rich young man and that will be that."

"And never have a career?"

"Don't be silly, why would she want one with the money we have?"

"Whatever happened to your ambition? There was a time when you wanted to train to become a family lawyer."

"I had your daughter remember, she takes up all of my time."

"In amidst your shopping sprees I suppose," Matt said sarcastically.

"That's it, Matthew, don't come back tonight, just stay over at the office, you're good at that." Carla marched out of the kitchen.

Christ, that's all he needed, yet another night in the office. He packed an overnight case and took it to work with him. As usual he had meetings with clients all day and only broke off for a quick thirty minute lunch. Picking up the newspaper, the headlines read: 'A Wedding fit for a princess, only one week until the magical day'.

Katie was on the front cover looking beautiful; Antonio had his arm around her, while her hand rested on his chest. The engagement ring was huge, it must have set de Marco back a big chunk of cash, he thought. He couldn't bear the thought of them getting married, he had to do something and fast.

Opening the safe he pulled out the silver box and unlocked it. He had to tell her everything and then it was up to her if she still wanted to go through with this sham of a marriage to a murderer and a liar. He had nothing to lose any more and if she despised him after this then so be it.

He made the call. The secretary at Casa Vita was trying her best to put him off. She was under instructions not to disturb her boss unless it was extremely urgent.

Meanwhile Katie was in her own world, finalising the wedding plans. The remainder of the year had passed in a total flash. The wedding plans were well under way and Katie was so excited that finally it was almost time to become Mrs Antonio de Marco. She had made several trips to Italy and had her final fitting two weeks before. The dress was absolutely incredible, handmade by an up-and-coming Italian wedding dress designer, recommended by Fran. Naturally it was made out of the finest Italian silk, with a boned bodice. Each pearl was hand stitched around the corset and finished off with embroidered delicate twists to the edging. It accentuated her tiny waist and then flowed into a five foot train. The veil was long and had tiny crystals hand stitched, strategically placed so that they would catch the light when she moved. Both Francesca and Nina had approved, so much so that they were both in floods of tears. She looked like a princess, radiant and glowing. Under the advice of Francesca she chose a crescent shaped bouquet, elegant and distinguished, made up of simple white roses, bergrass, ruscus, water arum and dragon tree variegated.

She was just approving the final touches to make the ceremony more special, if that was indeed possible, when her phone rang. "Wendy, what is it, I told you that I didn't want to be disturbed."

"I'm sorry, but the gentleman insisted."

"Oh, not the press again!" Katie was sick of the constant speculation about what she was wearing, how many bridesmaids, page boys, how many guests, which guests, it was slowly driving her out of her mind.

"No, it's Mr Carmichael, he said that it was very important."

"Oh, er, ok, I suppose you had better put him through then."

"Katie, how are you?"

"Matt, is that you?"

"Look, I'll cut to the chase, I need to see you, but it must be discreet."

"What on earth is going on, Matt, and why all the secrecy?"

"I just need to show you something and then you decide."

Katie was intrigued. "Ok, you've got my attention, tell me more."

"No, you must meet me, can you get away this evening?"

"Yes, Antonio is out of town on business. Is this about him, Matt, because if you're trying to split us up again then I don't want to know."

"Katie, you won't regret it, come to my office on West Strand Street, about eight?"

"I'm not sure." Katie put the phone down. Damn it this is all she needed, everything had been brilliant the last couple of years and now, once again she had a feeling that all of that was about to change.

Katie was fifteen minutes late, Matt didn't think she was going to turn up. He had ordered a pizza which arrived five minutes before Katie. He had whisky and a couple of bottles of wine chilling in the fridge. He didn't know what to expect, the love of his life was about to meet with him. What could he offer her? He loved every bone in her body, she was the world to him and much more, but he knew that she if she went through with this marriage she would be making a huge mistake. She wouldn't believe anything he said, but the evidence was real and she couldn't ignore it, if she did then so be it, she would get what she settled for, a murderer and a crook.

Katie pressed the buzzer, not knowing what she was doing there; if it was all about Antonio, then she would leave.

Matt let her in. "Katie, I wasn't sure that you would come."

"Neither was I, Matt, I don't need this, not now, Jesus I am getting married in two days."

"Maybe what I've got to show you will change your mind."

"Oh, Matt, for goodness sake, you have got to stop this resentment, this hate that you hold for the de Marcos."

"Perhaps you will change your mind once you see what I have to show you."

"Matt, I'm sorry but you are really trying my patience."

331

He led her into his office. "Sit down, glass of wine, something stronger, maybe?"

"Wine will be fine, thanks."

Matt poured the wine and never spoke, he studied this beautiful, confident young woman that had once been his. He wished he had married her years ago, he missed her so much. There was nothing he could do now, but tell her the truth and see how she reacted and what she was going to do about it.

"I haven't got all night, Matt, so tell me, what do you want?"

"I'm sorry, but you are not going to like what I have to say."

"I'm a big girl, I can handle it."

"Don't put that business head on Katie, I know you, remember."

"You know the old me, Matt, I've changed."

"Yes, I know you have."

"So, why are you doing this to me?"

"Lucy was your best friend and she was murdered."

"So, tell me something that I don't know." Katie was exasperated by Matt's tone.

"Did you know that it was Sasha Breschnevsy's car that mowed her down?"

"What, don't lie to me, Matt."

"It's true, the de Marcos covered it up, they even had the police on their side."

"Stop it, I can't bear this, I'm leaving."

"But there's more."

"What do you mean?"

"The drug trafficking, it was down to the de Marcos, poor Roberto Valetti was never involved."

"Stop this, this is insane, why are you doing this?"

"I told you that Gianni and a thug of his threatened me and that's why I had to dump you, I was scared for my life and Lucy's."

"No, no, stop it, you're lying." Katie was becoming hysterical.

"I wish I was, Katie, really, there's nobody more than me that would wish you all the happiness in the world, but you are making a huge mistake."

"What, for being in love with Antonio?"

"He is a murderer and a drug trafficker."

"Fuck you, Matt, you jealous bastard." Katie was beside herself, her brain couldn't take it in.

"Your lovely fiancé covered up Felicia's death."

"What?"

"They have many enemies, past and present, who they have screwed over. Lucy was deliberately killed and that's what happens to anyone who becomes close to them, it could be you next."

"No, Antonio would never let anything happen to me."

"Poor Felicia was six weeks pregnant and I had to cover it up on the instructions of your beloved Antonio."

"Oh, Matt, you've told me all this before and I don't believe it for one second."

"I'm so sorry, Katie, but it's true, this man you are about to marry isn't what he seems."

"But I love him, Matt, I truly adore him."

"So, you think that love is enough to get you through this, just don't let your heart rule your head. Promise me that you will hear me out, just this once. For old times sake."

"I have never seen that side of the de Marcos and if I did then you know that I wouldn't stand for it."

"Katie, I know you and I know that you wouldn't sit back and condone murder in any shape or form, but these guys are extremely dangerous."

"I can't bear to listen to this any longer." Katie grabbed her handbag.

"Katie, I am only scraping the surface, there's a lot more you need to know. Their family was killed in a rival attack in Umbria."

"Yes, I know that."

"The families were enemies Katie, they cut the brakes killing three people, the de Marco parents and their sister."

"I don't know what you think you are trying to achieve, Matt, but…"

"Please just hear me out, there's more." He paused waiting to see what she was going to do next.

She sat back down. "Ok, you might as well give it to me in one go, get it off your chest once and for all."

"Everything they touch turns to shit. Tania Horrocks was with one of the Calvi brothers when that car bomb went off, do you think that was an accident?"

"Calvi brothers, I met Georgio Calvi the first time I went to La Pregheira."

"What? Where at?"

"I was at the de Marco villa. Antonio was called back when Felicia was killed. Pesaro, the horse I was riding, threw me off and Georgio Calvi came to my aid."

"Do you think he had something to do with the accident?"

"I don't know, I suppose it's possible, after all he ran off when two of Antonio's minders came, Jesus he could have killed me."

"My God, this thing isn't over between the de Marcos and the Calvis, he'll be biding his time, wanting revenge for his brother's murder and you could be top of the hit list. You're about to become Antonio's wife, what better time to strike than at the wedding."

"You're really scaring me now, Matt."

"I'm sorry, but you have to face facts."

"Nobody would dare try anything, there'll be too many people there, somebody would recognise him."

"It doesn't have to necessarily be him, he could hire a hit man or arrange another little accident."

"This is supposed to be one of the happiest days of my life, what am I going to do?"

"I think you should talk to Antonio about everything."

"I'm not sure, what if he tells me that he was involved in all these things?"

"And what if he wasn't?"

"I need to mull things over, I wish Lucy were here, then I would have someone to talk to."

"You have me, Katie."

"Matt, I just can't believe that Antonio is mixed up in anything like this, he just isn't the type."

"Then, maybe you don't really know him after all."

Katie put a hand to her face, what if he was right.

"Another thing, watch out for that Sasha woman, her father is some kind of arms trafficker."

"What, you can't be serious, that quiet silver haired man?"

"You've met him then?"

"Just the once."

"You've got to wonder where all the de Marco money came from, surely?"

"No, I've never thought about it, they have a wine business that they ship all over the world, isn't that how they were able to invest in the clubs?"

"I don't know, you tell me."

"It's all supposition, Matt."

That was it, he'd said all he could and now it was up to her, after all it was her life and her choice.

"I must go now."

"Good luck, Katie."

Katie nodded and left his office, she felt sick to the pit of her stomach. What if Antonio confirmed everything Matt had told her, then what, would she have the nerve to walk away? She didn't think she was strong enough to do that.

That night she found it impossible to sleep, she was glad that Antonio was in Umbria, it gave her a chance to have a good look around. She pulled opened his bedside drawers, she didn't know what she was looking for but would know if she found it. Opening the wardrobe doors she checked the pockets of his suits. What the hell was she doing rummaging through his things, what did she hope to find? Exhausted she sat on the bedroom floor, wondering what to do.

Confronting him would be madness and he would demand to know who was filling her head with such nonsense. Once he knew that it was Matt he would go crazy and God knows what he would do to him. That was it, if there was any truth in any of this, then if she confronted Antonio, something could happen to Matt and she wasn't prepared to risk it. The rights and wrongs of it all were irrelevant to her. Taking a sleeping tablet she curled up in bed and hugged her pillow.

Chapter Ninety Seven

1990

Katie was in bed at the penthouse in London, she was dreaming, it was the day of the wedding, she was reliving it all over again.

She remembered slowly walking down the stairs in the villa in Umbria, her father had whistled at her. "Wow, you look wonderful, like a princess."

He had given her the pearls that her mother had worn on their wedding day. "For good luck," he told her.

They had travelled by horse and carriage to the little chapel. Most of the townsfolk were out, waving at her and wishing her luck.

As she walked down the aisle with her father she could hardly breathe. Antonio was facing her, wearing that dashing smile of his, waiting for her to finally come to him. They had spent time and deliberation, poring over the choice of wedding vows, until they both agreed on the perfect ones. After they each recited their individual vows, they spoke in unison. A hush fell over the entire chapel. *'Entreat me not to leave you, or to return from following after you. For where you go, I will go, and where you stay I will stay. Your people will be my people, and your God, will be my God. And where you die, I will die and there I will be buried. May the Lord do with me and more if anything but death parts you from me'.*

She remembered his kiss and felt blissfully happy, this is what she had always wanted. It couldn't have been more perfect.

After the ceremony was over and the photographs were taken, they were driven into the village square where they sat on either end of a long bench with a 'sawhorse'.

The crowd clapped and cheered as they were given a double handed saw and set to work in sawing the log apart. When they were finished it symbolised that they must always work together in all of life's tasks.

After an evening of speeches and partying they had sneaked off back to the villa. She smiled, remembering the struggle he had to open all of those little buttons in desperation to have her, seal their marriage as man and wife. It had been special and intense, she felt alive, really alive and it was the best feeling in the world to surrender body and soul to the man she loved.

She had ran them a bath filled with rose petals and bubbles, she was lighting the candles wondering what was taking him so long. "Antonio, where are you my husband?"

Wrapping the dressing gown around her, she opened the door. She was beaming, but not for long. The horrific sight that met her was too much to bear, there was a crimson tide of blood flowing down the silk bed sheets. Antonio wasn't moving, she noticed something glinting beside him. Not sure what it was she rushed over, but she seemed to run in slow motion. She tried to wake him, he was face down, not moving, she tried to scream but nothing came out. There was blood on her hands, blood on her dressing gown, she picked up the thing that must have killed him. A gun, on no, she dropped it onto the floor and that's when the police had arrived.

"No, no, no!" Shouting out in her sleep, the nightmare had wakened her, she was sweating, her heart was racing. But it wasn't a dream, it had really happened and now she was being accused of murdering him.

She felt sick; racing to the bathroom she retched her guts up. Nobody would believe her, everyone had stayed away from the police station she was held at in La Pregheira. She begged for her one phone call and that's when she had rung Matt. After hearing what had taken place Matt realised that the only way Katie would have a fair trial was if he arranged for it to take place back in the UK. He promised Katie to do everything in his power to make it happen and somehow, miraculously he did just that.

When they had landed at Heathrow, she was led off the plane in handcuffs, the press had been there taking her picture, she tried to keep her head down. People were shouting 'murderer' at her, it was like a living hell.

Chapter Ninety Eight

Katie had just finished dressing when the phone starting ringing; she was reluctant to answer it thinking that it must be the paparazzi, yet it was insistent, almost begging her to answer. "Hello."

"Katie, this is Gianni, please don't hang up, I need to see you."

"Gianni?" She was frightened, what did he want from her? "No, I can't, I'm not allowed to have any contact with the prosecution witnesses."

"Katie, I've changed my mind, I've been talking to Matthew Carmichael. I was crazy to think that you could have done it."

"What..?"

"Please, if not for me, then hear me out for my brother's sake."

"How do I know that you're not coming over here to kill me?"

"You have to trust me, I'll be there in an hour, oh and by the way Matt and Stevo are coming with me." He put the phone down.

Oh my God, what were they up to? Katie felt suddenly sick again and ran to the bathroom just making it in time. Christ, what was wrong with her, lately she couldn't stop throwing up. She was so nervous she could barely keep anything down.

Katie took a long look at herself in the mirror. Staring back at her was a girl she didn't recognise, pale, gaunt and thinner than ever. The signs of lack of sleep were starting to show with dark circles appearing around her eyes. Antonio's death was slowing sucking the life out of her.

The doorbell rang, making her jump. Holding her stomach she walked slowly towards the door. Looking through the spy hole she saw Matt. Quickly unlocking the door she let him in, he was closely followed by Gianni and Stevo.

"I'm sorry to think that I was dumb enough not to believe you, Katie."

"Better late than never, Gianni." She spoke quietly.

"I want to do everything I can to help you, we all do."

"What can you do, the gun has my fingerprints all over it!"

"We have to put on a united front, show the world we support you, and more importantly believe that you are not a murderer," Gianni told her. "In fact we are going to the club tonight and you are the guest of honour."

"No, I can't."

"But you must, it is the only way, we'll all be with you and I've already taken the liberty of inviting Nina."

"What do you think that will achieve?"

338

"It will achieve exactly the right publicity."

"Gianni is right," Matt backed him up. "After all the bad coverage you've had, to be welcomed into the club and sit with Antonio's brother and best friend, believe me, people will think twice about being so hasty to judge you."

"No, what's the point?" Katie couldn't bear the thought of going into the club.

Gianni was becoming impatient, they needed her. "It may draw out the real killer." There he'd said it, much to Matt's dismay.

"What do you mean?" If there was a real chance of revealing Antonio's murderer then she would do anything.

"We think either Gianni or you are next on the list," Stevo told her.

"What list?"

"Katie." He got hold of her by the shoulders and looked into her blue eyes, which were so full of grief. "This is serious, they plan to assassinate one of you, maybe both of you."

Katie fainted. "Shit, give me some help here," Stevo shouted.

"Is she ok?" Matt asked.

"She'll be fine, she just fainted."

"I told you not to tell her the truth; it's too much for her."

"You heard her, Matt. She wasn't going to budge; now we may have a chance."

"Don't tell her any more details, the less she knows the better," Stevo warned.

Katie was just coming around. "What happened?"

"It's ok, you passed out." Matt put a glass of water into her hands. "Here sip this."

"Thanks."

Sasha had followed Gianni to Antonio's apartment, what the fuck was he doing and with the other two in tow for christ's sake? Was he trying to help the bitch in some way, she hoped not or he would seriously regret it. She gripped the steering wheel so hard that her hands tuned white, forcing it into gear she sped off in a violent rage.

She wasn't alone, somebody else was watching with keen interest, waiting for a chance to strike. With a bit of luck, tonight would be that very night.

Chapter Ninety Nine

Gianni made the call. "It's on, just be discreet and I'll give the signal when the time is right." He picked up his brother's photo. "Justice will be done tonight, Antonio, I promise you."

He rang Veronica before setting off. "Did you organise everything just like I asked?"

"Yes, of course to the detail."

"I'll be there shortly."

Eddie Regan rang his contact. "Guess what, it's time for that next instalment, I've got something for you."

"Oh, yes?"

"I just heard, everyone is going to be here tonight, it will be a perfect opportunity to end this in one fatal swoop." He laughed menacingly down the phone.

"Good, just leave the door ajar and I'll do the rest."

"What are you going to do?"

"Wait and see." The phone went dead. This prick was getting to know nothing, he would go up with the rest of the club.

Gianni got into his car. "I think you better go with Fred and pick up Katie and Matthew, I don't want anything happening to her."

"Are you sure? I feel better coming with you."

"I'll be fine."

Stevo didn't like it one little bit, he had a horrible feeling something terrible was about to happen. "But...."

"See you at the club."

Feeling helpless Stevo did as he was told.

Gianni checked his rear view mirror, the car behind him was getting closer and they had their lights on full beam. "Who the fuck is this asshole trying to intimidate?" He accelerated hard to see if he could shake him off but to no avail. Slowing down at the traffic lights he tried to see where the car had gone, it just seemed to disappear. Feeling a little more relaxed Gianni set off again, he was just rounding the corner when a car came at him head on. The car spun out of control and ended up upside down on the embankment. The windscreen was smashed to smithereens and Gianni was barely conscious. He remembered being dragged from the car just before it exploded.

Jed shook him. "Boss, you ok?"

Gianni was bleeding and choking for breath. "I've been better. What about the driver?"

"It was Charlie Driscoll, he's dead, the impact flung his body out of the window into the path of an oncoming lorry." Jed pointed.

Gianni struggled to his feet. "What are you doing here anyway?"

"Stevo phoned me, he was worried. Just as well I came, man, eh, you would have been chargrill!" Jed laughed at his own joke.

"You better get me to the club, straight away, this may not be the end of it."

"What about the hospital?"

"It's just a few scratches, I'll be fine."

"You don't look too good, man."

"I told you, get me to the club and make it fast!"

Katie arrived with Matt and Stevo, as predicted the press were all over the place.

"Are you confident of being found not guilty, Mrs de Marco?" one of the journalists shouted.

"Where is Gianni de Marco, is he convinced of your innocence now?"

"No comment." Matt put his hand up as Stevo ushered Katie into the building.

"Thanks, Stevo."

Stevo wasn't paying much attention, he couldn't see Gianni's car and hoped that he was alright, he should have arrived before them.

Veronica greeted them in the foyer. "Katie." She hugged her. "My poor girl."

Stevo nodded at her. "Where's Gianni?"

"He called to say that he was on his way, but there's still no sign of him."

"No problem, we'll go straight to our table."

Veronica led the way, the other guests couldn't take their eyes off Katie, she looked so nervous and fragile.

"Good evening, Mrs de Marco." Sasha was in her face. "Soo nice to see you, where is Mr de Marco? Oh yes, I forgot you killed him didn't you?"

Matt had to hold Katie back, she was gunning for her; this woman had been the bane of her life.

"What the fuck is she doing here?" Stevo demanded. "Get that psycho bitch out of my face."

"I think you'll find that Gianni invited me!" Sasha exclaimed.

"No way, he finished with you, you mental case."

Veronica had to intervene. "Come and wait over here, Sasha, I'll get you a little table and we'll sort this out when Gianni arrives."

Reluctantly Sasha obeyed her. "I'll see you later, Katie."

341

"I can hardly wait."

"I'm sorry, Katie, it does seem that Gianni wants her here, but God knows why!" Veronica whispered. "I'll keep an eye on her."

Diana and Henry Brookstein, Ralph and Lorraine Anderson, Nina, Matt and Stevo were seated with her.

Nina stood up. "Are you sure this was wise of you, I mean to come out in public like this?"

"I know what I'm doing, Nina."

"My dear Katie." Ralph took her hand. "It must have been extremely difficult to come here tonight, I admire you."

"Yes, me too." Lorraine kissed her on the cheek.

Diana and Henry didn't know what to say. "My dear, it is with great courage and dignity that you have found it in yourself to attend tonight and we are so happy to see you." Henry's voice was full of warmth and genuineness.

"Thank you all, you don't know how difficult this is for me right now." Katie sat down.

Sarah came over. "Hello, it will be my pleasure to take your orders this evening."

"Thank you." Matt looked at Katie, she looked awful. "Please give us another few minutes."

"Certainly, whatever you wish."

Georgio Calvi slipped in through the back door, the one Eddie had so kindly left open for him. He planted the bomb and smiled to himself, at last he would finally have justice for the family that was taken away from him.

It would blow up the bottom floor of the club and with it take out Gianni de Marco, Stevo and Katie; he couldn't have felt happier. Now all he had to do was skip the country.

Gianni was stuck in a traffic jam. "Christ, what's going on tonight?"

"There's some concert on, so it may take a little time to get there."

"Just let me out, I'll walk, it will be faster."

"Don't be fucking stupid, man, you're liable to collapse the state you're in."

Gianni was insistent, so Jed let him out of the car. "I'll meet you there."

"Yeah, whatever." Gianni walked as fast as he could.

Eddie was trying his best to get Veronica out of the way, it was too late to get out without causing suspicion, and he wanted to spend his last moments with her. He made up an imaginary phone call that wouldn't wait.

"Ok, but I can't be long," she told him, frightened that she was going to miss something.

342

When she got to the office he locked them both in. "Eddie, what the hell are you doing?" she demanded.

"It's for the best, you'll see."

"Is there something you want to tell me?"

"Just that I love you, but I didn't want it to end like this."

"What?" Veronica was freaking out and made a dash for the phone. Eddie grabbed the brass eagle that she loved so much and smashed her over the head.

"I'm sorry." He hit her once more, she lay crumpled up in a heap on the floor. He kissed her on the lips. Taking the letter opener from her desk he slashed his wrists and slipped into unconsciousness.

Chief Superintendent Frank Mason had picked up Georgio Calvi, thanks to Gianni's tip off. He threw him into the back of the police van. "Just give it up, son, you've been caught, there's nowhere to go."

Georgio laughed in his face. "It's too late." He passed the rucksack to him. "They're all going up in smoke." He looked at his watch. "Any time now."

Chief Superintendent Mason frantically spoke into the walkie talkie. "It's a go, do you hear me, go, go now!"

The team moved in, but it was too late.

Gianni was just coming around the corner when he saw the building explode. The shock of it startled him and he collapsed in the street.

In the confusion Georgio Calvi managed to escape.

The Chief Superintendent contacted the fire brigade and several ambulances, but he feared the worst.

The bar area had taken the brunt of the bomb and there were many fatalities, among them were Veronica Lamont and Eddie Regan.

Katie and her companions had just made their way into the restaurant area and were sitting near the pillars when the bomb ripped through the building, shaking it to the core.

Stevo had instinctively pushed Katie out of the way; he saved her life. He remembered the promise he made to himself that after Lucy's death he would always look out for her and that's what he did. He was trapped, pinned down by chunks of debris.

The air was thick with dust and smoke, Nina scrabbled around, she couldn't see a thing. "Can anyone hear me?"

There were moans and groans all around her, but she was frightened to move in case something crushed her to death.

"Nina, Nina," Katie spluttered, reaching for her.

"I'm here." She crawled towards her voice. "Are you ok?"

"Yes, I think so."

343

"What about the others?" Katie asked.

"I don't know."

They huddled together waiting for help to arrive.

Chief Superintendent Frank Mason just heard that Gianni de Marco had been found lying unconscious in the street and was subsequently rushed to casualty.

It took almost two hours to get the bodies and the rest of the people out. Calvi had caused mayhem, killing innocent people and destroying the club.

Katie vaguely remembered being taken to the hospital, it was all a bit of a blur, she was suffering from smoke inhalation. The doctor ran some tests and was on his way to see her, to tell her the news.

"Mrs de Marco, how are you feeling?"

"A little sore, but I'll live."

"I have some news for you."

"What is it?" She pulled herself up in the hospital bed.

"You're pregnant."

Katie gasped, instinctively holding her stomach. "But, I can't be!"

"It's true, congratulations. Now I must go, it is very busy tonight."

Pregnant, pregnant? Katie could barely digest the news.

Matt was standing in the doorway with his arm in a sling.

"Oh, Matt, thank God you're alright, what about the others?"

"Stevo has a broken leg, if it wasn't for him, I don't know if you would have survived. And now you have something to live for, don't you?" He sat down beside her and held her hand. "You will make a wonderful mother."

Katie cried, she didn't know how to feel, but she knew that now she was expecting she would have to pull herself together, for the sake of her and Antonio's child.

"Everyone is ok, apart from a few cuts and bruises and of course smoke inhalation." He coughed. "But I am afraid that Gianni suffered some sort of seizure, he was found near the club, he's in a coma."

"What?"

"Apparently he was attacked by Charlie Driscoll."

"Who is that?"

"He is the one responsible for killing Antonio."

"How do you know?"

"I have been speaking with Chief Superintendent Frank Mason and you're in the clear!"

She flung her arms around his neck. "Oh, thank God, have they arrested him?"

"No, he tried to run Gianni off the road and ended up killing himself in the process. Just rest, the Chief Superintendent will explain everything to you all in due course."

344

"Will you do something for me?"

"Anything."

"Take me to see Gianni."

"Ok." He helped her out of bed and they walked slowly down the corridor to the Intensive Care Unit.

Stevo was already sitting by his bed in a wheelchair. "Katie, I'm glad that you are ok."

"I heard that if it wasn't for you then I may have been killed in the blast."

"It was nothing."

"You are a hero," Matt told him.

"How is he?" Katie asked looking concerned.

"The doctor says that he may come round in hours, maybe weeks, who knows."

Just then there was a knock on the door. "I have some news regarding Mr de Marcos girlfriend, Sasha Breschnevsky." The man looked very grave.

"You can speak freely, we are all friends here," Stevo spoke out.

"I am afraid that she just died."

"Thank you." Stevo nodded to her.

Katie was holding Gianni's hand. "You've got to wake up, I have some important news." She whispered in his ear. "I'm going to have a baby, you're going to be an uncle, we need you."

Gianni's eyes flickered open and he smiled. "Katie, an uncle you say?"

"Ssh, it's ok, just please get better."

"You go and get some rest, I'll take over for now," Stevo told her.

Matt helped her back to her bed and Nina was waiting for her. "Katie, we are so lucky to be alive."

"Yes, I know, we are." Katie patted her stomach and had that strange look only a pregnant woman could have on her face.

"You're going to have a baby?" Nina was astonished. "A new life on the way, that is amazing. He or she is going to be absolutely doted on."

Matt agreed. "Yes, we're all here for you."

"I know you are, I'm so lucky to be surrounded by the people I love most in the world."

Katie had a different dream that night, she dreamt of giving birth to a beautiful, healthy child, that would know everything about the great man their father was and how he would have loved them. She could finally lay Antonio to rest.

Georgio Calvi's flight had just taken off; he was sipping his champagne and reading the newspaper. Antonio had left an heir to the de Marco empire, it was incredible but true. He would watch with interest to see how this baby grew up.

The End